PRIDE *and* JUSTICE

Elizabeth Bennet doesn't need a hero – she already is one.

Timothy Bowden

Clan Destine
PRESS

First published by Clan Destine Press in 2024

PO Box 121,
Bittern Victoria 3918
Australia

National Library of Australia Cataloguing-In-Publication data:

PRIDE AND JUSTICE

ISBNs: 9781922904829 (paperback)
          9781922904836 (eBook)

Cover design by kimsol-digitalart

Design & Typesetting by Clan Destine Press

Clan Destine
P R E S S

www.clandestinepress.net

For Sandra

My very own superhero

VOLUME I

Chapter 1

While it is a truth universally acknowledged that a single man in possession of a good fortune must be in want of a wife, it is equally acknowledged – or at least, it is amongst those who choose to take up the mask and responsibilities of being a Vigil – that a villainous man, no matter the size of his fortune, must always be seeking to increase it.

So it seemed to Miss Elizabeth Bennet as she trudged home through the darkness. Her left hand was pressed to her leather jerkin, holding her aching ribs. The poacher she had just encountered had got one good punch in before she was able to gain a decent grip and throw him, thus taking the wind – and fight – right out of him.

His violence had rather surprised her, when she had come upon him setting snares. She had at first assumed him to be a local, one of the poorer folk she had caught before. She was ready to give at most a scolding when she laid a gloved hand on his shoulder, but when he turned, his eyes widening at her masked, leather-clad appearance, she did not recognise him at all. Before she could speak he was up and letting fly, and it was only when he lay gasping at her feet – having landed satisfyingly heavily – that she was able to speak to him.

Of course, 'speak to him' meant *rasp in a deep, throaty whisper*. For it was one of the particular difficulties faced by a female Vigil, she had found, that one was not taken as seriously by many of the criminals one faced. At least, not until one had unleashed enough violence to prove one's superiority. Better to disguise oneself as male and hope to avoid more fighting than was absolutely necessary. With her face masked, hair tied back, clad in leather trousers, her tightly buckled jerkin constricting her bosom, she was usually able to pass for a young man.

And so she had learned that the unseemly fellow had been drawn to the area by word in the London slums that a new villain had chosen Hertfordshire as a base of operations. The poacher was hoping for employment as a henchman. He did not know much more, except the name the villain chose to go by: Cain.

Elizabeth broke his snares, threatened to break several bones and hand him over to the constable if he ever returned, and sent him limping and cursing on his way. But what he said gave her pause for thought. A new villain...

The whole county was abuzz with the news that Netherfield Park had just been let by a wealthy young man from the north. Coincidence? It seemed unlikely. A villain moving to the area would need an alias, some kind of cover story. One couldn't go about as a costumed villain every hour of every day, just as it was impossible to remain disguised as a Vigil full time. Exposure for either equalled great risk: apprehension on the one hand, too much attention and even revenge on the other. So it seemed quite likely that this newcomer, this Mr Bingley, was probably in some way connected with the villain, Cain.

While the neighbourhood was humming with supposition about his marriageability, Elizabeth was much more concerned with his possible criminality. Hertfordshire had been quiet for some time. She did not like the thought of an interloping villain inserting himself like an infection in an otherwise healthy body.

An owl hooted nearby, and Elizabeth froze, ears straining. She cursed herself – she had been too deep in thought, not paying attention. The man may have had compatriots in the vicinity, despite his protestations that he was alone. But then she caught a flash of grey winging through the canopy – an owl, then – and so relaxed her tensed shoulders and continued on her long walk home to Longbourn.

The burst of energy released by the encounter had given way to a heavy fatigue when she arrived back at her darkened family home – no lights shone; even their maidservants would be asleep and oblivious at the rear of the building. As she climbed the trellis to her second-storey bedroom window, she felt slow and clumsy. She clambered gratefully into the warm, welcoming darkness.

'Lizzy?' came a soft voice from the other bed.

'All is well, Jane. Go back to sleep.'

Her sister sighed and turned over. Elizabeth sat on her own bed, fingers fumbling at the laces and buckles of her jerkin. She was stiff. She would have to look at adding some more padding beneath the leather to better absorb blows such as that. She couldn't get the first lace undone, leaned over to try to get it with her teeth, couldn't reach.

'Actually, Jane,' she whispered, 'would you be a dear?'

The topic at breakfast the next morning was, of course, the new occupant of Netherfield. But not for the same reason he was foremost in Elizabeth's thoughts as she yawned her way downstairs – no, instead it was because he possessed that most admirable of qualities, as far as their mother was concerned: he was deliciously single.

'My dear Mr Bennet,' said Mrs Bennet, pouring herself some tea. 'Have you given thought to when you shall be calling on him?'

'Calling on who, precisely?'

'Why, Mr Bingley of course!'

Mr Bennet made no move to look up from his newspaper. 'Bingley? I don't believe I know any Bingley. Moreover, I'm not sure I require to know any Bingley. I have made do so far without his acquaintance. I dare say I can manage a little longer without it.'

Elizabeth bit the inside of her cheek.

'Mr Bennet,' cried his wife. 'Consider your daughters!'

'How so? How do they factor into me knowing or not knowing Bangley?'

'*Bingley*! How can you be so tiresome? You must know I am thinking of his marrying one of them!'

Mr Bennet looked up, frowning. 'Marry one of them? How is he to marry one of them when he doesn't even know them? How are they to even meet?'

Elizabeth pressed her napkin to her mouth and coughed. Jane kicked her under the table. The other girls weren't really listening – Mary, the middle daughter, had her face in a book, and Lydia and Kitty, having only in the past year made their debut, were whispering and snorting together like children at the other end of the table.

'That is precisely my point,' cried Mrs Bennet. 'That is why you must call on him! Before everyone else beats us to him! Then we may call on him, and he will fall in love with one of the girls and marry them!'

Mr Bennet looked thoughtfully around the table. 'Really? As simple as that? I had no idea I had fathered such sirens. These girls? Are you sure?'

He winked at Elizabeth. She shook her head at him.

'Mr Bennet, how can you abuse your own children in such a way? You take delight in vexing me. You have no compassion for my poor nerves.'

'You mistake me, my dear. I have the deepest respect for your nerves. I count them as my oldest acquaintances. I know them like the back of my hand.' His gaze had travelled to his right hand as he spoke, and Elizabeth caught a sudden flash of some deeper emotion as he looked, then cleared his throat and shook out his newspaper. She looked down at her own reddened knuckles and quietly placed her hands in her lap.

Mrs Bennet burst into tears, threw down her napkin and ran from the room. Jane followed, her tone soothing, calling the youngest three girls to attend their mother. Mary stood and followed, still reading. Kitty hesitated, looking at Lydia, who rolled her eyes and pushed up from the table with a dramatic sigh. Mr Bennet and Elizabeth were left alone at the table.

'A curious thing,' said Mr Bennet as he stirred his coffee. 'I rose in the night and could have sworn I heard the trellis creak.'

'Perhaps it was the wind.'

'Perhaps.' He tapped his spoon twice against the edge of his cup, seemingly studying the eddies within. 'You seem to be moving a little slowly this morning, Lizzy.'

Elizabeth hesitated, a lie poised on her lips. But then her father looked up at her, his piercing gaze seeming to see directly to her core. She swallowed.

'Perhaps you ought to go call on Mr Bingley, Father.'

'Oh? And why is that?'

'A...man I spoke to last night mentioned someone moving into the neighbourhood.'

'A man you spoke to,' repeated her father drily.

'A poacher.'

'Lizzy...'

'He said that he had come to join a new criminal undertaking. I believe we have a villain moving into our midst. He didn't know much, but he thought the man's alias was Cain.'

'How very biblical.'

'And now this Bingley arrives–'

Her father held up his hand. 'Firstly, you know that I am not comfortable with you continuing in these activities.'

'Father, there has been a Vigil in this neighbourhood for upward of twenty years. I am simply continuing the trad–'

'I know full well how long this area has been...protected. And you know why I prefer this family to have nothing more to do with Vigils and Vigilism. In the past I have merely made my feelings known to you and hoped that would curb you. Do not now make me forbid you, Elizabeth.'

Elizabeth looked down at her lap. Heat rose in her cheeks.

'Secondly, this is not London. The chance of a high-level villain setting up here is very remote indeed. Surely this poacher was simply telling you what he thought you wanted to hear. Did you...did you *chastise* him?'

'Indeed, Father.'

Mr Bennet grunted. Was that approval? She searched his face, but it remained stern and unreadable. She looked away again, missing the flash of pain that shot across his eyes. He sighed.

'Now. Come. Let's not you and I quarrel, Lizzy. As it so happens, I have every intention of calling on Mr Bingley.' He held up a hand to forestall her as she looked up. 'But not to investigate him. If your mother is so determined that he is to be my first son-in-law, I had better get to know him sooner or later. But I dare say I shall get a feel for his character and may then be able to set your mind at rest. Now, in the meantime I shall be in my library. Hopefully undisturbed.'

Chapter 2

The next evening the family sat together in the drawing room, going about their various individual pursuits. Mr Bennet sat reading and Mrs Bennet had the girls sewing, though Lydia was more often trying to goad Kitty into seeing how far either could stick a needle into their thumbs, and Mary's hand kept straying to her book.

'I hope Mr Bingley will like it, Lizzy,' said Mr Bennet suddenly.

Elizabeth flushed, and it took all her self-control to remain still. For in her lap, beneath a disassembled hat, were some pieces of padding she was stitching to line the interior of her leather armour. She knew her father was unlikely to notice, but it felt as though she had been caught out. Luckily her mother unwittingly rescued her from further scrutiny.

'We are not in any way to know what Mr Bingley likes,' she said resentfully. 'Since we are not to visit him.'

'You forget, mama,' said Elizabeth, recovering. 'We are sure to meet him at the next dance. And Mrs Long will be sure to introduce him, if she has met him.'

'I do not believe Mrs Long will do any such thing! She has two nieces of her own to marry off. She is as bad as a villain when it comes to such things. She is such a schemer.' She rounded on Lydia. 'Oh, do stop that, Lydia! You tear my poor nerves to pieces! It is disgusting.'

'I think it is funny,' Lydia said, pouting and holding her impaled thumb aloft.

'Anyway, my dear, fear not,' said Mr Bennet smugly. 'You may play Vigil to Mrs Long's villain if she has such selfish designs, for you shall have the upper hand. *You* may do the introductions.'

'Impossible,' cried his wife. 'How am I to do that when I do not know him? Enough of your teasing, sir! Why, I declare I am now quite sick of Mr Bingley!'

'I am sorry to hear that. Why did you not tell me that before? If I had known that this morning, I certainly would not have called on him. Oh dear. As I have actually paid the visit, we cannot escape the acquaintance now.'

He smiled at the astonished silence that met this proclamation, but then frowned as the storm broke, and his wife and younger daughters screamed in delight and all started speaking at once.

Elizabeth caught his eye from across the room.

'And did you form any opinion on his character, Father?' she asked lightly.

'One cannot know what a man really is by the end of one visit. But he appears as one would expect. As opposed to what one may fear. You understand, Lizzy?'

Elizabeth nodded. But it was true – one visit was not enough to know.

'What an excellent father you have, girls,' cried Mrs Bennet. 'Lydia, my love, though you are the youngest, I dare say Mr Bingley will dance with you at the next ball. Yes, then you, Kitty. And Mary, well...Oh, we must have him to dinner!'

And thus the web is spun, thought Elizabeth as she listened to her mother's plans to monopolise the man. *Unless it is actually Bingley who is the spider, and we the flies.*

Elizabeth was unable to sleep. The thought of a villain in their midst – especially one operating under the cover of a desirable match for the local families with unmarried daughters – unsettled her greatly. She should trust her father's instincts, she knew – but then, he had been retired from investigating for quite some time. No, the only thing that would satisfy her would be to find the opportunity to get to know Mr Bingley herself.

Cain, who slew his brother. It was a worrying identity to adopt as an alias, hinting at a capacity for murder.

Her father was right in that it was usually in the cities, especially London, where the high-level villains tended to operate. That was where the richer pickings lay, and a readier supply of those willing for employ as henchmen. But that was also where the major Vigils hunted. Did it not make sense that some villains may choose to move into the countryside, hoping for easier prey?

She kicked at her covers and turned over, staring into the darkness. It worried her too that word had gone out on whatever system the criminal underbelly used – codes scratched under bridges and in the stables of seedy taverns, that kind of thing – that here might be the chance of employment. If more foul characters arrived, it would certainly be beyond the ability of the local constable to manage.

She had to be ready.

She sat up, listening for a moment to Jane's steady breathing. She slipped out of bed, pulled the window open and climbed swiftly down the trellis. By the subdued light of the moon she made her way to the old carriage house behind the stables and slipped inside. She felt about, located a lantern and flint, and, once she had light, made her way to the back. Here she approached what appeared a solid section of wall. She pressed, and a concealed hatch opened, which she slid aside. Ducking through, she lifted the panel back into position behind her. She opened the lamp fully and held it high.

Within the small windowless room was an array of training equipment. She hung the lantern on a hook and stripped off her nightgown. She slipped on a pair of workman's trousers left folded neatly on a bench, and a sleeveless vest. Next she picked up two strips of cloth and wound them around her hands and fingers, then stepped up to a large leather bag hanging from a beam.

She pressed her palms against it for a moment, feeling its weight, breathing in its familiar musty odour, then stepped back, knees bent, hands coming up in a boxer's stance. She began snapping out jabs with her left hand, each blow causing the heavy bag to tremble. She shuffled lightly about in front of it, adding more-powerful blows from her right that caused the bag to jolt and swing. She grunted with effort and satisfaction. Now her strikes came faster – double jabs and crosses, upper cuts into the middle of the bag, rips designed to strike the ribs – she felt the tightness still in her own left side from the poacher – and then she spun about, her right fist flying backhand, smacking heavily into the leather.

Now she stepped back a little, pivoted on the ball of her left foot, delivered a round sweeping kick, sinking her right shin into the bag at thigh height. The bag jerked. She kicked again, and again, then rapidly switched to her left, the blows arcing around at varying heights – knee, thigh, waist, even head. She followed with push kicks from her front leg, causing the bag to seesaw and the rafter to groan.

'I knew I'd find you here.'

Elizabeth spun around, cursing herself for not hearing the partition opening, not noticing the rush of cooler air. Then she relaxed – Jane was always very good at moving stealthily.

'Was any light visible?'

'No. Don't worry. You won't be discovered by Mother or the girls. Father may be another matter.'

'There is nothing wrong with keeping in shape. He can have no cause for objection. Hold the bag for me?'

Jane cocked an eyebrow but came and wrapped her arms around the bag. Elizabeth stepped away, turned and thudded a back kick into it.

'Oof,' said Jane. 'You are very strong now, Lizzy. Tell me, why are you out here? Why are you training so hard? I don't believe you are just staying in shape.'

Elizabeth wiped the sweat from her forehead with one arm.

'I do not know, Jane. I feel that something is coming. Someone–'

'By the pricking of your thumb?'

'Something wicked this way comes, yes.'

Elizabeth left off striking the bag and instead hefted a sack of grain from the floor, lifting it across her shoulders. She slowly squatted, then with a grunt stood upright, thigh muscles bunching. She repeated the movement. And again.

'But will Mr Bingley like it?' asked Jane, mock serious.

Elizabeth let out a gasp of laughter and let the bag slide from her shoulders. 'Don't make me laugh while I am doing this. You will cause me to injure myself.'

'Hm. Show me your hands.'

Elizabeth slowly unwound the wrapping from her fingers.

Jane grabbed her hands and turned them about in the light.

'Oh Lizzy,' she said, looking at the swollen red knuckles. 'The spring dance...'

'I told you, I have to be ready.'

'Then,' said Jane, 'if you are right, if there is some danger coming, then you should not be facing it alone. Every Vigil must have a companion...'

She looked away.

'Jane,' said Elizabeth, then more forcefully, 'Jane!' Her sister finally looked back at her, eyes shining in the lamplight. 'It was not your fault, sweet sister.'

Jane nodded slowly. 'Will you come back to bed?'

'Soon. I promise.'

Elizabeth kissed her on her forehead, then with a little push sent her towards the partition.

As Jane climbed through, she glanced back at her sister, who had taken up a long iron bar and was curling it up to her chin, her biceps standing out sharply in the flickering light.

Her sister looked strong and capable, sweat-sheened skin painted golden by the yellow light of the lantern. Yet Jane could not shake her own feeling of dread, of a mighty test to come. The strongest oak could be felled, should the storm prove wild enough.

Chapter 3

As custom required, Mr Bingley returned her father's visit, but all Elizabeth was able to do was catch a glimpse of him from an upstairs window, buffeted by her two youngest sisters as they oohed and aahed over his blue coat and black horse.

He was a young man, that was all she could learn. Still, not all villains were necessarily old. They all had to have started their descent into evil sometime. Some may have soured over time, reacting badly to life's experiences and pitfalls, slowly closing off and growing dark. Bitter. Wicked.

Others were perhaps naturally drawn to evil from their earliest days – no, that couldn't be right, that made it sound like a foregone conclusion, and Elizabeth couldn't accept that. For by that logic could one hold a villain to account, if performing evil acts was simply in their nature? No, it must be that some lacked the will to hold themselves back from acting on the baser urges – for surely everyone possessed some element of darkness – and the more they gave in to these, the more addictive they became. Then, just as an opium addict required more and more of the drug to obtain the result they craved, so too the evil accumulated in the villain's system, building up and rendering them capable of viler and viler acts.

The girls gathered with Mrs Bennet in her parlour while the visit continued below, all abuzz and full of supposition. Mr Bennet had avoided answering any questions after his visit to Netherfield, so they had been forced to make do with second-hand intelligence from their neighbour, Lady Lucas. Her report was highly favourable. Her husband, Sir William, had been delighted with him. Mr Bingley was quite young, wonderfully handsome, extremely agreeable and – best of all – meant to be at the next assembly with a large party. Nothing could be more delightful! To be fond of dancing was a certain step towards falling in love, after all.

'If I can see but one of you happily settled at Netherfield,' declared Mrs Bennet, 'and all the others equally well married, living happy, normal lives, I shall have nothing else to wish for.'

She fell silent, her mind obviously whirling with plans and stratagems.

It was indeed almost villain-like, thought Elizabeth, watching her mother.

Once Mr Bingley had departed, she attempted to corner her father, but he waved her off and retreated to his study.

The next move in the social game was an invitation to dinner at Longbourn, which was duly despatched and readily accepted. Mrs Bennet drove their cook, Hill, mad with her decisions and counter decisions on the courses to be offered, but then news came that certain matters suddenly demanded Mr Bingley's attention in London. Mrs Bennet could not, for the life of her, imagine what could drag him back to the city so soon after arriving in Hertfordshire.

Lady Lucas was able to calm her fears somewhat by suggesting that perhaps he had gone to London to organise a large party for the upcoming spring ball, and indeed reports soon followed that Mr Bingley was planning to bring 12 ladies and seven gentlemen back with him to the assembly.

Elizabeth wondered if this could be him reporting back to his cronies that Hertfordshire was indeed a suitable place for a lair, and the dance simply provided pretext for a sudden arrival of guests. That could mean a gang of 20 all together. The thought made her shudder. How could she prevail against such numbers?

When the night of the spring ball finally arrived, and all the local families were dressed in their finest and stuffed together in Meryton's rather smallish assembly room, it was with some relief to her – and to her sisters, who had dreaded an influx of fashionable ladies competing for the men's attention – that Mr Bingley brought only four others: his two sisters, the husband of one, and one other young gentleman.

Finally, Elizabeth was able to examine Bingley up close. He moved easily through the throng, with a smile and bow for all; a good-looking gentleman with a pleasant countenance and unaffected manners. Or at least, that was how he was presenting himself. His sisters appeared fine women, fashionable and confident. His brother-in-law, Mr Hurst, seemed fairly unremarkable. It was the last guest who drew the attention of the room, with his height, looks and noble mien. He was taller than Mr Bingley and Mr Hurst, and obviously well proportioned. His jacket hinted at a strong musculature. But whereas Mr Bingley exuded warmth and cheer, there was something icy about this man and his serious dark eyes. This, the gathering soon shared, was Mr Darcy.

Now Elizabeth had to reassess, for such was the difference between the men that she couldn't believe Mr Darcy was in any way an underling to Mr Bingley. It must be the other way around – if any of the men was Cain, surely it was this Darcy. That would fit: send in a lackey to hire a house as a base, then arrive as a simple guest, able to come and go as he pleased.

Unless, she thought with a frown, it was a double bluff, designed to throw off any investigator from looking too closely at Bingley in favour of his friend. Perhaps Darcy was too obvious...She rubbed her temples. Really, she was going to give herself a headache.

Mr Bingley soon made himself acquainted with all the principal people in the room and won them over; he was lively and unreserved, danced every dance, and talked of holding another ball at Netherfield at his earliest convenience. This was exactly the sort of young man the neighbourhood desired: all could agree on that.

Mr Darcy, on the other hand, stood silently to one side, staring straight ahead, answering any who spoke to him so shortly it bordered on rudeness. It appeared he felt himself above the company. He danced only twice: once with Miss Bingley and once with Mrs Hurst. Socially, his fate was thus decided: he was the proudest, most disagreeable man in the world, and everyone hoped he would not be staying long and would not come again.

Elizabeth, due to the want of a partner, was obliged to sit for two dances, and happened to overhear a conversation between Mr Darcy and Mr Bingley. The latter had just been dancing with Jane and came up red-faced and damp with sweat to speak to his friend.

'Come, Darcy,' Mr Bingley said. 'I hate to see you standing about by yourself in this stupid manner. You had much better dance!'

'I certainly shall not. You know how I detest it, unless I am particularly acquainted with my partner. At such an assembly as this, it would be unsupportable. Your sisters are engaged, and there is not another woman in the room who it would not be a punishment to me to stand up with.'

'Nonsense,' cried Bingley. 'You old stoat! Upon my life, I have never met so many pleasant girls in all my life as I have this evening!'

'You are dancing with the only handsome girl in the room,' said Mr Darcy, nodding towards Jane who stood fanning herself.

'Oh, she is the most beautiful creature I ever beheld! A little quiet, but beautiful. Listen, one of her sisters is sitting just behind you. She is very pretty and I daresay very agreeable. I'll ask Miss Bennet to introduce you.'

'Which do you mean?' Turning round, he cast his eye over Elizabeth as she quickly looked away. 'She is tolerable enough. Her build appears a little...solid for my liking. And I don't much fancy wasting my attention on a girl thus ignored by the local men. There is probably a reason. It is likely she is dull or poorly tempered. Go back and dance, Bingley, and leave me be.'

It was well the music was so loud, as Elizabeth ground her teeth together, and clasped her hands in her lap till the knuckles turned white. An image sprang to mind, of taking hold of Mr Darcy and throwing him over her back, but further imaginings were interrupted by a cry: 'Robbery! Oh, robbery!'

The musicians faltered to a stop, the sudden silence filled by shouts of alarm as Mrs Long was half-carried into the room by several servants and deposited in a chair. She appeared to be in a swoon. Mr Long was close behind, holding a white handkerchief, stained red, to his head.

'Robbery,' he cried again.

Glasses of punch were thrust into their hands. Mr Long slopped his as he held it in his shaking grasp.

Half the room was in uproar, asking what had happened, as the other half shushed them so that Mr Long could speak.

'Highwaymen!' he was at last able to gasp out. 'Here! In Hertfordshire!'

'Highwaymen,' cried half the room, while the other half angrily demanded that they do be quiet.

'We were running late,' continued Mr Long. 'And just coming over the bridge, when two men stopped us. I didn't know them, and thought at first they may be of Mr Bingley's party–'

Which they may, thought Elizabeth, her eyes darting to the apparently concerned expression on that young man's face. Behind him, Mr Darcy stood listening impassively.

'–and I thought they may wish directions to the dance, so I asked Rutherford to pull over. Well, the blighters – excuse my language – had daggers and a pistol, and threatened us. I protested, and one threatened to shoot me, and struck me on the head. Poor Rutherford was stabbed by the other – he is in the kitchen, I think. They ran off with my money belt and Mrs Long's jewellery.'

Mrs Long let out a loud wail. 'They took my mother's necklace! My keepsake of her!'

There was much hubbub, then Lord Lucas shouted above it: 'Let us all return to our homes and see to the safety of our families and our belongings! Travel in groups! Let none travel alone tonight, as...'

Elizabeth didn't hear the rest, as she was already moving, heading as fast as her dress would allow out through a side door. She lifted her skirts and ran swiftly to where her family's coach stood. Luckily there were no servants about – probably they were tending to poor Rutherford. She went to the back of the coach and squatted, feeling about beneath the rear luggage rack. A box was held in place there by two straps, which she swiftly undid. Grabbing one end of the box, she dragged it away into the darkness behind a nearby shed. She glanced about one more time, then reached to wrestle with the clasps on the back of her gown. If only there was time to find Jane, but she had to act swiftly. She dragged the garment over her head, feeling it tug at her hair, pulling strands loose. Once free, she grabbed a pair of black leather trousers from the chest. She thrust one leg in, but overbalanced, her haste making her clumsy. She fell backwards in the dirt, wincing at the thought of her fine undergarments, but then wriggled both legs in and pulled the trousers up – they were quite tight, to make it easier for her to run through woodland without brambles catching at her. Next came the black leather jerkin, swiftly buckled into place. Then the soft leather boots from the bottom of the chest, ideal for silent movement. Last was her mask – she pulled her hair back tightly and settled it into position.

As always, once she had the mask in place, the leather of her armour pressing on her muscles, she felt...*alive*. This was her moment, to show that Hertfordshire was still protected, and those who sought to threaten it had best beware. She stuffed her gown as neatly as she could into the box and shoved it further behind the shed.

She skirted the noise and torchlight at the front of the assembly hall and ran through the darkened streets for the bridge. Just over it, she cut left off the road and into a grove of oak that grew along the riverbank. As a Vigil, it was important to know your area well – she guessed that the highwaymen would not go far before wanting to stop and examine their takings, and she knew of a small clearing some half mile in, where the thicket was at its widest. She ran quickly as she dared, hands before her to ward off any low branches. Her night vision improved the further she was from the assembly hall, and the tree trunks stood out as blacker shapes in the gloom. Her breath came raggedly, exertion and nervous energy making it hard to settle into a controlled rhythm.

When she guessed that she was nearing the clearing, she slowed to a creep, sliding her booted feet to avoid stepping on any twigs. A dim light showed up ahead, and she fancied she heard voices – barely, over the thudding of her heart. She forced herself to breathe more slowly, and quietly, and glided forward through the shadows.

In the clearing knelt two men, a hooded lantern burning low beside them. There was the clink of coins, and then one held something aloft that hung glinting from his fingers – Mrs Long's necklace, no doubt. Elizabeth felt a blaze of anger – how dare they take something so precious from a lady!

She strode forward, growling, 'Drop that and surrender!'

She had misjudged – she saw it in an instant as the two men first jumped and cursed in fright, but then recovered and rose to face her. Local chancers would have dropped the loot and fled, to be pursued or not at her leisure, or maybe even surrendered, allowing her to bind them and leave them for the constable. These men appeared to be ready to fight.

She was committed now. There was nothing for it – she charged.

As she neared the closest, she launched herself, throwing one knee forward, and grimaced in satisfaction as she felt it impact with his sternum. He stumbled backwards, tripping and falling, and she just managed to avoid going down in a tangled heap with him. She spun, but the second man was already upon her – he was fast, faster than she had faced before. She brought her arms up in guard, but he had already struck – she felt a sharp blow in her ribs, a hot stinging – she glanced down to see the glinting blade in his hand. *Stab her – he had tried to stab her* – but the tough leather had held the blade, only allowing the very tip to break through and pierce her. The man grunted in surprise, expecting her to have fallen. She seized her chance and wrapped her arms around him. He tried again with the knife, but it was too late. She turned, getting her weight under him, then straightened her legs and pivoted, and he flipped over her back and landed heavily on the ground.

He had tried to stab her.

She needed to clear her mind.

She could be dead.

Something hummed past her face. There was a cry. The first man was back on his feet, a pistol in his hand – and a black arrow lodged in his shoulder. The pistol dropped from his fingers, and he stared at her in bewildered accusation. She whirled, crouching, staring at the void surrounding them. There came a thrum, and another arrow buried itself in the ground between her and the second man, who had rolled onto his belly and now lay wide-eyed.

A tall, shadowy figure appeared at the edge of the lamplight, cloaked and hooded, a hunting bow drawn to fire again. Elizabeth threw herself sideways, kicking out with her feet and smashing the lamp, plunging the clearing into total darkness. She heard cursing and crashing as the two highwaymen took their chance and plunged away into the night. She remained where she was, ears straining, eyes trying to pick out the black-caped man in the inky dark. She held her breath, and fancied she could hear deep, slow breathing, and then quiet steps as whoever it was stalked away.

When it had been quiet for some minutes, she slowly felt about, careful of the shards of glass from the lantern, until her fingers chanced upon the chain of Mrs Long's locket. She rose slowly, limbs suddenly weak and heavy. Her fingers felt along the side of her jerkin, found the small indentation where the knife had struck her. At least the cotton padding had saved her too much bruising, and no doubt it was soaking up whatever blood was coming from the tiny cut she had received.

Who was the man in the black cloak? Was this Cain? But why shoot his own man? Or was that just an accident while actually aiming at her? Either way it demonstrated his disregard for life.

The locket was gripped tightly in her hand. Was it worth it? She could have died tonight. Was this piece of metal worth her life? The knife, the arrow...She was lucky.

She lingered at the tree line by the bridge, and only returned to the assembly hall when the carriages had all departed. Her mother would be frantic, but Jane could be counted on to provide a cover story – most likely that she had accompanied their neighbours, the Lucases. She recovered her gown from the box behind the shed. It was an awkward armful to carry home, but she could hardly leave it, and it would be difficult to send a servant to fetch it without raising suspicions. She would also have to leave the necklace somewhere it could be found. A pity she couldn't deliver it personally, take the credit for it, but that was not the Vigil way.

Chapter 4

The soft, warm glow of candlelight illuminated their bedroom, outlining Jane's silhouette in the window, as Elizabeth limped down the dark carriageway. She was glad of her sister's helping hands when she reached the top of the trellis – the gown bunched under one arm made climbing difficult and her strength had left her in the wake of the night's action.

Jane fussed about her as she peeled off her leather garments, exclaiming in alarm at the small puncture in her side and the purple bruising surrounding it. She insisted on fetching water and sponging the wound clean. Elizabeth told her briefly of the night's action, but hesitated to mention her suspicions about the newcomers. Instead she sought to distract Jane from her worrying by asking how she had enjoyed the dance – at least, up until the moment of alarm. To her surprise, her sister allowed the change of subject and launched into warm praise of none other than Mr Bingley.

'He is just what a young man should be,' said Jane, 'sensible, good-humoured, lively. And I never saw such happy manners! So much at ease, with such perfect good breeding!'

'He is also handsome,' said Elizabeth drily, 'which I suppose helps, somewhat?'

Her sister missed her tone. 'I was very much flattered by his asking me to dance a second time. I did not expect such a compliment.'

'Did you not?' The words hurt her heart. 'I did for you. Why shouldn't he or anyone ask you to dance again? You are five times as lovely as every other woman in the room. I wish you could see that. And I know you are blushing now and wish me to be quiet. So. Bingley, eh? You have liked many stupider a person, I suppose.'

'Lizzy!'

'Oh! You are a great deal too apt to like people in general, you know. You never see a fault in anybody. All the world are good and agreeable in your eyes. I have never heard you speak ill of a human being in my life. Even knowing...even knowing what you do.'

Jane looked down, and Elizabeth cursed herself. She did not wish to bring discomfort but had strayed into dangerous, painful territory. She really wanted to question Jane more about Bingley's character, but felt awkward and did not want to risk further upset interrogating her. She wished she could accept that he was as he appeared, take her sister's obvious attraction to him as a sign of his essential goodness, but she was not blessed with the same lack of suspicion.

'And how did you find his sisters?' she asked at last, and was rewarded with a slight smile.

'Well, as I am sure you noted, their manners are perhaps not the equal of their brother's.'

'Jane Bennet!' said Elizabeth. 'Be very careful! That is nearly a criticism!'

Jane held up her hand. 'But they are very pleasing women when you converse with them. Miss Bingley is to live with her brother and keep his house. I think she shall make a charming neighbour.'

Elizabeth listened in silence but was not convinced. They may have seemed fine ladies, but they appeared haughty brats to her, proud and conceited. And while it seemed unlikely they could be villains, in league with Cain, she could not yet dismiss that possibility either.

As she climbed into her bed, still fussed over by Jane, she reflected on the oddness of being caught up in two such levels of struggle at once: that of good versus evil, and, at a more domestic level, that of politeness versus rudeness. Tonight she had faced both literal and social shafts from the cloaked man and the insufferable Mr Darcy.

She sat up.

'What did Mr Bingley and Mr Darcy do when the assembly broke up?'

Jane thought for a moment. 'I didn't see them. There was quite the hubbub. I expect they escorted the ladies back to Netherfield.'

Jane blew out the candle. Elizabeth lay back, hoping sleep would come quickly – her body was wretchedly tired – but her mind jumped about. It would have been easy enough for Bingley to send the ladies back with Mr Hurst and Darcy, then come to meet the highwaymen. Or for Darcy to do the same. She frowned. Was that one of them, beneath the cloak? By attempting to shoot her, whoever it was had proved beyond doubt his villainous – and murderous – intent. She shuddered. She must expose this villain as quickly as possible.

She had to be careful, be circumspect. Not only must she avoid alerting them to her suspicions (embarrassing if she was mistaken, potentially deadly if she was correct), she must also hide her actions from her family. On the one hand, her mother and the younger girls did not know the family secret. On the other, she did not wish to further alarm Jane. Then there was her father...She winced in the darkness. *Don't make me forbid you.* It had not been like this in the old days. Then, he would have been leading the investigation: the Foxhound of Hertfordshire, sniffing out wrongdoing. And they – she and Jane – his companions, the Pack, at his side.

It had all changed now. He had hung up his mask, refused to reveal the secret to the younger girls and train them, curb their ill-disciplined ways. And Jane was left changed.

And she?

She gritted her teeth. There was still one of the Pack on the hunt. And that would be enough. It would have to be.

Chapter 5

The Lucas family lived within a short walk of Longbourn. Sir William Lucas had previously been in trade in London where he had made a tolerable fortune. Unfortunately, this had brought him to the attention of a local villain there, who styled himself the Black Baron. The Baron's speciality was extorting money from successful businessmen: refusal was met with increasing acts of violence. Sir William had held out as long as he could, enduring in that process broken windows and foul messages painted on his warehouse. But when his foreman's arm and ribs were broken by hooded men, Sir William had grudgingly decided he must pay up. It was at this point he was contacted by a Vigil troop, the Red Robins, who requested he set up a meeting with the Baron in his warehouse and give them permission to prosecute the business as they saw fit. Sir William had agreed, even choosing to station himself within his warehouse at the time appointed to meet with the Baron, despite the risk.

The ensuing Vigil ambush resulted in the defeat and permanent crippling of the Black Baron, the death or wounding of half a dozen henchmen, and the destruction by fire of half the warehouse. When the Baron's hood was removed and he was revealed to be a local bishop, there was a great deal of consternation – not least among two of the Red Robins who happened to be vicars from within that very bishop's diocese (it was they who inflicted the worst of the beating). Some expressed surprise that he had not styled himself the Black Bishop, but those who made more of a study of villains and Vigils (there were many popular pamphlets printed on the subject) pointed out that a disguise was supposed to hide one's true identity, not provide such an obvious clue. Though, they conceded, the name was a good one and thus sure to be adopted by some other villain at a later date.

Sir William himself was unharmed, but left soot-stained and wondering how he was to go on. Shortly after, a representative of the King informed him that he was to be knighted for his service to law and order. Obviously one of the Vigils had been highly placed, or at least had friends in high places.

But the whole affair had given Sir William a disgust for business, and he had removed his family to a house about a mile from Meryton. As such they became the Bennet's nearest neighbours.

Lady Lucas was Mrs Bennet's dearest friend and greatest rivel. They shared proximity, a simplistic worldview, and the fact they both had several children. The eldest Lucas was a sensible, intelligent young woman named Charlotte – she shortly had become Elizabeth's closest friend.

The morning after the ball, the two families met to discuss the excitement. To Elizabeth's relief, it was the early part of the evening – the dancing – that the ladies preferred to discuss. She did not wish her disappearance to come up in the conversation, as she hadn't had enough time to pull Charlotte aside and explain her part in her alibi.

'You began the evening well, Charlotte,' said Mrs Bennet brightly. 'You were Mr Bingley's first choice.'

'Yes,' returned Charlotte with a small smile. 'But he seemed to like his second better.'

'Oh! You mean Jane, I suppose. Because he did indeed dance with her.' She smiled at Lady Lucas. 'Twice. That does rather make it seem he admired her. Such a gentleman. If only he would choose his friends more carefully – that Mr Darcy was a most frightful man.'

'Perhaps he just appears so,' said Jane.

Mrs Bennet pursed her lips. 'I am sure however he appears is exactly how he is.'

Discussion continued on the usual topics of who wore what, and who danced with whom, how lively were the musicians, and ultimately how disappointing that the affair should be brought to such a sudden end by the arrival of the distraught Longs.

'I'm sure I don't know why they just didn't go home after they were robbed,' said Kitty.

'Or at least waited until the dance was over to come in,' added Lydia. 'That would have been nice. It's not like he was that badly hurt.'

'Lydia!' said Jane.

'Well, Jane,' said her mother, 'it was a shame to have the night cut short...'

A little later, Elizabeth was able to signal to Charlotte, and they went out into the garden. They walked swiftly out of sight, lest Lydia and Kitty decide they were bored and seek to accompany them.

Dragging Elizabeth down onto a stone bench, Charlotte said, 'Now tell me the rest.'

With great relief Elizabeth told her about the fight in the clearing. In some ways she could be more open with Charlotte than Jane. Charlotte had grown to be such a trusted friend that it had seemed natural for Elizabeth to trust her with her secret when she had first taken up the mask. Now, when she finished, Charlotte lay her hand on Elizabeth's thigh and squeezed it.

'Lizzy, it sounds so dangerous. It is too much for one person.'

'I manage.'

'You need a companion.'

An image flashed unbidden into Elizabeth's mind: the stocky figure staggering out of the darkness, eyes wide with fear, the soaking-wet girl lying limp in his arms, her face so terribly pale amongst the clinging tendrils of her hair.

She forced if from her mind, met her friend's pleading gaze.

'I've told you before, Charlotte,' she said, her voice steadier than she expected. 'I know what I am doing. I am careful.'

'Train me. Let me help you. Every Vigil needs a companion – let me be yours.'

'Dear Charlotte. You know I cannot do that. I could not bear it if I exposed you to danger.'

'Yet I am supposed to bear you exposing yourself? Bear not being able to help you?' Charlotte stared at her intensely, something hungry in her gaze.

Elizabeth looked down where Charlotte's hand still lay on her thigh. Charlotte glanced down too, and drew it away. She clasped her fingers together.

'Charlotte...'

Charlotte smiled tightly. 'I am sorry. I don't mean to press you. I know you need an outlet, someone to talk to about these things and I am glad I can at least offer you that. But you can't stop me...worrying about you. Now. perhaps we should rejoin the others?'

When they entered the drawing room, it appeared the conversation had not moved on.

'Lizzy,' cried her mother. 'There you are! We were just speaking of that terrible Mr Darcy and his refusal to dance with you!'

'Well, Mother, he didn't quite refuse. It is just that he did not ask.' How she wished that the exchange had not been noted. Such public incidents became the currency of one's worth. Kept private, they were naught but small hurts, but once widely known and gossiped over in drawing rooms across the county, they very much affected how one was seen. At least in this case, it was being taken more as a comment upon the manners of the gentleman rather than her desirability as a woman.

'Well, I would not have you take his hand should he ever get another chance to ask,' said her mother.

'I believe, ma'am, I may safely promise never to take his hand.'

'He is prideful,' said Charlotte, 'but I suppose that is natural with everything being in his favour. Wealthy, well built, with a good family – is it any wonder he should think highly of himself? Perhaps he has a right to be proud.'

'That is very true,' replied Elizabeth, 'and I could easily forgive his pride if he had not trodden quite so heavily on mine.'

'Pride,' cut in Mary, 'is a very common failing, I believe. By all that I have read, I am convinced human nature is particularly prone to it. If we consider–'

'Oh, do be quiet, Mary!' said Kitty. 'You quite make my head ache when you go on.'

'Now, now,' said Mrs Bennet, but she did not encourage Mary to continue.

'You know, if I were as rich and strong as Mr Darcy,' said Lydia, 'I should set myself up as a great villain and become wealthy as some Persian king, with slaves and servants and henchmen galore to do my every bidding!'

'You would do no such thing,' said her mother crossly. 'You, become a villain? The very idea!'

Elizabeth shot a look at Jane, who smiled and shrugged slightly.

'You could be a Vigil,' suggested Kitty.

'Certainly not that either!' said Mrs Bennet.

'Ugh,' said Lydia. 'How boring that would be. No, I should much rather be a villain.'

Mrs Bennet again countered that she would not, and the argument ended only with the conclusion of the visit.

Chapter 6

Elizabeth's next opportunity to observe the newcomers was at a party hosted by the Longs, who were determined to show themselves unaffected by their ordeal. A number of the wealthier families were invited, along with the party from Netherfield. On the morning, a message came for Jane from Mrs Hurst and Miss Bingley, the two sisters, stating their hope that she would be attending and their great excitement at the opportunity to further their acquaintance. No mention was made of Elizabeth or any of the other girls.

Though Jane expressed doubt that such elegant ladies could find someone such as she interesting enough to wish to spend time with, Elizabeth could see she was quietly flattered by the attention. It was obvious watching her put a little more care in her preparations that afternoon, as one of the maids helped them don their better gowns – Elizabeth's had thankfully avoided any damage or stains after being carried home the week before – that seeing Mr Bingley was also on her mind.

Elizabeth had to find out the truth as soon as possible – if Bingley was a criminal, the sooner she thwarted him the less heartbreak for Jane. And if it turned out that he was not Cain, then she could, with relief, allow her sister to love where she would.

Later that afternoon they joined the throng gathered in one of the

Longs' tastefully appointed rooms. Mrs Long took the opportunity to joyfully show off her mysteriously returned locket, and the party then spread out to enjoy the company and refreshments.

'Bingley likes your sister,' said Charlotte, sitting beside Elizabeth. They both looked over to where Bingley stood chatting with Jane.

'And she likes him.'

'She may.' Charlotte hesitated. 'But Bingley may not be aware of it.'

'Not be aware of it? How could he not be aware of it? It's obvious.'

'Remember, Eliza, that he does not know Jane's disposition as you do.'

'Meaning?'

'Meaning, much as I adore Jane, she can come across a little...subdued.'

Elizabeth frowned. 'Well, I am far less concerned whether he should understand her character than that I should understand his.'

'As a potential brother-in-law?'

'Firstly that he is just as he appears.'

'Well,' said Charlotte, 'should he prove to be so, I wish Jane success with all my heart, and if she were to marry him tomorrow, I should think she had as good a chance of happiness as if she had been studying his character for a year. Happiness in marriage is entirely a matter of chance.'

'You make me laugh, Charlotte. You would never leave your own happiness to such chance as you describe. No, you would be sure to know your future husband's character as well as you know mine.'

Charlotte simply smiled, but Elizabeth was slightly confused, for there appeared to be an inexplicable trace of sadness in her friend's eyes.

Before she could question her further, Charlotte was drawn away by her mother, and Elizabeth found herself instead standing near a Colonel Forster, whose regiment was soon to be encamped several miles beyond Meryton. At the same moment she suddenly became aware of Mr Darcy standing close behind her. Her back twitched at his cold presence – frankly, she disliked anyone standing there, it wasn't safe – but she resolved not to let him upset her.

'I believe, Colonel,' she said lightly, 'that we will all soon be able to sleep much more soundly, knowing that there is such a strong military presence in the neighbourhood.'

'How do you mean?' asked the Colonel, smiling.

'Why, no villain would dare raise his head with the might of His Majesty's redcoats stationed not far down the road.'

There was a sudden burst of coughing behind her.

'Are you unwell, Mr Darcy?' she asked, turning.

That gentleman regarded her coolly. 'No,' he said. 'I do not get sick.'

'No, of course you don't.'

'I'm afraid,' said the Colonel, glancing between them, 'that I must disappoint you, Miss Bennet. We are not permitted to intervene in civil matters.'

'Oh, really? How disappointing. Well, if you can't do that, and if we are currently not at war with anyone, what *can* your regiment supply?'

'Would a large number of handsome young officers suffice?'

'For some. But without activity provided alongside them, they may be more of a nuisance. Do you think you might include a ball?'

She was rewarded by a brief wince crossing Mr Darcy's face. *Touché*.

'That we can do,' said the Colonel with a smile. 'All work, as they say...'

The Colonel bowed, and moved off, leaving Elizabeth awkwardly alone with Mr Darcy. He was staring at her intently. She felt increasingly uncomfortable and fought the urge to touch her face. Was there something wrong? She didn't think she had any bruises, nor bags under her eyes. Luckily at that moment Charlotte reappeared beside her.

'Did you wish to say something, Mr Darcy?' Elizabeth said.

'About what?'

'A ball. Or...wishing to feel safe to sleep at night?'

'Why would you think yourself in danger at night?'

'Because you never know who may be skulking about in the darkness.'

Darcy frowned. 'Indeed.'

'If you don't mind, Mr Darcy,' said Charlotte, taking her arm, 'I am going to open the instrument. And, Eliza, you know what follows.'

'You are a very strange friend! Always wanting me to play. If my vanity had taken a musical turn you would be invaluable. As it is, I would rather not perform in front of those who are no doubt in the habit of hearing the very best performers and are all too ready to point out my many faults. But if it must be so, it must.' She glanced gravely at Mr Darcy. 'It has been a pleasure conversing with you, sir, but I fear we have talked so much I am quite breathless, and I must save some for my song.'

She turned her back on him, feeling quite pleased with herself despite the prickling sensation up and down her spine that told her he watched her the whole way to the piano.

Her performance was pleasing enough, though her fingers were stiff from her recent fights and stumbled through some of the more difficult sections. After two songs, and before she could reply to the entreaties of several guests that she should sing again, she was eagerly succeeded at the instrument by her sister Mary, who practically barged her aside.

Mary was always impatient to display her knowledge and accomplishments, for it had not escaped her notice that she was the least attractive of the five Bennet girls. She sought to overcome this deficit via working hard to attain a higher level of skill – any skill. Unfortunately reading the room was not one of them – she launched into several lively Scotch and Irish airs, belting them out at top volume. Lydia and Kitty eagerly grabbed some of the other younger folk and began dancing at one end of the room, but the rest of the audience found their ability to converse constrained. Mary ploughed on, loud and undaunted.

Elizabeth found her eyes drawn to Mr Darcy, who stood emanating indignation. Sir William appeared beside him, straining on his toe tips to shout in his ear.

'What a charming amusement for the young people this is, Mr Darcy! A welcome distraction from the recent incident. There is nothing like dancing. I consider it as one of the first refinements of polished societies.'

'Every savage can dance.'

Sir William smiled, a little uncertainly, but gamely continued. 'Your friend performs delightfully,' he said, nodding at Bingley, who had joined in with the dancers. 'And I do not doubt that you are an adept in the art yourself, Mr Darcy.'

'You saw me dance at Meryton, I believe, sir.'

'Yes indeed! And very pleasing it was to watch. You move very well. Very well indeed. Very...fluid.' He looked up and down at Darcy's muscular form. 'Do you dance often at St James?'

'Never, sir. I am generally occupied by far more important matters.'

Mr Darcy fell silent, and even Sir William felt the divide between them. But at that moment he noticed Elizabeth, and took hold of her arm.

'My dear Miss Eliza, why are you not dancing? Mr Darcy, you must allow me to present this young lady to you as a very desirable partner. You cannot refuse to dance when so much beauty is before you.' He took her hand and attempted to place it in Mr Darcy's. That gentleman, caught by surprise at this suggestion, appeared about to take it automatically. But Elizabeth glanced down at her reddened, slightly swollen knuckles, and instantly pulled her hand back before Darcy could see.

'Indeed, sir, I have not the least intention of dancing,' she said. 'I entreat you not to suppose that I stood here in order to beg for a partner.'

She turned away, aware of Sir William, somewhat flustered, pausing then wandering off behind her. She would have moved further away herself, but out of the corner of her eye saw Miss Bingley approaching Mr Darcy and so hovered, that she might listen in.

'I can guess the subject of your reverie,' said Miss Bingley.

'I should imagine not,' replied Mr Darcy.

'You are considering how unbearable it would be to pass many evenings in this bumpkin manner. Indeed, I am quite of your opinion. I was never more annoyed! The insipidity, and yet the noise! I know you well!'

'Perhaps my mind was more agreeably engaged. Perhaps I was meditating on the pleasure a pair of fine eyes can bestow.'

'Oh really?' said Miss Bingley, fluttering her lashes. 'Who could you mean?'

Elizabeth swiftly looked away as she felt him glance in her direction.

'Her?' Miss Bingley's voice was sweet, but icy. 'I am all astonishment! How long has she been the favourite?'

'Don't be ridiculous. But...there *is* something about her eyes...' mused Mr Darcy, more to himself than her. He frowned. 'Where–'

'And am I to wish you joy?'

His attention snapped back to Miss Bingley, and his eyes were cold. 'That is exactly the sort of thing I would expect you to say.'

At that she relented, but remained fastened to his side for the rest of the evening, like some villain's personal bodyguard.

Chapter 7

The town of Meryton was only one mile from Longbourn, a most convenient distance for the young ladies, who usually walked there three or four times a week. In the case of the younger sisters, it was to pay their respects to a favourite milliner. In the case of Elizabeth, it was to visit Aunt Phillips.

Aunt Phillips was known as the sister of Mrs Bennet, and understood to have been married to a Mr Phillips, a clerk in business, now deceased. What was not known outside of the Bennet family was that in fact Mrs Bennet had no such sister. The person known as Aunt Phillips was, in reality, an old Vigil associate of Mr Bennet's, who, needing a safe location to retire to and reinvent themself in, had moved to Meryton under the guise of a widowed sister.

Mr Bennet's family was well known locally so it had not been possible for a sister to suddenly appear from his side. It was therefore necessary that she be ascribed to Mrs Bennet, who would greet mention of the name with compressed lips. However, despite her distaste for the arrangement, this was one of those occasions where she found her husband to be most obstinate and mysterious.

So when Elizabeth mentioned her intention of walking into Meryton to see Aunt Phillips the morning after the dance, Kitty and Lydia expressed their delight in accompanying her.

'But only to the village,' Lydia told Elizabeth. 'We don't want to see Aunt Phillips. She is very strange. I sometimes wonder–'

'Well don't,' snapped Elizabeth.

Thankfully Jane elected to come along to keep the younger girls in line.

The walk into Meryton was pleasant, the early springtime weather comfortably cool so that young ladies in long gowns need not fear unsightly perspiration. The path took them along lush green meadows and through a small wood. It was while passing through this that Jane fell back alongside Elizabeth, who had been trailing a little.

'What is the matter? Why do you keep looking behind?'

'Do you not feel it? Like we are being watched?'

Jane glanced around. 'No, I do not.'

'Jane, I think we are being followed. Keep the girls going, I will catch up.'

'Elizabeth–'

But it was too late. As they passed by a large tree surrounded by some thick bushes, Elizabeth darted off the path and pressed back into the foliage. Jane hesitated, and Elizabeth was about to hiss at her, but then she strode quickly off after their sisters, whose high, piping voices and laughter carried easily through the trees.

Elizabeth shifted awkwardly in her dress, pulling the fabric up above her knees, exposing her white undergarments. It was ridiculous. The dress made swift movement almost impossible. It was so frustrating that the very clothing she must wear by day should hamper and constrain her so. A male Vigil would not be so compromised in his normal daywear. At least at night, in her leather, there was a kind of equality.

A twig cracked nearby, and she held her breath. Was that the stealthy tread of someone on the path? She leaned to the side, craning her head, trying to catch a glimpse, and was then struck by the strong feeling that someone was standing just on the other side of the tree, listening. An ant tickled her, crawling across the back of her neck, but she dared not move. She thought she heard a faint scuffing, of something rubbing against the tree. Should she jump out and surprise whoever it was, demand to know why they were following them? Now was the time, *now*. Action was always better than inaction. She would at least get a look at whoever it was. She made to spring forward, but the bracken dragged at her, slowing her, one branch catching her hair, and as she fought her way clear she heard light footsteps running away deeper into the trees. By the time she was free, whoever it had been was long gone.

Cursing the lost opportunity, she tidied herself as best she could and then strode after her sisters.

'Oh Lizzy!' cried Lydia as she exited the wood. 'Did you really need to pass water that badly? How very wicked and wild of you!'

Kitty laughed, and Jane reddened and scolded them, but they were in high spirits and continued to laugh loudly the rest of the way into the village. Elizabeth was quite glad to leave them.

She made her way down a lane to a small house with a somewhat overgrown front garden. She knocked on the door and waited, and after a short while a gruff voice bade her enter.

'Hello, Aunt,' she said to the large figure seated knitting in the front room.

'Eliza,' said Aunt Phillips in a deep, rasping voice. 'A social call, or have you come to train?'

There was an eager glint in her eye.

'Train, please, Aunt. If you have the time.'

Aunt Phillips dropped her knitting. She looked at the door behind Elizabeth hopefully.

'No one else with you?'

'No, dear Aunt. Just me.'

'Oh. No matter.' Aunt Phillips nodded, her heavy jowls seeming to sag.

'Jane is still...Well, frankly, we need her to keep an eye on Kitty and Lydia. Those two are becoming quite impossible. Their heads are full of nothing but fashion and young gentlemen. And Mary is, well, Mary.'

'And your father?'

'Oh, Aunt. I am not sure he will ever return.'

'Ah well,' said Aunt Phillips, and she rose from the chair, her large frame seeming to fill the room. 'Let us begin.'

Elizabeth followed her through the house to a room at the back. What was once a sunny sitting room had been transformed. There was little furniture, just racks holding a variety of implements. The floor was covered in stitched canvas. Elizabeth slipped off her shoes before entering, her feet sinking a little into the cushioning. Aunt Phillips was pulling her gown roughly over her head, and Elizabeth copied her, hanging the garment on a peg by the door. Aunt Phillips gestured to the middle of the room, and they stood side by side, facing a portrait of a stern moustachioed gentleman hanging on the far wall.

'We bow to our master, Sensei Barton-Wright, who brought the teachings of the East to London for the betterment of gentlemen. And gentlewomen. As Sensei Kunichiro taught him, and he taught me, so now I teach you. We gratefully receive this training.'

They bowed, then Aunt Phillips turned to face Elizabeth, and they bowed again.

'Prepare,' she said, and rolled her large, muscular shoulders and cracked her thick knuckles. 'Now, basics.'

She gripped Elizabeth by the vest of her undergarments, and Elizabeth grabbed hold of her in return. One of Aunt Phillips' feet flashed past her, seeking to scythe around behind her knees and trip her up, but Elizabeth swiftly stepped clear, tugging sharply down on Aunt Phillips' sleeve and tapping her ankle with a foot as she staggered, off balance. She only just avoided losing her footing, and grunted approval. They swept around the room in this odd dance, each seeking to trip up the other. Aunt Phillips would suddenly step in and pivot, wrapping an arm around Elizabeth's waist to throw her, and Elizabeth would jump clear of the danger. She, in turn, would duck in, seizing one of Aunt Phillip's legs, and turn, forcing the other to hop wildly to avoid a fall.

'Very good,' said Aunt Phillips. They were both panting now. 'Now let me teach you this one – it is advanced, but you are ready.'

Gripping tightly, she lifted one foot and planted it up against Elizabeth's stomach. Elizabeth had a moment to look at it in surprise, but then Aunt Phillips abruptly sat backwards onto the ground, pulling her down. At the same time, she straightened her leg, and Elizabeth found herself being propelled in a somersault over the top of her aunt. She had the sense to tuck her head forward, but still landed quite heavily on the mats. She found her aunt sitting astride her – somehow she had maintained her grip and used Elizabeth's own momentum to follow her over and end up on top. And now her grip was locked in the collar of Elizabeth's undervest, twisting it until the edges of Elizabeth's vision grew blurry and the blood thumped in her temples. She tapped her aunt's thick wrist. The grip relaxed, and her vision restored.

'*Tomoe nagi*,' said Aunt Phillips. 'Circle throw. If you keep your grip and think of doing a backwards somersault, you ride your opponent's movement and finish in mount.'

'Teach me,' said Elizabeth.

They kept at it for the next half hour, alternating throws with basic boxing and kicking techniques. Aunt Phillips fairly purred with pleasure at Elizabeth's form.

'Good, very good. You are better than Jane ever was. Better even than your father. Why, if I had had you as a student in London...'

Aunt Phillips' eyes lost focus as she sank into memory. A cloud appeared to cover her face, the pleasure gained in the physical contest suddenly lost.

'Aunt Phillips,' said Elizabeth. 'I was thinking – I believe it is time to add a weapon to our training.'

That shook her aunt from her reverie.

'A weapon? No. A weapon is separate to you, and dangerous. It may be taken and used against you. Better to be the weapon yourself.'

'Things are changing. The danger is greater. I believe I need it.'

She told her aunt about the highwayman with the knife.

Aunt Phillips looked down, twisting her hands. 'My child, it is one thing to inflict a necessary beating upon a miscreant. It is another thing altogether to take someone's life. Do not rush into that nightmare.'

'Then what about a weapon less likely to kill? Not a knife or sword, but something else?'

Aunt Phillips' expression lightened. 'Hm. I suppose, yes, a very good idea. That we can do. But what to choose? Something from the French style? They are masters of the stick – *La canne*? Fighting with a walking stick? Still, a young lady, carrying a cane...It would attract attention. Unless you faked an injury, perhaps? Affected a limp? An excellent cover that would be; none would suspect you were a Vigil then.'

Aunt Phillips caught the expression on Elizabeth's face.

'Ah, but of course. You do not wish to limp. What young lady wishes to limp? We must make allowances for vanity, too, must we not? Then, perhaps, *la baton court*? The short stick? Yes. It could be short enough for you to hide it up one sleeve, yet strong enough to inflict quite a blow.'

Aunt Phillips rummaged about in a chest, finally coming up with a small club around 15 inches long.

'*Brise*,' she cried, swinging it. '*Croise tete*! *Enleve*!'

Elizabeth was pleased to see the light blazing in her aunt's eyes.

'Will this do?' asked Aunt Phillips.

She took the proffered weapon. The wood was stained the colour of dark honey. It was smooth in her grip, of pleasing weight. Her fingers tightened about it. It felt...natural.

'It will do very well indeed,' growled Elizabeth. 'Now, show me the strikes.'

Later, there was, of course, time for tea. Elizabeth sat nursing her cup with one hand while rubbing her thigh with the other.

'Is it very bad, my dear?' enquired Aunt Phillips, solemn-eyed beneath her thick brows.

'It is fine, Aunt.' Her aunt had caught her in the leg with a roundhouse kick that had knocked her to the matting and left her thigh aching and numb.

'It is called "corking",' said her aunt. 'Painful, but not permanent. I'm sorry I became a little overenthusiastic.'

There was a rattling sound across the roof, and Elizabeth slopped some of her tea as she jumped. Aunt Phillips remained still, her eyes slightly closing. Another rattle followed the first.

'What is that?' Elizabeth made to stand, but her aunt motioned her to sit.

'It is nothing. Just some of the neighbourhood children, who find me... inexplicable.'

'Does this happen often?'

'No, my dear. More cake?'

'You should go to their parents.'

Aunt Phillips pursed her lips. 'I prefer to keep a low profile. Besides, teasing an old widow is fairly traditional, isn't it?'

But that ought not be so, thought Elizabeth, though she held her tongue, as her aunt clearly did not wish to discuss it.

When it was time to meet her sisters. Elizabeth washed in a basin and towelled herself dry, then pulled her gown back on. Finally, she took up the baton and slipped it up one sleeve. If you were looking for it, you might see the shape, but Elizabeth found if she walked with her arms crossed, it was unnoticeable. Pleased, she kissed her aunt goodbye, lips brushing the rough cheek, and walked into the centre of town. The day had changed – dark clouds had begun to gather on the horizon. She found the others already waiting for her, Lydia and Kitty laden with several hat boxes.

'Lizzy,' yelled Lydia when she saw Elizabeth coming. 'You will never guess the news! The innkeeper's daughter has run away!'

'Lydia, shush,' cried Jane, looking about. 'Do not shout such things aloud.'

'But its true!' said Kitty. 'She has gone! Some say she has run away to London.'

'Isn't it exciting?' said Lydia.

'It is not,' said Elizabeth. 'A young girl on her own in London...It isn't safe.'

'So do not treat it like it is something to be excited about,' added Jane.

Lydia and Kitty rolled their eyes at each other, but fell largely silent for the remainder of the walk home. Once back with their mother, however, they could not restrain themselves from blurting out the news.

'From all I can collect by your manner of talking,' said Mr Bennet, who had just exited his library, 'you must be two of the silliest girls in the country. I have suspected it some time, but now I am convinced.'

'I am astonished, my dear,' countered Mrs Bennet, 'that you should be so ready to think your own children silly. They are all, in fact, very clever.'

Mr Bennet fixed his wife with a particularly owl-like stare, and Elizabeth feared how he may respond, when all was saved by the entrance of the footman with a note for Jane from Netherfield. Mrs Bennet's eyes sparkled with pleasure, and she was eagerly calling out even as Jane opened it.

'Well, Jane? What is it about? What does it say? Make haste and tell us, my love, tell us!'

'It is from Caroline Bingley,' said Jane 'She writes that if I do not come and dine today she and Louisa will be in danger of hating each other for the rest of their lives, as much as a Vigil hates a villain. I am to come as soon as I can. Oh. Her brother and the other gentlemen are to dine with the officers.'

'With the officers,' cried Lydia.

'Dining out,' said Mrs Bennet, 'that is very unlucky.'

'May I have the carriage?' asked Jane.

'No, my dear, you had better go on horseback, because it seems likely to rain, and then you must stay all night.'

'Mother,' broke in Elizabeth. 'The coach is safer.'

Jane shot her a look.

'I would be perfectly safe on horseback.'

'But–'

'I am not a child, Lizzy. I shall be fine on horseback.' She turned to her father. 'I shall not require the coach after all, Father.'

'Wonderful,' murmured Mr Bennet. 'You mean I shall actually have the use of the horses about the tenant farms? That business for which they were originally purchased? Marvellous.'

Elizabeth pursued Jane up to their room.

'Jane,' she said to her sister's back. 'While you are there, keep an eye out, won't you? Not everything may be as it seems.'

Jane straightened, but did not turn around. 'Elizabeth,' she said, 'some things can be allowed to be ordinary, can't they? Not everyone hides a secret.'

'I didn't mean–'

Jane kissed her cheek, then before Elizabeth could say anything else, ran lightly down the stairs, calling for her horse.

Mrs Bennet's hopes were answered: Jane was not long gone before it started raining hard. Elizabeth was uneasy, but Mrs Bennet was delighted. The rain continued the whole evening without intermission: Jane certainly could not come back.

'This was a lucky idea of mine indeed,' chortled Mrs Bennet, more than once. The next morning, however, breakfast was scarcely over when a servant from Netherfield (drenched and shivering) brought a note for Elizabeth:

My dearest Lizzy,

Please do not say 'I told you so', but there was an incident on the way here. Do not worry, I am unharmed but feel very unwell this morning. My dear friends will not hear of me returning home until I feel better. Please tell our parents that it is nothing more than a headache and sore throat.

Yours, &c.

Upon reading this, Elizabeth's mind was in turmoil. What could have happened? There was definitely villainy afoot, but nevertheless she did as Jane bade and only told their parents that Jane had taken ill in the night. She was reassured by a mark in the corner that signified it was indeed Jane herself writing the note, and all her letter 't's were formed in such a way that said she was not writing under any duress. Elizabeth was thankful that she had remembered these basics of their father's training.

'Well, my dear,' said Mr Bennet to his wife. 'At least if Jane should die, it will be a comfort to know it was in the pursuit of Mr Bingley, and under your orders.'

'Oh! I am not afraid of her dying at all. People do not die of trifling colds. She will be taken good care of. I will go and see her, if I may have the carriage.'

'Let me go,' said Elizabeth, jumping to her feet.

'And do you also require the carriage?' asked her father.

'No, I shall walk.'

'Ha! Then that seals it. You may walk, your mother may remain here to brighten our days, and I may have the work horses for a second day in a row.'

Elizabeth ran upstairs and, in the privacy of her room, dressed in her leather armour and then threw her gown back over the top, tucking her mask and baton into a small bag. This chance to investigate Netherfield seemed almost too good to be true, and she wished to be prepared for anything. As she descended the stairs, she was accosted by her mother.

'How can you be so silly? In this weather? You will not be fit to be seen!'

'I shall be very fit to see Jane, and that is all I want.'

With that, she left before anyone else could say another word to her.

Chapter 8

Elizabeth walked at a quick pace, feeling a little warm in her triple layers of leathers, dress and cloak. The rain held off, but the clouds were still threatening. On foot she could take a short cut rather than stick to the road. She crossed several fields, jumping over stiles and springing over puddles, then joined a track that ran through some rocky, hilly ground. At one point, where it ran between some rough hillocks, she came upon a small tree lying across the way. It looked too conveniently placed to be accidental. The stump was too smooth for the tree to have simply snapped and fallen: someone had to have deliberately cut it down. *An ambush site?* She scanned the ground, saw that it was hacked up – there were both hoof and boot prints discernible in the mud. Jane could well have taken this track rather than follow the road all the way around in the rain, she may have been accosted here as she came upon the barricade. Only the fact that she already knew from Jane's note that she was alive and well kept her from panicking. Then something flapping caught her eye – a piece of parchment tangled in some brambles. She squatted, trying unsuccessfully to hold her dress clear of the muck, snaked her hand in, gaining a number of scratches in the process, and managed to pull it free. Though stained, she could still make out some strange text written upon it:

Now pray with faith. Doubt bishop shall hear people 30. Pagan gains. Never prepare own useless identity. Now joyful end of just human use. Xenophon found the main zion. May pain discover loss.

It made no sense that she could see – a code then? Surely linked to whatever had happened to Jane. She tucked the note into her sleeve and strode swiftly on, more determined than ever to investigate. Eventually, with weary feet, dirty stockings and a face glowing with the warmth of the exercise and her feelings of concern, she came within view of the great house.

She was shown into the breakfast parlour, where all but Jane were assembled, and where her appearance created a great deal of surprise. That she should have walked three miles so early in the day, in such dirty weather, and by herself, was almost unbelievable to Mrs Hurst and Miss Bingley; Elizabeth was sure they held her in contempt for it. Nevertheless, on the surface they were all politeness, and Mr Bingley's manner was warm and kind. Mr Hurst did not speak, giving his attention to his rather late breakfast of kippers and coffee. Mr Darcy appeared to be staring at her. *No doubt in disgust.*

As soon as she could, Elizabeth asked to see Jane, and a maid led her to her sister's room.

'Elizabeth!' said Jane from her bed as she entered. 'I am so glad to see you.'

Elizabeth sat herself on the edge of her sister's bed and felt her brow.

'How are you, Jane? Are you being well treated?'

'Very well indeed. Have no fear on that account. The whole company have been nothing but kind to me. Honestly, Elizabeth, I do not believe they can in any way be associated with any villainy. Though, there certainly is something afoot.'

'What happened, dear sister?' asked Elizabeth, squeezing Jane's hand. 'What was the incident that happened on the way? Was it by the fallen tree?'

Jane looked at her. 'Why, yes. I had to dismount there to lead the horse around it. But then someone grabbed me from behind.'

'An ambush! I knew it!'

'There was a man. He had a cloth in his hand that he was pressing to my face – there was something on it; there was a sharp chemical odour. I held my breath as he attempted to drag me from the path. Thankfully he was not well-trained, his balance was all wrong, so I was able to spin and throw him down. I'm afraid I was a little...overwrought. I kicked him, rather a lot. Thankfully my horse hadn't been too frightened and was standing not far away. I managed to grab her and ride on. I was intending to ask that servants be sent back to apprehend the man, but I'm afraid the combination of the rain, the drug and the exertion were too much, and I felt quite ill by the time I arrived here. And I didn't want, well, I don't know what Mr Bingley or his sisters quite think about that kind of thing.'

'Oh, Jane!' Elizabeth looked at her sister with tears pricking her eyes. 'My beautiful Jane! Mr Bingley cannot mind that you are able to defend yourself!'

'Perhaps, but you know how many men – and women – view such things. They don't see it as appropriate. Elizabeth, there is something else.' Jane shuddered. 'The man spoke to me as he was attempting to subdue me. He said: "You're a fancy one, you'll do nicely for the Wicker Man."'

'Wicker Man? Who on earth is the Wicker Man?'

'I was thinking, perhaps he is an accomplice of this Cain?'

Elizabeth frowned. There had certainly been many pairings of villains, even trios, in the past. Often a villain's natural greed prevented them from forming alliances, but it was not unknown – the Bronze Men, the Grey Friars – but their aliases tended to match, whereas these, Cain and Wicker...

'Jane!' she said excitedly. 'They may be one and the same! When I questioned that poacher, I thought he referred to *Cain,* but maybe he meant *C-a-n-e*! Don't you see? He was unsure of the name himself, he got it mixed up: wicker, cane. It could well have been this Wicker Man that he was actually referring to!'

'Perhaps,' said Jane. 'Though I don't know if this helps you get any closer to his true identity. Or hers.'

She looked away, blinking.

'No, that is correct, my dear Jane. We must always remember that it is possible for a woman to be a villain. It is just so much less likely.'

But not because of any natural, more caring sentiment, she thought. Rather because society made it much more difficult for a woman seeking to exert influence in the world, even as a criminal. No, for most women the battleground remained at a smaller scale: the drawing room and assembly hall. Though the conflicts that occurred there were no less vicious, the wounds no less damaging.

When the clock struck three, Elizabeth unwillingly decided she should go. When she announced her intention, Miss Bingley offered her the use of a coach, which was pleasing to Elizabeth, as her leg was feeling quite stiff from the combination of the training session with Aunt Phillips and the long walk to Netherfield. Jane, however, was loath for her to go, and so Miss Bingley grudgingly converted the offer into an invitation to remain the night. Elizabeth thankfully consented – it meant not only getting to stay with Jane, but to also more time to observe Bingley and Darcy.

A servant was dispatched through the drizzle to Longbourn to inform the family and bring back a supply of clothes.

At half past six, Elizabeth was summoned to dinner. There were many enquiries as to Miss Bennet's health, and Mr Bingley in particular appeared to be pleasingly concerned. However, she had to inform them that Jane was in no way better. The sisters, on hearing this, repeated three or four times how much they were grieved, how shocking it was to have a bad cold, and how excessively they disliked being ill themselves, but then appeared to give no more thought to the matter. Elizabeth felt increasingly justified in her dislike for them.

Mr Bingley was the only one of the party she could regard with any favour. His care for Jane was evident and his attentions to herself warm and pleasing. The others paid her little attention. Miss Bingley hung off Mr Darcy, seeking to make him smile with her animated conversation. Mrs Hurst was the same, though Elizabeth could hardly blame her, for her own husband, Mr Hurst, sat belching and indolent in the corner.

At one point Elizabeth became aware that the attention of the three seemed to be directed surreptitiously in her direction. It was quite humorous, to see the two ladies shooting sideways glances at her, thinking she was not picking up on the attention. While smiling at Mr Bingley, she strained her ear in their direction.

'And did you see her petticoat? Six inches deep in mud,' Miss Bingley was whispering.

'What about walking all that way?' asked Mrs Hurst. 'In the dirt, all alone. What could she be thinking?'

'You wouldn't want your sister doing that, would you, Mr Darcy?'

'That...would hardly be possible,' said Darcy quite loudly, his voice sounding hard and angry.

The sisters shushed him, glancing at Elizabeth, who pretended not to notice.

'I am afraid, Mr Darcy,' observed Miss Bingley in a half whisper, 'that this adventure has rather affected your admiration for her fine eyes.'

'Not at all,' he replied, 'they were brightened by the exercise.'

'But what of this so-called "aunt" living in Meryton? Have you not heard the rumours?'

At this point Elizabeth could take no more and excused herself to check on Jane. She ran up the stairs, seeking to discharge the anger that burned in her breast. She allowed herself a pleasing fantasy of forcefully knocking the two sisters' heads together, and as for Darcy...She paused at the door to Jane's room. What was that? Some mocking comment about her eyes? What was wrong with her eyes? She touched them gently – they did feel a little puffy. She shook her head. The man was nothing but rude and cold.

But was he more?

When she peeked in, she found Jane in a fitful sleep. With the others entertained downstairs, now might be her best chance to conduct a quick reconnaissance. She hesitated – she could move faster and more quietly in her leathers, but it would be impossible to explain if she were caught. It would be almost as difficult to explain herself if caught snooping about in her dress, but it seemed she must risk it.

She stole along the hallway, past the staircase, towards the other guest rooms. At the first door, she pressed her ear against the wood, then turned the handle slowly, wincing at the loud click the lock made as it disengaged. She peered in – it appeared to be Mr and Mrs Hurst's room, with casually discarded trousers and piles of hat boxes. She closed the door and moved on. The next was neater, with a nightdress already laid out on the bed – Miss Bingley's room. She felt a childish urge to slip inside and wreak some small revenge – unpick a seam, cause a crease – but time was of the essence.

The next room was undoubtedly Darcy's. It was neat, but there was a definite masculine tone. She crept inside, crossing first to a writing desk, and, after checking carefully for any tells, such as a hair stuck across a drawer to alert the owner if it had been opened, searched it quickly. There were quills, ink and a bundle of letters. She leafed through them without undoing the knot – it may have been set in a particular way. The letters were all addressed to Darcy, with the salutation 'Dear brother', and signed off 'Georgiana'. The hand was definitely different to the scrap of code she had found at the ambush site.

She moved to a large standing wardrobe. As she opened it, the smell of the man surrounded her. It was not unpleasant. She pulled some coats aside – there was a large travelling trunk at the bottom, secured with a padlock. She knelt, and slid her fingers underneath the trunk, trying to get a sense of the weight – it felt quite heavy. Not the empty conveyance of his clothing, then. And stored here, in his room, rather than in the cloakroom or baggage store – the contents were something he wanted to keep nearby.

She had to see inside.

She felt on top of and under the wardrobe, and in all the pockets of his coats and trousers, hoping to find a key, but alas, there was nothing. She checked the obvious places in the room, but it could be anywhere, and her nerves were fraying. Like all large old houses, this one was full of creaks and groans, and it was easy for the mind to assemble them into a veritable army of nosy servants advancing down the hall to catch her in the act. Or worse still – Darcy himself. If he was the Wicker Man, or one of his henchmen, it would not do to be caught going through his room.

She would need to try again tomorrow night, with the proper tools. A plan was already forming in her mind to that effect. The only problem was, picking locks had never been her forte. She paused at the doorway, looking back to check if anything appeared out of place from her search, then quickly let herself back out into the hall.

When she returned to the drawing room, she found the others at cards. She was immediately invited to join them, but declined. Her mind was back on the coded note she held up one sleeve. She took up a book, and, once seated, unfolded the note inside it so that she could peruse it.

'Do you prefer reading to cards?' asked Mr Hurst. 'That is rather singular.'

'Miss Eliza Bennet,' said Miss Bingley brightly, 'despises cards. She is a great reader and has no pleasure in anything else.'

I would take great pleasure in throwing you to the ground, Elizabeth thought, but said aloud: 'I deserve neither such praise nor such censure. I am not a great reader, and I have pleasure in many things.'

'In nursing your sister I am sure you have pleasure,' said Bingley, 'and I hope it will soon be increased by seeing her quite well.'

Thankfully, their attention drifted from Elizabeth, leaving her free to stare at the strange text, occasionally pretending to turn a page. The question was whether the words themselves meant something, or if each signified something else, or whether the number of letters in each word were the key, or…The permutations were many. It was very vexing, and her attention wandered back to the card game.

'Is Miss Darcy much grown since the spring?' Miss Bingley was asking.

'She is,' answered Darcy.

'How I long to see her again! Such a countenance! Such manners! So extremely accomplished for her age!'

'It is amazing to me,' said Bingley, 'how young ladies can have the patience to be so very accomplished, as they all are.'

'*All* young ladies accomplished?' asked Miss Bingley, with a sideways glance towards Elizabeth.

'I am very far from agreeing with you,' said Darcy to Bingley. 'I cannot boast of knowing more than half a dozen, in the whole of my acquaintance, that are really accomplished.'

'Your criteria sound quite severe, sir,' said Elizabeth. Her cheeks reddened as the party all turned to look at her. Why couldn't she hold her tongue?

'Oh, I agree!' said Miss Bingley, turning back to Darcy. 'To be considered accomplished a woman must have a thorough knowledge of music, singing, drawing, dancing, and the modern languages. She must also possess a certain something in her air, and manner of walking, and tone of voice, or the word will be but half deserved.'

Elizabeth supposed that boxing, savate, jui jitsu and baton work did not figure in Miss Bingley's list, which made her stifle a smile. But neither, she thought glumly, was it likely to figure in many men's.

'All this she must possess,' cut in Darcy, 'and to this she must add something more substantial: the improvement of her mind. Through reading.'

'Then it is no wonder you know so few,' said Elizabeth. 'Indeed, I am surprised you know any at all.'

This brought the full attention of the card players onto her again. She made a show of closing her book, aware of Darcy's cold stare and the sisters' shared smirk. Claiming to be weary from her long walk, she bade them goodnight and left the drawing room. But outside the door she lingered, shamefully pressing her ear against the wood – she could hardly pretend this was about exposing the villain. She just wanted to hear what they said about her.

'Eliza Bennet,' Miss Bingley was saying, 'is one of those young ladies who seek to promote themselves to the other sex by running other women down. It is a very mean art.'

'Undoubtedly,' answered Darcy, and Elizabeth's hands curled into fists. 'There is meanness in all the arts which ladies sometimes condescend to employ for captivation. Whatever bears likeness to cunning is despicable.'

She didn't wait to hear any more but ran lightly up the stairs. There was a feeling of great pressure in her heart and her stomach, and she was loath to try to understand the reason for such an internal storm. In her room, she threw off her clothes and crawled beneath the covers, eyes open and staring up at the shadows cast flickering on the ceiling by the candle burning by her bed. It took some hours for sleep to finally claim her.

Chapter 9

In the morning, Elizabeth was relieved to see an improvement in Jane, and happily sent the news via the maid down to the others. She also sent a message to her younger sisters.

Lydia and Kitty arrived shortly after breakfast – accompanied by Mrs Bennet. Possibly some stirring of guilt had prompted her to come and see Jane's condition for herself. Or a determination to do what she could to make the stay as long and productive as possible.

While their mother sat on the edge of the bed, chatting with Jane, Elizabeth drew Lydia and Kitty aside.

'Did you bring the bag I asked for? The small brown one from beneath my bed?'

'Oh, Lord! That ugly thing?' said Lydia. 'We found it, but you can't take something as horrid as that somewhere like Netherfield!'

'I brought my old Chinese patterned one,' said Kitty. 'It is much more stylish. You will find it far superior. I was going to give it to you to keep, but now that I look at it again, I find I do still like it. But you may borrow it while you are here.'

Elizabeth ground her teeth. 'I really, really wanted the brown one. With my...sewing.'

'Oh, we brought all that,' said Lydia. 'We tipped all your stuff inside Kitty's bag – I say!'

Elizabeth snatched the proffered bag from Kitty and dug her fingers down inside. Amongst the sewing paraphernalia, her fingers brushed a small packet that held her lock-picking tools. She sighed with relief.

An invitation then arrived from Miss Bingley for the visitors to please join her in the breakfast parlour, and Jane was left to continue resting. Elizabeth followed, on edge at having her mother at the mercy of the London ladies' tongues. She was relieved when Bingley joined them, professing his hope that they had not found the patient worse than expected.

'Oh indeed I have, sir,' Mrs Bennet answered. 'She is a great deal too ill to yet be moved. We must trespass a little longer on your kindness.'

'Removed,' cried Bingley. 'It must not be thought of! My sister, I am sure, will not hear of her removal.'

Elizabeth caught the slight flare of Miss Bingley's nostrils before she spoke.

'You may depend upon it, madam,' said Miss Bingley with cold civility, 'that Miss Bennet shall receive every possible attention while she remains with us.'

Mrs Bennet was profuse in her acknowledgements.

'Jane is so fortunate to have such good friends. She suffers a great deal, you know. Though she has the sweetest temper I ever met with. I often tell my other girls they are nothing to her. You have a sweet room here, Mr Bingley. I do not know a place in the country that is the equal to Netherfield. You will not think of quitting it in a hurry, I hope.'

At that point Darcy entered the room, and Elizabeth felt her cheeks colour at his arrival. The knowledge of her planned invasion of his privacy must be the cause of such a bodily reaction, she supposed. Though she ought not to feel guilty when she was simply acting to ensure the safety of the neighbourhood. She suddenly felt quite fidgety.

'Well, at present I consider myself quite fixed here,' Bingley said. 'But I must warn you, I can be quite impetuous when the mood strikes! I can be off in five minutes!'

'You move about a great deal, then?' asked Elizabeth, fixing her attention to Bingley. 'I wonder what compels you?'

A slight smile pulled at the corners of his lips. 'A spirit of adventure?'

Darcy shot Bingley a look.

Elizabeth wondered: *What did that mean?*

'Then I must question your decision to settle in Hertfordshire,' she said. 'We boast many things, but I would not think opportunities for a young man to experience adventure is one of them.'

'Lizzy, that is not so,' cried Mrs Bennet. 'I assure you, sir, there is quite as much going on in the country as in the Town. Why, we even have our own villains, I would have you know. And not just your average henhouse thief or sheep duffer. Oh no, we have proper murderers and everything. Or *murderesses*, I should say.'

This protestation was met by stunned silence. Bingley blinked and looked at the table. Darcy, after staring at her for a moment, turned silently away. Elizabeth, reeling herself from her mother's words, observed this, and wondered.

Mrs Bennet, fancying she had won a victory of sorts, ploughed on.

'Oh yes. We had several murders in the neighbourhood – well, nobody realised they were murders at first, of course – all the work of one villain. A woman: the odious Miss King! She died, too, of course. You see? How is that for adventure, sir?'

'Mother,' cried Elizabeth, and her eyes shot to ceiling, in the direction of Jane's room, but Jane was asleep, Jane was safe.

'What? What on earth is wrong with you, Elizabeth?'

Elizabeth saw Bingley struggling to hold in a smile. His sister was less delicate, directing her eye towards Mr Darcy with a smirk. Desperate to distract her mother from continuing on this topic, she now asked if Charlotte had been to Longbourn, looking for her.

'Ah, Miss Lucas,' said Bingley, nobly joining her in changing the subject. 'She seems a very pleasant young woman.'

'Oh yes,' said Mrs Bennet. 'But you must own she is very plain. Lady Lucas herself has often said so, and envied me Jane's beauty. It is as well she spends so much time with Elizabeth, rather than Jane, so the difference is less stark, though still there nonetheless.'

Elizabeth could think of nothing to say. She trembled, lest her mother should continue speaking so and expose herself again. But luckily Mrs Bennet began repeating her thanks to Mr Bingley, and soon after called for her carriage.

During the whole of this conversation, Lydia and Kitty had been speaking earnestly in the corner, and now, as they began to leave, accosted Mr Bingley about his past promise to hold a ball at Netherfield.

'I assure you, I intend to keep that promise,' the gentleman told them. 'Once your sister is recovered.'

Their delighted squeal caused all but Mrs Bennet to wince.

Once the carriage was finally out of sight, and Elizabeth was back upstairs sitting by her sister, she realised just how tight her muscles were. Must her family always leave her feeling so?

Chapter 10

When the ladies removed to the drawing room after dinner, Elizabeth first ran back up to Jane and was heartened to find her feeling well enough to spend a little time downstairs. When they entered, the Bingley sisters fell upon Jane with many solicitations, but later, when the gentlemen came in, their attention immediately shifted. Miss Bingley's eyes were instantly turned towards Darcy, and she pounced on him before he had barely entered the room.

The gentlemen expressed their gladness at seeing Jane up – Bingley, in particular, was full of joy and attention. He fussed over the fire and Jane's position in relation to it.

'Shall I set up the card table?' asked Mr Hurst.

'Not now,' said Miss Bingley brightly, clearly feeling that she had safely trapped Darcy in a corner of the room.

'I thought we were going to play,' said Mr Hurst, somewhat truculently. 'Aren't we?'

'Not. Now.' Miss Bingley smiled at him, though it was somewhat frozen.

'Bingley?' said Mr Hurst. 'Cards? Eh?'

'What?' said Bingley. 'Oh, I don't think – unless, of course, Miss Bennet wishes to play?'

Jane smiled and shook her head.

Mr Hurst looked about the room.

'I very much thought we were going to play.'

'William,' cried his wife. 'No one is playing cards. No one has any interest in playing cards.'

Elizabeth watched the exchange with some delight.

Tea arrived, and afterwards Mr Hurst stretched out on one of the sofas and promptly fell asleep. Darcy took up a book. Miss Bingley did the same. Mr Bingley continued to converse with Jane. Elizabeth took up some sewing to pass the time, though her fingers were starting to shake at the thought of what she intended a little later, and also to watch Miss Bingley's next move.

She did not have long to wait. Miss Bingley spent more time watching Darcy than actually reading her book. Several times she made small noises of interest, obviously hoping he would speak to her, but Darcy did not bite. Finally, covering a great yawn, she said: 'How pleasant it is to spend an evening in this way! I declare after all there is no enjoyment like reading! How much sooner one tires of anything than of a book!'

She looked about, but no one made any reply. She frowned, then tossed her tome aside. Seeing her brother in enjoyable conversation with Jane, she butted in.

'By the bye, Charles, are you seriously thinking of a ball at Netherfield? I do think you should consult the rest of the party. There are some amongst us to whom a ball would be a punishment rather than a pleasure.'

'If you mean Darcy,' said her brother, 'he may go to bed if he chooses. Before it even begins, perhaps, so our spirits are not dampened by his dour aspect.'

Elizabeth looked to Darcy, but he merely smiled. It appeared some degree of banter was usual between the two – or more correctly, some teasing of Darcy by Bingley – but both gentlemen seemed to take it in good part and there appeared nothing malicious about it.

But if they were such close friends as that implied, what did that mean? The implication was that either both were involved in villainy, or neither. She really needed to search that trunk. She was wondering if she might take her leave soon when Miss Bingley got up and began pacing about the room. Her figure was elegant, and she walked with some fluidity, but Elizabeth bet she couldn't throw a decent punch to save her life, nor lift a heavy feed bag on her shoulders. She was thus caught looking when Miss Bingley suddenly turned to her.

'Miss Eliza Bennet, let me persuade you to follow my example and take a turn about the room. I assure you it is very refreshing after sitting so long.'

Elizabeth supposed Miss Bingley's game was to catch Darcy's attention and perhaps to even show herself in better light by direct comparison. What had Darcy said about her – a little 'solid' for his taste? However, her leg was stiffening up and could do with a stretch, so she allowed Miss Bingley to hook her arm and pace with her about the room. She noticed that Darcy had lowered his book and was watching them – no, watching *her*. A fact not lost on Miss Bingley.

'Won't you join us, sir?' asked Miss Bingley brightly.

'I shall not,' he replied.

'And why not, sir?'

'I would not wish to interfere with your designs.'

'What can he mean?' said Miss Bingley, turning towards Elizabeth but watching Darcy. 'I am dying to know his meaning. Do you understand him?'

'Not at all,' answered Elizabeth, 'but since he is so keen for us to ask, our surest way of disappointing him will be to not.'

As she suspected, however, Miss Bingley was not about to give up Darcy's attention now that she had finally snared it.

'Pray answer, sir!'

'Very well,' he said. 'You are conscious that your figures appear to the greatest advantage in walking. If you wish me to admire you, I can do so much better as I sit by the fire.'

'Wishing for you to admire us?' cried Miss Bingley. 'Outrageous! How shall we punish him?'

Elizabeth had no wish to be part of this one-sided flirtation, but looked at Darcy sitting so composedly, and said, 'Laugh at him.'

'Laugh at him? Laugh at Mr Darcy? Why, he is the best of men! Oh no, he is not to be laughed at!'

'A pity,' said Elizabeth, holding Darcy's eye. 'I dearly love a laugh.'

'Miss Bingley gives me too much credit,' he said. 'Besides which, even the best of men may be made the butt by a person whose aim is to render everything a joke.'

'Certainly,' replied Elizabeth. 'There are such people. But I hope I am not one of them. I hope I never ridicule what is wise or good. Follies and nonsense do divert me, it is true, and I laugh at them whenever I can. But these, I suppose, are precisely what you are without.'

'Perhaps that is not possible for anyone. But it has been the study of my life to avoid those weaknesses which expose one to ridicule.'

'Such as vanity and pride?'

'Yes, vanity is such a weakness, indeed. But pride – where there is a real superiority of mind, pride will always be under good regulation.'

And there it is, thought Elizabeth. The kind of arrogance that caused some men to believe they sat above others. And it was from that lofty position that they believed their actions beyond reproach, and thus villainy was so often born.

'I have faults enough,' Darcy continued, his gaze having slid from her to the fire. 'My temper I dare not vouch for. I cannot forget the vices and follies of others as soon as I ought. My good opinion once lost is lost for ever.'

'Do let us have a little music,' cried Miss Bingley, seemingly tired of a conversation in which she had nothing to share.

'Perhaps in every person there is a tendency to some particular evil,' he mused. 'A natural defect, which not even the best education can overcome.'

Elizabeth frowned. Was this not some guilty conscience speaking? An attempt at rationalisation?

By then the pianoforte had been opened, and Mr Hurst sat up with a start as the two sisters began to loudly play. Shortly after, Jane announced herself to be very weary, and Elizabeth rose to escort her to bed.

She hastened her sister upstairs and under the covers as quickly as she could, kissed her, took up her little packet of tools, removed her shoes and padded silently down the hall to Darcy's room. The strains of piano music reassured her that the whole party was still downstairs – for surely if Darcy had left, Miss Bingley would have stopped playing to pursue him.

She stole into his room and straight to the wardrobe. The chest was inside, just as last time. She knelt before it, opened her packet and withdrew a pair of thin bent rods. With her tongue between her teeth in concentration, she fished about with them inside the padlock, seeking to shift the tumblers within. The lock was well-made, obviously expensive, and was reluctant to open for her. The longer it took, the sweatier her fingers became, and she had to pause to wipe them on her dress. With growing frustration she tried to force it, slipped, and speared her thumb on the end of one rod, drawing a bead of blood.

She sucked on it and tried to calm down. This was not her skill. She had spent very little time with the strange travelling tinker her father had tasked with teaching her and Jane the secrets of lockpicking. Jane always had been better at it.

She shut the wardrobe and ran lightly back to Jane's room. In the lamplight, she saw that Jane was already fast asleep, the poor thing. It felt cruel to wake her, but still, she had to know.

'Jane,' she whispered, shaking her sister with increasing firmness. 'Jane!'

'Elizabeth?' Her sister blinked, rubbed a loose strand of hair from across her eyes. 'What is it?'

'I need you,' said Elizabeth. 'I need you to open a lock.'

'What lock?'

'A chest. In Darcy's room.'

Jane's eyes came fully open, and she regarded her younger sister seriously. 'What do you mean? What chest? What is going on?'

'Jane, we do not have much time. Someone may come along. There is a locked chest in Darcy's room. I want to open it to see what is inside.'

'You do not persist in this idea that Mr Darcy is some kind of villain, do you? Even now? After spending all this time with them?'

'Why not? One may smile and smile, and still be a villain. And Darcy doesn't even smile very often.'

'But don't you see, Lizzy? He and Mr Bingley are such great friends. There is no way he could be hiding a secret villainous identity and Mr Bingley not know. And if you are suggesting that Mr Bingley is involved...'

'Then let us just do this one thing to prove me wrong, to prove he is innocent. Or at least guilty of nothing worse than being a conceited, arrogant man.'

'No, Lizzy.'

'Jane!'

'No! Don't you see? Don't you understand? I don't want to do this anymore. Do not misunderstand me: I am grateful for knowing how to defend myself – that skill came in very handy on the way here. But I do not want to be a Vigil anymore. I want to be a wife. I want to be normal. I want a house and a family. No more masks, no more secrets, no more... death.'

She looked away, blinking tears from her eyes.

'Jane–'

'No more death, Lizzy,' said Jane, her voice rough with emotion. 'You weren't there.'

'I wish that I had been,' said Elizabeth quietly. That image in her head again – her father, carrying the pale, half-drowned girl. The long wait by her bedside, waiting to see if she would survive.

Jane shook her head.

'No. I would not wish that on you. Father wouldn't let you come, he said you weren't ready–'

'I was!' An old argument, but a story Elizabeth had to let Jane tell.

'We tracked her to the mill.' Jane's eyes were unfocussed, or rather, focussed within. The words tumbled from her. 'It was late – near midnight. But the moon was very full, and very bright. I felt excited: the Foxhound and the Pack, on the chase. Our quarry cornered. The "odious Miss King" – killer of several poor, lonely men. I went up the outside staircase to the top floor while father searched downstairs. And she was there, just standing, waiting for me. She smiled when she saw me, and put a flask to her lips. I thought it was something to steady her nerve, to make her fight better. I told her to surrender, that she must account for the murders she had done. She just shook her head, so sadly, and said "If you only knew why...", then fell silent. I don't know what she meant. I didn't ask, didn't give her a chance to explain.'

Jane shook her head.

'She appeared a pale ghost in the moonlight with the window behind her. I went to take hold of her, and in that moment she embraced me, put her lips to mine. And I tasted it then, in that most bitter of kisses, the poison she had consumed. I felt it enter me, and I was so frightened. I called out to Father, but she grabbed me fiercely, and we fell backwards and crashed through the window, down into the black waters of the pond below. I went under, and it seemed that the weed clutched at me, seeking to pull me further under, and she was there too, fighting me. We surfaced, close by the great turning wheel, and I saw that it had her, was pulling her. At first I gripped her hand, to try to pull her clear, calling and calling for Father, the water burning my lungs. But I realised she was caught, and trying still to pull me in with her, to take me too. "Why?" I gasped. "Why not?" she replied, and then the wheel dragged her below the surface, and, in her grip, I followed. The cold. The dark. I don't remember any more for a long time after that.'

'Father jumped in and pulled you free, but was too late for Miss King. He carried you all the way home. I saw him from our window. Saw him carry you down the drive. We sat, he and I, till dawn, watching to see if you would survive. We told Mother you had taken ill during the night.'

Jane nodded.

'So you see, Lizzy, I have seen that murderous intent, that utter villainy. I do not see it in Mr Darcy. And I certainly do not see it in Mr Bingley.'

Elizabeth smiled sadly and stroked her sister, felt the tension in her muscles.

'Dear Jane. My dear, sweet Jane.' Then her voice caught in her throat, and she buried her face in her sister's neck and felt Jane's own tears running down the valleys created by their closely pressed faces.

But when she could, when she felt Jane slowly relax and then drift off into sleep, she disentangled herself as gently as possible and crept from the room. She had to try the chest again; there was nothing else for it.

She crossed the landing and stopped dead.

Darcy was on the stairs. He stared at her, her feet bare, skirts lifted. She opened her mouth, but nothing came out. They stayed like that for a moment, but then she remembered who she was, whose daughter she was, and dropped her skirts, smoothed them into place, straightened her back, and met his eye, chin jutting in challenge. He inclined his head and slowly turned and descended the stairs, the thud of each step like a hammer in her ribcage. She stood frozen in place till he was out of sight, then finally took a breath. Body rigid with tension, she withdrew to her bedroom. There would be no more searching for clues this night.

Chapter 11

In the morning, Jane declared herself well enough to travel, and Elizabeth consequently wrote to their mother, requesting the carriage. While no nearer to discovering the truth, Elizabeth was glad to quit Netherfield and escape the embarrassment of being in Darcy's presence.

But then a note returned from their mother stating the carriage could not possibly be spared before next Tuesday, and so if Mr Bingley and his sisters pressed them to stay, she could spare them very well.

'We're going,' Elizabeth growled to Jane, 'if I have to carry you on my back.'

Jane sent a request to Mr Bingley, who swiftly agreed to the loan of his own carriage, though it was with real sorrow he heard of their plans to go and wondered if it would be safe for her to leave so soon.

She is perfectly safe with me, thought Elizabeth crossly.

The moment of departure arrived, and Elizabeth noticed that Miss Bingley's civility towards herself and affection for Jane increased the closer it came to them leaving.

The ride back was uneventful, though Elizabeth spent it quietly fingering the baton hidden up her sleeve. It was unlikely that a man who attempted to abduct a lone female traveller out in a rainstorm would attempt two in a carriage with a driver in the morning sunshine, but it didn't hurt to be prepared.

Abduct two...

'Jane,' she said, grabbing her sister's arm. 'The innkeeper's daughter!'

'What of her? Is there news?'

'What if the same man who tried to kidnap you has her?'

Jane frowned. 'You believe there is a connection?'

'Yes! Why didn't I see it straight away? One girl goes missing – everyone thinks she has run away to London. But then you are attacked, the man appearing to wish to abduct you, rather than rob or...or assault you.'

'For what purpose?' asked Jane, shivering despite the warm sunshine.

'I do not know, but nothing good. If only we could read the code on the note I found!'

'We should give it to Mary. You know how she prides herself on her intelligence. Perhaps she can crack it.'

'You mean tell her – Father has not given us permission to bring her in.'

'No, we need not tell her where it came from, or why. Just set it as an intellectual challenge.'

Elizabeth nodded. It was worth the risk. The stakes appeared to be rising, along with a sense of fear within her. Wicker Man. Why that name (assuming she was right)? It brought to mind pagan rituals of burning, sacrifice. Not all villains were purely interested in money; others had darker, twisted motivations.

They were not welcomed home very cordially by their mother. She met them with a stony face and twisted lips. She admonished them for causing so much trouble by taking Mr Bingley's carriage. Elizabeth was tempted to fire a salvo back by pointing out their own carriage was indeed standing idle in the carriage house, the horses grazing in the field nearby, but it was generally better to let the storm run its course.

They found Mary deep in a book and presented her with the note, simply saying they had found it and wondered if it was important, and how to find its owner?

Mary smoothed the crumpled paper and stared at it for some minutes before looking up at them owlishly.

'It's a code,' she said.

Jane squeezed Elizabeth's arm. 'Yes, dear, that was our impression too. Alas, when we attempted to solve it, we found ourselves quite unable to.'

'Leave it with me,' said Mary smugly.

Kitty and Lydia also had news they wished to impart in breathless fashion. The regiment had arrived. There were red-coated officers everywhere. Their high spirts drove their father to his study even earlier than usual, and Jane and Elizabeth to their room.

Chapter 12

'I hope, my dear,' said Mr Bennet to his wife at breakfast, 'that you have ordered a good dinner today, because I have reason to expect an addition to our party.'

'What do you mean, my dear? I know of nobody that is coming, I am sure. Unless Charlotte Lucas should happen to call in, and I hope my dinners are good enough for her. Indeed, I do not believe she often sees such at home.'

'The person of whom I speak is a gentleman and a stranger.'

Mrs Bennet's eyes sparkled. 'A gentleman and a stranger! You mean Mr Bingley, I am sure, though he is no stranger to us now! Why, Jane! You never dropped a word of this, you sly thing! But – good Lord! How unlucky! There is not a bit of fish to be got today! Lydia, my love, ring the bell! I must speak to Cook!'

'It is not Mr Bingley,' said her husband. 'It is a person I never saw before in the course of my life.'

He waited for their astonishment to die down before continuing.

'I have received a letter from my cousin, Mr Collins. It is he who, when I am dead, may turn you all out of this house as soon as he pleases.'

'Oh,' cried his wife. 'Odious man! I cannot bear to hear him mentioned.

How cruel, that your estate should be entailed away from your own children to a man that no one cares anything about! If I were you, I should have tried to do something about it.'

'It certainly is a most iniquitous affair, but such are the terms of the inheritance, and thus such is the law. But let me tell you what he writes. You may be perhaps a little softened by his manner of expressing himself.'

He read:

Dear Sir

The disagreement between yourself and my late honoured father always caused me great unease. Now that we have lost him, I believe the time is ripe to heal the breach. I have held back a little while, fearing it may seem disrespectful to his memory, but my mind is now made up on the subject. I have been fortunate after my recent ordination to be distinguished by the patronage of the Right Honourable Lady Catherine de Bourgh, whose beneficence has preferred me to the rectory of this parish. As a clergyman, I feel it my duty to promote peace on all within my influence, and on those grounds, I flatter myself that my present overtures of goodwill are highly commendable.

I cannot be otherwise but concerned at being the means of injuring your dear daughters, and beg leave to apologise for it, and assure you of my readiness to make every possible amends (more on that later – and on another matter I am most delighted to discuss with you).

I propose myself the satisfaction of waiting on you and your family, Monday, June 18th, by four o'clock. Thankfully, Lady Catherine is not opposed to my occasional absence.

I remain, dear sir, with respectful compliments to your lady and daughters, your well-wisher and friend,

William Collins

'So we shall shortly be expecting this peace-making gentleman,' said Mr Bennet as he folded up the letter. 'He seems a very polite young man.'

'Though it is difficult,' said Jane, 'to guess in what way he means to make amends, the wish, at least, is to his credit.'

'There is something very pompous in his style,' said Elizabeth. 'Apologising for something he has no control over. Is he, do you think, a sensible man, Father?'

'Oh, I hope not,' said Mr Bennet. 'I have great hopes of finding him quite the reverse. There is a mixture of servility and self-importance in his style which raises my hopes.'

'I declare he writes very well indeed,' said Mrs Bennet.

Mr Bennet's eyebrows shot upward. 'Do you indeed, my dear? Well, they do say the pen is mightier than the sword. Here I was, ready to tell him to beware and be ready to defend himself bodily from your attack, and he has already won you over with mere words! If only all villainy could be brought down by well-written contrition!'

Sometimes, when her father teased her mother without that lady being aware of it, Elizabeth felt a small stab in her heart. It had worsened since he retired, when he no longer had an outlet for his sharp, restless mind. While her mother could be very vexing, Elizabeth was not sure she deserved to be held up to ridicule in such a way before her children. She was aware that her closer relationship with her father, begun quite young and ultimately resulting in the Vigil secret shared with he and Jane, had positioned her to see her mother in a less flattering light. Her parents' relationship had caused her many times to reflect on what she herself wanted in a partner. True, there was affection between them still, but she wanted more than that. She wanted a true partnership. But was it possible?

Mr Collins arrived punctually at four o'clock. Elizabeth watched him walk up the drive, clad in his black and white clergyman attire. He had an oddly stilted gait, more like a man acting at walking than just walking naturally. She fancied he was one of those people who imagined themselves to always be observed, and so performed every action as though for an audience. In this case, of course, he was quite right – she was watching. She dropped the curtain of her bedroom window as her mother called shrilly from downstairs for them all to come down.

Face to face, Mr Collins was a tall, heavy-looking young man of five and twenty. His air was grave and stately, and his manners very formal. He had barely taken a seat in the drawing room before complimenting Mrs Bennet on having so many fine daughters, that he had heard of their beauty, and that the descriptions had fallen short of the true mark, and added that he had no doubt she would see them all, in due time, well disposed of in marriage. Elizabeth looked at Jane and rolled her eyes, but Mrs Bennet accepted the compliments most readily.

'You are very kind, sir. I wish with all my heart that it may prove so, for otherwise they will be destitute, one and all.'

Elizabeth groaned internally: it had not taken long for her mother to bring *that* up.

'You allude, perhaps, to the entail on this estate,' said Mr Collins gravely.

'Ah! I do indeed, sir. Such a grievous affair for my poor girls. Not that I find fault in you, of course, but you must confess it is most grievous for them.'

'I am very sensible, madam, of the hardship possibly faced by my fair cousins, and I would say more on the matter, but do not wish to appear forward and precipitate. But I can assure the young ladies that I come prepared to admire them. At present, I will say no more.'

He was interrupted anyway by the summons to dinner. On the way through, it did not seem they could pass anything without Mr Collins admiring it: the hall, the dining room, all the furniture. Lydia openly stared about, trying to understand how their everyday, ordinary things could be worthy of such lavish praise. Kitty kept giggling behind her hands. Mrs Bennet took it all a little more coolly, no doubt suspicious that such admiration may be coming from one who would one day hope to own it all himself.

The dinner, too, was in turn highly admired, and he begged to know which of his fair cousins was responsible for the excellent cookery. Here, Mrs Bennet assured him with some asperity, they were very well able to keep a good cook, and her daughters had nothing to do in the kitchen. Mr Collins begged forgiveness from all of them, and despite Mrs Bennet assuring him they were not offended, continued to apologise for the next quarter of an hour.

Company meant Elizabeth was not able excuse herself as soon as she would have liked, but when she could, she stole out to the carriage house. She had formulated a plan, and it was time to take some action. In the privacy of the training room, she carefully removed her attire and dressed in her leathers. Over this she tugged on a serving girl outfit she had obtained from the maid. With her baton inserted in her sleeve, she exited the room, settling the secret panel back into place, and after a last glance towards the house, ran lightly down the drive and into the dusk.

Once well clear, she stopped running and started walking in the middle of the lane, doing her best to emulate a tired – and thus vulnerable – young serving girl. She kept her head down, but all the while her eyes were scanning side to side and her ears straining for any sounds of movement about her. Passing through the wood where she was sure she and her sisters had been followed recently was particularly stressful. But the evening passed uneventfully – she walked all the way to Meryton without issue. Once there, she hesitated briefly while she considered visiting Aunt Phillips, but then turned and walked back towards Longbourn by a different route. Again, nothing transpired.

Once she reached home, she was about to turn around and do it all again when she caught sight of Jane walking quickly among the outbuildings. Jane spotted her in the same moment.

'There you are! I've been looking for you! Father wants to speak to us.' Jane looked her up and down. 'What on earth are you wearing? What are you up to?'

'Tell Father I will be in directly. I'll explain all to you later, I promise.'

Jane frowned, but nodded and went back towards the house. Elizabeth trotted into the old carriage house and froze – the sliding partition was open and light spilled out from inside. A trap? She glanced about – no, it made no sense. There had been ample opportunity to attack her on the way here, and to advertise one's presence by lighting a lamp...

She ducked cautiously through the opening.

'My dear Miss Elizabeth,' beamed Mr Collins. 'How delightful!'

The clergyman stood in the middle of the training room, a lamp throwing his shadow across the walls like a stain.

'Mr Collins,' replied Elizabeth evenly. 'What are you doing here?'

'Indeed, indeed. Though, if one may be so bold, I may enquire the same of you? What brings you to this...interesting room at this hour? And so attired?'

Her hand went to the plain dress she wore. She chose not to answer the question – a breach of social etiquette, perhaps, but so was skulking about in your host's outbuildings, surely.

'I informed your dear father that I wished to take an evening stroll about the grounds. He was most gracious to give me leave to do so, quite eager in fact, which I do thank him for – very kind of him to be so solicitous of my good health. Anyway, as I walked about, I could not help but notice that the exterior dimensions of this delightful carriage house do not match the internal. And so, I confess, my curiosity piqued, I chose to investigate further. And here I am. Or rather, here *we* are.'

'What do you want, Mr Collins?'

Mr Collins drifted over to the heavy bag and tapped it lightly – the bag didn't move and he frowned, looking at his knuckles.

'It is not what *I* want, Miss Elizabeth. I do not claim ownership of the issue, though as you will see, I do have, let us say, an interest in the outcome. No. You have no doubt heard me speak of my patron, Lady Catherine de Bourgh?'

'Indeed, sir. I believe you may have mentioned her once or twice in passing.'

'She is all affability and condescension. She is reckoned proud by many people, but such is her position and bearing that I see no fault there. She is, truly, of the best.' Mr Collins shot her a look. 'Do you take my meaning?'

'I'm afraid I do not, sir.'

He nodded, sucking at his cheeks. 'This room,' he said, looking about. 'This is not tack or other gardening tools. These are training devices, am I correct? For martial pursuits?'

'Yes,' Elizabeth replied guardedly. 'Is it so unheard of, in these times, for people to practise defending themselves?'

'Why, no,' said Mr Collins. 'But this goes further than that, does it not? May I speak openly?' He tapped his finger to his nose. 'This is for the advancement of Vigilism, is it not?'

Elizabeth did not know how to answer.

Mr Collins saw her struggling to come up with a suitable refutation and smiled.

'My dear Miss Elizabeth, you have nothing to fear from me. I know only too well that Vigilism is best served by anonymity. As does my patroness, Lady Catherine de Bourgh. Come, let us show our cards. I know that the Bennet family has been involved in Vigilism for the past decade or more. More to the point, Lady Catherine knows it, too. She is patroness of a grouping of Vigils, known as the Best Men, who operate across the countryside, restoring order where there is chaos. She has heard of the Foxhound and his good works in this neighbourhood, and, though your family is a little lower down the scale than those she typically considers for membership, I was able to speak up on your father's behalf and obtain an offer.'

'You, sir?'

'Yes. It may interest you to know that I am a Vigil myself. Of a sort. I am what you would call an investigator. As such, I rank below an actual Vigil and his companion, as Lady Catherine was kind enough to explain to me when she recruited me to the role. She said that I had certain qualities that made me ideally suited to the part. A keen eye, a sense of curiosity, and, of course, a dedication to the betterment of English society.'

Elizabeth had to admit that Lady Catherine was on to something here – who would suspect someone like Mr Collins to be engaged in any investigation?

'You may imagine my delight when Lady Catherine charged me with coming to speak to your father, providing as it did a chance to become acquainted with you all and see if there is not a mutually advantageous solution to the issue of the entailment. A number of birds slain with a single stone, you see.'

'And have you spoken to my father of this, Mr Collins?'

'Indeed I have. And here my delight turns to chagrin, for I have found him somewhat reluctant to take up the offer. I expressed great surprise at that. I admit, the prospect of rebuttal had not entered my mind at all as a possible outcome. Linking with the Best Men would provide a network of information, of material aid, that would be of great benefit. Not to mention the pride that would come from helping one such as Lady Catherine to achieve her aims.'

'I'm afraid you are too late, Mr Collins. My father is retired. He does not act as a Vigil anymore.'

'Ah,' said Mr Collins. 'Just so. Just as he told me. But, Miss Elizabeth, he is not the only Vigil in the family, is he?'

'It is common enough knowledge that the Foxhound hunted with a companion. Or two.'

'Which, in the absence of sons, means his daughters. His two eldest daughters, to be precise. Now, that is a piece of information I have played down with her ladyship. Direct involvement of women in Vigilism is not something she condones. No, a woman's position at most is to act as an assistant to a Vigil – a kind of administrative role, a little below that of the humble investigator.'

'Well, Lady Catherine need have no concerns as far as that goes. As I said, the Foxhound is retired, and so too are his companions.'

Mr Collins beamed at her. 'Your attempts at what you see as protecting your family do you credit, Miss Elizabeth, and I do understand your caution. But is it not so, that you yourself are indeed an active Vigil? One of the Pack, as it were?'

'I–'

'Nothing escapes Her Ladyship! We have heard from our sources that someone is active in this neighbourhood. Dear Lady Catherine naturally assumed it was your father, but I had my suspicions, given certain physical descriptions, subsequently borne out. Why, your dress at this moment suggests you are currently engaged in an operation, are you not?'

'Mr Collins, I do not know what to say. You have truly caught me off guard with all of this.'

'I do not wish to cause you any vexation, Miss Elizabeth. I merely wished a chance to speak with you, to explain what it is that I offer. Well, what I offer in this first place. But more of that later, at a more suitable time. For now, I will bid you good evening. I believe your father wishes to see you. Pray, please do impress on him the benefits of the Bennet family joining the Best?'

'Mr Collins, Father will not wish to come out of retirement, no matter the offer.'

'Retirement? He is not so old. But if he has lost his taste for direct action, he may still provide leadership and experience to younger members.'

'Jane is done with Vigilism. As for me–'

'You misunderstand me. I did not mean you or your sister. That would be out of the question. Lady Catherine would install new members. There would be no more running around in the night, dressed as you are. You will have to give up the mask.'

'*As I was saying*...As for me, Mr Collins, I will always do that which I believe to be right for this neighbourhood.'

The clergyman frowned. 'A rather wilful attitude, though I do hope you will forgive me for describing it as such. I can only assure you that Lady Catherine's view on all matters is most sagacious and worthy of notice. Surely you must see that someone such as yourself, from a family such as yours–'

'A family such as mine?'

'–thinking she can speak with equivalence to one such as Lady Catherine, well...'

There was a moment of silence. Mr Collins felt he had landed the telling blow. Elizabeth was struggling to not deliver an actual blow of her own. Finally the clergyman smiled broadly, bowed, and stepped to the hatch.

'Oh, Mr Collins?'

He paused, midway through, looking back at her awkwardly.

'As an investigator, have you heard anything of a villain styling himself as the Wicker Man?'

'Wicker Man? How very pagan. No, I have not heard of any such fellow.'

'Are you sure?' Elizabeth pressed, halting him again. 'Lady Catherine has not spoken of him either? Or maybe he is known as Cain?'

'Pagan or biblical, eh? No, Miss Elizabeth, I can assure you that I do not know the name. And if the fellow has not come to Lady Catherine's attention, then he either does not exist – for, you know how the popular mind likes to concoct villainy where there is none – or does not pose any great threat.'

'He does to the women in this neighbourhood.'

'How so?'

'Someone attacked Jane. And the innkeeper's daughter has been kidnapped.'

'Ah, so this is why you dress in this manner. You are offering yourself as bait, are you not? With no companion? Does your father know and approve of this plan? This is exactly the sort of amateurish theatrics that Lady Catherine seeks to eradicate through her company. As I said, certain changes will certainly have to be made to the running of this operation. Now if you will excuse me?'

Elizabeth watched him go, and when she was sure he was out of earshot, strode across the floor and launched herself at the bag, delivering a punch that caused it to creak and swing, its shadow dancing about the room.

Once changed, she joined Jane in her father's library.

'Elizabeth!' said Mr Bennet. 'I am in urgent need of sensible conversation. That man...He is indeed as absurd as I had hoped, and I enjoyed him for a good quarter hour or so. But then the dose was enough, and I was in desperate need of respite.'

'He is a well-intentioned though, is he not?' asked Jane.

'If his intention is to make me loathe Lady Catherine without ever having met her, then yes. What would you like to know about her? Or her sickly daughter? I have many details available with which to educate you.'

'What about the Best Men?' asked Elizabeth quietly.

'Ah,' said her father, peering at her owlishly. 'You know about that, do you? He accosted you, too?'

'Yes.'

'Who or what are the Best Men?' asked Jane.

'Lady Catherine's personal Vigil company,' explained Elizabeth. 'She has some very particular views on the matter.'

'Oh,' said Jane.

'I told him that the Foxhound hunted no more,' said Mr Bennet quickly. 'I am retired, and mean to remain so. And of course, I spoke for the two of – I spoke for the Foxhound's companions, too.'

'Thank you, Father,' said Jane quietly.

Elizabeth felt her father looking at her, and nodded.

'Now if only that were the end of it,' said Mr Bennet. 'Unfortunately, I suspect Mr Collins is here on a joint mission. He may have been thwarted in one endeavour, but I fear he has not given up on the other.'

Jane and Elizabeth looked at each other. 'We do not know what you mean,' Elizabeth said.

'You will,' said Mr Bennet gravely. 'If I am correct, I'm very much afraid you will.'

Chapter 13

That Mr Collins was indeed not a sensible man became abundantly clear to Elizabeth the more time she was forced to spend in his company. Jane tolerated him kindly, Kitty and Lydia ignored him, her mother fawned over him, her father took him in small, delighted doses then sought to avoid him, and Mary engaged in awkward intellectual conversations with him where neither seemed to understand the point the other was trying to make.

The 'other mission' soon became obvious: Mr Collins intended to marry, and in seeking reconciliation now that his miserly father was dead, he meant to choose a Bennet. He approached the matter with a smugness that suggested he found his plan of making amends for one day inheriting their father's estate by marrying one of them excessively generous and disinterested on his part.

His sights fixed on Jane, as the eldest, and Elizabeth watched his clumsy and awkward attempts to engage with her with a mixture of amusement and horror. Mrs Bennet observed them as well, obviously wrestling with the securing of Longbourn versus a chance at Netherfield. Really there was no contest – she had multiple daughters, but only one shot at so magnificent an estate. So she quite gently but firmly let it be known that her eldest daughter was very likely soon to be engaged, and thus with other daughters being available, his attention shifted down the line.

Whatever feeling he had convinced himself he had for Jane now settled upon Elizabeth like a clammy fog. He was such a mixture of pride and obsequiousness, self-importance and humility. She did not believe that it could be any kind of act designed to help him as an investigator – a kind of bumbling manner designed to lull others into a false sense of security. No, she felt sure that what you saw was what you got, and if this was Lady Catherine's idea of good recruitment, then she was sure they were better off remaining independent.

Next morning Lydia announced an intention of walking into Meryton, and the other girls except Mary agreed to go with her. Elizabeth excused herself and ran upstairs to her room, to swiftly pull on her leathers beneath her gown. If they should be followed or accosted, she wished to be ready. When she came back downstairs, she was alarmed to see Mr Collins waiting with the others, walking stick in hand, hat upon his head.

'Mr Collins is accompanying you,' said Mr Bennet, closing the door of his library. He had the grace to look a little guilty as he did so, but not greatly so.

Jane caught her eye and smiled sympathetically. 'If you like, I can accompany the girls, and you can stay here. I'm sure we will be safe.'

'No,' said Elizabeth gloomily. 'In that case he will find an excuse to stay as well, and I will be trapped, just the two of us. At least this way his attention is watered down a little.'

The walk into Meryton seemed to take forever. Mr Collins was a fairly brisk walker, but slowed when he was pondering some point, which seemed to happen fairly regularly as he held forth on various topics. Lydia and Kitty forged ahead, with Jane occasionally calling them to come back.

When they reached the wood, Lydia spun around with a gleeful look.

'Lizzy! Remember last time? When you were so busting you stopped to–' She looked at Mr Collins and clapped her hand to her mouth, giggling wildly.

'Lydia!' Elizabeth felt her face go red.

Jane bustled after the two younger girls, grabbing them by their arms and walking them forward, her tone low and angry. Elizabeth found herself alone with Mr Collins.

'Some private joke, I imagine,' he said. 'Humour is, of course, greatly to be valued. However, one must be careful to maintain appropriate levels of decorum. Lady Catherine says that any humorous comment resulting in a lady opening her mouth in more than a smile is best left unuttered.'

'And for gentlemen?'

'Hm?'

'Does her Ladyship maintain a similar rule for gentlemen?'

Mr Collins frowned. 'I'm not sure I follow. Anyway, as we find ourselves temporarily alone – though not in any untoward manner, of course – for, a gentleman and a lady out walking with other fair members of her family, and with the approval of both her parents, may find themselves together like so from time to time...Well, I do hope you have given thought to our conversation of the other evening. Of the part you could play in Lady Catherine's grand design.'

'It was my understanding, sir, that under her rules there would be no part for me to play.'

'Then the error was mine, and mine alone, in not explaining her vision adequately. There would be a very important role for you to play. Imagine a great wheel, with Lady Catherine at Rosings acting as the central hub, and avenues of information reaching out into the countryside, alerting the Best Men to any villainy in need of attention.'

To Elizabeth it rather conjured up images of a giant web, with Lady Catherine squatting like a fat old spider in the centre.

'All of the information would require collation and annotation. That would be the role of the wives of the investigators.'

'And these wives – you said they rank below the investigators in this hierarchy?'

'Naturally. Just as their wedding vows place them at the service of their husbands, so too would this role follow the same path.'

'And where would this collation and annotation take place?'

'Why, in their own homes, of course. That way there need be no disturbance of the smooth running of the household. Lady Catherine is very firm on that point. Indeed, she would take a most active interest in ensuring that.'

'Plucking at the strands.'

'I am afraid I do not understand.'

'Never mind.'

Thankfully they had by then caught up with Jane and the other two, and Mr Collins fell silent on the issue with a conspiratorial smile at Elizabeth. She tried to avoid looking at him after that – the sense of sharing anything with him was not a comfortable one. The fact he appeared to enjoy this little intimacy was quite repellent to her.

Once in Meryton, the younger girls' eyes were immediately wandering in the quest for the bright red of officers. Only a very smart bonnet or really pretty new muslin in a shop window could draw them from their pursuit.

Despite the happy chatter from the girls, Elizabeth felt unsettled. She looked at Jane, but she did not appear perturbed. Yet something was pricking at her mind. She felt tense, and it wasn't just because of Mr Collins. In the warm sunshine, time seemed to slow like treacle. Things felt hazy. Some village children ran by, playing a ball-bouncing game, their high voices chanting:

'Run, run as fast as you can
'But you can't escape from the Wick–'
'Look! It's Denny,' cried Kitty.
Elizabeth shook her head to clear it.
'And who is that with him?' said Lydia.

Along the street came a young officer obviously already well known to the younger girls, and with him a young gentleman with a confident, attractive air. Denny bowed towards the young ladies, and Lydia and Kitty seized the moment to rush across to a shop on the other side of the street, so as to cause a meeting. Jane and Elizabeth were forced to follow, Mr Collins trailing disapprovingly in their wake.

Denny greeted them and was pleased to introduce his good friend, a Mr George Wickham, who, he was happy to say, had recently accepted a commission in their regiment. Kitty and Lydia blushed and giggled, no doubt already imagining him in his uniform – for that was all that was missing to make him completely charming. He was handsome, with a trim figure and warm, open manner. His dark eyes swept the group, and as they met Elizabeth's, and his smiled widened warmly, she felt a thrill run though her. There was something quite compelling about him – it wasn't just his looks; something put one quickly at ease, so that even though the acquaintance had just been made, one soon found oneself sharing a little joke about the township, and it seemed the most natural thing in the world that he should lean in to make a comment, his breath warm and sweet upon one's face.

They may have been standing talking for minutes or hours when the clopping of horses' hooves broke the spell. Wickham glanced up, and there was such a change in his face, like the sun had passed behind a sudden storm cloud. The warmth and life were gone, and the eyes that had twinkled with such delight were now cold and dead. Elizabeth frowned, confused, and turned to look over her shoulder – Darcy and Bingley were riding down the street. In the same moment, she saw Bingley notice them, speak to Darcy, and direct his mount towards them. She turned back to say something witty about Darcy to Wickham, but he was gone. Denny and the girls were still chatting, Jane was smiling and stepping towards Bingley, Mr Collins had retreated sulkily further along the street, but Wickham seemed to have disappeared.

'Miss Bennet,' called Bingley. 'We were just on our way to Longbourn to inquire after you.'

'That is very kind of you,' said Jane. 'I am quite recovered, as you see.'

Elizabeth watched the two of them talking together, he leaning down from his saddle, she looking up at him, a gentle smile on her face. It was indeed a pleasant thing, she reflected, spending time talking with a handsome young man. Then she looked up at Darcy, and in that moment caught him staring at her. As their eyes met, he flicked his gaze away, his posture rigid. His horse stamped impatiently beneath him.

'Bingley. Let us ride on,' he said, his eyes fixed down the street. He kicked his horse and trotted off.

'Darcy! For goodness' sake, wait!'

Bingley grinned apologetically at Jane, saluted the group, and urged his horse after his friend.

Later, when they had prised the two younger girls away from Denny and the hunt for any other young men in red coats, and were walking back to Longbourn, Jane leaned in close to Elizabeth.

'I saw how much attention Mr Wickham was paying you,' she said. 'And it did not look to be ill received.'

Elizabeth opened her mouth to refute the accusation, but Jane smiled at her so sweetly, her eyes wide and inquiring, and she had to admit, the attentions of such a handsome young man had indeed been quite pleasurable. All the worse that it should be terminated so abruptly. By the arrival of Mr Bingley and Mr Darcy? What could it mean? Or was it just coincidence: Wickham probably had myriad tasks to perform in taking up a commission. Though he could have said goodbye...

At least Mr Collins appeared to be in quite a sulk and hardly spoke the whole way home.

Chapter 14

A cold night. Stars were twinkling distantly in the purple sky, and a maid paced along the road, head down, weary from her long day. She was quite alone. Quite vulnerable. If a wolf lurked in the darkness, she must appear irresistible.

Elizabeth smiled to herself. Felt the comforting weight of the baton. Felt the energy tingling through her body. Felt so very alive. The deepening gloom was not frightening to her. It was her domain. Let the wolf come, for it would find its teeth matched in kind.

It was a relief to escape the house. If she heard one more thing about Lady Catherine de Bourgh and her exquisite taste, she feared she may explode. Her father had retreated quite early to his study, and even her mother and Jane had battled to maintain an interest in the silly man's droning stories. Even worse were his attempts to engage her in the conversation – she had been forced to feign a headache to extricate herself, while Jane shot her a reproachful look.

She sighed happily – and just caught the whisper of running feet before a body slammed into her, an arm wrapped around her waist, another clasping to her face. A cloth, a cloth in his hand, and though the impulse was to breathe, to draw breath, she stopped herself in time. She felt a stubbled chin rasping against her ear, hot, ragged breathing. She flopped forward, bending over the man's arm, a dead weight. He grunted in surprise, dropping his other arm from face to waist to hold her up. She reached back between her legs, beneath her skirts, and caught hold of one of his feet. In one motion, she yanked it forward and up while thrusting herself backwards – back he fell, crying out in surprise. She spun as she followed him down, meaning to thrust her knee into his midriff, but she tangled in his legs and her own skirt and fell sideways. She kicked away, kept rolling, and tore at her costume, feeling the weakened stitches give way as planned. With her other hand she dashed her hat from her head and pulled her mask down over her face.

'Another fighter, eh?' said the man, coming up onto his knees. 'Well, I reckon he likes 'em feisty.'

He came at her, fast. She was just kicking the dress clear as he barrelled into her, sending her backpedalling until she hit a tree. The air exploded from her lungs, and at the same time he was thrusting that damned cloth into her face again. She squirmed, turning away, sucking in some desperate air from the corner of her mouth, felt the cloying bite of chemical fumes. She reached to her wrist and grabbed the end of the baton where it sat in a leather sheath. She wrenched upward, her elbow connecting with his chin, snapping his head back, just enough to continue the movement, the baton catching his jaw with a crack. He cursed and staggered back, mouth opening and closing like a landed fish.

'You will pay for that, you–'

She leapt at him, striking for his head. He lifted an arm in defence and the club landed solidly across his forearm. His arm dropped, deadened by the blow. He made a grab at the baton with his other hand, but she turned it and cracked him on the fingers. She stabbed forward, driving the end into his solar plexus. He folded, hands on knees, swaying and drooling saliva.

'Now, talk,' she rasped. 'Where did you take the girl? Where is your boss?'

He stopped swaying.

'Speak, damn–'

He charged. She was too close. She brought the club down, but across his back, and he was already grabbing her around the waist and tackling her to the ground. She tried to spin as they fell, to land on top of him, but failed. She cried out in anger and frustration as they crashed down. She let go of the club, the thong around her wrist keeping it close. She started shifting beneath him, seeking the moment where she could overturn him.

'Hold or die!'

The voice was loud, compelling. The man on top of her froze, then looked over his shoulder.

'Now then, squire, no need for all–'

'Get up,' growled the voice.

The man rolled off her and slowly stood. She could now see who he was talking to – the tall, cloaked figure from the night of the ball stood before them, a grim, dark shape in the moonlight, the bow in his hands, cold light glinting on an arrowhead pointed in their direction.

'You get up, too.' The figure dropped his aim towards her.

The man beside her bolted.

It happened so fast – he dashed for the shadows, and the bowman quickly corrected his aim, the ends of the bow straining back as he pulled to full draw. She rolled onto her knees and desperately twirled the baton over her head by its thong, heard the thrum as the string was released, and then a crack – so satisfying – as the baton made contact with the arrow in mid-flight, sending it spiralling away harmlessly into the night.

'That,' said the figure, 'was foolish.'

Elizabeth knelt, weighing her chances. The archer had not yet reloaded. She inched the baton back into her hand by its thong and slipped her hand free.

'You would shoot a man in the back?' she spat. 'Murder him in cold blood?'

'He chose to run.'

'No wonder, seeing how you keep trying to kill your own henchmen.'

'*My* henchmen?'

'I suppose you hope to silence them. But it won't do you any good. I will learn who you are. You will face justice.'

The figure appeared to be staring at her from beneath the dark hood.

'And who exactly are you?' he rasped.

'Your doom,' she snarled. 'Wicker Man.'

'Wicker what?'

She snapped her arm back and hurled the baton with all her might, straight at the black hood. He flinched back, barely managing to knock the baton aside with his bow, but she was right behind it, launching at him with a flying knee. She struck true, sending him staggering, the bow dropping from his gloved hands. The baton lay just to the side – she seized it and faced him. He grabbed the edge of his cloak and flicked the bottom of it at her – it hissed through the air, fast and heavy – must have lead shot sewn into the bottom seam. She jumped backwards – straight into a pair of arms.

'Bingo,' said a voice triumphantly in her ear. She was lifted high into the air, and before she could react, dashed heavily to the ground. The air left her lungs for a second time. Winded, she couldn't move.

'Don't hurt the young fellow too much,' said the cloaked man. 'I think he was trying to help.'

'He's just a bit battered. He will be fine. I didn't drive his head into the ground or anything.'

'I believe he thinks I am a villain.'

The second man laughed. 'It's your manner, I told you.'

The cloaked man grunted. 'Sit on him so we can get some answers.'

Elizabeth steeled herself. The man who had grabbed her dropped down astride her. She gasped.

'Awake are you? Don't struggle, there's a good fellow.'

'Get off me,' growled Elizabeth. The man on top of her was wearing a dark jacket, possibly blue, and a mask below a tricorne hat.

'Questions first. Who are you? What are you doing out here?'

'That is none of your business.'

'You are going about masked and wearing black at night. That makes it very much our business.'

'Not to mention twice now you have prevented me bringing down a criminal,' the cloaked man added.

'I stopped you murdering them!'

'Murder? It is no crime to kill a rabid dog. It is execution. This is the fate they choose when they adopt a life of crime. Now answer the question: who are you? What are you doing, going about at night masked like a villain?'

The accusation caused Elizabeth to strain against the man on top of her, but he had her well pinned. 'I am no villain! I am a Vigil!'

The two men looked at each other and laughed.

'No,' said the cloaked man. '*We* are Vigiles. We are the watch keepers, the firemen. You are a silly young boy playing games who keeps getting in the way.'

'Wait. So you are not...you are not the Wicker Man?'

The cloaked figure drew himself up taller, flicking his cloak so it flared behind him in the night breeze, eyes glinting from behind his mask.

'You are in the presence of the Dark Archer, nemesis of all those who choose the path of villainy.'

'And Bingo Boy,' said the man on top of her.

The cloaked figure grunted.

'What?' said the other.

'That just does not...' He shook his head. 'Enough, we are wasting time. I want answers, boy. Speak the truth and we will let you go. Where did you learn the fighting arts? Do you have associates? How do you always come to be associated with these henchmen?'

'I'll tell you nothing until I am sure—'

'We don't have time for this. You may think this is all great fun, but I assure you, this is not a game we are playing. Time is wasting. Let's cut to the chase – black ball him, please. He'll talk soon enough.'

'Certainly,' said Bingo Boy. He adjusted his weight, and to her horror, Elizabeth felt him slip one hand down between her legs. 'Best you do talk quickly, because this will of course hurt you more than me – oh I say!'

He reared in shock.

Elizabeth seized her moment. She bucked upward and twisted, sending the man sprawling. She rolled, snatched up her baton and sprinted off the road, the shrubs tearing at her as she made her escape.

Behind her, she heard the blue coat say, 'Uh, that – that was no boy.'

Chapter 15

All the long walk home, she wrestled with it.

She must of course tell Jane.
On no account must she tell Jane.
Would Jane even believe her?
Jane would have to believe her.

It was Darcy and Bingley. Of course it was Darcy and Bingley. Jane would ask her: *Did she actually see their faces?* She had not, she would be forced to admit. But two new Vigils appearing, obviously gentlemen by their manner of speech? And what of their names? *Dark Archer* and *Bingo Boy*? Darcy and Bingley?

She had to shake her head at the pride and arrogance of some men, that they held the rest of the population in such low regard. It just seemed so obvious. She was honestly amazed their identities had not been published in the pamphlets, with all the ensuing attention which was in essence death to Vigils – for how could one operate when one's every move was watched by admirers and enemies alike? When one's home, instead of being a sanctuary, became both a theatre and a target? Not to mention the risk to loved ones, surely the easiest way for a villain to thwart any who opposed them.

Perhaps she ought to be glad that there were more Vigils in the area to disrupt whatever evil was gathering. True, they were rude to her – *more than rude*, she thought, her cheeks reddening at the memory of Bingley groping at her – but they had obviously dismissed her as some local youth playing at heroes. Or they *had*...Would knowing she was female change that? What would they make of that discovery? It was likely, she supposed, that they would think her some crackpot, some girl giddy and overexcited by unlikely stories she had read in Vigil fan pamphlets now trying to act out her fantasies. No one to be taken *seriously*.

And where did this leave her? Angry, now she thought of it. She had had the kidnapper in her grasp, and their interference had forced her to actually assist in his escape, to prevent his death. But it had been the right thing to do, of that she was sure – she could not stand by while a man was murdered before her eyes. It was not for those who took up the mask to act as judge, jury and executioner.

She really needed to talk to someone about this. But Jane was best left out of it for now. She couldn't talk to her father – engaging in melees with kidnappers and outsiders would not please him.

And so at breakfast the next morning, after a restless night spent kicking at her bedclothes, she announced her attention to go into Meryton again, to take tea with Aunt Phillips.

'We'll come too.' said Lydia, around a mouthful of toast and marmalade.

'I would like to come as well,' said Jane.

Mrs Bennet, who had been frowning, suddenly lit up with a smile. 'What a capital idea! Perhaps you shall see Mr Bingley out riding again, Jane!'

Jane blushed. Of course that was the motive for her decision, but she didn't like it stated openly.

'Mr Collins?' said Mr Bennet, refusing to meet Elizabeth's eye. 'Perhaps you would care to again accompany the girls?'

'Delighted!' replied their guest, drawing breath to no doubt hold forth on the virtues of exercise and discourse. 'However, if I may comment on what is seemly for young ladies–'

'If you are all coming with me,' cut in Elizabeth, 'then you are all coming to visit. Aunt Phillips will be glad of some company.'

Mrs Bennet pursed her lips, and the younger girls fell silent.

'Just...tea?' asked Jane.

'Yes, Jane. Just tea.'

'Capital,' said Mr Bennet, looking at Mr Collins and his smug smile. 'I'm sure she will enjoy a visit.'

Just to be sure, a messenger was despatched to Meryton and soon returned with the happy news that Aunt Phillips would be delighted to have them for tea. Still somewhat shaken by the events of the night before, Elizabeth pressed their father for the use of the carriage and was most relieved when he acquiesced without a single complaint – though of course he was probably just hoping to be rid of them as quickly as possible.

All five girls (Jane hounded Mary from her room) and Mr Collins boarded the carriage at a suitable hour to be conveyed to Meryton. Elizabeth tried to avoid sitting next to the clergyman, but it was not to be. As the motion of the carriage bounced her against him, she wondered if she should ask if he knew of Vigils styled the Dark Archer and Bingo Boy, for she could not help worrying that they had lied to her. If what they said was true, then Lady Catherine's esteemed investigator may have heard of them. She turned towards him, but paused. This close she could see the sweaty dampness of his skin, the hairs growing in tufts from his ears. The thought of whispering a question to him, bringing her lips close to his head, caused her to shudder and turn away. She shook her head at herself. That she should have the courage to engage men in combat but not the stomach to speak to Mr Collins – what kind of Vigil did that make her?

They arrived, and Aunt Phillips threw open the door to greet them. Lydia and Kitty did their best to duck the hugs and rough kisses that Aunt sought to bestow on their cheeks. Mary seemed rather oblivious, but Jane returned the embrace with a warmth that pleased Elizabeth – she could see the tears pricking in the corner of Aunt Phillips' eyes. She was engulfed in that muscular hug herself, and then drew back to enjoy the spectacle of the meeting with Mr Collins.

That good gentleman had doffed his black hat, but now stood somewhat frozen as he took in Aunt Phillips for the first time: the size. The bluish chin. His eyes darted at the girls then back to Aunt Phillips, up and down, then remained fixed squarely on her face.

'And you are Mr Collins?' asked Aunt Phillips gently.

'Indeed, uh, madam. Delighted. Delighted to make your acquaintance. Any...any relative of the Bennets is naturally...uh...'

The spectacle of Mr Collins, red-faced and lost for words, was almost too delicious, though Elizabeth worried he may blurt something out and offend Aunt Phillips. But her aunt was practised in dealing with such awkwardness and smoothly led them inside to the drawing room. Someone was already sitting there.

'I have taken the liberty,' announced Aunt Phillips, 'of inviting another guest. I believe you have already made his acquaintance.'

Wickham smiled at them broadly from a stuffed armchair, a teacup balanced on one knee. A surge of energy ran through Elizabeth – why was he here? Was his purpose to mock Aunt Phillips? Her jaw tightened. But then she observed his easy, gentle way with her aunt, and she felt a different thrill run through her as he stood and requested she take the seat beside him. As Aunt Phillips bustled about, pouring tea and handing around plates of cakes and neatly cut sandwiches, Wickham kept up a steady stream of small talk about the weather and the likelihood of a wet evening, and it seemed to Elizabeth that even the dullest topic could be rendered interesting by a skilled speaker.

Mr Collins did his best to compete, attempting to gain the attention of the entire company, but Elizabeth noticed Wickham was skilled at appearing to listen for a short time and then smoothly directing his attention instead to Elizabeth and starting a new conversation whenever the clergyman paused for breath. It seemed Mr Collins had recovered from his initial shock at meeting Aunt Phillips, though he shot curious glances at her whenever he didn't think she was looking.

'Oh la!' said Lydia, throwing herself into a seat near Elizabeth. 'You have had the attention of Mr Wickham long enough, Lizzy. Let the rest of us talk to him too!'

Wickham smiled at Elizabeth, who flushed a little with embarrassment. She also felt quite annoyed – Lydia could be a most determined talker when an officer was the target, and she had to admit she had been enjoying the attention the young man had been bestowing upon her. It was not something she generally sought, not at the balls and assemblies and tea parties in crowded drawing rooms. Indeed, she was normally disdainful of those young women who so obviously hungered for male attention, that currency decreed so vital for an unmarried girl. But then Wickham turned to Lydia, took one of her hands – Elizabeth found herself biting her lip – and gently tapped it while smiling at her and looking deeply into her eyes.

'Dear, dear little Miss Lydia,' he said. 'I think I know what you want. I think you would enjoy some cards with Mr Collins. Don't you?'

Elizabeth almost laughed out loud. Lydia had not the patience for most card games, nor a good enough memory of the rules. Usually if she played, her attention was only half on the game and half on whether anything else more interesting was going on anywhere else.

'Play with Mr Collins?' asked Lydia, her face screwing up at the thought.

'Yes. I think you can beat him. I think you would enjoy beating him.'

Lydia stared at Wickham for a moment longer, then pulled her hand away. 'Fine,' she said. 'Perhaps I will.' And with that, she got up and seated herself at the whist table nearby with Mary, Jane and their clergyman cousin.

'I am impressed,' said Elizabeth. 'Lydia is not well known for doing what she is told.'

'Indeed?' asked Wickham, his gaze sliding over Lydia before returning to meet Elizabeth's eyes. 'Must be my new military bearing, I suppose.'

'You impress me in other ways as well,' she said, and then blushed – it sounded forward. 'Your manner with Aunt Phillips,' she went on hurriedly. 'You are very kind to her. Not everyone is as...understanding.'

'I find her absolutely charming,' said Wickham, and he turned and raised his teacup in salute to Aunt Phillips, who waved in return. She was trying to help Lydia play correctly.

'Your manner with others may be somewhat different, however. You disappeared rather abruptly the other day.'

'I hope I didn't offend you. I recalled some rather urgent business and did not wish to interrupt the conversation.'

'Was it...was it in any way because of the two gentlemen who appeared? Mr Bingley and Mr Darcy?'

'Ah,' he said, playing with his cup, tracing his finger along the creamy lip. He had nice fingers – long, but not too long. They would no doubt feel rather nice stroking one's hair...

He met her eyes, and she jumped a little. He smiled. 'How long has the latter gentleman been in the area?'

'About a month,' said Elizabeth, and then, when he didn't seem about to speak again, added: 'He is a man of very large property in Derbyshire, I understand.'

'Yes,' replied Wickham. 'His estate there is a noble one. Very beautiful.'

'You speak as one who has seen it?'

'I speak as one who is very familiar with it indeed. In fact, I have been connected with his family since my infancy.'

Elizabeth was astonished. 'Yet you did not care to greet him yesterday?'

Wickham looked at her. 'Are you much acquainted with Mr Darcy?'

'As much as ever I wish to be,' she said. 'I have spent quite enough time in his company. He is...' The strong black figure inserted itself into her thoughts – the casual cruelty, so quick to shoot at a fleeing man or order his companion to grab her – '...very disagreeable.'

'I shouldn't say anything,' said Wickham. 'I have known him too long and too well to be a fair judge. But no doubt you are in the minority, and he is held in high regard here abouts?'

'Not in Hertfordshire! Everybody is disgusted with his pride. You will not find him favourably spoken of by anyone.'

Wickham smiled thinly. 'I cannot pretend to be sorry. The world is often blinded by his fortune and consequence, or frightened by his high and imposing manners, and sees him only as he chooses to be seen rather than his true nature. I wonder whether he is likely to remain in the country much longer.'

'I do not know. But I hope that your plans with the regiment will not be affected by his being in the neighbourhood.' And she saw that it was true – she was enjoying talking to this handsome young man and already wondering when she might see him again. A thought bubbled up that this made her perhaps not so different to Lydia and Kitty, but she thrust it down.

'Oh no, I will not be driven away by Mr Darcy. Though it would cause me pain to have to meet him socially, so I may choose to avoid him when possible. I can be rather good at avoiding notice when I find it necessary.'

'Mr Darcy should be the one who is driven away!'

'Indeed. And if I told the world what he has done...His father, Miss Bennet, the late Mr Darcy Senior, was one of the best men that ever breathed, while this Mr Darcy, well, his behaviour towards me has been scandalous. But I believe I could forgive him anything and everything, except for his disappointing the hopes and disgracing the memory of his father.'

Elizabeth's eyes widened. She hungered for more detail – it all made such sense, Darcy *was* an evil man – and luckily Mr Wickham seemed happy to divulge more.

'My friend Denny persuaded me to join the regiment. He told me of the great attentions Meryton had bestowed upon them. Society, I admit, is necessary to me. I have been a disappointed man, and my spirits will not bear solitude. Military life is not what I was intended for, but here we are.' Wickham looked across at Mr Collins, who was trying to explain some finer points of the game to an increasingly exasperated Lydia. 'The church ought to have been my profession. I was brought up for it, and I should at this time have been in possession of a most valuable living, had it pleased the gentleman we were speaking of.'

'Really!' She tried to hold herself back, not appear overly eager.

'Yes. The late Mr Darcy bequeathed me the best parish in his gift. My father looked after the estate, you see, and Mr Darcy Senior was my godfather and excessively attached to me. But when he died, the position was given away to someone else.'

'Good heavens,' exclaimed Elizabeth. 'But how could that be? How could his will be disregarded? Did you not seek legal redress?'

'The terms of the bequest were just vague enough to give me no hope. A man of honour could not have doubted the intention, but Mr Darcy chose to doubt it. He claimed that I had forfeited all claim by extravagance, imprudence, in short anything or nothing. But I have done nothing to deserve losing it. I admit I have a warm, unguarded temper, and he may have felt the end of it once or twice because of his own coldness towards his father in his dying days, but I can recall doing nothing worse. The fact is, we are very different men. He hates me.'

'This is quite shocking! He deserves to be publicly disgraced!' The thought of that pompous pride being pricked was quite delicious.

'Some time or other he will be, but it will not be by me. Till I can forget his father, I can never defy or expose him.'

Looking at Wickham's noble, handsome face, turned to the side as his eyes went distant – goodness, they had brightened with unshed tears – Elizabeth bit her lower lip.

'But what,' she asked, after a pause, 'can have been his motive?'

'It is awkward for me to say,' replied Wickham, 'but I suppose it must be jealousy. Had the late Mr Darcy liked me less, the son might have liked me more. But his father's admiration for me irritated him. He saw us in competition for his father's affection and could not bear losing to someone such as me.'

'I had not thought Mr Darcy so bad as this! I have never liked him, and thought he despised his fellow creatures in general, but did not suspect him of descending to such malicious revenge, to such...injustice!'

'And yet you will hear him described as liberal and generous, as a kind and careful guardian of his sister. But it is all a front.'

'What sort of a girl is she, this Miss Darcy?'

He shook his head. 'I wish I could call her amiable. It gives me pain to speak ill of a Darcy, but she is too much like her brother. Very, very proud. As a child, she was extremely fond of me, and I devoted hours and hours to her amusement. But she is nothing to me now.'

Elizabeth knew she should change the subject. True, Wickham appeared to feel no qualms continuing his revelations about the Darcy family, but gossip made her feel uneasy. Yet, she found she could not help reverting to the subject again as she glanced across at Jane.

'I am astonished at his intimacy with Mr Bingley. How can Mr Bingley, who is so amiable, be in friendship with such a man? How can they suit each other? Do you know Mr Bingley?'

'Not at all.'

'He is a sweet-tempered, amiable, charming man. He cannot know what Mr Darcy is.' As she said the words, she remembered the feeling of Bingley's hand and thrust the thought away – he was all she had said, just obviously easily manipulated on top of that.

'Probably he does not,' said Wickham. 'But Darcy can please when he chooses. He can be companionable if he thinks it worth his while. Especially when among the richer of his friends.'

There was a loud burst of laughter from Lydia. She had apparently beaten Mr Collins, who was trying his best to smile and assure the rest of the company that they were not to be concerned, the money lost was a mere trifle. His eyes were blinking somewhat rapidly.

'I know very well, madam,' he assured Aunt Phillips, who was tutting over him with concern, 'that when persons sit down to a card table they must take their chances, and happily thanks to Lady Catherine de Bourgh, I am not in such circumstances as to make five shillings any object.'

'It's your deal,' said Lydia.

Mr Wickham observed Mr Collins for a few moments longer, then turned back to Elizabeth, asking in a low voice if she was at all acquainted with the family of de Bourgh.

'Not directly,' laughed Elizabeth. 'Though I feel I know her Ladyship very well indeed from the number of times she has been mentioned.'

'Your Mr Collins certainly seems well enamoured of her.'

'He is not *my* Mr Collins,' said Elizabeth, a little too quickly. Wickham smiled at her. She continued, 'You will find that there is not a topic of conversation to be had that does not in some way relate in the end to Lady Catherine.'

'She is Darcy's aunt, you know.'

'Indeed, I did not know!'

'I believe the plan is for Darcy and Lady Catherine's daughter to marry, thus uniting the two estates.'

This information made Elizabeth smile, as she thought of poor Miss Bingley. All her efforts, all her attention, wasted in the face of such monumental familial plans.

'Mr Collins,' she said, 'speaks very highly of both Lady Catherine and her daughter. But reading between the lines, I suspect his patroness is a somewhat arrogant, conceited woman.'

'I believe her to be both to a high degree,' replied Wickham. 'I have not seen her for many years, but I very well remember that I never liked her. Her manners were dictatorial and insolent. You are a perceptive and shrewd judge of character, Miss Elizabeth Bennet.'

His praise warmed her. Some small part of her mind was trying to alert her to how free and easy she was being with a man she barely knew, but it was quite easy to thrust that part back. Why shouldn't she enjoy his attention? This is what a girl of her age and class was supposed to do, wasn't it?

'You two are very deep in conversation,' said Aunt Phillips, having left the card players and wandered over to join them.

'Forgive me if I have neglected the rest of the company and your good self, Aunt Phillips. It is all too easy for me to become somewhat fixated when the company is as enjoyable as Miss Bennet's.'

'Not at all, sweet boy. There is no offence. You enjoy talking to a pretty girl – it is only natural.'

Elizabeth could feel her cheeks reddening.

'I am a firm believer in doing what is natural, I assure you,' said Wickham.

'You know,' said Aunt Phillips wistfully, 'I spent many, many years not living true to my nature. It was very difficult.'

'I can only imagine, madam. And let me say to you, that I find you the most charming hostess, and will be sure to inform the other officers of the regiment that here lives a most gentle woman indeed.'

Aunt Phillips smiled, eyes suddenly bright, and patted Wickham on the shoulder. She returned to the card table, where Lydia was again in loud argument with Mr Collins as to the rules of the game.

'Thank you,' said Elizabeth. 'I mean it, thank you.'

Wickham smiled at her. 'We should all live by our own true nature, don't you think?'

'In this specific case, yes of course. More generally? I suppose it depends on what one's nature is, whether it is good or evil.'

'But if a thing is natural, surely it is always correct, and thus good?'

'Not necessarily. What if someone's nature is to do harm to others?'

'Perhaps in that case, it is the nature of some to be harmed. The nature of the wolf is to eat the sheep. Perhaps the nature of the sheep is to be eaten.'

The card party was breaking up, Lydia loudly declaring she was bored with games and wanted to go and look at hats, Mr Collins asserting just as loudly that playing correctly was the way to gain the most enjoyment at cards, and that patience was a true virtue. While the cards and table were packed away, Elizabeth thought about what Wickham had said – in a world of wolves and sheep, what was she? But that was too narrow a choice: did it not follow that where those two existed, there were also hounds? And it was the nature of the hound to protect – yes, that was her. That was the heart of the Vigil: to protect, to hunt. This, then, was her nature. She could feel it. She was born to be a hunter.

When they left, Mr Collins was disappointed to find that they were not heading straight back to Longbourn, but must instead walk about the street as Lydia and Kitty surged ahead, looking in shop windows. Mr Wickham bade them farewell, and it was only once he had disappeared from sight – my, he had a noble, soldierly bearing – that Elizabeth realised she had failed to speak to Aunt Phillips about the events of the evening before. No matter, another time.

When they had finally coaxed the younger girls back into the carriage, she realised Mr Collins was sulking again. He made one terse comment that he hoped he was not crowding her, then spent the rest of the trip sitting legs spread, hemming her in to the side of the carriage while he stared angrily straight ahead. His mood was probably not alleviated by Lydia's non-stop recount of her victories, and how if cards were that easy to play, then Lord, perhaps she would play more often, and how funny it was taking other people's money!

After dinner, sensing his mood, in a moment of indulgence Mr Bennet invited him to read aloud to the ladies. Mr Collins graciously assented, and after some deliberation chose Fordyce's *Sermons*.

Lydia gaped as he opened the volume, and before he had, with very monotonous solemnity read three pages, turned to her mother and interrupted with:

'Do you know, mama, that another girl has disappeared from the village?'

'Lydia,' hissed Jane. 'Hold your tongue!'

'Wait!' said Elizabeth, ignoring the pained expression on Mr Collins' face. 'What did you say?'

'I heard it this afternoon while we were in town. I forgot till just now, isn't that funny? It was the milliner's daughter. She is quite vanished!'

'I hope this isn't some sort of trend,' cried Mrs Bennet. 'Good young girls all running off to London! Scandalous!'

Elizabeth clutched her stomach. 'You say vanished? Are you sure?'

'Lord, Lizzy, what is wrong with you? You look ghastly,' said Kitty.

Mr Collins cleared his throat loudly. 'I have often noticed how little young ladies are interested in books of serious stamp, written, I may point out, solely for their benefit. It amazes me, I confess. *Oh, and now Miss Elizabeth?*'

She was on her feet. She was on her feet, and the room was filmed with scalding tears.

'May I be excused?' said Elizabeth, a hand to her brow. 'I need to go.'

She stumbled from the room, ignoring the questions from her mother, the disapproving glare of Mr Collins and Jane's worried look.

Another girl. Another girl gone.

And it was all her fault.

Chapter 16

There would be pain.

(She pulled the lacing of the jerkin tight.)

She had known that, right from the beginning. There would be pain.

Learning how to punch, and kick, and throw. Bruises to be hidden from Mother. Aching muscles more used to the dance and the leisurely stroll, becoming strengthened, taut, reformed. Good pain. Honest pain. Achievement. The smile from her father. Approving nod from Aunt Phillips.

(The gloves now, pulled into position. Fingers flex. Make a fist, feel the leather pull tight across the knuckles.)

There would be other pain, too. Pain at seeing the despair of a farmer's family, their prize stock stolen. Empathic pain of loss and helplessness.

(The boots next. Stamp the feet, make sure they are snug.)

Pain inflicted. Gasps and grunts – met at the time with savage joy and satisfaction, but later, in the quiet night, that nagging internal pain of having inflicted hurt on another being, no matter how deserved. Pain of having caused another to fear.

But this was worse still: the pain of responsibility, of guilt.

(The final piece, the mask, slipped down over her eyes. Elizabeth no more.)

Or perhaps more fully Elizabeth than at any other moment?

There would be pain. Tonight.

Her desire for it almost frightened her.

It was as if she had wings, so suddenly was she down the drive and running towards the town. She did not try to keep to the shadows. She had no need of stealth tonight. She knew she would find him.

It did not matter who. The kidnapper. Wicker Man. Dark Archer. It did not matter. All had been stirred together in her mind into one dark stain falling across the neighbourhood she loved. She was the hunter. It was her nature.

The moonlight was dim, but enough. The gravelled road glowed white.

Someone would pay tonight.

She slowed, ribs pressing with each breath against her leather. She drew the baton from its sheath. Stood ready in the middle of the road. This was her land. She was the neighbourhood.

And he came.

A patch of deeper darkness resolving itself from the gloom into the form of the tall cloaked figure.

'So,' he growled. 'You again.'

'That is close enough,' she said, husking her voice, when he was some 12 feet from her. Close enough to hurl the baton if needed. He did not appear to be carrying his bow. He stopped, hands on hips, watching her.

'Where is your friend?' she asked.

'Possibly behind you.'

She fought the urge to turn her head, saw a certain tension rise and fall in his stance. He nodded his cowled head.

'Not falling for that one? Very well then, how about this: what if we attempt some honest discourse?'

'I'm not sure that is possible with a man hiding under a cloak.'

'Says the...person...in a mask. As a mark of good faith, I will go first: my companion is otherwise engaged. There is only I. Now it is my turn: are you indeed a woman? Or was it just that my friend's aim was poor?'

'Why does it matter?'

'That means yes,' he said. 'A young man wrongly identified as the weaker sex would protest vociferously. My friend was thus correct, and that means I must apologise both for him and myself. Though you choose to garb yourself thus and run about in the night in a way that is not becoming for a woman, still it is not acceptable that you should have been...dealt with in that manner.'

'Your apology appears to come wrapped in an array of insults.'

'Does it? I believe I merely state the facts.'

She ground her teeth. 'My turn. Are you involved in the kidnapping of the girls?'

'You seek to insult me? As I already told you, I am a Vigile.'

'That doesn't answer my question.'

'Yes, it does. If you had better sense, you would know it does.'

'Again, the arrogance.'

'How you perceive my actions and my words is up to you. My turn again – are you in league with anyone? Are you another's companion?'

'I am no companion. As *I* told *you*, I am a Vigil.'

'No. You think you are one, but what you are doing is merely playing. One such as yourself, especially a woman, could easily be manipulated into thinking you do good, when really you are but a pawn in a more calculated game. You have not recently come under the sway of someone from outside this neighbourhood? Someone who has ordered you to watch for me?'

'No! I would not assist a villain–'

'But that may be his cunning. You may think him charming. Or harmless. He would seek to take you in. Use you.'

'I can assure you, sir, I am my own person.'

There was a pause. Elizabeth realised she had been holding her muscles tensed and slowly breathed out, trying to relax a little.

'My turn,' she said. 'Do you *know* anything of the missing girls? Do you know where I may find them? Who has them?'

'Technically that is three questions. But I will indulge you. Though I confess to not understanding why it matters so much to you.'

'Why it matters? They are young, they are just girls!'

'Who were walking about in the dark by themselves.'

'So it is their fault they were taken? They were not taking the air! They are working girls, walking home after long hours serving their employers! They may not be wealthy, but they have worth!'

'To you, maybe. But in the greater scheme of things, they do not. I do not know anything about them. I am not concerned with them. I am after a far more important prize.'

'And what,' she spat, 'is so important that you can so casually dispense with others' lives? Gold? Land?'

'Vengeance.' He hissed the word.

She laughed, but her eyes stung with tears behind her mask. 'That is not a thing. That is a construct. That is vanity.'

He suddenly took two long paces towards her.

'Do not speak of what you do not – *cannot* – understand. You will anger me.'

'Should I care about your feelings? What of mine? If all other Vigils were like you, then–'

'Vigiles.'

'What?'

'You are pronouncing it incorrectly and displaying your ignorance. The correct term is "Vigile", not "Vigil". If you intend to continue with your dress-up and wish to be taken seriously, I suggest you learn the correct terminology.'

Unbelievable.

'What are you talking about?'

'I am a Vigile. A watchman, like the brotherhoods who served as firemen in Ancient Rome. I watch for the fires that would destroy our country. *Vigile.*'

'Vigil is just the same.'

'No, it isn't. It is a vulgar corruption of the original, just as the calling has been vulgarised by too many inappropriate individuals thinking they are worthy to wear the mask.'

'You think me unworthy? You do not know me.'

He appeared to be about to continue the lecture, but his stance shifted, and she felt his contemplative gaze fall upon her.

'No. I do not know you. But, I must confess, I am a little intrigued. Who are you, that acts and speaks so boldly? Who is it beneath the mask?'

She slid her baton back into its sheath and stood before him, arms held out to the sides.

'You really wish to know? Then lift my mask.'

He hesitated, then stepped forward again. In the cold moonlight she looked up into the darkness of his cowl, saw his eyes glinting behind his mask. He slowly lifted his gloved hands, and tentatively, almost tenderly, brought his fingers to the sides of her leather mask–

Taking hold of his jerkin and sleeve, she pivoted sharply, her back to him, stabbed her leg across in front of his knees and turned, tugging him downward. Caught off guard, he tripped over her leg and fell heavily on his side. She dropped onto him, all her weight behind her knee, and heard him gasp. He sprawled onto his back, and she was astride him. He tried to push her off, but she swam inside his arms, drove her forearm down across his throat.

Gurgling, he tried to roll away, and she let him turn, came down upon his back, her arm snaking around his neck. She fell sideways, pulling him with her, her legs locking around his middle. He fumbled at her arm, but it was already too late. She had cut off the blood supply to his brain. He was already sinking into unconsciousness.

'You wish to know who I am?' she snarled. 'More than a match for you, that is who.'

He grunted, and his arms fell to his sides. She quickly released her grip and pushed him aside. He was lying heavily across one of her legs, and she struggled to pull it free while he twitched and snorted. Once clear, she stood, gazing down at him. There really was no doubt, surely, as to his true identity – that pompous, conceited arrogance – and there was not much time before he woke. But still she bent, pulled the hood and mask aside, and stared for a moment into the face of Fitzwilliam Darcy.

Even unconscious, the face appeared smug, disdainful, lit wanly as it was by the half moon. Her fists bunched. She could ruin that face. Pound the certainty from it. Make him pay...

For what, though? Insulting her? Was that now a crime? She felt herself on the edge of a precipice. Was this how it began, the slide from Vigil into something else, something darker? How many of those who now took on the title of villain had once supposed themselves something else entirely?

But what about Wickham? Surely Darcy should pay for that. But a broken nose would not restore what had been taken. And was too easily explained as a nasty fall while riding at hounds, or some such. She could hardly go around the town boasting that it had been her that caused the bruising.

He groaned, stirred some more. He would be coming around soon. There was little time. She would leave him here, she decided, lying as he was, and when he woke, he would fear who had seen him there. A wicked thought struck her – pull his breeches down? But she instantly burned with shame at the thought, her stomach rolling over strangely. Instead she bent and pulled the mask so it was askew – let him know that while he did not know who she was, she had definitely seen his face. Let him wonder. Let him worry.

So she left him, and strode away into the night.

Chapter 17

Elizabeth hadn't had time the night before to relate to Jane all that Mr Wickham had told her, but the next day, following breakfast, she drew her elder sister aside. Jane listened with astonishment.

'I can't believe it.' She shook her head. 'That Mr Darcy should prove to be so unworthy of Mr Bingley's regard.'

Elizabeth controlled her face – Jane managed to bring most things back to Mr Bingley.

'Yet I cannot question the honesty of Mr Wickham. Oh, the poor man! To have endured such unkindness! But perhaps it is a mistake? Perhaps they both have been deceived in some way or other that we cannot make out. Interested parties have perhaps misrepresented each to the other. Some act of villainy, designed to sunder a deep childhood bond?'

Elizabeth sighed. 'Much as you would have them both blameless, I do not think it possible. I fear we are going to have to be allowed to think ill of somebody. Honestly, you tie yourself in greater knots than Aunt Phillips could upon the mats.'

'It is distressing. One doesn't know what to think.'

'I beg your pardon, one knows exactly what to think. Darcy is a terrible man. Almost a villain.' The image of Darcy lying unconscious the previous evening flashed into her mind. *Served him right.*

The conversation was interrupted by news of visitors. Mr Bingley and his sisters had arrived to personally invite the Bennet family to the promised ball, to be held at Netherfield the following Tuesday. Elizabeth watched the two Bingley women fuss over Jane, declaring it an age since they had last seen her, while doing their best to ignore Mrs Bennet's interjections on how wonderful it all was to have such neighbours, and how really they ought to see far more of each other. They had scarcely sat before the two ladies had risen and declared the need to go, much to the surprise of Mr Bingley, who was left to smile apologetically at Jane and hurry after them.

Jane was all smiles, picturing a happy evening with her two new friends and basking in the attention of their brother. Elizabeth herself imagined how nice it might be to take a turn or two upon the dance floor with Mr Wickham – for surely all of the officers of the regiment would be present, and in those numbers he need not worry about getting too close to Darcy. Lydia and Kitty, of course, were very happy – a ball was a ball to them. Even Mary declared herself not disinclined to attend.

Such was her good mood, Elizabeth made the mistake of asking Mr Collins if he meant to join in the dancing. She was teasing him, but recognised her mistake as soon as she spoke, for his eyes lit up as he beamed at her.

'I am by no means of the opinion, I assure you,' he said, 'that a ball of this kind, given by a young man of character, to respectable people, can have any evil tendency. I am so far from objecting to dancing myself that I shall hope to be honoured with the hands of all my fair cousins in the course of the evening.'

Elizabeth forced herself not to smile as she caught sight of Lydia and Kitty looking at him in horror behind his back. She frowned a little as Lydia pretended to throw up.

'In fact,' continued Mr Collins, stepping closer, 'I take this opportunity of soliciting yours, Miss Elizabeth, for the first two dances especially. A preference which I trust my dear cousin Jane will attribute to the right cause and not to any disrespect for her.'

Elizabeth cursed herself. Why could she not have kept her mouth closed? The first two dances? Those dances held social power – who danced with whom for those dances said much about where one stood, where one's favour lay. She had intended being engaged by Wickham for those dances – to have Mr Collins instead! But it was not the sort of invitation one could easily turn down without causing serious affront. There was no help for it. She would simply have to grit her teeth and delay her own happiness till she was able to offload her cousin onto one of her sisters.

It was only after walking away that the choice of his words truly struck her – the 'right cause'? Dear Lord, there appeared no avoiding it – she had indeed been targeted as the potential Mrs Collins. Doomed to be nothing more than some kind of secretary to Mr Collins as he investigated whatever matters Lady Catherine deemed suitable? And share a life, a...a bed with *him*? She shuddered.

Over the next few days Elizabeth observed his increasing attention, his frequent attempts to compliment her. She found herself holding her tongue, aware of Mr Collins hovering on the edge of his seat, almost bursting with the desire to heap praise upon whatever utterance she made, however banal. Worse, the way her mother smiled and nodded led her to believe she was fully in favour of such a match – indeed, was encouraging it.

The situation was perilous. She could see the danger, the coming attack was obvious, but there was no counter she could think of to avoid it. It was maddening. She was well aware that a serious dispute must be the consequence of any proposal. And strangely, that kind of open disagreement as a young woman was in some ways harder to take than a fistfight at night, masked and anonymous.

Chapter 18

Till Elizabeth entered the glittering, elegant drawing room at Netherfield and looked in vain for Mr Wickham's trim figure, it had not occurred to her that he may not be present. That evening she had found herself dressing with more than her usual care, and was in such high spirits that even Mr Collins' insistence of sitting beside her in the carriage had failed to dampen her mood. She had not fully realised how much she was craving speaking to Mr Wickham again until she found he was not there. At the realisation, a wave of cold anger washed over her – the insult, for all the other officers of the regiment to be there, except him. How could Darcy dare it – how could Bingley support it? Her jaw tightened.

'Ladies!' said Denny, coming towards the sisters with a smile. He complimented them all, and, in answer to Lydia's query, explained that Wickham had been obliged to go to Town on business and was not yet returned. 'Though I do not imagine his business would have called him away just now, if he had not wished to avoid a certain gentleman here.'

So. He had stayed away by choice, to save himself the upset of seeing Darcy lording it about. But it was so unfair that he should be the one missing out, when it should be Darcy skulking off with his tail between his legs. And by extension, her own evening was now the poorer. She could barely speak to Mr Bingley when he arrived to welcome them and thank them for attending.

At least Charlotte was there, and Elizabeth could take pleasure in seeing her friend. Charlotte listened to her complaints about Wickham's absence sympathetically.

'Well, Lizzy, I know you are disappointed. But I doubt you will be wanting for partners. I believe one is coming your way even now.'

'Oh no,' groaned Elizabeth. 'That, dear Charlotte, will be my cousin, Mr Collins.'

The doors through to the ballroom were thrown open, and the musicians struck up the first air. She had no choice but to take the clergyman's hand and be led through to take their places on the polished wooden floor. The first two dances were mortifying. Mr Collins was awkward and solemn, frequently apologising and not paying attention. He would step in the wrong direction, jostle other pairs, and remain seemingly unaware of it. Numerous frowns were shot in their direction, and she felt shame and misery until they were done. It was surely a metaphor for what it would be like to be married to him.

Such an ecstasy of escape when the musicians stopped and the dancers lightly applauded...

'Perhaps, Miss Elizabeth, I may be so bold as to ask if we may not dance–'

'Elizabeth,' said Charlotte, arriving at her side. 'You must not keep your cousin to yourself all of the night! I am sure you will not mind if you yield?'

Elizabeth looked gratefully at Charlotte and felt such an urge to hug her. Mr Collins looked nonplussed and was about to speak, but Charlotte was already taking his hands and leading him into position for the next dance.

Her evening improved then, for she danced next with an officer who was a refreshingly good partner, and had the delight of talking about Wickham and hearing that he was universally liked by his fellows. Indeed, so glad were they to have him in their regiment that they sometimes even relieved him of some of the more tedious duties. She occasionally caught Charlotte's eye when the two couples were near each other, but Charlotte merely smiled at her in response to her own raised eyebrow.

When that pair of dances was over, Elizabeth immediately sought her out.

'You, my dear Charlotte, are indeed a worthy friend. To sacrifice yourself like that.'

Charlotte laughed. 'He is not so very bad. More like a large clumsy child than one who means any harm.'

'Well, you are more patient than I. I was afraid I would be trapped all evening and find an offer made by the time of the last dance.'

'Really? He has designs?'

'I'm afraid so.'

'He may not be the only one with you on his mind,' said Charlotte.

'Whatever do you–'

She realised there was someone directly behind her. She spun – and found herself face to face with Darcy. It was all she could do to not drop into a fighting stance.

'I wish to apply for your hand,' said Darcy, face stiff and implacable. 'For the next two dances.'

She was so taken aback she could not speak, but then felt Charlotte nudge her in the back and found herself tightly nodding her agreement. That he should seek her out...Did he suspect? He walked away immediately, leaving her to fret over her own want of presence of mind while Charlotte tried to console her.

'I daresay you will find him agreeable enough.'

'I do not think that is at all possible.'

At that point, the musicians made ready, and Darcy cut back through the throng towards them, his black eyes fixed upon her.

'At least he is a man, not a child,' observed Charlotte drily. 'Now do not be a simpleton and allow your fancy for Wickham make you appear unpleasant. He is rich and handsome, and thus you are the envy of nearly every young woman in the place – your stocks rise. Rejoice.'

Elizabeth made no answer, but took her place in the set opposite Darcy. She was keenly aware of the curiosity of her neighbours, who were no doubt wondering why he should seek her out. But if she was hoping for some sign from him as to the answer, she soon saw she was to be disappointed – he did not speak to her, and it appeared that the silence may continue for the entire two dances. So he was not there to confront her. But why should he suspect her? Why, from his perspective, the masked young woman he had encountered could be any girl at the ball – or maybe not even there, for it was probable his pride could not conceive that a girl who had defeated him could also appear just like any other eligible young lady in town. And so the silence was welcome, and she resolved not to break it herself, but as her comfort level grew, so too did her desire to punish him further by forcing him to speak to her.

'A most delightful dance,' she said at last.

He grunted something in reply, maintaining a steady gaze somewhere between her right ear and temple. After a pause of some minutes, she spoke up again.

'It is your turn to say something now, Mr Darcy. I talked about the dance, and you ought to make some kind of remark on the size of the room or the number of couples.'

He looked at her for a moment or two, then answered: 'I assure you that whatever you wish to be said shall be said.'

'Very well. That reply will do for the present. Though later I may have other observances to make, so start planning something witty for your next utterance. For now we may lapse back into silence.'

'Do you talk by rule then, while you are dancing?'

'Sometimes. One must speak a little, you know.' She realised that his attention was torn between attending to her and scanning the other women as they danced by. So. He was indeed seeking her and did not realise she was in fact literally in his grasp. He must be wondering who knew his secret identity and what they intended to do with the information. 'It would look odd to be entirely silent for half an hour. And be quite uncomfortable.'

He did not reply. Feeling the desire to prick him a little more she said: 'When you met us in Meryton the other day, we had just been forming a new acquaintance.'

'Ah yes. Some officer no doubt,' he said dismissively.

'Why yes. Including one you did not see, but who did see you. One who knows you well. Mr Wickham?'

The effect was immediate. It was as if a silent thunderbolt had gone off within him. His whole body jerked, but he appeared to master himself with great effort, his face stiff. She had expected some reaction, but not one as powerful as this. She found herself unable to go on taunting him. At length Darcy spoke again, grinding the words out between his teeth.

'So Wickham is here?'

'In the neighbourhood? Yes. Here tonight? No. Your presence appears to have seen to that.'

'As well it might. Where is he staying? Do you know?'

'He is serving with the regiment. His brother officers are quite taken with him. He seems a very likeable sort of man.'

'So. Surrounded by soldiers, is he? Mr Wickham seems to be blessed with such happy manners as may ensure his making friends wherever he goes. Whether he is capable of keeping them is less certain.'

'He has certainly been so unlucky as to lose your friendship,' replied Elizabeth, 'and in a manner which he is likely to suffer from all his life.'

'Mr Wickham suffers, you think?'

'To be robbed of a promised living? Bequeathed by a loving man? Yes, I should think that qualifies as suffering.'

'And you think yourself qualified to make such judgements? To see him as the innocent party, and me as some kind of villain? Me? The Dar–'

He bit his lip, dark eyes staring over her shoulder. She pulled him a little closer.

'Careful,' she whispered. 'Your mask is slipping.'

This time the effect was different. It wasn't energy that coursed through his body, but freezing ice – not just cold, but the power of an iceberg. He slowly pushed her from him, staring into her eyes, and at that moment she felt a stab of…was it fear? She found she could not maintain his gaze, and so looked aside herself. Then he pulled her swiftly to one side – a short, sharp tug no one else would have been likely to notice. She instinctively caught her balance without stumbling, and she heard the long hiss of his exhalation. Next he took hold of her hand and held it up before his face. She paled – her knuckles were still red and swollen. The sort of knuckles one did not get from playing the piano.

'*You,*' he snarled.

She didn't know what to say. She hadn't meant to give away her advantage, to reveal herself so. Aunt Phillips would shake her head. She had foolishly allowed herself to become caught up in the moment.

'You,' he said again.

'Yes, me,' she snapped. 'And you. What of it?'

She went to pull away, to leave the floor, no matter how remarked upon it would be, but he held her tightly. Breaking his hold was at least socially impossible, if not physically so.

'You have had training in Barton-Wright's oriental ways. How is that possible? A mere girl from such a neighbourhood as this. Who has taught you?'

'There's that pride again, Mr Darcy. You think only London has the best to offer.'

He opened his mouth to speak several times before finally finding the words.

'About Wickham. I must warn you–'

At that moment, Sir William Lucas appeared, red in face, and caught hold of Darcy's arm.

'Forgive the interruption,' he said, 'but, sir, I must compliment you on your dancing and choice of partner. I hope we see this oft repeated, especially when a certain desirable event has taken place.' And here he stopped and nodded meaningfully to where Jane and Bingley danced nearby. 'But let me not interrupt you further! You will not thank me for detaining you from the bewitching conversation of this young lady, whose bright eyes are also upbraiding me!'

And with that, he moved on, leaving Darcy and Elizabeth to lapse back into an awkward silence. She realised he was staring at Jane and Bingley. When would this wretched dance end? All she had wanted was to rattle him, prick his pride, but now she felt desperately uncomfortable and almost a little guilty. It was as if she had waded into a river and found currents below the surface dangerously stronger than expected.

Finally, mercifully, the music did end, providing an opportunity for escape. She curtsied, and Darcy's attention shot back onto her.

'Wait. I must speak to you about Wickham.'

'I have heard the story, Mr Darcy. I doubt there is anything you could say in your defence that would change my mind.'

The stone returned to his face. But there was pain behind it, a look in his eyes, that sucked some of the breath from her and made her feel a little ill.

'Indeed?' he said. 'Such is your prejudice against me, is it? Then there is nothing more that needs be said, and I will bid you good evening.'

He bowed, short and sharp, spun on his heel and stalked off. Elizabeth looked about in vain for Jane or Charlotte, but both were occupied with partners. To avoid being asked to dance by anyone else, Elizabeth retreated to the edge of the room and seated herself among the older women who sat fanning themselves around the wall.

Supper was called, though Elizabeth had no appetite. Whatever little she had was squashed when she took her place at the long table in the dining room and found she was seated almost across from Darcy, with her mother beside her and Lady Lucas next along. Mrs Bennet immediately launched into an animated though one-sided discussion of her expectation that Jane would soon be married to Mr Bingley.

'I shall have him!' she declared. 'Or rather, Jane shall have him! Mark my words!'

Elizabeth winced at the volume of her mother's words. Darcy, who had been scrupulously ignoring her, surely overheard every embarrassing remark.

'For heaven's sake, madam, lower your voice!' she begged when she could bear no more, but her mother simply turned to glare at her momentarily before returning to her topic.

Elizabeth blushed and blushed again with shame and vexation. She was so far from holding the upper hand now – she had been revealed and exposed. She could not help glancing frequently at Mr Darcy, though every glance convinced her of what she dreaded for although he was not looking at her mother, she was convinced his attention was fixed upon her. The expression on his face changed gradually from indignant contempt to a composed and steady gravity.

At last Mrs Bennet ran out of things to say on the topic, despite repeating the same information a number of times. Lady Lucas, who had long been yawning, was finally able to give her full attention to her plate of cold ham and chicken. Elizabeth's nerves had almost begun to settle when supper was over and singing was talked of. To her mortification, Mary was at once on her feet, rushing to the piano in undignified haste. Elizabeth watched her as she sat heavily on the piano stool, hunching forward, squinting at the music.

Mary's powers were by no means fitted for such a display: her voice was weak and her manner affected. The music and the performance must grate on anyone possessing the least knowledge and appreciation of the art. She looked at Jane, to see how she bore it, but Jane was very happily talking to Bingley. She looked at his two sisters, their mouths twisted in derision, rolling their eyes at each other. She dared look last at Darcy and found him to be looking at her. As soon as their eyes met, he looked away. She felt sick. What a freak show her family must appear.

Mary came, pounding, to an end, and before she could begin again, Elizabeth found herself on her feet. Mary pretended not to see her coming and was placing her fingers on the keys again when Elizabeth reached her, gently but firmly covering her hands with her own.

'Well done, Mary,' she said, 'but let some of the others have a turn. You have delighted us long enough.'

Mary looked set to argue, but Elizabeth closed her grip around her younger sister's fingers and squeezed, then drew her to her feet and away from the centre of attention.

'It isn't fair,' said Mary. 'I have been practising. Ow!'

'Yes, well, I wish you had spent a little less time practising and a little more on trying to solve that puzzle I gave you.'

'That old thing? That was nothing.'

Her stomach dropped.

'*What?*'

'I worked that out days ago. You just had to take the first letter of each word, then count back–'

'Why did you not tell me?'

'I didn't think it important. You never said!'

'Mary, listen.' Elizabeth took hold of her arms. 'It *is* important. I should have told you. Now, this is vital – can you remember what it said?'

Mary screwed up her face, sniffed. 'Not really.'

Elizabeth slumped – she would have to wait till the end of the ball, and no doubt their mother would be in no hurry for them to leave.

'But it doesn't matter, as I think I have it here in my reticule.'

Elizabeth stared at her, torn between the urge to shake or kiss her.

'May I see?' Her voice was unsteady, her hand shaking.

'Hold on, hold on.' Mary dug through balled-up handkerchiefs, some darning wool, and finally withdrew a tattered, folded slip of paper. 'It was quite a snap in the end, once I–'

But Elizabeth was no longer listening. She turned away, unfolding the paper. Beneath the nonsensical words, Mary had neatly printed the translation of the code. It read: 'Meet 30th of the month midnight to move the cargo. Westly Lock.'

Her stomach lurched. It was the 30th tonight. They were moving the girls from wherever they had been keeping them tonight. Westly Lock? So, they were intending to use the canal – down to the river, and then on to London. Where they would be lost forever.

She must act. The hunter had the scent. She knew where the wolves would be.

She was ready to rush from the room, but then paused. She must think. Westly Lock was some miles away – it would take too long to get there on foot. And she did not know how many men may be there. Could she be sure she could handle them all alone?

She looked rapidly about the room. Jane was talking still to Bingley. She could not ask her – could not ask dear sweet Jane to come away now and risk her life. She looked to her father. He was standing talking to Lord Lucas, punch in hand, swaying a little, his face red. No, he was in no fit state.

There was only one here tonight she could ask for help.

She looked about – she could not see him. Where was he? She swiftly stood on a chair to scan the room. People turned to stare at her but she ignored them. There, he was there, speaking with Miss Bingley. Or being spoken to by her. She stepped down and thrust through the crowd to him, all the company seeming to conspire to stand in her way. He saw her coming, and stared. Miss Bingley turned and looked at her in astonishment as she arrived before them and took Mr Darcy by the hand. She pulled him into an empty sitting room.

'Have you gone mad?' he asked. 'Have you no sense of propriety?'

'Listen to me! I need your help. I have found out that the Wicker Man's henchmen are moving the girls tonight – soon! I don't know how many there will be. I need your help.'

'What on earth are you talking about?'

'There is no time! Please – we need horses. We must get to Westly Lock by midnight. They are moving the girls. We must save them!'

'We? I told you once before, I do not share your desire to become embroiled in some petty local scheme. I have a larger goal.'

'Yes, yes, your stupid vengeance. But I need you tonight. Now. Will you come?'

He stared at her, frowning.

'Mr Darcy! You say you are a Vigil – act like one!'

'Vigile,' he muttered automatically.

There was no time for this. She ran from the room. Her outfit was again boxed beneath the family carriage outside. There would be no time to unhitch one of the horses, so she was resolved to borrow one. The ends must justify the means.

Chapter 19

Westly Lock was lit by a series of torches and lanterns. Elizabeth could count six men from where she lay in the thick undergrowth on a ridge overlooking the canal. A roofed barge sat tied in the lock, and near it a small wagon pulled by a pair of horses, stamping nervously. A light shone from inside the lock keeper's hut on this side of the waterway.

The men all appeared to be hooded in some fashion, confirming they were up to no good. As she watched, two pulled a long blanket-wrapped bundle from the back of the wagon. The bundle kicked and bucked, and she realised it was a person, tightly bound. The man carrying the feet dropped them and stepped forward. He drew his hand back and brought it down with a mighty whack across the bound figure's head, and the figure became still.

Elizabeth's knuckles tightened around her baton, and she went to rise to her feet – but a hand caught her around the ankle and hauled her back down. Hissing, she rolled onto her back, kicking backwards. The man behind her grabbed this leg, too, and pinned both down.

'Stop kicking,' whispered the man. 'That hurt.'

'*Darcy?*'

He released his hold, and she pulled free of his grasp.

'Please refer to me as the Dark Archer out here.'

He was indeed in his Vigil outfit of black cloak over leather armour.

'You are a fast rider,' he observed. 'But your forest craft needs work. I was easily able to locate you. Be thankful they do not have a roving patrol in the tree line who may also have discovered you as easily.'

'Thank you for the tip,' she snapped. 'Now if you are quite finished, let's go down there and rescue the girls.'

He shook his cloaked head.

'Not just like that. Passion will only take you so far. And not far enough to triumph. There are too many of them.'

'I'm not afraid.'

'I didn't say you were. I just observed there are too many of them. I do not doubt your courage or your martial skills – I am simply stating the truth that whatever strength or skill a person may hold, these may always be overcome by numbers.'

'I will not let you stop me. I am going to save them!'

'I have not come necessarily to stop you, though, looking at the situation here, I do believe it would be the wiser choice to follow the barge rather than attempt to overwhelm them now. No, I have come to make sure you do not risk your life needlessly.'

'What do you care!'

'Oh, but I do. You are a woman of character, no matter the unfortunate relatives who surround you. I cannot stand idly by while you put yourself in harm's way, even if I disagree with your choice of mission.'

'Then what do you propose? You will help me?'

For answer he pulled a wrapped bundle from behind him and unrolled it. Within lay his short hunting bow and a handful of arrows.

'I propose to even the odds a little.'

'No. No killing.'

'You are being amateurish and foolish. These men will have little hesitation in taking your life. Even if they knew you were a woman, it would make little difference.'

'It is not my way.'

'Then you are choosing to make your way harder than necessary. I have not followed you here to be knifed in the back by some common henchman. Especially not for the sake of some silly, common girls.'

'I take back my request for your help. I do not need you.'

'Oh, but you do. Think, Elizabeth. Choose your battles more wisely.'

'I choose this one!'

A cry from the lock caught their attention. The girl had been loaded down in the hold of the narrow barge. The torchlight glinted on a padlock being snapped shut on the entry hatch. Two men standing on the barge took up long poles, while another on the bank started to untie the lines.

'We are wasting time!'

Elizabeth swiftly rolled clear of Darcy's reach, then sprinted down the slope towards the cover of the hut. She was counting on the men's attention being on the barge, and that the circles of light from the torches and lanterns blinded them to the deeper dark beyond. She did not know if Darcy followed or not. She tried not to think how many there were opposing her. She needed a distraction.

She slammed against the wall of the hut, ears straining, but could hear no cries of alarm. She slipped around the far side to where a lantern hung off a hook set in the wall. She lifted it clear and was pleased to feel it sloshing full of oil. She used her baton to slowly push open the shutter on the nearest window. There were at least two men inside – she glimpsed a strange, pale face and a larger man in some kind of headdress. She turned her head away, smashed with her baton at the window glass, heard it shatter and the shouts of surprise from within. She flung the lamp into the interior. The cries turned to alarm as oily orange flame blossomed within.

She dashed around the corner, crashed into the back of a hooded man. She recovered, kicked him behind the knee and felled him with a blow from her baton as he went down.

'Who the devil?'

She spun – one of the men from the hut stood in the doorway – another figure disappeared in the flickering smoke. This one was wearing a wolf skin as a headdress – how apposite. He held an old blunderbuss with a flared muzzle, pointed right at her.

'This will mess your pretty mug, whoever you are.'

He cocked the hammer and pulled – she flinched – an arm encircled her, and a black cloak like a giant wing furled around them. Darcy! He pulled her to him, turning his back, and she heard the gun go off with a muffled thud. Darcy grunted, staggered, then released her, whipped his arm, and the weighted end of the cloak slashed back, knocking the barrel aside. He whipped again, with the other side, and the lead weights cracked across the wolf-man's temple, sending him to his knees.

'Go!' gasped Darcy, straightening painfully.

'You've been shot!'

'Behind you!'

Feet running – she turned, one man almost on her. She took his arm as he came at her, spun, pulling, and threw him to the ground. She jumped, landing with both knees full on his belly. He croaked like a giant frog, vomited, and writhed gasping for breath as she rolled clear. Another was right there, a blade in his hand. He stabbed – she swatted his hand down, jumped back. He thrust again – a mistake, never repeat the same attack twice, never make a pattern. She swatted down again, jumped forward this time, sliced her elbow across his nose, felt it crack – where was his knife hand? Turned, caught it, slipped a foot behind his and wrenched. Down he went. She still had his knife hand, snapped it back across her knee. His numb fingers dropped the blade and she kicked it away.

A grunt behind her – Darcy wrestling with another ruffian. He thrust the man back, then kicked out with his heavy boot, catching the henchman square in the solar plexus.

Darcy pointed. 'The barge!'

She turned – the pole men were moving the barge away from the side of the canal. Another was at the rack and pinion, to release the water from the lock and let the barge through to the lower part of the canal.

She ran for the edge of the canal, jumped, and landed heavily on the rear deck of the barge, sending it rocking. The closest man thrust his pole at her like a pike, striking her in the head. Sparks went off behind her eyes. He drew back to strike again. She braced, ready to move inside his reach, but arms grabbed her from behind, lifting her off her feet.

'Chuck him over,' yelled the poleman.

She smashed backwards with her head, felt it impact the man's nose, but he held on, growling. She tangled her feet back through his, and he stumbled. She dropped her weight, slipped down through his grasp, grabbed one of his legs, lifted and drove him backwards. Over the side he went, hitting the dark canal water with a mighty splash. A blow took her in the kidney – the pole again – and she was on her hands and knees. She heard him coming for her, rolled onto her back – he came in too close, and she kicked him square on the knee. He squealed, grabbed at it, and she kicked again, her shin landing flush against his head. He staggered, stumbled and went over the side.

'Just set the bloody thing on fire,' bellowed the rough voice of the wolf-man from near the hut.

The man at the lock mechanism ran for one of the torches and snatched it up. He ran towards the barge.

'Darcy,' she screamed.

He was there, by the burning building, his bow in his hands. He drew back, full stretch, released, and the arrow sped across the gap, burying itself in the runner's back. The man took two more stumbling steps, then went sprawling. Darcy nocked another and faced the remaining couple of henchmen. Both hesitated, glanced at their fallen comrades and then at each other, then took to their heels.

'Devil take you,' snarled the wolf-man, still on his knees, holding his head where Darcy's weighted cape had struck him. Darcy aimed his arrow square in the man's face. The leader sat back, holding up his hands in surrender.

Elizabeth rose painfully to her feet and took up one of the abandoned barge poles. She thrust it into the water and strained, grunting. Slowly, slowly, the end of the barge shifted back towards the side of the canal. When it bumped, she dropped the pole, caught up one of the lines and clambered onto the side of the lock, where she lashed the barge into place. She moved to the hatch, then cursed when she spotted the padlock – who had the key? She rattled it furiously, then stood and looked about. Silhouetted against the burning cottage stood Darcy, still aiming at the seated figure of the wolf-man. One man lay on the bank, an arrow in his back, but all the rest had crept away.

'Hold on,' she called down into the narrow seam around the hatch. She couldn't tell if anyone answered.

'There is a padlock,' she told Darcy as she limped over to him.

He nodded. 'Bind this one. Then we shall deal with that.'

She cast about, eventually removing a spare line from the barge and dragging it over. She tied the man's hands and feet. Darcy groaned, and relaxed his draw.

'Are you all right?' she asked.

'Search him,' grunted Darcy. 'He may have another key.'

She patted at the man's filthy pockets – he stank of sweat – but found nothing.

'Watch him,' said Darcy. He walked slowly over to the windlass mechanism and removed an iron bar from it. He carefully stepped down onto the barge and jammed the bar into the soft wood of the door frame. He heaved, grunting with pain, and with a splintering crack the hinges came loose. He staggered, narrowly avoiding falling backwards into the water.

'Da–Dark Archer! Let me!'

He paused, looked at her, then waved her over. They passed on the side of the lock, he returning to guard the wolf-man, she climbing onto the barge.

'I'm opening the hatch now,' she whispered into the hold. 'Do not be afraid.'

She pulled open the broken door, and could barely make out four pale faces in the dank gloom. They retreated further into the dark, and she could hear muffled crying. She quickly made a decision, and pulled her mask from her face.

'Don't be afraid,' she said again, stepping slowly down. 'I am here to save you. Some of you know me, or know of me. I am Elizabeth Bennet.'

One of the girls there in the dark – yes, there were four of them – leaned forward, her wide eyes searching Elizabeth's face. Her mouth was gagged, but she squawked as she recognised her. Elizabeth in turn saw that this was the milliner's daughter.

When she had untied all four, she stopped them before they climbed from the barge. She settled the mask back into position.

'Now listen. I must ask something of each of you. You must not tell anyone that you saw me tonight. You must only say that you were helped by the Dark Archer and another Vigil. You must not name me. If you do, you make it impossible for me to help others such as yourselves. Do I have your word?'

The girls all swore, and she led them from the cramped and stinking hold, up onto the bank and into the trees where her horse was tied. She bade them wait for her there, and returned to Darcy.

'How are you?' she asked him. 'Are you badly injured?'

He waved her off, and she turned her attention to their prisoner.

'So,' she growled. 'You call yourself the Wicker Man?'

The wolf-man stared at her for a moment, then cackled loudly, revealing a mouth filled with blackened teeth.

'Wicker Man? What you talking about? I'm the Wolf! You bloody fools!'

'You are our prisoner,' said Darcy. 'So keep a civil tongue in your head.'

'But you work for the Wicker Man?' Elizabeth persisted. 'You were kidnapping these girls for him?'

The Wolf snorted. 'Sonny, you don't know nothing, do you? It ain't Wicker Man. It's the *Wicked Man*. And you have no idea what you are up against.'

She reeled. Again – she had been chasing the wrong name again. Not Cain, or Cane, or Wicker Man – it was the *Wicked* Man all along.

The children's song...

Run, run as fast as you can
You can't escape from the Wicked Man

'Then where is he? Where is this Wicked Man? Answer!'

She had found her baton on the way back, and now thrust it under the man's chin. He grinned at her.

'Well, he was right here a minute ago. Having a pleasant little chin wag in the hut, we was, till one of you heroes tried to burn us alive. That wasn't very nice. Nor was shootin' poor Egbert in the back. Very bloody heroic, ain't yer?'

He had been in the hut? An image – the other figure with the strange, pale face, behind the Wolf, slipping away in the smoke...He had been right there. If she had gone around the hut the other way, she would have run right into him. Would have seen him. Could have him tied on the ground right now.

'Well, it is over for you,' she said. 'You have failed. The girls are safe.'

'There's always plenty more girls,' the Wolf snarled. 'Though I must say, these ones were quite tasty.'

Of its own accord, the baton lashed out, striking the man across the head. His lips curled back in grimace.

'Couldn't help sampling the wares meself–'

And she struck him again, harder. This time, there was a flicker of fear in the man's eyes, but after she struck a third, fourth and fifth time, this too had faded, and after that she wasn't counting, till she became aware of Darcy dragging her backwards, and realised the scream she heard filling the night sky was coming from her own raw throat.

Some time later, Elizabeth was sitting miserably on a rock by the road a mile or two outside of Meryton when Darcy returned. He swung painfully down from his horse and stood before her.

'You have escorted the girls back to the town?' he asked her.

'Two come from further away,' she answered dully. 'But they will stay with the innkeeper's family tonight.'

He stood in silence for a while.

'So. There was no killing, as you wished. I deposited the two injured scum with a cheap apothecary. The one may die yet of blood poisoning, may never have full movement back in his arm after they get the arrow out of his back. The other, well, he will probably never be quite the same either. He will probably end up in a workhouse or begging in the street. Are you pleased?'

Her heart was as cold as his tone.

'No, I am not pleased. But better that than be a killer.'

'That is my point. A quick, clean kill would be kinder in the end, if such things concern you, and less cost.'

'Who are we to judge who lives and dies?'

'I am a Vigile. I decide.'

'By what right?'

'Exactly. By what is right, that is how I decide.'

'But who will watch the watchmen?' she mumbled into her hands, rubbing her face. She had never felt so tired. She could feel a sob building. 'What I did to him-'

Was this how the slide into the abyss began?

'Was no more than he deserved,' said Darcy curtly.

'But I-'

'Think no more of it.'

'As easily as that?'

'If you wish to be effective, then yes.'

She forced herself to sit up straighter, to look at him. 'What of you? Did the apothecary tend to you? And how is it you are not injured more badly? He shot you in the back.'

'With an ancient fowling piece loaded with bird shot. I imagine it was more to keep the girls in line than for combat. But since you ask, this is how.'

He spread his cloak out before her. It was shredded by the pellets, and the moonlight glinted on small squares that clinked within the material.

'Enamelled panels, sewn into the lining,' said Darcy. 'They stopped most of the shot getting through. Though I daresay I have three or four pellets lodged in my back. And no, I did not let that apothecary touch me.'

'Let me see,' she said unsteadily.

'No. I shall have Bingley remove and dress them when I return to Netherfield.'

He let his cloak fall back into place and held out his gloved hand to her. 'Come. I will escort you to your home.'

'What of the Wicked Man?' she asked. She would have stood by herself, but relented and allowed him to pull her to her feet. 'Should we not go after him?'

Darcy shook his head. 'His operation here is destroyed. I doubt he will be able to employ any other henchmen when news of what occurred here gets out. No, he is finished. He will slink off somewhere far away and lick his wounds. Your neighbourhood is safe.'

It seemed too easy, in some ways, but she was too tired to argue. All she wanted was her own soft bed. To take off this leather armour, wash the dirt and ash from her skin.

If only she could as easily wash away the feeling of her baton colliding with the Wolf's head. And the awful, awful feeling of dark pleasure it had given her.

Chapter 20

Unfairly, the very next day saw an attack on a different front: Mr Collins made his move.

Elizabeth had been thankful to find she had arrived home before the rest of her family. The Longbourn party had been the last to depart from Netherfield, due to a manoeuvre by Mrs Bennet. She managed to volunteer their carriage for another's use, guaranteeing Jane additional time with Bingley. So by the time the Bennets returned home, Elizabeth was fast asleep.

When she came down for breakfast, Jane was lying in wait.

'Now will you tell me what happened? Where did you go? Mary said something about the note. You didn't go after the kidnappers alone, did you?'

'I was just checking something,' replied Elizabeth. 'But it turned out it was nothing.'

'Nothing? I see. Yet whatever it was had you hurry off without informing me. You are lucky that I am adept at covering for your disappearances with mother.'

Elizabeth kissed her forehead.

'I am indeed very lucky. As I said, it was nothing. Though I do believe the kidnappers have gone now.'

Jane stared at her suspiciously, but then allowed the subject to drop as they passed into the morning room.

Elizabeth lingered over the breakfast table, feeling an ache deep in her body and soul. She was trying to take pleasure from the victory but found herself hollow and dispirited. The loss of self control she had fallen victim to horrified her. She glanced up as the door opened, realising that it was just she, her mother and Kitty left at the table. Mr Collins strode into the room, with his stiff peacock gait.

'May I hope, madam,' said he, addressing Mrs Bennet, 'for your agreement when I request the honour of a private audience with Miss Elizabeth this morning?'

At the mention of her name, Elizabeth suddenly felt overly warm. There was an intensity about the clergyman that filled her with dread.

Oh not now, she thought, *please not now*. When she was at her lowest ebb.

'Oh dear! Yes – certainly – I am sure Lizzy will be very happy – I am sure she can have no objection! Come, Kitty, I want you upstairs.' Gathering her sewing, Mrs Bennet was hastening to leave when Elizabeth stood and called out in a strained voice:

'Dear Mother, do not go! I beg you – Mr Collins must excuse me – but he can have nothing to say to me that anybody need not hear. In fact, I was just leaving myself, so–'

'No, no, nonsense, Lizzy. I desire you will stay where you are.' And upon seeing how Elizabeth's gaze darted wildly about the room, added firmly, 'Lizzy, I insist upon your staying and hearing Mr Collins.'

How could she oppose such an injunction? After a moment's consideration she realised it may be better to get the encounter over as soon and as quietly as possible. She sat down again, resignedly. Mrs Bennet dragged Kitty out the door, and as soon as they were gone, Mr Collins began.

'Believe me, my dear Elizabeth, your modesty, rather than doing you any disservice, adds to your other perfections. You would have been less amiable in my eyes had there not been this seeming...unwillingness. You can hardly doubt the purport of my discourse, however your natural delicacy may lead you to dissemble; my attentions have been too marked to be mistaken.'

Hunted, thought Elizabeth, slumping into her chair. *I am hunted.*

'Almost as soon as I entered this house, I singled you out as the companion of my future life.' He looked about and dropped his voice. 'And that is even putting aside your obvious utility to me as an assistant in my work as an investigator for Lady Catherine de Bourgh and the Best Men. But I must be careful lest I am run away by my feelings.'

He paused for breath, and she would have tried to use this gap to forestall him but was so taken aback by the idea of Mr Collins being at the mercy of his feelings that she had to struggle not to laugh out loud.

'I think it is right for every clergyman to marry,' he continued, 'to set the example of matrimony to his parish. Apart from this, I am convinced it will add very greatly to my happiness. But the key reason, of course, is that it is the express wish and advice of the very noble lady whom I have the honour of calling patroness. I refer here, you realise, to Lady Catherine de Bourgh. She directed me to choose an active, useful sort of gentlewoman as a wife, and, Miss Elizabeth, you must admit that you indeed fit those qualities! Of course, Lady Catherine does not approve of young women styling themselves as Vigiles, as this is the proper domain of men. But you will still feel useful, taking notes for me, and possibly – though I do not wish to raise your hopes too high – delivering them to Lady Catherine yourself, with all the humility and respect her rank inevitably excites.'

The pressure was mounting. She barely heard his words, just waited for an opportunity to reply.

'Now, you may wonder why I chose to look here, rather than my own neighbourhood, where, I may inform you, there are many amiable young women who would be more than adequate. But the fact is, that since I am to inherit this estate after the death of your honoured father, I resolved to choose a wife from amongst his daughters, that the loss might be felt as little as possible. This has been my motive, my fair cousin, and I flatter myself to think it meets with your approval. And now nothing remains for me but to assure you in the most animated language of the violence of my affection. To fortune I am perfectly indifferent and shall make no demand of dowry on your father, since I am well aware it could not be complied with. On that head, therefore, I shall be uniformly silent, and no ungenerous reproach about it shall ever pass my lips when we are married.'

It was like facing a relentless series of blows. It was absolutely necessary to interrupt him now.

'You are too hasty, sir!' said Elizabeth. 'You forget that I have made no answer. Let me do so now. Accept my thanks for the compliment you are paying me – I am very sensible of the honour of your proposals, but I must decline them.'

There. It was done.

'I am well aware,' replied Mr Collins, smiling at her, 'that it is usual for young ladies to reject the addresses of the man whom they secretly mean to accept when he first applies for their favour. "No" actually means "yes", as it were.'

Elizabeth took a deep breath, but Mr Collins held up a hand.

'And sometimes the refusal is repeated a second or even a third time. I am therefore by no means discouraged by what you have just said and shall hope to lead you to the altar ere long.'

'Upon my word, sir,' said Elizabeth. It was as if she knocked him down, but he just kept getting back to his feet unfazed. She needed to be more direct: 'Your hope is rather an extraordinary one. I am not one of those young ladies – if they exist. I am perfectly serious in my refusal. You could not make me happy, and I am convinced that I am the last woman in the world who would make you so. Were your friend Lady Catherine to know me, I am sure she would find me in every respect unsuitable for the situation.'

'If she did, that would certainly be difficult,' mused Mr Collins. 'But I cannot imagine that her ladyship would at all disapprove of you. And you can be certain that when I have the honour of seeing her again, I shall speak in the highest terms of your modesty, economy and other amiable qualifications. And though she will be disappointed that your father did not agree to her most generous offer of recruitment, she will surely be somewhat mollified to know that I will have such an able assistant to provide support to me in my lesser but not unimportant role.'

'Mr Collins, all praise of me will be unnecessary. And Lady Catherine will have to accept that my father is retired and I have no desire to enter into her service, including through marrying you. I wish you happy and rich and, by refusing your hand, do all in my power to prevent your being otherwise. The matter may be considered, therefore, as finally settled.'

She rose, very desirous of quitting the room, but Mr Collins addressed her again.

'Until the next time I speak to you on this subject. At which time I hope to receive your actual answer, in the affirmative.'

It felt as if the floor tilted beneath her feet. How did one battle such an opponent? An urge sprang to mind: to take hold of his waistcoat and shake him until his teeth clattered in his head.

'Mr Collins,' she cried instead. 'If what I have said seems like encouragement, then I do not know how to express my refusal in such a way as may convince you of its being one.'

'My dear cousin, you must give me leave to flatter myself that your refusal is merely words. It makes no sense otherwise. It does not appear to me that my hand is unworthy of your acceptance. Indeed, my circumstances compared to yours are highly in my favour. You should also take into consideration that in spite of your manifold attractions, it is by no means certain that another offer of marriage may ever be made to you. Your portion is so unhappily small that it will in all likelihood undo the effects of your loveliness and amiable qualifications. And I believe you may find other gentlemen not as understanding and forgiving as I of your previous *less gentle* activities – indeed, for many it would be quite off-putting. As I must therefore conclude that you are not serious in your rejection of me, I shall choose to attribute it to your wish of increasing my love by suspense, according to the usual practice of elegant females.'

Elizabeth laced her swollen fingers together, to keep her hands still. Her gown felt tight. So much more painful, wasn't it, when a lesser opponent was able to sneak a telling blow past one's defences? For he was right: who indeed would want her? Who would understand and allow her to live as she wished? Her stomach lurched at the alternatives – trapped in unhappy marriage, or left unwanted, labelled as an old maid, with all the social opprobrium that came with such a title.

'I assure you, sir,' she said quietly, 'that I am being sincere. I thank you again for the honour you have done me in your proposals, but to accept them is absolutely impossible. My feelings in every respect forbid it. Can I speak plainer? Please, do not believe I am playing some game. Please see me as a rational person speaking the truth from her heart.'

'You are uniformly charming,' cried Mr Collins, but there was an edge of awkwardness to it. 'I am sure that when sanctioned by the authority of both your excellent parents, my proposals will not fail of being acceptable!'

She found she could not speak. To open her mouth again was to risk a scream, and if she let it out, she feared that she may never stop. Such wilful self-deception...Here was villainy of a different sort – to subject a woman to such pressure. Lucky it was her – how would someone kinder than she deal with a man such as this, who was so caught up in seeing the world his way, he could not – *would not* – see any alternative view point, especially a woman's? She walked stiffly from the room – seemingly one of the few acceptable ways to exercise her autonomy left available to her.

Chapter 21

'We are all in an uproar,' cried Mrs Bennet, dragging Elizabeth into Mr Bennet's study. 'You must make Lizzy marry Mr Collins, for she vows she will not have him, and if you do not make haste he will change his mind and not have her!'

Mr Bennet looked up calmly from his book.

'What are you talking about?' he asked his wife.

He sat impassively as Mrs Bennet launched into a passionate description of the morning's events, that a marriage was all but secured, but that Lizzy had declared she would not have Mr Collins, and Mr Collins had begun to say he may not have Lizzy, and that Mr Bennet must speak to her and insist she marry him.

'My child,' said her father. 'It is true? Mr Collins has made you an offer of marriage?'

Elizabeth nodded miserably.

'So. And this offer of marriage you have refused?'

'I have, sir.'

'Very well. We now come to the point. Your mother insists upon your accepting it. Is that not so, Mrs Bennet?'

'Yes. Or I will never see her again!'

Her breath caught in her throat. That her mother should play such a card as this, to force both her father's and her own hand.

'An unhappy alternative is before you, Elizabeth,' said Mr Bennet gravely. 'From this day you must be a stranger to one of your parents. Your mother will never see you again if you do not marry Mr Collins. And I will never see you again if you do.'

There was a beat, and then came a great wailing from Mrs Bennet. Elizabeth fought to keep a relieved smile from her face.

'Mr Bennet! What do you mean? You must insist upon her marrying him!'

'No, the only thing I insist on is being left undisturbed. I am quite content that Lizzy knows her own mind. And heart.'

Mrs Bennet stormed from the room, but when Elizabeth went to follow, Mr Bennet held up a hand to forestall her.

'One more thing. I received a note this morning, Elizabeth, from an acquaintance. An acquaintance from *the old days*. He thanked me for my services in securing the release of a tenant's daughter last evening. It appears she was being held captive by some ruffians. Given I am retired, and was at a ball last night, it certainly had nothing to do with me. Do you know anything about it?'

'Sir?' was all she felt she could venture.

'I dislike the idea of anyone being held against their will, and so am relieved to hear this young lady is home and safe, but I even more deeply dislike the idea of one of my daughters being in danger.' He fixed her with a penetrating gaze, and for a moment she remembered him as he had once been. 'Are you in danger, Elizabeth?'

'Sir,' she said slowly, 'it is the opinion of other interested parties who probably deserve credit for whatever has occurred, that whatever danger there was has now passed.'

He stared at her for some moments, then slowly nodded. 'Well then. If we have averted two dangers this day, then it is a day well seized indeed.'

'Two dangers?'

'Aye. A kidnapping, and welcoming Mr Collins as my son-in-law!'

The following day Charlotte came to visit, which was a most welcome distraction for Elizabeth. The atmosphere in the house had been quite tense, between Mr Collins' stiff, injured pride and her mother's silent fury, and so she was glad to retreat to her room with her oldest friend.

'Oh my dear Charlotte! I have so much to tell you!'

'I'm afraid Lydia has already beaten you to it. She caught me on the stairs and told me she was glad I had come, for there has been such fun here.'

'Fun,' cried Elizabeth.

'Yes, she said: "What do you think has happened? Mr Collins has made an offer to Lizzy, and she will not have him".'

'Can you believe it?'

'So it is true, then?'

'Yes! He cornered me after breakfast. I had to be quite firm in the end to get him to see that I really did mean to refuse him.'

'Oh dear. I hope you didn't hurt him too much.'

'He thinks too well of himself for that. I am sure he will be fine. You are as bad as Jane, always caring so much for others' feelings.'

'Well,' said Charlotte lightly, 'unrequited love is a very painful thing.'

'Love? He did speak of love, but he cannot mean it. He does not know me. He has an idea of me, but it is a poor fit for the real thing. Can you truly love someone you do not know?'

'It is true,' said Charlotte slowly, 'that perhaps the deepest love comes from knowing another so well, almost as much as one knows oneself.'

'And there is more. There was a fight. Last evening. I had to save the village girls, but in so doing–'

'What? Is that why you disappeared? What happened? Were you injured?'

'No, I am fine. Bruised and shaken, but physically whole. But, I did things–'

'You must not risk yourself like that. I have told you: you need help.'

'I had help. I enlisted the aid of another.'

Charlotte flinched.

'Who?'

'I think, at this moment, I had better not say. It is complicated.'

'Complicated.' Charlotte pulled back a little. 'I see.'

Elizabeth was confused. A gap seemed to have opened between them.

'You know I trust you, Charlotte. But...'

The silence stretched between them.

'So,' said Charlotte finally. 'I nearly lost you.'

'I told you, dear Charlotte, I was not hurt–'

'I meant to Mr Collins.'

'Never! He is a fool.'

'But still, if not him, then soon some other. You will marry. And then you will be gone.'

'Well, some day, I suppose. But honestly, it is hard to see–'

'Elizabeth,' said Charlotte, looking her in the eye with a piercing gaze. 'Elizabeth. You must allow me to tell you how ardently I admire and… and…'

Charlotte stopped. Her hands twisted. She was searching Elizabeth's face, but Elizabeth could only frown in confusion.

'Charlotte?'

'No,' said Charlotte, shaking her head. 'No. Of course not.'

'My dear–'

'Please!' She held up a hand, could not meet Elizabeth's eye. 'I am being foolish. Forget that I spoke. We were talking of you, not I. Or perhaps we should go downstairs?'

Elizabeth assented, desperate to escape the brittle atmosphere that had descended upon them. Charlotte almost ran down the stairs ahead of her. They entered the breakfast room to find Mrs Bennet seated within.

'Aye, there she comes!' said Mrs Bennet. 'Looking as unconcerned as may be. Pray, Miss Lucas, persuade your friend to accept her family's wishes. Nobody is on my side, nobody takes my part. I am cruelly used; nobody feels for my poor nerves.'

'I am sure it is very hard for you, ma'am,' said Charlotte. 'But we all wish, above all else, that Elizabeth should be happy.'

'I tell you what, Miss Lizzy,' hissed Mrs Bennet. 'If you take it into your head to go on refusing every offer of marriage in this way, you will never get a husband at all. Then what will become of you? You shall end up an old maid!'

There was a cough, and Mr Collins entered, head thrown back in a manner even more stately than usual.

'Oh Mr Collins,' cried Mrs Bennet.

'Madam,' he said, fixing his gaze upon her after letting it sweep imperiously over Elizabeth and Charlotte. 'You will not, I hope, consider me as showing any disrespect to your family by the withdrawing of my offer for your daughter's hand. I have meant well, seeking only to share some of the fortune arising from my association with my benefactor, Lady Catherine de Bourgh. If that was wrong, I beg leave to apologise.'

With that, he announced an intention to go for a long walk – Lady

Catherine having many times recommended physical activity as an integral part of maintaining one's wellbeing – and left. Charlotte also made her goodbyes, and Elizabeth let her go, despite the urge to ask her to stay, to try to repair the awkwardness that had come between them. But she found herself weary to her core: there had been too many assaults upon her, from too many quarters.

The next day showed no abatement in Mrs Bennet's ill humour and a continuation of the same stiff manner and resentful silence from Mr Collins – though he at least disappeared early for another 'constitutional'. When Kitty and Lydia suggested a trip into Meryton, Elizabeth found she was most grateful – her younger sisters' endless chatter was far preferable to listening to her own thoughts.

'Perhaps we shall find Mr Wickham has returned,' said Lydia with a sly smile, and though Elizabeth doubted she meant it for her sake, the thought was cheering nonetheless. It would be nice to talk to someone who liked her.

On the walk into town, she had to admit that Darcy may have been right – there did not seem to be the same air of menace she had previously felt. Perhaps they had indeed driven the troublemakers from the neighbourhood.

The younger girls made a bee line for the milliners, but no sooner had they their noses to the glass than the door flew open and the milliner's daughter stood there, staring at Elizabeth. Elizabeth shook her head warningly, and the girl nodded, but then darted forward and thrust a piece of lace into her hand before rushing back inside.

'Lizzy?' said Kitty. 'Whatever–'

'I say! It's Wickham,' cried Lydia.

And that was a very welcome pronouncement indeed, coming as it did on the heels of the risk of exposure.

'My dear Miss Bennets!' said Wickham, walking over to them with a grin. 'I have just called upon your charming aunt. And now I find more members of my favourite family in the neighbourhood here in Meryton itself!'

'We missed you at the ball!' said Kitty. 'Didn't we, Lizzy?'

'Why did you have to go away?' Lydia said with a pout. 'You promised me a dance.'

'Alas,' said Wickham, 'heavy is my heart that I should be the instrument whereby you learn that not all promises can be kept in this world. Another time?'

'Two?'

He smiled. 'Of course. Two dances, another time. Now allow me to walk with your older sister while you two terrorise the good shopkeepers of this town.'

They laughed, all flashing teeth and eyes, but did run off.

'What of you?' he asked her. 'Did you miss me at the ball?'

'The company was certainly poorer for your absence. Were you really called away by business?'

'Well,' he said. 'I found, as the time drew nearer, that I had better not meet Mr Darcy. Even in the company of others. To be in the same room with him for so many hours together might be more than I could bear, and scenes may have arisen unpleasant to more than just myself.'

'In which case I can only approve of your forbearance.'

'Was it very dull?' he asked. 'Or exquisitely exciting?'

'Oh,' she said, 'there were moments of both, I suppose.'

'Oh! Tell me,' he said, 'of the moments of excitement.'

She caught herself. Had she really just been about to tell him what transpired that evening?

'Actually,' said she. 'Upon reflection, those moments were perhaps merely slightly less dull.' It struck her then how differently the evening could have turned out – if he had been there, would she have spoken to Mary and discovered the clue in time? Or would those poor girls, even now…It did not bear thinking about.

Wickham coughed, grimacing slightly.

'Oh dear! Are you unwell?'

'Do not have any pity,' he said. 'It is a self-inflicted wound. I confess to catching up with some old acquaintances in London, which included rather too much time spent in a cigar salon. Matching their capacity has proved challenging.'

'Was it necessary to attempt to match them?'

'Match for match. Yes, it was. The nature of men, I suppose. But do not women compete, too?'

'Ah, you have me there. I am afraid that we do indeed fight our own battles. Who plays the prettiest. Who sings or sews or dances best. It can be quite violent.'

'You see? Then it is in our nature to compete. In whatever arena society provides us.'

'How very gladiatorial!'

He laughed. She enjoyed making him laugh. How very, very different he was to Mr Collins, or Mr Bingley. Or Mr Darcy.

She was surprised when it was time to head home. The couple of hours they spent strolling about Meryton slipped by so easily. Wickham elected to walk them most of the way back to Longbourn, and even having Lydia and Kitty competing for his attention did little to spoil her lightened mood.

In the house, though, she found Jane sitting red-eyed and pale in their room, folding and refolding a letter in her hands.

'It is from Miss Caroline Bingley,' she said as soon as Elizabeth entered the room. 'What it contains has surprised me a good deal. The whole party has left Netherfield and are on their way to London. Without any intention of coming back again.'

'What? Oh, dear Jane! What does she say?'

'She writes that business has called Charles back to town, and that since they believe once there he will have little inclination to leave it again, they are going with him.'

'I do not believe it. Jane, I am sure that Mr Bingley will return as soon as he can. It will not matter to him if his sisters follow or not. Mr Darcy is still here, isn't he?'

'No, she says the whole party has left. She is quite adamant in her writing that they will not return. Though she writes that she hopes to lessen the pain of separation by a very frequent correspondence–'

'A pox on her correspondence!' So, Darcy gone too. She wondered if perhaps he was more badly hurt than he had let on and gone to seek medical care. 'Anyway, it is evident that Miss Bingley means to stop him returning.'

'Why do you think that? It must be his own doing. He is his own master. But you do not know all – I will read you the passage which particularly hurts me: "Mr Darcy is impatient to see his sister, as are we. Miss Georgina Darcy has no equal in beauty, elegance and accomplishments. It is our hope of one day welcoming her as a sister. Our brother admires her greatly already, and will now have the opportunity of seeing her more frequently. Nothing should then prevent the happiest of events."'

Jane choked, and crumpled the paper in her hand.

'What think you?' she asked thickly through her tears. 'Is it not clear enough? Caroline Bingley neither expects nor wishes me to be her sister. She is perfectly convinced of her brother's disinterest and seeks to put me on my guard, less I become too attached.'

'And it is rather too late for that, isn't it?' asked Elizabeth gently. Jane nodded. 'Will you hear my interpretation?'

'What other interpretation can there be?'

'This: Miss Bingley sees that her brother is in love with you, and wants him to marry Miss Darcy. She follows him to Town in the hopes of keeping him there and tries to persuade you that he does not care about you.'

Jane shook her head.

'Indeed, Jane, you ought to believe me. No one who has seen the two of you together can doubt his affection. Miss Bingley, I am sure, cannot. If Mr Darcy had shown her a quarter of that affection, she would have ordered her wedding clothes. But the case is this: we are not rich enough, or grand enough, for them. She hopes to get Miss Darcy for her brother in the hopes it makes her own match with Mr Darcy more likely.'

'But Elizabeth, even if this were all so, how could I be happy in accepting a man whose sisters and friends are all wishing him to marry elsewhere?'

Elizabeth knelt by Jane's side.

'Jane! You are allowed to sometimes have what *you* want. Would upsetting them really allow you to turn him down if he asked?'

Jane smiled faintly. 'Though I should be exceedingly grieved at their disapproval, I daresay I could withstand it. If it meant I could have him.'

'There is the Jane that I know and love.' She rose and kissed her sister's forehead. 'Now come, you must break the news to Mother, and that is going to take far more courage than wearing a Vigil's mask.'

Chapter 22

For the next day or two, Mr Collins was scarcely to be found, for which
Elizabeth was grateful. Between her mother's wailing at the loss of Mr
Bingley – she swung between blaming Jane and hugging her to her tear-
dampened bosom – and her reproachful comments about how she had
gone from two daughters good as married to none, and what must people
now be saying of the Bennets and their inability to land a man, Elizabeth
was glad of any break.

Then finally the time arrived for his departure. Mrs Bennet told him with
great politeness that they should be very happy to see him at Longbourn
again, whenever his other engagements might allow him to visit them.

'My dear madam,' he replied, 'this invitation is particularly gratifying,
because I do indeed have an engagement in the vicinity which will very
soon necessitate my return. I shall therefore avail myself of your kind offer
as soon as possible.'

There was a moment of stunned silence from the assembled Bennets.

'But...but is there not the danger of Lady Catherine's disapprobation
here, sir?' croaked Mr Bennet. 'You are better off neglecting your relations
than risk offending your patroness.'

'My dear sir,' replied Mr Collins 'I am particularly obliged to you for this friendly caution, but can assure you that I shall take no steps without her ladyship's express approval.'

'Still, sometimes better not to even ask, eh? For fear of annoyance? We shall cope without you, and look forward to meeting again at some...future occasion.'

The leave taking and thanks took some time, but then he was finally gone. Mrs Bennet was cheered by the thought that he may mean to return and look to one of the younger girls. Mary might be the better choice, she mused, as she did already resemble what one might imagine a clergyman's wife to look like.

The next morning, the sunlight seemed particularly refreshing to Elizabeth as she came down to breakfast. She found she had a good appetite, and a knot of tension that she had been carrying appeared to have eased. She was particularly pleased when it was announced that Miss Lucas had come to see her.

'Well,' said Charlotte brightly as soon as Elizabeth joined her in in the drawing room. 'What do you know? I'm engaged.'

Elizabeth stopped dead in her tracks.

'What?' She paused, giddy. 'I don't know what to say. I didn't...Who on earth to?'

'Why, to Mr Collins, actually,' answered Charlotte. Though her smile was bright, her eyes held a different emotion.

'Mr Collins? Impossible!'

Now Charlotte recoiled, stung.

'Why impossible? Do you think it impossible that he would procure another woman's good opinion just because he failed with you?'

'Well, no, but Charlotte, surely–'

'Oh, don't worry, Lizzy. I know I am the second choice. Or third, even.'

There was an awkward pause. Elizabeth came further into the room and sat beside her friend. She struggled to find what to say, aware of how she had blundered already.

'I am just trying to understand. When has he spoken with you?'

'On several occasions. You just didn't notice. At the ball. Walking me home from here. And he has visited me these last few days.'

'So that is where he went skulking off to.'

'Skulking? I prefer to think he was trying to save your feelings by not proceeding in your plain sight.'

'And...and do you feel he loves you? Do you love him?' *Can you love him?*

Charlotte stared out the window.

'Love?' She rose and paced about. 'Aye, there is the crux of it. What would you have me do, Lizzy? Shall I stay fixed here, waiting, always waiting, never to have...To answer, I do not know if he loves me. But he will care for me. He will not make any great demands of me. He will let me play some part in something greater, as an assistant to his investigations – yes, he told me about that. It isn't what I wanted, no. What I wanted was to be your companion. But you turned me down. What I wanted was to be your...' She stopped, biting her lip.

'Oh, Charlotte...' said Elizabeth, her heart stabbed with pain.

'In many ways you are so unorthodox,' Charlotte continued shakily. 'So for a long time – too long – I fooled myself into thinking that you could be more unorthodox still. But I was wrong. That will never be. Instead, one day, you will marry, and leave. And I will be alone. I don't want that, Lizzy. I don't want to be sad and alone. And so I am going to be the one to leave instead. Now, embrace me and wish me well.'

Elizabeth rushed into her arms, and they pressed tightly together, but the tears that flowed were not the happy tears expected at the news of a friend's engagement.

The following days were difficult. Lady Lucas, triumphant, called at Longbourn rather oftener than usual. Mrs Bennet received her with increasingly gritted teeth. A polite battle would take place between them as Lady Lucas sought continuously to steer the conversation towards marriage (oh, the comfort of having a daughter well married!) while Mrs Bennet desperately fought to talk about anything but.

Between Elizabeth and Charlotte there was a restraint that kept them mutually silent on the subject, and Elizabeth worried that no real confidence could ever exist between them again. Meanwhile, her worry grew for Jane, who became increasingly fragile and anxious as the days since Bingley left passed by with no further word.

Wickham, at least, provided some relief from the turmoil. Naturally, one couldn't always expect to see him in Meryton or riding about the countryside: his duties as an officer must sometimes keep him busy. But she encountered him often enough – perhaps by placing herself where he might be found – and his light, attentive conversation acted as breaks of sunlight through the gloom of her mood.

'I've heard some most exciting talk,' he said on one occasion, a week after the scene with Charlotte.

'Oh?'

'Yes.' He glanced about. They were strolling past the shops on the high street of Meryton. 'Did you know, there is a Vigil in the neighbourhood?'

'Really?' she replied, her tone light.

'Don't you find that interesting? A masked doer of good deeds, fighting evil. Only, I'm not sure there is enough evil around here to be fought.'

'Perhaps they are a part-time Vigil, then.'

'Perhaps so. What do you suppose such a person does with the rest of their time? It must seem very dull, by comparison.'

'But serve as a useful disguise.'

'Who do you think it might be?'

She laughed. 'I am sure I do not know. I am not even convinced one exists.'

'Use your imagination! Someone fit, strong, bold...probably good looking.'

'Is that a necessary part?'

'I should think so. At least, it is in my imagination. Ruins the whole image, otherwise.'

'Perhaps you are describing yourself, and this is all a game before you admit to me that you are the Vigil.'

He laughed. 'I'm too fond of my sleep to be leaping about at night in a mask.'

Thankfully, he moved on to other topics. Though, later, she mused on what it would be like to tell him her secret. How would he react? Would it make her more – or less – attractive in his eyes?

A mere week later Mr Collins returned, much to Mrs Bennet's annoyance. It was inconvenient and exceedingly troublesome, and she hated having visitors when her health was indifferent – and lovers, of all people, were the most disagreeable.

Her irritation led her to speak more frequently of Mr Bingley, totally oblivious to Jane's pained silence and the warning looks Elizabeth shot her. Where was he, Mrs Bennet demanded to know; when was he returning?

If he was returning, thought Elizabeth, though she did not speak such fears aloud to Jane.

One blessing was that Mr Collins spent the greater part of every day at Lucas Lodge, and he sometimes returned to Longbourn so late he barely had time to make an apology for his absence before the family went to bed.

Since the battle at the canal, no more girls had gone missing, so it seemed Darcy was right and they had driven the Wicked Man away. If only, she reflected, she could defeat the daytime villains – the Bingley sisters, the conceited Mr Collins – as handily. But such combats required a different set of moves, more subtlety. If only Aunt Phillips could arm her with the skills for this arena as well.

VOLUME II

Chapter 1

Finally, like a shot to the head, Miss Caroline Bingley's letter put an end to all hope. The colour drained from Jane's face as she read it, then thrust it towards Elizabeth. The very first sentence confirmed the family being settled in London for the remainder of the year, while the last reported her brother's regret that he had not had time to pay his respects to *all his various friends* in Hertfordshire before he left.

Elizabeth's hands trembled as she read it. It was just as well that Miss Bingley was well out of reach, for if she were in the same room as her...Mr Bingley really cared for Jane, she was sure of it. But she could not think without anger, contempt even, on how easily he was manipulated by his designing friends, and thus the deep hurt he had inflicted on Jane. Jane, who already carried enough. Jane, who deserved to be happy.

She kept up her night patrols. Not as often as before, which was as well – the dark bags that had seemed to be taking up permanent residence under her eyes were finally receding – but enough to give her an outlet for the frustrated energy Jane and Charlotte's situations were causing to roil within her. She was aware of a need for caution – she understood herself well enough to know that she was seeking an outlet for her anger. She would have to make sure she kept a firm hold on herself. She would not become like the Dark Archer, inflicting more harm than necessary while pretending it was all in the name of what was good. She must be her own watch-keeper.

So it was on one cold evening, several days after Caroline's letter had devastated Jane, that Elizabeth was near the bridge on the outskirts of Meryton, on the lookout for highwaymen, when she encountered a familiar figure staggering down the middle of the road.

It took her longer to notice him than she would have liked. The evening had been difficult, as Mrs Bennet had latched back onto the subject of Netherfield and its master, and how irritated she was by his behaviour, and talked long and loudly on the subject, till Mr Bennet had closed his book with a snap and Jane fled to their bedroom to escape. Elizabeth had been ruminating, her mind drifting, and had to mentally shake herself now. She stepped out to block the figure's path.

He was an older man, poorly dressed, smelling strongly of drink.

'Good evening, Daddy Warwick,' she growled.

'Who's that?' cried the man, reeling back. He squinted in the moonlight. 'Oh! *You*! I ain't done nothing wrong. Don't you dare harass an elderly gennelman going about his lawful business.'

'Well, as long as your business doesn't include poaching, stealing or fencing, you and I have no issue. Do you need help getting home?'

'Ha,' cried the old man. 'Not a chance! You ain't coming into my home, sniffing around. You go bother some other poor, decent folk with your... your pugilistic, pugnacious, p...p.... I ran out of p's...Though speakin' of which...' He turned to the side of the road, fumbling at the front of his pants.

Elizabeth turned away. 'Good night, then, Daddy. Please keep to the right path.'

She walked by him, onto the bridge.

'Hey,' he called after her. 'He was askin' about you.'

She stopped, pivoted.

'Who was asking?'

The old man was stuffing the front of his shirt back down his breeches. 'Very nice fellow. Very generous. Offered to buy me a drink, but I said "Thank ye, sir, but no, I have given up the stuff for my health."'

'It seems to me you have drunk quite a bit. I can smell you from here.'

Daddy stared at her and scratched his head. 'So I did...Well, hard to refuse such a pleasant fellow.'

'And you saying he was asking about me?'

'Yes, that's right. Was right keen to know about any Vigils in these parts. But I said to him "Sir, I am no friend to any Vigils, I can tell you that. I have no truck with those who go about sticking their beaks in others' business. But I ain't giving information to folk who are not from round here neither. I ain't no dripper."'

'When was this? Where? Tell me more. What did he look like?'

He caught the tension in her tone as she came back to him, and retreated a couple of steps.

'I dint do nothing wrong. I dint tell him anything. I said, "Who the Hound is ain't for me to say. Because I don't know. And even if I did know, I wouldn't tell no stranger."'

'He knew about the Hound? He said the name? Or did you say it first?'

Daddy frowned. 'I can't remember. I told him the Hound had not been active for quite a spell, but one of his companions, one of the Pack, was still around. He wanted to know who you are.' Daddy stared at Elizabeth. 'He promised good money for giving your real name – good money. I don't suppose...' He reached out a quivering hand towards her mask.

She slapped it away.

'You have told him quite a lot then.'

'Did I? I suppose I did.'

'Now tell *me* something. Tell me what he looked like.'

Daddy shook his head. 'Now that I can't do. I thought there was something wrong with his face at first, then I saw he was wearing a mask.'

A cold sensation was spreading through her midriff.

'He was masked?' Perhaps it was Darcy...but no, he already knew who she was. He wouldn't be buying someone like Daddy drinks. Some other Vigil then? 'What did the mask look like?'

Daddy shrugged. 'Nothing. It was just blank. Dead and blank.'

'Would you recognise him again if you saw him? His height? His manner?'

'I doubt it. He was a generous fellow with the drinks. But...' He smiled at her slyly. 'If you want me to keep an eye out, maybe tell you if he comes calling again, maybe we could come to an arrangement?'

She looked from his gap-toothed smile to his outstretched hand. She felt herself on a precipice. To give money to an old crook like Daddy Warwick went against her sense of what was right. But the prickly feeling of being hunted was worse than that. She kept a few coins in the belt of her leather breeches, just in case. She dug one out and handed it to the old man, who crowed with delight.

It had to be the Wicked Man. Who else would be so intent on finding out who she was? So, he wasn't gone, as Darcy had thought. He was looking for her. Looking for revenge. She must be more careful from now on.

The wedding took place. It seemed a strange, strained affair to Elizabeth. On the one side was Lady Lucas, almost bursting with satisfaction, and on the other was Mrs Bennet, bringing as grey a cloud to the proceedings as she could. Mr Collins beamed smugly throughout and informed them many times over how Lady Catherine herself would have been present, such was her approval of the arrangement, were Hertfordshire not so inconveniently far from Rosings. Several times Elizabeth looked at Charlotte to find her friend watching her, but as soon as their gaze met, Charlotte's eyes would slide away, and she would laugh brightly at something Mr Collins had apparently said.

Then it was time for the bride and groom to depart for Kent. They settled in their carriage, but Charlotte leaned out, desperately scanning the small crowd. Elizabeth had already taken a step forward when Charlotte saw her and thrust out her hand. Elizabeth rushed forward and took it, and Charlotte gripped her tightly and pulled her in, right beside the carriage. They embraced, and Elizabeth felt tears leak onto her cheek, mixing with her own.

'I shall depend on hearing from you very often, Eliza,' said Charlotte shakily.

'That you certainly shall.'

'Will you come and see me?'

'Of course!' said Elizabeth.

'Goodbye, my dear Eliza,' and her lips brushed Elizabeth's ear.

Then she pulled back into the carriage, and the horses stepped off. Elizabeth held up a hand in farewell, but Charlotte was now staring straight ahead.

A distraction from her low mood arrived a week later in the form of the girls' favourite aunt, Mrs Gardiner. Married to Mrs Bennet's older brother, she was an intelligent, elegant woman. Having heard of Jane's disappointment, she and Mr Gardiner had arrived to take her back to London with them. They hoped a change of scene would cheer her up.

Elizabeth was grateful. Watching Jane suffer caused her a great deal of pain. It was as if Bingley's departure had poisoned her anew. But now she had hope. *All girls*, she thought, *ought to have such an aunt* – especially those with a mother like Mrs Bennet.

Mrs Gardiner displayed great patience as she gave attention to the three younger sisters, nodding seriously as Mary held forth on some esoteric subject, sitting through a fashion show put on by Lydia and Kitty – but she made sure she gave equal time to the older girls, too. So it was that she asked Elizabeth to accompany her on a walk into Meryton. Jane had been invited too, but professed herself not up to the excursion.

'Some time away with you will do her the world of good,' said Elizabeth to Mrs Gardiner as they strolled along the path. *At least, I hope it will.*

'There seems to be a shadow hanging over you too, Elizabeth, if you don't mind my saying so,' said Mrs Gardiner.

'Oh, I am fine. It is just worry for Jane.'

Mrs Gardiner cocked an eyebrow at her.

'I admit, there have been a number of personal difficulties recently.' Elizabeth wished she could tell her aunt everything, but Mrs Gardiner did not know of the Hound and the Pack.

'Yes, your mother had much to say on the topic of certain proposals,' said Mrs Gardiner, giving her a squeeze. 'It occurs to me that Mr Gardiner and I will later be returning this way, to undertake a tour of the Lakes. That is rather too far away to be a useful escape to you now, but the offer to accompany us is there. But now, dear Elizabeth, if you wish I shall pretend to look into this shop window, for that young man over there appears to be eager for your attention.'

Elizabeth looked over her shoulder, and her heart lifted to see Wickham standing by the corner. She kissed her aunt's cheek and went to meet him.

'Is there not a ball some time soon?' Wickham asked as she approached. 'I find myself full of impatient energy, which could best be dispelled through dancing.'

'Do your duties as an officer not furnish ample opportunity for exercise?'

He grimaced. 'Not in any interesting way. Not in any way involving delightful female companionship.'

'Oh dear. Well, I do hate to be the bearer of bad news, but I am afraid I know of no balls any time soon.'

'Damn it,' said Wickham. 'Oh, I do beg your pardon. Forgive my language. I am around rough infantrymen far too often.'

'I believe my ears will survive the onslaught.'

'That is what I like about you, Elizabeth. You are not like most of the boring fish I encounter.'

'I suppose that is flattering.'

'It should be. There is a spark about you, a liveliness. You must promise me never to let it go out. Never let some dull man like Darcy snuff out your flame.'

'You have my word on that! Darcy! Why mention him?'

'He is ever on my mind.'

'Better to think of dancing, perhaps.'

'Indeed! In fact...' He bowed towards her.

'What are you doing?'

He held out his hand. 'Let us dance.'

'What? Here? In the street?'

'Yes!'

'With no music?'

'Only the music that flows through us! Yes! Come!'

'Mr Wickham, you are a terrible tease.'

'I am not teasing. I am serious. Come. Dance with me.'

'No.'

'Dance with me!'

'No!' But did her feet seem to shift forward of their own accord?

There was a pause. Their voices had both risen a little. Then his eyes softened, and he smiled dazzlingly.

'Your pardon again, Miss Bennet. I have no desire to make you feel uncomfortable. I am not seeking to make a joke at your expense. Put it down to youthful exuberance. It is not done, of course, for young men and women of good character to dance in the streets.'

'You are forgiven.'

'You keep glancing towards that lady, and she to you. Is she a friend?'

'My aunt. Please allow me to introduce you.'

When the introductions had been made, it turned out that Mrs Gardiner had spent time in the part of Derbyshire that Wickham hailed from, had seen Pemberley and known of the late Mr Darcy. Wickham was delighted to hear her praise for the father and eagerly asked what she knew of the son. Mrs Gardiner frowned, but admitted carefully she had heard him to be a reserved sort of young man.

Walking home, Mrs Gardiner looked sidelong at Elizabeth, and said, 'You are a sensible girl, Lizzy, so I do not need to tell you to be careful.'

'Thank you for the compliment. However, I feel you are about to add a "but".'

'But...I would have you be careful not to fall in love with Mr Wickham.'

'This is serious talk indeed!'

'Yes, I am being serious. I can see that he is a handsome, charming sort of fellow, but there is something about him...I cannot quite put my finger on it.'

'Have no fear, dear aunt. He is a very agreeable young man, but I am not about to fall in love with him.'

Mrs Gardiner looked sharply at her, but said no more.

The Gardiners stayed a week at Longbourn and then returned to London with Jane, who had readily accepted their kind offer.

On the third morning after they had left, one of the maids knocked on Elizabeth's door and announced there was a serving girl come to see her, wouldn't give her name, wouldn't give a message, but wouldn't go away neither. What did Miss Elizabeth wish?

Elizabeth hastily finished pulling her gown into place, thanked the maid and hurried downstairs. There was no one at the front door, but then she realised her mistake and went through the rear of the house, out through the scullery, to the outbuildings. Here she found a nervous-looking young girl, tucked away out of sight, biting at her nails. She looked familiar.

The girl stared at her.

'Is it you?' she asked.

'What do you mean?' asked Elizabeth. 'Who are you? Do I know you?'

The girl came closer. 'Size is about right,' she said, mostly to herself. 'And you said your name. That night.'

The last was almost a whisper. Elizabeth glanced about, but they were alone.

'Were you one of those girls? At the canal?'

The girl nodded her head sharply, gaze darting about and back to Elizabeth. Elizabeth let out a long breath.

'You didn't need to come. In fact, it would be better that you hadn't. I told you that night, I must keep my identity secret, or I am powerless. I thought you understood.'

'He has a message for you.' The girl's bottom lip quavered.

Elizabeth felt her stomach lurch. 'Who?'

'*Him.*'

'The Wicked Man?'

Again the quick nod.

'You have seen him again?' She spun about – was he here? Had she been betrayed? Her right hand had gone automatically to her left sleeve, but the baton wasn't there – it was upstairs, with her armour. Her legs tensed to run.

'Yesterday evening,' the girl said. 'On my way home from work.'

Not here then. She relaxed a little.

'Did he...did he do anything to you? What happened?'

The girl reddened, but she shook her head.

'Nothing like that. I was just walking home, and it was getting dark. I was nervous, because, well, I'm always nervous walking there now.'

'You should walk a different way.'

'There is no other way!' There was a flash of anger from the girl. 'Am I meant to walk another five miles, every morning, every night, just in case? Why must I be the one?' She knuckled tears from her eyes. 'Sorry, miss.'

'No, I am sorry,' said Elizabeth. 'It was a stupid thing to say. It isn't your fault, it is his. Did he have anyone with him?'

'No. He was alone. Just standing by the roadside. I didn't see him at first, then I spotted that weird pale face and I...I just froze. And when he saw that, he laughed. And that made me so angry and so scared at the same time.'

'I can only imagine. What did he say?'

'He said...he said that he wasn't there to take me again. He said his buyer had lost faith in him, so there was no money in it, and fun as it would be to keep me as a pet, he had nowhere to keep me.'

'He was toying with you.'

The girl nodded. 'I was looking around, getting ready to run, but he pulled out a pistol and said he would shoot me if I moved. He said: "See how easy it was for me to find you again? I can find you and hurt you anytime that I want. So you better do what I say."'

Elizabeth's fingernails were digging into the palms of her hands. Her jaw was so tight it took an effort to speak.

'Go on.'

'He asked if I knew who you or the other man, the big man in the cloak, was. I said no. He came right over close to me, I could see his eyes, and he asked me was that the truth – it was, I didn't know you, miss, I couldn't even remember your name, though you said it that night. He said he wanted to meet you, so I had better find you.'

'How did you find me?'

'The milliner's daughter. In Meryton. I remembered she knew who you were. I went to see her and told her what happened.'

'Had she seen him too?'

The girl shook her head. 'I reckon she ain't been outside much since it happened. I'm trapped.' The girl's breath caught in her throat. 'He's right, miss. He can get to me anytime. I have to work, with my mam sick and all, and I have to walk that way, it is the only way. What am I going to do? I don't want him to hurt me.'

'He won't hurt you,' said Elizabeth. 'I won't let that happen.'

The girl looked at her, fear and hope mingling in her red eyes. 'You'll see him? You'll stop him?'

'Yes. Did he say where he wished to meet me?'

'Yes. At the old bridge.'

Elizabeth nodded to herself. It made sense. The old bridge was some miles beyond Meryton, superseded by the newer, wider one closer to town. It was an isolated spot now, especially at night.

'He said he would be there at midnight on the next Sunday. He said you must come alone, as will he.'

That was in three days' time.

'You have done well,' Elizabeth told the girl. 'Wait here, and I will find a coin for your trouble.'

'Begging your pardon, but I don't want your money, miss,' said the girl. 'I just want you to kill him!'

Elizabeth started at the sudden venom in the girl's voice.

'I...I don't kill.'

The girl looked at her in surprise. 'How else are you going to stop him? You must kill him, miss. You mustn't let him hurt me again. Or any of the other girls.'

Elizabeth looked at the girl's fear-sharpened face. 'What is your name?'

'Meg.'

'I won't let him hurt you, Meg,' said Elizabeth shakily. 'I promise you, whatever happens, he won't hurt anyone again.'

Chapter 2

'I don't like it,' said Aunt Phillips. 'Not one bit.'

'Dear Aunt–'

'It is too dangerous. It is obviously a trap. And he was armed, you say?'

'Which is why I have come to see you.'

'I should at least come with you.'

'No, Aunt. He said for me to come alone.'

'Ha! Definitely a trap!'

'I'm not so sure. I do believe he wishes to speak to me.'

'To what end?'

'I don't know. But if he just wanted to attack me, he could have used the girl to set a trap. And remember, he is on the back foot. He is the one who was defeated, his henchmen run off.'

'You still haven't told me about your mysterious companion,' grumbled Aunt Phillips.

'I apologise for that,' said Elizabeth. 'I have my reasons. Now, will you help me?'

'Your father would kill me, if he knew what you were up to.'

'Best he does not know, then. Aunt, I will take every precaution. You know me: I am no great risk taker. I want to see if there is a way to persuade him to surrender, or to at least leave the neighbourhood. Father devoted many years to the defence of this place. I am simply following that tradition. Will you help me?'

Aunt Phillips tapped her fingers on the arm of her chair, eyes drifting over to the wall of the drawing room. 'There may be something. A little something, just in case.'

On the day that Elizabeth intended to meet the Wicked Man, she received a letter from Jane.

'My dearest Lizzy,' wrote Jane, 'I am sure you will take no triumph when I admit that you were right about Caroline Bingley. I wrote to her as soon as I got to Town – and yes, I admit it, in the hope that renewing our acquaintance might allow me to see Mr Bingley again. However, I did not hear from her for days, despite writing a second and third time (you must imagine how I now curse my weakness in doing so). Finally I engineered a meeting – I staked out her dwelling and managed to appear to accidentally run into her. It was very evident that she had no pleasure in seeing me. She was so altered a creature it was almost as if some villain had taken her place and was masquerading as her. But now I wonder if the "friend" I met at Netherfield was in fact the imposter, and this was her true self revealed. She left as soon as she could, with no offer for me to meet Mr Bingley or to visit with her again. Why she singled me out in Hertfordshire I do not know, and it was very wrong of her if it was not real and she had no intention of continuing the friendship. So, anyway, it appears I am done with all those bearing the name Bingley and matter to none of them in the least. Let me hear from you very soon. Yours, &c'

Elizabeth shook her head. She indeed took no joy from having been proved right. It was as well she had the meeting this night – she was full of a need for action. The irony of the situation was not lost on her. She could don her mask and fight to defeat those villains who concealed their identity and hid in the shadows, but she was almost powerless against these other foes who fought their battles in broad daylight with more subtle stratagems. Her own sister was suffering, and all her fighting skills, her strength, her armour and weaponry, were unable to defend her and make it right.

Elizabeth arrived at the old bridge on dusk. This was a complicated task, involving first a cover story for her whereabouts for her family, in particular to put off Lydia and Kitty who were always seeking something to divert their attention. At Aunt Phillips' insistence, she had reinforced her armour, meaning it was thicker and heavier and thus harder to wear beneath a gown, but as it was too early for her to walk about in it, and she wanted to be in position well before the scheduled time of the meeting to see if she could spot any attempts to set up an ambush, she must make do. This meant wearing her older, least flattering gown in order to disguise her jerkin and leggings, which in turn meant Lydia, when she saw Elizabeth descending the stairs, remarked: 'Lord, Lizzy, you are looking fat!' It took great self control to not push her sister down the staircase.

And so, once through Meryton and on the path that ran beside the river, she darted into the undergrowth and pulled the gown off as soon as she could. She bundled it and tucked it neatly as she could out of sight behind a tree, settled her mask in place, pulled her hair back, and continued on. As she neared the old crossing, she left the path and cut through the trees, moving as stealthily as she could.

She found a good position, concealed by bushes at the base of a large oak tree, from where she could observe the bridge. For a long while, nothing happened. Her stomach grumbled – she was going to miss tea, and one thing she had not thought to do was bring provisions. Her muscles cramped, and she stretched each leg out in turn. She also became aware of a growing need of nature's call – it was no good, there was no denying it forever. She glanced about to make sure she was truly hidden, and unlaced her trousers, pulling the stiff leather down as far as necessary and squatted in the undergrowth. She giggled at the thought of Miss Caroline Bingley encountering her thus – probably all her suspicions of Elizabeth's barbaric character would be confirmed. Her smile faded as she considered how much less amusing it would be if the Wicked Man had a similar idea of arriving early and picked the same vantage spot. She finished up as quickly as she could and squirmed to pull the trousers back up without having to stand upright. Lord, how much easier to be a man at such times.

A figure appeared on the far side of the bridge. She quickly crawled back into her hide to observe whoever it was. It appeared to be an older man, carrying a pack, like a tinker. A disguise? She watched the man approach the stone bridge and stride out onto it. Midway across he stopped and looked about. He leaned over the side, gazing down – was he looking to see if anyone lurked beneath the span? Her nostrils flared in disgust as he hawked, then spat a glob of sputum into the water below. The man hoisted the pack higher on his back and walked on, crossing to her side and continuing along the path towards Meryton. He clanked by her, quite close – she could have leaned out and touched his boot as he passed. She waited a moment, then eased herself out of her hidey hole so she could observe him – he was far down the path, and soon it turned aside and he was lost from sight. It seemed he was just a traveller.

She returned to her position and studied the bridge. It had been built many decades before. Too narrow now, hence the construction of the wider bridge closer to Meryton, with low stone abutments. It was a place the mothers of Meryton ordered their children to avoid lest they fall into the river below.

Dusk slowly gave way to evening, and the stars began pricking the purple expanse of sky. Elizabeth had to admit she was very, very bored. Watching the bridge had sounded like an excellent idea, the sort of thing a professional Vigil would be sure to do, but the reality of sitting still in one spot with nothing to do but watch was very different. Insects buzzed in her ears. Small creatures, which she hoped were not rats, rustled through the undergrowth around her. She pictured her family in the warm sitting room, imagined herself sitting trying to read while Lydia and Kitty shrieked and laughed and Mary plonked away on the piano. She thought of her dear father, sitting in his library. And Jane, dear Jane, sitting alone at the Gardiners', hoping for a visitor who would never come.

The moon had risen high. It must be getting late now. She slowly levered herself to her feet, up against the tree trunk. It was chilly. She flexed her fingers, kicked her legs, getting the blood flowing again. She looked back towards the bridge...

...and there he was.

A lone figure standing in the middle of the span. He had managed to get that far before she had seen him. She cursed herself: what if a gang of henchmen had managed to infiltrate nearby as easily? But no, she had only looked away for a moment.

She swallowed, and stepped out onto the path. She walked towards the bridge, trying to inject strength and confidence into her gait. It was one of the things Aunt Phillips drilled into her – if one wished to project a commanding presence to awe miscreants into submission, one needed to walk a certain way, and that wasn't like a lady, with small, delicate steps as if one feared to leave any mark upon the world.

Her plan was simple enough: let him talk (since men always seemed to want to talk about themselves), hear why he wanted to meet her, see how much he would reveal, then subdue him and tie him. In the morning she would send word to the constable that the kidnapper was waiting, bound like a gift.

As she stepped upon the flagstones of the bridge, the figure turned towards her, pale face gleaming in the moonlight. And so, here, finally, was the villain she had been hunting. The Wicked Man himself.

He was clad in an assortment of loose grey clothing, looking almost like a character from a pantomime. It meant that she was unable to get a true sense of his body shape beneath the material. And his face – he appeared to be wearing a full face mask, such as one would indeed see in a theatre, with some kind of coating that looked like skin, but wasn't.

'Ah, here he is,' said the Wicked Man, his voice pitched high but muffled slightly by the small opening at the mouth. 'How nice to see you. Can you see how pleased I am? Hold on a moment.'

He reached up to his face and squeezed the mouth into a terrible rough caricature of a grin.

'You see?'

The mask was coated in some kind of putty, which he could obviously manipulate into different shapes. The combination, along with his disguised voice, meant it would be very difficult to recognise him out of costume. She had to admire the cunning behind it – even if people knew it to be a mask, he could leave an impression of, say, a large nose or pointed chin, and it would be difficult to shake that impression.

'You are the Wicked Man?' she growled. Amusing that she should disguise her voice and gender by deepening her voice, while he disguised his with a higher pitch.

He performed a deep, mocking bow.

'The same. And you? I don't believe we have been formally introduced. You are?'

'Who I am doesn't matter. What I am is more important.'

'Oh dear. And that is? No, let me guess...My doom? My downfall? My own date with destiny?'

Elizabeth paused. 'Mock all you like. You will not succeed in any of your plans in this neighbourhood.'

'*So far*, you should say. I haven't succeeded *so far*. Who knows what the future may hold? Ah, no closer, thank you.'

He held up a warning hand and took a step back. Elizabeth had barely realised she was moving herself into attacking range. Old habits.

'Why did you want to meet me?'

'I'm pleased you received the message. I wasn't sure the girl would be up to it. It is hard to get good help. Especially when you and your large chum did such a job on my loyal assistants recently. Where is your friend, by the way? Not lurking about back there in the trees, is he?'

'I'm here alone, as you requested.' *And if he were here, you would have an arrow in you by now, no doubt.*

'Which is admirable of you. Brave and admirable. Now, I wanted to meet you, specifically, to discuss where to from here. You see, we are at a critical point in the tale. I am in need of money and wish to pursue certain activities to obtain it. I would prefer you not to get in the way again. Your disruption of my little operation the other night has cost me a great deal of good will in the circles I wish to move in.'

'Your "little operation"? The kidnapping and assault of innocent girls!'

'What? They were all quite low class. Surely they weren't friends of yours?'

'No, but–'

'Then why so upset? For God's sake, it is only by pure luck that they were born here in the middle of nowhere instead of the city, otherwise they would probably already be earning their way on their backs there.'

She went to go for him then, but his hand flashed out from beneath his clothes, a large pistol locked in his grip. It was in her face as she stepped forward, and she saw it was double barrelled, the twin muzzles like black eyes staring into her own. She raised her hands and stepped back.

'Behave yourself, young sir. I don't want to kill you, but I will if I have to.'

She nodded, keeping her hands in the air.

'Now where was I? Yes, well, your efforts destroyed one revenue source and scared off my little band of supporters. If I am to do anything from here, there are a number of steps that need to be taken.'

'Why don't you just leave? Your kind are not welcome here.'

The Wicked Man sighed. 'Now how are we going to work together with that attitude?'

'Work together? You must be mad!'

'No, I'm not. I am completely and totally sane. I am the sanest person I know.' He paused for a moment, as if waiting for her to agree. She stayed silent. 'What would be madness would be for us to waste our energy locked into some kind of ongoing battle. I have no interest in being your nemesis.

You know what happened in York, of course? Between the Sword and Shield, and the Master of the Hunt?'

'Why not enlighten me.'

'You really don't know? Are you sure you are a real Vigil? The battle between the two Vigils and the villain there destroyed half the city and cost all three their lives. Not to mention a score of others. No thank you, not for me. I don't believe that is a path we wish or need to go down. I have another idea.'

'Which is?'

'I want you to help me run my next enterprise.'

'Help you kidnap more girls? You absolute, disgusting monster–'

He gestured with the pistol. 'Again. This disrespect will not do. Not for your future employer. And I'm unsure if I wish to kidnap any more girls at this point. That depends if there is any money in it. No, I was thinking opium this time. Or perhaps something involving children, since they are easier to handle.'

Elizabeth was speechless.

'Don't be so morally superior. I am merely seeking to provide what people – people with money – want. A fair exchange. And that is the joke – I may be the Wicked Man, but you should think of me more as a mirror, reflecting back the wickedness that already resides in man's heart. My face is every man's face. My face is your face. After all –' he stepped closer, and Elizabeth could see the glint of his eyes within his mask – 'I know there are things that you desire. Things that you dare not speak of. I can help with that. I can help satisfy the undisclosed desires of your heart.'

Elizabeth felt herself sway forward, but wasn't sure if she had actually moved from the spot. What she desired...To have what she desired...Why not? Didn't she deserve to be happy too? But then there was a clash within, a crash, for what she desired was impossible. Was both the sea and the rock, the wave and the shore, and she existed, trapped, in that space where they met, where they continually smashed and roiled and seethed, joined but unreconciled, unreconcilable. No. It wasn't possible.

'And more,' continued that high, foul voice, 'think of it: I am offering you the chance for a generous business arrangement. Everything becomes possible with more money; you must know that. That is the first step, that you join me or at least agree to stay out of my way. The second is, I need to know who your large companion with the bow is.'

'Keep on with this villainy, and I think you will meet him soon enough.'

'Yes, well, I'd rather meet him when he isn't expecting it. He has displayed a certain proclivity for lethal violence. Which is surprising. It goes against everything else I have heard about him.'

'What you have heard about him?'

'The Hound? Well, I had heard that he didn't kill. But then, the other night...'

Her breath caught. He thought Darcy was the Hound. Her mind whirled. If he discovered that her father was the Hound and mistakenly thought he was responsible for the attack at the canal, her family would be in danger.

'You see, there needs to be a sacrifice for what you both did. You are young, and I can use you. He was the one with the bow, so it seems fair that he pays the price, not you. I need to know who he is. Who he really is.'

'You honestly think I would tell you anything about him, so that you could assassinate him?'

'Well, it makes sense. I've outlined my preferred course of events. But there are other paths we could take. Let me put it this way: someone needs to die. I'd prefer it was him, but, it could be you.'

The pistol was still pointed at her face. She noted that he must be reasonably strong, for it was a large piece, but it had barely wavered. A terrible picture crowded into her mind, of her body lying here upon the bridge, waiting to be discovered. What would it do to her father, to Jane? What did she owe Darcy? The man who had destroyed her sister's happiness, insulted her. Why not offer him up? Let the Wicked Man go hunt him in Town – it would remove him from the neighbourhood, save her father, save her family, save herself. Serve Darcy right.

'That's good,' said the Wicked Man. 'That's right. Think about it. You want to tell me who he is. You don't want to die here.'

'I don't want to die here,' she said softly.

'No. So cold here. So lonely here. And so? His name?'

'His name?' she said, and her hands came together behind her head. 'His name is...'

'Yes?' The Wicked Man stepped forward hungrily, but still out of reach. 'Yes?'

Her fingers found what they were looking for, hidden in her hair. Drew it clear. Curled around it. There would be but one chance. Quick now.

Her hand flashed, and she dropped to the ground in the same movement. There was a sharp crack above her head, a stabbing flash of light, the stink of powder – and a high cry of pain. She came up – there was the second barrel to contend with. The Wicked Man stood holding his gun hand, the dart she had thrown stuck through the webbing between his thumb and forefinger. She launched in – he swung the pistol as she came, and it caught her a glancing blow across the top of her head. Bright light behind her eyes. She had her hands around the back of his knees then, lifted and drove, and down they went. She heard the pistol go clattering on the stones. He punched at her wildly, but she buried her head into his chest, crawled up him, seeking to pin his arms with her knees. He roared and tried to thrust her off, but she swam down inside his arms, locked her arms behind his head.

Like a marionette doll with cut strings, all the fight seemed to leave his body. He relaxed beneath her, hands resting lightly on her waist. Incongruously, he giggled, then gasped.

'I admit it, you are a better fighter than I. You are a proponent of that oriental trickery, I see. What a bundle of surprises. How does a young chap in the countryside learn such things, I wonder?' He coughed. 'I am having...trouble breathing. Do you think you might get off me?'

She lifted a little of her weight from his ribcage – and felt a tremendous stab of pain in her side. She cried out, rearing, and the Wicked Man kicked his way out from beneath her.

'Got you,' he cried wildly, getting to his feet. 'You aren't the only one with a pointy little surprise!'

Her fingers went trembling to her side – there was something stuck in her, between the bottom of her jerkin and the top of her trousers. He must have been feeling for the gap while he distracted her with his talking. She grabbed the end of the object and pulled it free, crying out in pain – it was a hat pin, not as long and lethal as the ones some ladies wore for self defence, but easy to conceal beneath layers of clothing. She threw it from her, teeth set in a snarl.

'Now,' said the Wicker Man, pulling on some gloves he had produced from another voluminous pocket. 'Now, come on. Let us see you try your tricks again.'

He adopted a boxer's stance. He looked like he knew what he was doing. She slid the baton from the sheath on her sleeve, wound the thong around her wrist.

'Oh, now!' he said. 'That's cheating!' He glanced about for his pistol.

She lunged, striking for his head. He punched at the club as it descended, and glove and stick collided with a crack that jarred her arm. She pulled back. He shook his hand, flexing his fingers.

'Sap gloves,' he said. 'Not the best sensation, but – Oh, wait a moment.' He reached up to his face, dragged the corners of his putty lips down into a frown. 'I am not happy with you anymore.'

'You talk too much,' said Elizabeth, and came for him again.

His footwork was fast, and his left fist jabbed out towards her face if she got in too close. She was careful not to swing too wildly, lest he catch her out. His right fist suddenly flashed forward – his reach was long, and she barely pulled back her chin in time. She kicked at him, catching him in the stomach and making him grunt. She risked a second kick, saw too late he was less hurt than she supposed, and he punched down into her knee. Her turn to grunt, feeling the lead sewn into the knuckles of his gloves crunch into the joint. His jab came out again, just catching her mouth, connecting hard with her teeth. She slashed with the baton, fending him off, and they circled each other, breathing hard.

He bent swiftly, reaching for the pistol near his feet. She threw the baton, letting the thong slip from her wrist. The short heavy club hit him on the crown of the head. He clapped one hand to the spot, but his other kept scrabbling for the gun, found it! Too close to run, only one thing do – she dove at him. Totally committed now. She landed on him and they went down. She felt him trying to get the muzzle against her. She took hold of his arm, pulled it up, the pistol now pointing above her head. Spun over him, locking her legs over his body, fell back, pulling his arm down with her and arching her hips. The elbow went – broken or dislocated she couldn't say, but she felt something pop and he screamed out in pain and anger. She rolled clear, and he was coming up too, eyes black with fury behind the mask.

'I'll kill you,' he roared, one arm flopping like a broken wing.

She jumped forward, knee rising to catch him in the centre of his chest. He staggered back, hit the abutment and tumbled backwards, down into the rushing black water below.

She limped to the edge and looked down. No sight of him – then, a pale face rose from the depths, but she saw it was just the mask. It turned and bobbed away. The man himself was nowhere to be seen, swallowed by the cleansing black rush of the water.

It was as well that Jane was away, she thought as she dragged herself into their room. Jane would kill her. She peeled off her leather, gasping at the effort. Every part of her felt sore, abused. Sitting at the dressing table, a candle lit, she surveyed the damage. There was a puncture wound in her side, but it appeared to have gone only into the fleshy bulge that always formed at the top of her trousers. That bulge usually annoyed her, there no matter how hard she trained her stomach muscles. Now she was thankful for it, for it may have helped prevent the pin from sinking into an organ. She would bathe the wound and bind it, must watch it did not turn septic. She examined the angry red of her lips. She avoided looking herself in the eye.

What have you done?

She recoiled from the internal question, leant forward and inspected her teeth. One of her bottom premolars was quite sore, and, pushing against it with her tongue, she felt it shift loosely. She pushed a little harder, and gasped as it bent horizontal to the others. Panicking, she grasped it with her fingertips, tried to gently coax it back into position, but as she bent it back, she felt a small snap and it came away in her fingers.

She looked in horror at her reflection in the mirror, the black gap where the tooth had been.

Who would want you now?

No more than you deserve...

What have you done?

It was all she could do to not wake her father and tell him all. And what? Beg his forgiveness? Ask his help? Weep in his arms?

Father, I may...I have...

...killed a man tonight.

No. Not a man. A villain. Someone who sought to impose his cruel will on others, with no care for the damage he did. Surely such a one deserved to die.

'*We never,*' said Mr Bennet, as she and Jane sat with him in the training room, '*take a life. We are choosing to act as guardians of the people, of what is right, and we must never stray from the path of righteousness. We may employ violence when necessary, but always with restraint. We never allow our passion to rob us of our reason, of the very thing that makes us human.*'

She had failed in that basic tenet. She was not worthy of his teaching, of Aunt Phillips'. Not fit to wear the mask and take the name Vigil.

She just wanted to go away.

Sleep was a long time coming that night, and her pillow was soaked in tears by the time it arrived.

Chapter 3

Awaking the next morning she felt dreadful. Every muscle ached and she felt sick at heart. Her mouth was sore and swollen – her tongue went straight to the gap where her tooth had been; it wouldn't be possible to always hide its loss from her family forever.

And so, when she was sure they were all sitting down to breakfast, she entered the drawing room gingerly with a bloodied kerchief held to her mouth.

'Lizzy! What have you done?' shrieked Mrs Bennet.

'A stupid mishap,' she said, waving off Mary and her father who had risen in alarm. 'I rose in the night to use the privy and walked into the door. I'm...I'm afraid I have dislodged a tooth.'

'Let me see,' said Mary, gently prising Elizabeth's hand from her face. 'Oh, it is so bruised!'

'Now what are we to do?' cried Mrs Bennet. 'Missing a tooth? You have spoiled your looks!'

'Mother!' said Mary.

'Can we see?' said Lydia. 'I want to see.'

'Oh, that you turned down Mr Collins!' wailed Mrs Bennet. 'My nerves! You could be settled at Hunsford and be normal. But no, you had to refuse. And now, well, you make it harder and harder to find someone who will have you!'

'Oh, Mr Wickham may not mind,' said Lydia with a smile. 'Do you not think, Lizzy?'

'Why did you not just use your chamber pot?' asked Mary with a frown.

'Enough,' said Mr Bennet, rapping the table with his knuckles. 'Elizabeth, a word after breakfast if you please.'

Elizabeth looked around at their faces.

'I realised my courses had started,' she said. 'So I was in a rush.'

'Oh,' said Mr Bennet, looking down at his plate. 'Well then.'

Lydia and Kitty giggled behind their hands. Mrs Bennet cleared her throat pointedly and the meal continued quietly.

After they had eaten, Mary followed her as she headed to the library.

'I thought our courses usually came around the same time,' she said. 'I thought yours had already started two or three days ago.'

'No,' said Elizabeth. 'You must be mistaken. One cannot argue with nature.'

She kissed her sister on the cheek and entered the library. Her father was waiting behind his desk.

'So,' he said. 'You walked into a door.'

'No,' she said. 'That is not what happened.'

'Ah. I didn't think so.'

'I went to do some training with Aunt Phillips, and I confess I was not paying enough attention. She accidentally hit me too hard. She is mortified, the poor dear.'

'I can imagine.'

They sat in silence for some minutes.

'Well,' he said finally, 'you are still beautiful to me.'

She had to leave quickly then, as tears burned behind her eyes.

Then two days later, a letter in Charlotte's hand waiting for her at breakfast came like a small ray of sun piercing the leaden cloud. She tore it open and found, as she had hoped, a repeat of Charlotte's request that she come visit Hunsford. Her parents gave their assent, and the thought of spending time with her dear friend gave her such a warming spark of pleasure that seeing Mr Collins seemed a very small price to pay. And why should she not seize this opportunity to go, to regroup and rest now the girls and the neighbourhood were finally safe.

Safe, because she–
No.

Charlotte wrote that her father and younger sister were shortly coming to visit and that Elizabeth could accompany them on the journey. Elizabeth knew her father would miss her, especially with Jane away as well. But she was feeling such guilt in his company that an escape from that too would be welcome.

The one thing she would really miss was spending time with Mr Wickham. She sent a note to tell him that she would be going away, but received a reply from Denny instead informing her that Wickham was called again to business in London. She felt annoyed that he had not told her himself before he left, but such was his manner. And it wasn't as if there existed any reason why he must account for his comings and goings to her. It was not as if they were engaged or anything of the sort.

At first, she had resolved to leave her Vigil armour behind, and packed nothing but gowns and underclothes into her trunk. But as she closed the lid, she was struck by such a strange sensation of incompleteness, of emptiness, despite the box being quite full. She sat back on her bed, then slowly reached beneath it and drew her mask from where it lay hidden. Holding it, the eye holes seemed to stare back at her knowingly. Then before she knew it, she was kneeling by the trunk again, pulling every neatly folded item out onto the floor. She dragged her leather armour from its hiding place, noted how tattered it was becoming. She laid it in the bottom of the trunk, then buried it under her gowns.

Just like me, she thought: *light and feminine on the outside, battered and stained on the inside.*

But...she felt *better*. What did that say of her, that even after what had occurred, she still felt she needed this secret part of her?

Her excitement at finally being under way was soon dampened by the tediousness of the journey. Sir William Lucas and his younger daughter, Maria, were not particularly interesting companions. The girl was about thirteen, but much quieter than Lydia and Kitty, and spent much time just staring at Elizabeth in some awe. Sir William was pleasant but not a good conversationalist. Elizabeth found herself unconsciously tensing her muscles as she willed the chaise to go faster.

Finally, after many hours, they left the high road for the lane to Hunsford, with the fence line of Rosings Park as their boundary on one side. Elizabeth smiled at the recollection of all she had heard of its inhabitants. At length the parsonage became visible, a pretty house standing in a garden that sloped down to the road. Mr Collins and Charlotte appeared at the door, and the carriage stopped by a small gate, which led by a short gravel walk to the house. In a moment Elizabeth was out of the chaise, rushing into Charlotte's familiar warm embrace. It was some minutes before she could bear to let go and greet her cousin.

She saw instantly that Mr Collins was the same as ever: his pompous, formal civility was just as it had been. He made a short speech of welcome, enquired after each member of her family, paused to point out a number of features of the front garden, then they were finally allowed into the house. As soon as they were in the parlour, he welcomed them a second time with ostentatious formality to his humble abode, and punctually repeated all his wife's offers of refreshments.

It seemed to Elizabeth, as he stood describing the good proportion of the room, its aspect and furniture, that he addressed himself particularly to her, as if to point out what she had lost by refusing him. She looked at her friend – whenever Mr Collins said anything particularly embarrassing, Charlotte appeared not to hear, though once or twice she could discern a faint blush. After sitting long enough to admire every piece of furniture in the room, Mr Collins invited them to take a stroll in the garden, which was large and well laid out. He talked at length about its cultivation, to which he attended himself.

'Do you spend a great deal of time in the garden then, Mr Collins?' asked Elizabeth innocently.

'Oh yes,' said Charlotte. 'It is very good exercise for him. I encourage him to spend as much time in the garden as possible.'

Mr Collins beamed. Elizabeth tried to catch Charlotte's eye, but her friend was then busy pointing out something to her father. As they strolled about, Mr Collins kept up a constant description, not pausing long enough to receive the praises he asked for. Every view was pointed out with mind-numbing detail. He could number the pastures in every direction. But of all the views his garden could boast, none could compare with the sight of Rosings, glimpsed through an opening in the trees that bordered the park opposite the front of the parsonage. Elizabeth studied the distant house with its high dome and long wings and had to admit it was impressive, speaking of a great deal of wealth. All that saved them from a detailed description of the house at this point was the hint that they should soon be afforded a much closer view.

Mr Collins was keen to walk on, and Sir William was of the same mind. The ladies instead returned to the house, and Elizabeth was very glad of this chance to spend time with Charlotte. Maria soon dropped behind, and Charlotte took hold of Elizabeth's arm and squeezed it.

'Are you happy?' asked Elizabeth, gently pressing her friend's arm in return.

'I am content,' said Charlotte, and then she turned to ask Maria a question and urge her to catch up.

They toured through the rest of the house, which, while small, was well built and comfortable. She could see the hand of Charlotte in the decoration and layout of the rooms. She imagined that at those times that Mr Collins was absent, it would be most pleasant. Finally, Maria went off to look at the chickens, and Elizabeth and Charlotte were left alone in the drawing room.

'And what of you?' asked Charlotte. 'How is Miss Elizabeth Bennet?'

Elizabeth's voice caught in her throat, and her eyes suddenly grew hot.

'Oh Lizzy,' cried Charlotte. 'Whatever is the matter?'

'Oh Charlotte,' she said. 'I have done some things...questionable things...'

Charlotte came and sat by her, and hugged her.

'I know you,' she said. 'So I know that whatever you may have done, however much it may pain you now, you did it at the time because you believed it to be the right thing to do. Your doubt of yourself and your motives are what keeps you grounded and stops you from becoming arrogant. You are Elizabeth Bennet, and that is your way.'

Elizabeth laughed a little through her tears. 'My way sounds a little torturous.'

Charlotte brushed her lips against Elizabeth's temple. 'It is one of the best things about you. Now, tell me everything.'

So Elizabeth told her first about Jane and her heartbreak, and Charlotte was suitably angry at the behaviour of Caroline Bingley and Darcy. Then she spoke of Wickham and Charlotte arched her eyebrow. And, finally, Elizabeth spoke of the events on the old bridge.

For a while, Charlotte was silent.

'Then it was self defence,' she said finally. 'As simple as that.'

'No. Not simple as that. I chose to push him into the river, knowing he was badly injured. Not knowing if he could swim. I didn't have to do that.'

'It sounds to me that *this* you, who has the luxury to sit and analyse and question, is asking an awful lot of *that* you, who had to make decisions on the spot. He was trying to kill you.'

'I know that. But it doesn't make it easier.'

'Surely, in such a fight, these things happen.'

'Charlotte! I am not looking for excuses.'

'No, instead you are looking for a rod to beat yourself with. I don't know what to say to you. I don't know what you want of me.'

Elizabeth gestured helplessly. 'Just to listen. That is all.'

'Well, that I can do. But I cannot help having opinions, either, nor of speaking of them when I think you are being unjust to yourself. You are a true Vigil, Elizabeth.'

'I do not know about that.'

'You are. You are brave, and honest, and empathic. You are exactly the right sort of person to take up the mask, to take up that burden.'

Elizabeth smiled, then swiftly stopped herself, her tongue going to *that* spot. 'You think Lady Catherine may take me into her fold?'

'Well, I wouldn't get my hopes up there. She has rather strong opinions on such things. Elizabeth, correct me if I am wrong, but are you missing a tooth?'

Elizabeth's hand shot to her mouth before she could stop herself.

'Is it very noticeable?'

'Only when you smiled just now. Oh, Lizzy.'

Strangely embarrassed, Elizbeth waved away her concern. 'And what of you? Have you been involved with the Best Men, as you wished?'

'Not greatly. Not yet. We did spend several days on the west coast – Lady Catherine gave us the trip as a wedding gift. She wanted Mr Collins to look into a smuggling operation there while pretending to tour local ruins.'

'Oh!' said Elizabeth. 'So you got to...'

'I mostly stayed at the inn while Mr Collins went about. Writing up his notes, for her ladyship.'

'Did you find anything? Did you crack a smuggling ring?'

Charlotte's lips tightened ever so slightly. 'I do not know. Lady Catherine believes in compartmentalising information. I do not know what part I may have played.'

Further discussion was thwarted by the breathless return of Maria, who wished to tell them of the fight she had witnessed between two of the chickens.

'No, dear,' said Charlotte. 'Not fighting. That was the rooster.'

Elizabeth covered her mouth with her hand.

The evening was spent chiefly in talking over Hertfordshire news. Later, in the solitude of her chamber, Elizabeth had time to meditate on Charlotte's degree of contentment and her comments. She noted as she lay herself down, that it was with a lighter heart. The company and change of scene had indeed done her some good.

In the morning, Mr Collins was almost beside himself – the party had been invited to dine at Rosings the very next day! His excitement meant an almost non-stop commentary on their great luck, until Charlotte, recognising Elizabeth's increasing exasperation, took her and Maria for a walk into the village.

'And how do you find Lady Catherine?' asked Elizabeth once they were clear of the parsonage.

'She is very good to us,' said Charlotte, then fell silent.

'I cannot help but feel there is a "but" attached to that reply.'

Charlotte grimaced. 'No. She is very generous. Once could hardly ask for a better neighbour. And, if she is rather used to being listened to, it is only because of the position she has achieved and the respect she has earned.'

'Well, I will not press you further. I do not wish to seem as if I am attempting to make you speak ill of your husband's patron.'

A pretty young woman came along the path towards them, head down and walking quite quickly.

'Good day, Emily,' said Charlotte warmly.

The woman glanced up nervously and mumbled a reply but walked on faster. It was enough for Elizabeth to see a large bruise on the side of her face.

'What is that?' she asked. 'She looks like she has been on the end of a training session with Aunt Phillips!'

'Her husband,' replied Charlotte.

'Wait, what? What do you mean? He struck her?'

'Quite often, I am afraid.'

Elizabeth stopped. 'Then what is being done about it? To stop him?'

'Well, Mr Collins has spoken to him about it, but – Elizabeth, wait! Don't go after her. She will not wish to speak to you about it. She is a very private person.'

'She is a very abused person! By her husband!'

'Elizabeth, these things happen. They are wrong, yes, but it is not uncommon. As a clergyman's wife, I suppose I am now more exposed to such things.'

'It isn't right.'

'No, of course not. But marriage is complicated.'

'Someone has to make it right.'

'It – Wait, what are you saying? Maria, do walk on ahead!'

The girl had been trailing just behind them, and now slowly walked out of earshot.

'Elizabeth, you are here for a rest and to visit with me. You are not here to put all the wrongs of the world to right. Besides, you don't even have – oh, no. You brought your outfit, didn't you?'

'Where does he live, Charlotte?'

'Elizabeth...'

'Just a little talk, that is all. You know the woman, you care about her, I can see it. Why just sit back and say nothing more can be done, when we haven't tried everything?'

'More violence won't solve anything.'

'Who said anything about violence? I said a talk. But, Charlotte, as a Vigil, I can tell you that there are people on this earth who listen only to force. And tell me honestly: wouldn't you like to see a man like that pay?'

Charlotte met her eye, and Elizabeth nodded as she saw the gleam within.

Harold Tisdale stumbled home. His back ached, his rotten molar throbbed, and the ale he had drunk sat sourly in his stomach. There had better be some stew on the fire and bread on his plate, that was all he knew.

He frowned as he came up the path to his cottage. Hang her, she'd forgotten to light a lantern to guide him home. The path was perilous – lots of loose stones to roll under your foot and jar your poor back – and yes, blast it, he'd look to fix it when he was damn well ready to. In the meantime, how hard was it to hang a damned lantern so he could get home damned safely? She needed reminding. Again. You would think the stupid woman would learn.

'Harold,' said a voice.

He stopped, turned unsteadily. 'Who's there? Who is it?'

'You are Harold Tisdale, husband to Emily Tisdale?'

He squinted. There was someone standing there, someone dark.

'What you want?'

'A word.'

'What about?'

'Your wife.'

'What about her? What's the slut done?'

'Nothing. This is about what you have done to her.'

'Ain't none of your business. Off with you. I'm going to bed.'

Harold turned, started up the path again. He heard the rush of feet behind him, and something caught him low in the back. He cried out and fell sprawling. The stranger was on his back. An arm snaked around under his chin.

'Oh, but it is my business,' growled the voice in his ear. 'I'm making it my business.'

Panicking, Harold shoved up, trying to get to his hands and knees. He felt his attacker twist behind him, and he found himself flipped over, staring up at the night sky. The dark figure was under him, behind him, but the thin arm was still wrapped around his throat. It squeezed, and he could feel the thudding of his heart in his temples.

'You need to treat her better, understand? You are not to strike her, or touch her, ever again. Do you understand?'

Harold grunted. He clawed at the arm, but it just tightened further. The black night was getting blacker still, tinged with red.

'Do you understand?' hissed the voice.

'Yes...' he squeezed out.

Suddenly the pressure was gone, and he sucked in a huge lungful of cold night air. That started him coughing, and he didn't even notice the attacker shove him aside and writhe out from underneath him.

'Devil take you,' he muttered. 'Fight fair...Fight like a–'

'A man?' The voice was cold. 'Very well. Stand up, if you want.'

Harold got to his feet, fists clenched. The figure darted in, and a fist smashed into his nose.

'There. That's how you do it, isn't it?'

He flailed, swinging wild punches. The other ducked under them, came up, caught him across the jaw. He felt a stab of lightning through his molar. He roared, went to rush the devil – a stone rolled under his foot and he went down on one knee, hard. And the attacker was back on him, throwing out hooks that snapped his head side to side.

'This is what it is like, Harold, to be dominated by someone better than you. Or bigger than you. Do you like it?'

Harold started to shove himself up, but a foot lashed out, connected with his cheek, and he was down on his hands and knees again.

'I asked you a question. Do you like it?' The figure moved, as if to kick again, and Howard flinched.

'No,' he spat.

'So is this enough?' rasped the voice. 'Do you understand?'

He cowered, holding up his hands. 'Enough,' he grunted, spitting blood. 'I understand.'

And he was surprised for a moment that he actually did.

'This was just a taste,' said the figure. 'I mean it. If you touch her, I will hear of it. And if I do, I will come back for you. Devil take me, did you say? Well, I *am* your devil, and I *will* take you.'

Harold collapsed backwards. He heard light, quick steps, and then nothing. After a while, he heard the door open and the strike of a flint. He shut his eyes against the sudden flare of lantern light. He sensed Emily standing over him.

'Sorry, Em,' he mumbled. 'I'm sorry.'

'Sh,' she said, and he felt a cool, wet cloth on his face, and that was nicer than any kiss.

Chapter 4

'Do not make yourself uneasy about your appearance, my dear cousin,' said Mr Collins to Elizabeth the next day. 'Lady Catherine is far from requiring that elegance of dress in us, which becomes herself and her daughter. I would advise you merely to put on whatever of your clothes is superior to the rest, from your point of view. Lady Catherine will not think the worse of you for being simply dressed. She likes to have the distinction of rank preserved.'

Elizabeth was still blinking at that when Mr Collins stepped closer in, his breath tickling her ear. 'And perhaps you might not stand in such a... mannish manner. A more feminine way of comporting yourself while in her ladyship's presence would not go astray. Nor would it hurt if you were to smile a little more, dear cousin. People do like to see a young lady smile.'

Elizabeth dutifully pulled the corners of her mouth upward, keeping her lips firmly pressed together. Mr Collins looked as if he would say more, then thought better of it. Perhaps he had noticed something in her eyes. Still, while they were dressing, he came two or three times to their different doors, urging them to be quick, as Lady Catherine very much objected to being kept waiting for her dinner.

As the weather was fine, they had a pleasant walk of about half a mile across the park. The landscape with its green fields and stands of trees was truly beautiful, though Elizabeth could not be in such raptures as Mr Collins expected the scene to inspire. He seemed perpetually disappointed by whatever praise she gave.

'Do you know,' said Mr Collins, turning to Charlotte. 'I passed Harold Tisdale on my morning walk. It was most extraordinary.'

'Oh?' said Charlotte.

Elizabeth's ears pricked up.

'Yes. He looked as if he had been run over by a chaise and four. I asked him what had happened, but he just said he had taken a fall.'

'Did you happen to see Emily?'

'Yes! That was the extraordinary thing. She was with him. They were walking arm-in-arm. They looked most...companionable.' Mr Collins frowned, and glanced towards Elizabeth. 'Cousin, you did not...'

'Sorry, Mr Collins?' She met his eye calmly and held his gaze till he shook his head and smiled.

'Nothing, nothing. Well, dear Charlotte, it would seem my counsel had the desired effect!'

Charlotte glanced towards Elizabeth. 'Well, that is good news, dear husband.'

Elizabeth felt a rush of pleasing warmth race through her body, and it was enough to sustain her even through Mr Collins' enumeration of the windows in the front of the house and what the glazing had cost. Part of her wished she could speak up, take credit for the apparent change in Harold Tisdale, but that was all a part of taking up the mask. No, she must be satisfied with the knowledge that although it was early days, it appeared she may have done some good.

When they ascended the steps to the hall, Maria was wide-eyed with fright and even Sir William appeared nervous. Elizabeth found herself feeling quite calm – after all, she had been shot at and stabbed: this display of money and rank she could witness without trepidation. Even Lady Catherine's position as patron of the Best Men need not intimidate her. Look what she had accomplished lately herself...Though her mind had to skitter past the memory of the bridge.

From the echoing entrance hall with the curve of the dome several stories high overhead, they followed the servants through an antechamber. Mr Collins kept up a steady description of the fine proportions and exquisite ornaments as they went, in case their own eyes failed them.

And then they were ushered into a magnificent room, in the centre of which sat Lady Catherine herself, with her daughter seated alongside, and another woman flanking her. Her Ladyship rose to receive them. She stood smoothly – somehow Elizabeth had been expecting someone more infirm – and Charlotte provided the introductions, having begged that honour of her husband. Elizabeth suspected it was to avoid the embarrassment of the abundant thanks and grovelling apologies that would have made any introduction by Mr Collins take thrice as long.

Sir William, apparently awed by the grandeur, both human and architectural, surrounding him, could manage only a very low bow before taking his seat without saying a word. Maria perched on the edge of her chair, eyes darting about the room, looking for all the world as if she might suddenly bolt for the door at any moment. Elizabeth coolly observed the three ladies before her.

Lady Catherine was a tall, large woman with strong features. Her manner of receiving them made no effort to make her visitors forget their inferior rank. When she spoke, it was in an authoritative tone that marked her as one who very much believed in her own self-importance. There were definitely traces of Mr Darcy about her.

The daughter, by comparison, was thin and small. There seemed very little likeness between parent and child. She looked cross and sickly and in need of some exercise.

The third lady was introduced as Mrs Jenkinson, a lady's companion for Miss de Bourgh. She was a plain, serious-looking woman who watched them all with blank eyes. She appeared more bodyguard than lady's companion. Elizabeth wondered if she had any training.

After sitting for a few minutes, then being directed to stand and go over to admire the view from a particular window (Lady Catherine shouting from her seat at Mr Collins to point out particular features), they went through to dinner.

It was very fine. The plate on display and number of dishes and servants were just as Mr Collins had promised. He himself was seated at the bottom of the table and looked as if nothing could give him greater pleasure. He carved, and ate, and praised fulsomely. Every dish was commended first by him and then by Sir William, who was now seemingly recovered enough to at least repeat everything his son-in-law said. Elizabeth wondered how Lady Catherine could bear it, so gushing was this joint praise, but she seemed gratified by their excessive admiration and smiled graciously.

Elizabeth kept glancing sideways at Charlotte, but being seated beside her could not easily read her expression. It was as if her husband was more infatuated with his patroness than his own wife.

When the ladies returned to the drawing room, there was little to be done but listen to Lady Catherine talk, which she did without any intermission till coffee was served. She delivered her opinion on every subject in so decisive a manner that it allowed no other viewpoint. She enquired into Charlotte's running of her household, down to what and how often she was feeding her chickens. It seemed nothing was beneath this great lady's attention – at least, not when it provided her with an opportunity to dictate to others. At last she turned her eye to Elizabeth.

'She appears a genteel, pretty kind of girl,' she remarked to Charlotte, all the time looking Elizabeth up and down without a hint of embarrassment. Though she felt her cheeks reddening, Elizabeth held the lady's gaze. Lady Catherine smiled slightly. 'Yes. It is there. From the father, no doubt.'

The grand dame's eyes flicked across to Maria and back to Elizabeth.

'Your father has somewhat disappointed me, Miss Bennet. But that is a topic for another time. Now then – your family estate is entailed on Mr Collins.' She turned to Charlotte. 'For your sake, I am glad of it, but otherwise I see no occasion for entailing estates from the female line. It was certainly not happening in the de Bourgh family, I assure you.'

Elizabeth bit her lip. It seemed like an accusation of some sort of failing among herself and her sisters that they had not prevented an arrangement made before they were born.

'Do you play and sing?' Lady Catherine asked Elizabeth.

'A little.'

'Then some time or another we shall be glad to hear you. No doubt our instrument is far superior to the one you are used to. It shall be a treat for you to play it. Do you draw?'

'No, not at all.'

'What? It is one of those refined accomplishments a young lady ought to possess.'

'Alas, I have not the skill.'

'Skills can be learned, with correct instruction. It is the duty of your parents to provide it, via a suitable governess and exposure to the benefit of suitable masters.'

'We never had a governess.'

'No governess! How is that possible? Five daughters, brought up without a governess. It is no wonder you are lacking in the expected accomplishments.'

'I have other skills,' said Elizabeth, her voice coming out more sharply than she meant.

Lady Catherine's eyes gleamed. 'I see. And yet you are unmarried, are you not?'

'Your Ladyship knows that I am.'

'Then one must question the usefulness of such skills, do you not think? Tell me, are any of your sisters out?'

'Yes, ma'am, all.'

'All! What, all five out at once? Before the first is married?'

'I think it would be very hard on younger sisters that they should not have their share of society and amusement just because the elder had not had the opportunity to marry. Yet. To be kept back, I think it would not be very likely to promote sisterly affection.'

'Upon my word,' said her Ladyship. 'You give your opinion very decidedly for so young a person. You know so little of the world.'

'With all due respect, Lady Catherine, I may have seen more aspects of the world than you give me credit for.'

'There it is again,' cried Lady Catherine. 'It borders on impertinence!' She held her hand up at Charlotte, who looked about to speak. Maria looked as if she wished the floor would open up and swallow her. 'How old are you?'

'With three younger sisters grown up,' said Elizabeth with a smile, 'your Ladyship can hardly expect me to answer that.'

But Lady Catherine did appear to expect an answer, and was indeed quite astonished at not receiving one. Elizabeth fancied the disbelief was akin to the first time she had forced Aunt Phillips to submit during a sparring match. But whereas her aunt had been pleased, Lady Catherine's brows creased into formidable canyons.

'You cannot be more than twenty,' she barked. 'Therefore, you need not conceal your age.'

'I am not one and twenty.'

Lady Catherine grunted, satisfied, not realising that Elizabeth had chosen to yield the ground. Age was a strange thing for women, Elizabeth mused. While considered a girl, it was a thing to boast of, alongside one's accomplishments: one could dance a quadrille and was just 13. One could play a Scottish air and was but 15. But once you slipped past girlhood into womanhood, it became a secret best hidden, a growing blemish that slowly but surely tarnished the carefully polished fruit.

The gentlemen joined them, and the magnifying glass of Lady Catherine's attention was diverted by cards. She commanded Sir William and Mr and Mrs Collins to play with her, and so Elizabeth was left to join Maria, Mrs Jenkinson and Miss de Bourgh. It felt rather like being relegated to the children's table. Lady Catherine kept up a monologue highlighting the mistakes in the play of her companions or else relating some anecdote about herself. Mr Collins was employed in agreeing to everything her Ladyship said and complimenting her on every play she made.

When Lady Catherine had played as long as she chose, the tables were broken up, and the carriage offered and gratefully accepted. With many thanks from Mr Collins, and bows from Sir William, they departed. As soon as they had pulled away from the door, Elizabeth was called upon by her cousin to give her opinion of all she had seen at Rosings. But anything she could offer by no means satisfied Mr Collins, and he was very soon obliged to take her Ladyship's praise into his own, more practised, hands.

Chapter 5

Sir William stayed another few days at Hunsford, then returned home, taking Maria with him, satisfied his eldest daughter was comfortably settled. Elizabeth was a little sorry to see him go, for while he was there, Mr Collins had spent a good portion of each day driving him about in his gig to show him the country. She feared Mr Collins would now devote more of his attention towards Charlotte and herself. But as it turned out he spent a good deal of his time in the garden, or else reading and writing, and watching out the window of his book room, which fronted the road.

The room in which the ladies most often sat was at the back of the house, which Elizabeth had first thought rather strange: the front parlour seemed a nicer room. It was larger, with a more pleasant aspect. But she soon saw her friend had an excellent reason for what she did, since the front room was just across from Mr Collins' study, and he would have undoubtedly found more frequent reason to call in on them if they were more conveniently located. As it was, he satisfied himself by clomping down the hall to announce whenever Miss de Bourgh was passing by in her phaeton, an event that happened almost every day but which still seemed to necessitate reporting.

'Did Lady Catherine know of how that Tisdale man treated his wife?' Elizabeth asked Charlotte one morning when she was sure they were alone.

'I would say so,' said Charlotte. 'Mr Collins knew, and–'

'And what Mr Collins knows, Lady Catherine knows?'

Charlotte smiled, and shrugged, and went back to her sewing. Elizabeth watched her pull a stitch taut.

'Charlotte,' said Elizabeth. 'Charlotte, are you–'

'Elizabeth,' said Charlotte firmly. Her eyes were suddenly bright and dark. 'You are my dearest friend, and I am so glad to have you here with me. And there was a time when...a time when I...but I am here now, and content. I have this room, I have this home. I have a life that I can be satisfied with. But please, do not press me on certain subjects.'

Elizabeth felt a pain in her heart. There still existed this space between them that she could not seem to bridge. After a moment, she cleared her throat and returned to her original line of questioning.

'If Lady Catherine was aware that Tisdale was beating his wife, why did she not do anything about it? She has the resources of the Best Men at her disposal.'

Charlotte frowned. 'I suspect she believes that what occurs between a man and his wife is private and none of her business.'

'But why not? Especially when a woman's safety is involved?'

'I cannot answer that.'

'But do you think it is right?'

'What I think hardly has any bearing on Lady Catherine's actions, I can assure you.'

'But it isn't just her, is it?' Elizabeth got to her feet and strode about the small room. 'We all of us turn a blind eye to such things.'

'Mr Collins did go to speak to him.'

'Yes, that is true. But talking wasn't enough. Charlotte, I believe I see something here, something I can do.'

'You mean by going around beating men who beat their wives?'

'Why not? Why not? If that is the lesson they need, and no one else will step in because they don't think it is their business. But every woman's life and happiness should be our business. What have I learned all these skills for, if not for this?'

'But you cannot stop every such man. Will it make any difference?'

'It will make a great deal of difference to the women I can help. Charlotte, surely doing something is better than doing nothing?'

'But what if you make things worse? What if they take it out on their wives? Or children? What if they don't change?'

Elizabeth paused. 'That is a risk, I grant you, but one I am willing to take.'

'Yes, but it won't be you bearing that risk! Lizzy, can you be sure that this isn't just some excuse for you to...to release some rage on some easy targets?'

'Rage? I am not angry!'

'Oh Elizabeth! You are full of it! Or frustration, or maybe even passion, whatever you want to call it. You are overflowing with it. Can't you see?'

'You know, once you said you wanted to join me, to be my companion. I don't understand how you have come to be so changed.'

'That was when...' Charlotte shook her head, as if to clear it. 'Things are more complicated. I see that now. I am no pacifist, I assure you. You think I haven't wished to punch that stupid ox Tisdale in the head myself? You think I don't wonder what it was like, to beat him to his knees?'

'Then let me inform you: it felt good. It felt right. And I think it has worked. But that is one man, one woman. I can do more. We can do more.'

'What do you mean?'

'Find more men like Tisdale. Give me their names and addresses. Mr Collins is bound to know.'

'I can't!'

'Why not?'

'Lady Catherine would not hear of it!'

'Lady Catherine most certainly need not hear of it! I do not require her assistance. Or her permission.'

'In your own neighbourhood, maybe. But not here, Lizzy. Once, you can get away with. Hopefully. But more than that? It is asking for trouble. Lady Catherine has very strong views–'

'As do I.'

Charlotte smiled. 'I know. And that is why I love you. Come, please, let us not argue about this anymore. I needed to see you so much, Lizzy. I don't want to spend the short while we have like this.'

Elizabeth smiled at her friend, and nodded, though inside a storm blew through her. Was it rage? Who cared what name it was given – it was energy. It was purpose.

There came some unexpected news, delivered by Lady Catherine herself on one of her passing visits: her nephew Mr Darcy was expected to visit shortly. The way she spoke of him, in terms of the highest admiration and satisfaction, it was obvious that from Lady Catherine's point of view, he was destined to marry her daughter. Elizabeth had to stifle a laugh as she thought of poor Miss Bingley's frustrated designs and the prospect of Darcy having to sit through evening after evening with the dull Miss de Bourgh.

'Does something amuse you, Miss Bennett?' asked Lady Catherine.

'I am simply pleased to learn of Mr Darcy's imminent arrival. It will be my pleasure to renew our acquaintance.'

'Renew?' Lady Catherine's lower lip quivered. 'What do you mean, *renew*? How can you possibly have spent time previously with Mr Darcy?'

'Indeed, it is true, ma'am,' said Charlotte gently. 'While accompanying Mr Bingley in Hertfordshire, both gentlemen appeared at the local assemblies.'

And not just that, thought Elizabeth. We fought together. She remembered his strong arm pulling her close, the swirl of his cloak, the blast of the gun. Then she thought of Jane and her aching sadness, and Darcy's cold stare. Her hand squeezed into a fist behind her back.

Lady Catherine sniffed. Evidently, while she knew that Darcy had travelled in those parts, she had not thought he would stoop to meeting locals so far below him on the social scale. Annoyed at having her news so undercut, she left shortly after.

Two days later, word reached them that Darcy and another of Lady Catherine's nephews, a Colonel Fitzwilliam, had arrived. Mr Collins immediately put on this hat and rushed to Rosings to pay his respects. He had not been gone overly long when Charlotte called down to Elizabeth from an upstairs room – he was returning, and there were two gentlemen with him.

'I have you to thank for this honour, Eliza,' said Charlotte, joining her downstairs. 'I can't imagine Mr Darcy coming so soon just to wait on me.'

Elizabeth was trying to come up with a suitable reply when she heard the front door open and the voice of Mr Collins thanking them for their great kindness in visiting his home and hoping the walk had not overtaxed them. And then the gentlemen entered the room.

Mr Darcy looked as he ever did: well-dressed, well-groomed, cool and confident. If his back gave him any trouble from being previously peppered with birdshot, one could not tell due to his customary stiff, upright manner. He paid his compliments to all present, and Elizabeth curtsied in return, then he presented his companion.

Colonel Fitzwilliam, a handsome, well-groomed man with an open, easy manner, greeted Mr and Mrs Collins warmly, then turned his eyes onto Elizabeth.

'And this is *the* Elizabeth Bennet, at last.' He held his hand out to her, and she felt the strength in his warm, dry grip. He turned to Darcy. 'Is this an open conversation, Darcy?'

Darcy looked about the room. 'If you wish it so. To a point.'

'I'm not very good at remembering who is in the know and who isn't,' said Colonel Fitzwilliam with a smile. 'I look to Darcy to keep tabs on such things. It is a pleasure to finally meet you. I have heard quite a deal about you.'

'Indeed? I find that quite surprising, sir. I cannot imagine how I occupied any of Mr Darcy's thoughts. Perhaps you have not spent enough time with him to hear him on a broader array of topics.'

'Our recent foray required some rather long nights on watch. And he may not look it, but our Mr Darcy can be quite the chatterbox in the dead of night.'

'Perhaps you are mistaken, and he was actually speaking of my sister, Jane.'

Darcy shot her a look.

'You have been on a mission for her Ladyship, sirs?' asked Mr Collins. 'Of course, I am never directly in the know, but I do hope that perhaps in some small way my own endeavours have been useful in yours.' He dropped his volume. 'Were you involved in the business on the west coast, pray?'

'No,' said Darcy.

'South, actually,' said Colonel Fitzwilliam. 'Lyme Regis. No, it was definitely you he spoke of, Miss Elizabeth.'

'It is just with my sister having been in London these past weeks, I thought it may have been her he spoke of, since I was sure Mr Darcy was bound to have seen her.'

'Fitz, we should be heading back.'

'You did not see Jane then, Mr Darcy? I am surprised, since I know how much time you spend in the company of Mr Bingley's sisters, and–'

'I did not see her. We must go, Fitz. Now.'

'As you like. But you've forgotten our main mission!' He turned to the others. 'Our dear aunt requests your company at dinner tonight.'

'How gracious,' cried Mr Collins. 'Mrs Collins, is that not the height of benevolence? To be invited to the first dinner along with her dear nephews! We are delighted! Delighted! Are we not?'

'We are delighted,' said Charlotte with a smile.

'Right,' said Colonel Fitzwilliam. 'Good, then. Until this evening.'

The gentlemen left, Darcy without a single backward glance at Elizabeth, who was both fuming at him and perplexed at the colonel's words. Why on earth would Darcy be speaking of her?

At the proper hour, they presented themselves at Rosings and joined Lady Catherine and her visitors in the drawing room. Her Ladyship received them civilly, but it was clear that their company was not so acceptable as when she could not get anybody else, for she was almost totally engrossed by her nephews, speaking to them, especially Darcy, more than any other person in the room. Given her plans, one would have assumed she would try to bring her daughter into the conversation, but she appeared content to leave her sitting silently to one side.

Elizabeth withdrew to a settee. Colonel Fitzwilliam excused himself and strolled over to join her with a smile. For a while they spoke of books and travel, and Hertfordshire, and Kent, where he came from. But then Elizabeth changed the topic – she was not in the habit of spending time openly with other Vigils.

'Are you permitted to speak of the business that took you to Lyme Regis?'

He laughed. 'Of course. We are all friends here. Nothing particularly interesting, I'm afraid. We were seeking to break up a smuggling ring.'

'It sounds somewhat exciting.'

'It may sound it. But sitting huddled in cloaks on a cold beach, at night, in the rain, with no company but Darcy...He can be a bigger wet cloud than anything the sky can produce.'

'I heard that.'

They both looked up as Darcy joined them.

'Well, you know it is true,' said Colonel Fitzwilliam.

'Someone must take the matter seriously, if their companion is at such great pains to be flippant.'

Colonel Fitzwilliam laughed heartily. 'That may be. But don't call me companion. The Blue Jack is no man's companion, whatever our dear aunt may hope. And before you speak, yes, I know, that stiff neck of yours means the Dark Archer would never consent to being considered the companion in the partnership, either.'

'Why can't Vigils work as equals?' asked Elizabeth. 'Why must one in the partnership be considered the companion?'

'Vigiles,' said Darcy and Colonel Fitzwilliam at once.

'It is just the way it is,' said Colonel Fitzwilliam. 'There is a Vigile, and there is his companion.'

'But just because it has been that way, why must it stay that way? Aren't things allowed to change?'

'Change for change's sake must be avoided,' said Darcy. 'Maintenance of the status quo is synonymous with order and peace.'

'Rigidly adhering to custom, seeking to make it a rule, is better?'

'Undoubtedly.'

'You seem very sure of yourself.'

'Because I'm right.'

Elizabeth paused for a moment, looking at his controlled face. She was suddenly furious.

'He came back.'

Darcy frowned. 'Who?'

'You said he was done. You said he would leave. But he didn't leave. He came back. He didn't follow your rules. Do you want to know what he did next? What I...what I had to do?'

'What happened?' Darcy's eyes were big and dark. 'Tell me.'

'I–' said Elizabeth.

'What is it you are speaking of over there?' called Lady Catherine. 'What are you all saying? Let me hear what it is.'

'We are speaking of Vigilism, Aunt,' said Colonel Fitzwilliam.

'Of Vigilism! Then pray speak aloud. I must have my share of the conversation. After all, I am the patroness of the foremost stable of Vigiles in the country.'

'We know, dear aunt. After all, are not the Dark Archer and Blue Jack stalwarts of that very group?'

'Vigilism,' continued Lady Catherine as if he hadn't spoken, 'is the utmost expression of service to the nation. It is only proper that those of the right rank and breeding should shoulder the burden of lifting the common man from his sordid state by providing exemplars of excellence in character, spirit, word, action and physical prowess. It pains me, Miss Bennet, that I cannot count your father among such specimens, given the unfortunate news that he has chosen to retire.'

'He is not so young as he once was, your Ladyship,' said Elizabeth.

'Then he should have taken on a companion who was able in time to succeed him. That is one of the key functions of the companion.'

'There was the Pack,' said Elizabeth, her gaze drifting beyond her Ladyship's shoulder.

'The Pack? Never heard of them. What kind of companion can that be, if they are never heard of?'

'We were still training. Father wanted to wait until he was sure we were ready, but then–'

'*We*? Are you referring to yourself? Do you mean to tell me that you fancied yourself some sort of companion? A mere girl?'

'Some sort of companion, yes.'

'And your father allowed it? This is frankly astonishing. I am astonished. A girl has no place in the ranks of the Vigiles. If she wishes to serve, then she may do so, as an aide to an investigator, like Mr Collins' wife here. That is an acceptable woman's role.'

'Yet you are in command of a troop of Vigils, are you not?' asked Elizabeth.

'Vigiles,' said Darcy and Colonel Fitzwilliam at once.

'Do not seek to compare yourself with me,' said Lady Catherine.

'My dear Lady, I'm sure my dear cousin did not–'

'Quiet, Collins,' her Ladyship said. She turned back to Elizabeth. 'If I had known your father harboured such extreme views, then I would have saved myself the trouble of making an overture in the first place.'

'One must remember that not all neighbourhoods can boast the level of wealth and breeding that surrounds Rosings,' said Mr Darcy.

'You mean to make allowances? Well, I suppose you did say there was nothing but daughters. However, the only way Vigilism can remain true is that it is restricted to the best of men. Mind you, even if any of the lower classes were given the opportunity to don the mask, I doubt you would find many with the moral courage to do so.'

'They do not have the time,' said Elizabeth. 'The whole point is, that those of us who wear masks do so because we have the luxury of time to do so. To train, to patrol–'

'Sitting on a freezing beach in the rain? Not very luxurious, I assure you,' said Colonel Fitzwilliam.

'Ordinary people are working from sunup to sundown to provide for themselves and their families. We cannot blame them for not being able to find time to police their neighbourhoods as well!'

Lady Catherine stared at her. 'What a singular piece of work you are, Miss Bennet. I am glad that my daughter does not share such wild ideas. Or your sister, Darcy.'

'I don't know,' said Darcy, looking at Elizabeth. 'Is passion such a bad thing?'

'Yes! When it leaves reason behind! This girl, who likes to play at Vigilisim–'

'I don't play, I assure you. I am a Vigil.' She looked at the men. 'Don't say it!'

'Come, Miss Eliza,' said the colonel. 'Running about in a mask is one thing, and I for one applaud you for it, but true Vigilism involves great danger–'

'I have killed a villain.'

There was a beat of silence.

'What on earth do you mean? What on earth does this girl mean?' asked Lady Catherine.

Elizabeth and Darcy locked eyes.

'The Wicked Man.' Her voice was shaking. She hated it. 'I killed him.'

'You think you killed him,' said Charlotte softly. 'He could have swum away.'

'When was this?' asked Darcy tersely.

'When he came back. He threatened the girls. He was looking for us. Us!'

'What are you speaking of?' barked Lady Catherine. 'I do not understand! Who is this Wicked Man? Have you heard of him, Fitzwilliam?'

'Not I,' said the colonel, looking from Elizabeth to Darcy. 'Archer? What is going on? Who is he?'

'A nobody,' said Darcy. 'A nothing, playing at being a villain.'

'A nothing?' Elizabeth couldn't get enough air into her lungs. 'What he did–'

'What he did was very little. He kidnapped a few common girls. We concern ourselves with weightier matters here.'

'So their lives don't matter?'

'In the larger scheme of things, compared to the security of the realm–'

'What, like smuggling? Stopping cheap brandy coming into the country is more important than–'

'Enough,' cried Lady Catherine, her face white. 'Young woman! Take command of yourself. This is most unseemly.'

'My dear Lady Catherine,' said Mr Collins, 'allow me on my cousin's behalf to offer a thousand apologies–'

Lady Catherine erupted onto her feet and swept towards Elizabeth, who flinched, but the lady passed by her and flung her hand at the mantelpiece above the fire.

'Do you see this?' She pointed with a long nail to a silver plate on a stand. 'Do you? This was gifted to me by His Highness himself! Come here and read it!'

Elizabeth reluctantly stood and stepped forward, habit and training keeping her as far from Lady Catherine as could be while still reading the inscription etched into the silver.

'Read it aloud,' ordered Lady Catherine.

'"In recognition of the great service done to the Kingdom, by the B. of M."'

'You see' cried Lady Catherine triumphantly. 'Proof of our worth! Royal validation of all that we – all that *I* – have achieved!'

'Lady Catherine, I–'

'We are so far above anything you and your father could ever hope to achieve!'

Lady Catherine's finger was right in her face. Elizabeth was aware of Darcy and Colonel Fitzwilliam shifting uncomfortably behind their aunt.

'This plate, this level of recognition, is something you can only dream of, chasing down your pickpockets and poachers. Call yourself Vigiles? You are nightwatchmen at best.'

For emphasis the old lady flicked the plate and made it ring.

'Perhaps we could talk about something else,' said the colonel gently. 'What about that sister of yours, Darcy? How is she?'

'Yes!' said Lady Catherine, stalking back and sinking into her chair. 'Tell us all of Georgiana. Is she practising her music? You know, I should have been greatly proficient if I ever learnt to play. As would Anne, had her health allowed her to apply herself. I am confident she would have performed delightfully. How does Georgiana get on, Darcy? You must tell her from me that she cannot expect to excel if she does not practise a great deal.'

Elizabeth let the talk wash over her. She stood looking at the plate on the mantel, struggling to control her breathing, her heart thudding in her ribcage. She was aware of Charlotte's worried eye upon her.

'I assure you, madam,' said Darcy, 'that she does not need such advice. She practises very constantly. As you know, music is a balm to her.'

Elizabeth was barely listening but noticed a catch in Darcy's voice. She glanced his way, but a wicked thought had struck her.

The plate was sitting in pride of place on the mantel. Unguarded. It would be such a shame if something happened to it.

Mr Collins was fuming on the coach ride home. He barely said a word, and Elizabeth could feel his dark eyes darting towards her. Obviously he felt her behaviour had not been becoming. She felt weary and hoped to avoid any long-winded lectures that might make her wish to crush his larynx, but luckily he seemed to decide that affecting a wounded silence was punishment enough. Charlotte at least smiled at her kindly before ascending the stairs to bed.

In the darkness of the night, the Wicked Man came for her. She lay paralysed in bed as she heard the door creak open downstairs. She heard his laboured, gurgling breathing, and a terrible flopping sound. She knew that he was crawling up the stairs, his arm limp and boneless, dripping river water that ran in black rivulets, puddling on the floor like blood. She knew he was in her room, dragging himself to the bed, and soon would pull himself up and onto her, his dead face behind the mask pressing against her cheek, breath reeking, repulsively intimate, drenching her with the corrupted water soaking from his skin–

She jerked awake. Her bedclothes were tangled around her legs, her nightgown stuck to her body with sweat. She pressed her hands into her face.

Just a dream.

Harmless.

Chapter 6

In the morning, Elizabeth sat by herself in the front room, writing a letter to Jane. Mr Collins, clearly still sulking at breakfast, had stiffly demanded that Charlotte accompany him on some business in town. Charlotte had looked at Elizabeth, who simply smiled and shrugged. She was happy to have some time to herself, to enjoy the morning light that spilled into the drawing room.

All was quiet, and so she was startled by a ring at the front door, for she had heard no carriage. At least it couldn't be Lady Catherine coming to admonish her. It was likely to be someone seeking the clergyman – or so she was thinking, until the door opened and Mr Darcy strode into the room.

'I apologise for the intrusion,' he said, sitting, and then instantly standing again. 'Would you please accompany me outside?'

He was gone before she could really answer, and so she was forced to put aside her half-finished letter and go in search of him. He wasn't out the front, on the path, and so she cut around to the side of the house where there was a large section of open lawn. There stood Darcy, a long package lying beside him. He turned as she approached, the hem of her dress swishing through the grass.

'If you are going to insist on facing villains – of whatever calibre –

on your own, then I insist on you learning how to dispatch them from a distance.'

He bent, untied the bundle and rolled it open. An unstrung bow and sheaf of arrows clattered onto the lawn.

'Your offer is most generous, Mr Darcy, but I have no interest in learning how to shoot someone full of arrows.'

He frowned. 'Why not? It is a good weapon: silent, quick. I'm sure with practise you could reach a reasonable level of skill.'

'I have no interest in killing anyone.'

The man falling back off the bridge into the river...

'But *they* may have an interest in killing *you*. Or in killing someone you care about. Would you be so squeamish if the life of one of your sisters was at stake?'

They stared at each other for some moments.

'Why do you care?' Elizabeth finally asked. 'Is this a guilty conscience for leaving when you did?'

'Certainly not. I left because I was required elsewhere for a more important mission. And yes, I know this Wicked Man was important to you, and I also know that your particular sense of proportion means you are not able to see that there may be some matters that are weightier still.'

'If the events in our neighbourhood were so small, it is a wonder they attracted your interest at all. Why get involved in the first place then? Why come and help me at the canal?'

'Symbolism,' said Darcy. 'It is important that the Vigiles are always perceived to win – at least in the end. It is what makes us effective. So even a young woman with delusions of grandeur must triumph over a masked kidnapper and his filthy henchmen.'

'Delusions? You think me deluded? For caring what happens to the people in my neighbourhood?'

'No, of course not!' Darcy's fists clenched and unclenched in frustration. 'I misspoke. It is to your credit that you care. But it is not generally a role for a young woman to play.'

'When the need arises, someone must stand up.'

'Yes. A man.'

'There were no men standing! So *I* stood! *Me*!'

'And again,' said Darcy, deliberately lowering his voice and holding his hands out and open, 'that is to your credit. It is just a shame that your father did not have any sons.'

'Isn't it?' Her hands were balled into tight fists.

Darcy looked at them, frowning. 'I believe I have offended you. It was not my intention.'

'You do a good job of it without intention. I would hate to see what you were capable of if you meant to cause offence.'

He stared at her and then his face creased into a small smile.

'Of all the powers that one may have,' he said, 'I own it is limited in its usefulness. Now please, let me show you?'

He took up the bow, placed one tip against his boot and bent it down, his bicep bunching within his jacket. He slipped the looped bowstring over the other tip, settled it into its notches and plucked it lightly, causing it to thrum.

'This is a spare,' said Darcy. 'The draw weight is quite high, but I believe you to be quite strong.'

'While a compliment on my looks would be more traditional, I suppose I must make do with what I can get,' said Elizabeth. She had the unexpected pleasure of seeing him flush slightly. 'What are we to shoot at? Mr Collins' prize petunias, perhaps?'

'I think at this point we shall content ourselves with firing into the lawn itself.'

'Ah, then I suppose I am unlikely to miss.'

Darcy smiled. 'Then you have not seen Bingley attempt to shoot.'

Elizabeth's jaw tightened at the casual mention of the name. She held out her hand for the bow, and Darcy, noticing her darkened face, quietly gave it to her along with one of the arrows.

'Now, nock it and hold it with–'

'Yes, I know, thank you!' She thrust her left arm out and pulled on the string, feeling it dig into her fingertips. It took more force than she expected to draw it back towards her cheek, causing her braced left arm to tremble – the arrowhead bounced off her knuckle, the shaft sliding along her arm. 'Bother,' she cried. She flicked her hand several times, got the arrowhead back resting on her fist, aimed vaguely down the lawn, let go – and yelped in pain as the string stung her left forearm. The arrow fell clattering onto the ground at her feet. 'Damnation!'

'Will you allow me to help?'

She grunted, and Darcy moved to stand behind her. His gentle touch corrected the angle at which she held the bow, tipping it slightly so the arrow rested more securely. His cool fingers curled lightly around her right wrist.

'Stand more side on. Now draw back to your cheek. Breathe. *Breathe.* Release.'

She opened her fingers, and the arrow buried itself thrumming in the grass some 20 yards away.

'Good,' said Darcy. Their bodies bumped together.

Elizabeth took a step forward and turned, pretending to examine the bow.

'I will find something for a target,' Darcy said. 'Or better yet, you must come to Rosings. I have a full archery field there.'

'I am not sure your aunt would approve.'

'She has no issue with young women engaging in sporting activities – within reason.'

'But she would very much mind if she thought you were teaching me to hunt villains?'

'I am not teaching you to hunt villains. You know my opinion on the matter. I just prefer that you are capable of defending yourself.'

'I am entirely capable of defending myself, thank you.'

'With your little stick? Yes, you do have skill with that, and your Barton-Wright techniques, but they may not always be enough. I would hate to hear you had been killed because you chose to trust to those when your opponent preferred to trust to a musket or pistol.'

'For that, one must be seen. I assure you, I am very good at not being seen.'

He smirked. 'Perhaps by those who don't know what they are looking for. I have had no trouble finding you in the past, as you recall.'

Elizabeth bit her lip, holding back the retort that threatened to erupt.

'Come,' said Darcy. 'Let us not quarrel. Try some more shots.'

'I don't think so,' said Elizabeth. 'Thank you for the lesson, Mr Darcy. As ever, you have definitely asserted your superiority over me.'

She handed him the bow and walked back towards the house, feeling his eyes upon her the whole way.

That pride, that abominable pride. The same as Lady Catherine's. How she wanted to prick it.

Chapter 7

In the light of the crescent moon, Rosings sat like a silver mountain. One or two windows in the massive wings glowed with faint yellow light where staff on night duties went about their work, but most were dark, drapes drawn like lidded eyes. The massive front doors were likewise closed and no doubt bolted. The walls of the front of the house rose sheer and straight. There were no trellises interlaced with climbing plants here, as at Longbourn.

But Elizabeth had no intention of trying to enter from the front. Standing well back, in the shadows of a hedgerow, she studied the house for some time. There did not appear to be anyone on watch that she could see. Her heart was drumming within her breast, her ribs creaking against the leather of her jerkin with each breath – it was possible she had put on weight, in the absence of her usual exercise. Her limbs tingled. It was one of those magic nights when the rich turf had seemed to propel her forward as she jogged from the Collins' cottage to Rosings. The air was cool and clear, intoxicating.

Satisfied, she skirted the house, keeping to the grass rather than the gravelled paths, her soft boots making little sound. Around the rear of the house, the two wings extended back, framing a number of outbuildings between them. Here, out of view, the architecture was more functional and thus easier to scale. She waited and watched again for some minutes, then sprinted lightly across the open space between the back garden and the nearest building.

At the back wall of the house proper, in the corner formed where the wing connected, a drain pipe ran upwards. If one took hold and didn't stop to think too much, let the energy coursing through one's body carry one upwards, it was possible to climb the several stories to the roof. At the top she faced an awkward moment, getting a firm grip on the gutter and hauling herself over the edge. And finally she was there, on a small, flat section of the upper roof. She lay on her back for a moment, waiting for her heaving lungs to quiet, then sat up, shaking her hands to get the blood flowing again into her outraged fingers.

Standing, she surveyed her surroundings. The roof flowed off on either side in a series of slanted and flat sections over the two wings of the house. Before her, above the centre of the main house, stood the mighty dome. This was her target.

She stepped out onto an angled section of slate tiles, felt them shift a little beneath her weight. Continuing carefully, she reached the dome and found, as she had hoped, a walkway around it. Someone had to come up here to clean the windows that studded its side. And she hoped that someone had left at least one of them open. She paused a moment, looking out across the countryside. Fields and stands of trees, dimly moonlit, surrounded the great house in all directions. Further out, points of light in the deeper dark showed where houses stood, the occupants likely doing those personal jobs there was no time for during the day – the darning and repairing. It looked so peaceful.

No doubt somewhere within that bucolic scene, there was strife. People were suffering. She felt a strong sense of something welling up inside of her, a desire to reach out to these people. Provide them what measure of protection she could. There came a momentary pang as she reflected that her current mission wasn't necessarily in keeping with that loftier feeling, but she was committed now.

She placed her hands on the nearest window, the glass cool beneath her palms, and pushed – not the slightest give. She repeated the move at the next. And the next. And the next. It was possible, given Lady Catherine's patronage of the Best Men, that her security was better than average and Elizabeth would not easily find entry. But on the other hand, sometimes – the next window cracked open slightly at her upward thrust. She pushed again, and it opened further with a slight shriek of protestation. There was enough gap for her to get her fingers under it now, and she bunched her muscles, forcing the swollen wood to give an inch at a time. In the quiet, it sounded as loud as a scream to her, but any large, old house would be full of strange noises in the night. When the gap was wide enough, she slithered through onto the cool floor inside. She was on a narrow circular walkway that ran around the inside of the dome. Across from her she could see a darkened recess that must mean a doorway.

Peering over the inner railing, she could see the entry hall far below. The white marble of the floor seemed to glow in the darkness. She could not make out any servants on duty. Pressing back close to the wall, she stole around to the opposite side – sure enough, a small alcove hid an access door. She turned the handle, felt it click open, and thrust it slowly inwards. Within lay a narrow staircase, steeply descending into the black. She felt she could afford to leave the door ajar to let in what little light there was, but she soon passed beyond into pitch black and had to feel her way carefully. She fought against a childish sense of something waiting for her in the dark, idiotically grinning at her as she fumbled towards it – she forced an image of the Wicked Man standing just ahead, dripping wet, mask curved into a malicious smile, out of her mind.

And then she was at the bottom of the staircase, and could feel a door before her. At first she could find no handle, her fingers becoming increasingly desperate as they brushed across its surface. Then she simply pushed against it, and it swung open, revealing a dimly lit hallway. The door was disguised to look like the rest of the wall, one of those discrete access points for staff to be able to go about their business without getting in their employer's way.

The occasional lamp provided some soft light, and so she was able to see that the hallway was empty. The thick runner down the centre meant she could move quickly and quietly as she headed for the main staircase. No doubt there were other servants' passages leading down, but she felt it more likely she would run into one of the staff on night duty there than in the house proper. Neither Lady Catherine nor her daughter struck her as the type likely to be up and about at night. The two nephews were another matter, of course, but she felt she could trust in their arrogance to assume they were safe at Rosings.

And they were safe, too. They weren't what Elizabeth was after.

When she reached the main staircase, she paused again for some minutes, ears straining to catch any sounds of movement. She heard a faint cough, some distance away, possibly from a bedroom in one of the wings, but then nothing more. She started down the staircase, fighting the urge to break into a sprint. She kept close to the wall, soft boots padding lightly. A surge of nerves as she passed the second floor – no one about – then down again, finally reaching the entry hall. A thrill ran through her – nearly there. She ran across to the drawing room on her toes. Cracked open the door – there sat her prize, gleaming on the mantelpiece.

She crossed the room and reached up, taking the engraved plate off its wooden stand.

'Utterly predictable,' drawled a voice behind her. She spun, nearly dropping the plate. A deeper, darker shadow sat in one of the tall armchairs. Darcy – or rather the Dark Archer, dressed as he was in his Vigil outfit. She cursed herself – she hadn't checked, hadn't noticed. Too impetuous.

'Now,' said Darcy rising, cloak flaring. 'Be so good as to put that back, Miss Bennet.'

She looked around the rest of the room. 'Where's the Blue Jack?'

'Asleep. Where you should be, rather than engaging in this ludicrous and childish attempt to insult my aunt. How did you get in, by the way? There are bells on all the doors.'

So he didn't realise she had come via the roof.

'Insult? I just thought to show one shouldn't make assumptions.'

'I see. Well, that is over. Put the plate back, and I will show you out. We will not speak of this.'

She nodded, hefting the silver in her hands. 'But I did get in, didn't I? I made it right to this room.'

'Yes, you have some skill as a burglar, it seems. But now you are caught.'

'Caught?' She fairly buzzed with energy. Her legs tensed. 'I do not agree that I am caught. Yet.'

Darcy went very still. 'Do not be foolish.'

'Seems to me, the Best Men were unable to stop me getting to this plate, and I see no reason to believe they can stop me taking it.'

'Miss Bennet,' he growled, 'Do not!'

She bolted for the door. She felt him lunge for her, but she dove through the narrow gap, kicking the door closed behind her. It slammed, loud as a pistol shot in the quiet night. But she needed the delay – she was at the staircase as she heard the door fling open behind her, but up she ran, sprinting, pumping her legs with all her might. The thump of his steps and grunt of his breathing told her he was close behind, gaining. She hit the second-floor landing, turned tightly and was up the next flight, Darcy running slightly wider, slowing him marginally. Lungs bursting, she came out on the third floor and raced down the hall, the carpet masking their footfalls. She wondered briefly why he didn't shout out, raise the alarm. How would she explain this to her father, should she be caught? She then pictured Mr Collins' face, purple and bursting, and a wild laugh escaped her lips.

Where was the servants' passage? She trailed her fingers along the wall, trying to remember how far down it was – there! She pulled it wide, dove into the gloom and started up the dark staircase as fast as she dared. The plate rang as it banged against the wall. Darcy was in behind her, his breath hoarse in the confined space. At the top, she shoved the door and came out onto the circular walkway. She skipped around, watching over her shoulder – Darcy emerged, big and black against the pale wall. He looked about, looked over the edge, then stepped back. They faced each other across the circular gap.

'Very clever,' he said. 'You have proven yourself to be faster than me, and have a good knowledge of the layout of the house. I salute you for both those things. Now may we call this done? Or must I chase you round and round this dome till one of us collapses?'

'We cannot be done until you admit I have won.'

'You haven't won. You have bought yourself a little more time, is all.'

'Then on we go.' Elizabeth went through the open window head first, holding the plate before her, and rolled forward, her own weight squashing her fingers beneath it. She spun, reaching to shut the window, but heard one of the windows on the far side slam open hard enough to shatter. An unidentifiable thrill ran through her – he was coming, around the dome, his feet ringing on the circular walkway. She ran across the rooftop, but realised she couldn't head for the site where she had climbed up, not yet. She would be too slow in trying to climb down safely – had to gain more time, had to lose him somehow. She ran fast as she dared past the section where she had climbed up and kept going onwards to the western wing of the great house.

Behind her she heard the clinking of the tiles as Darcy followed, heard the sharp intake of his breath and a muffled curse. She laughed, feeling gleeful as a child. He was strong, but bigger and slower. She felt fast and light, fluid as quicksilver. Ahead, the rooftop was a jumble of pitches and slants. She leapt from one to another, slid down one long section on her bottom, dodged around dormer windows and sprinted across small plateaus. Behind her, the crunch of his steps was relentless. She heard the impact as he jumped, the rasp as he slid down the tiles behind her.

She was running out of roof – it would not do to be caught against the edge. On a small, flat section, she paused – and heard a soft beating in the air above her like a mighty wing. She flung an arm above her head as the moonlight was cut off by a black shadow, and Darcy's cloak fell heavily across her. The unexpected weight of it brought her to her knees, but her upthrust arm kept it from entangling her. She thrust herself upright, whipping her arm to tangle the cloak around it, took a moment to glance back at him: to throw it, he had stopped, and now she had her space, *now* – she sprinted by him, cloak and plate in hand, running full pelt across a sloping section, trusting to the magic of the night to keep her upright.

He was after her again, close behind, tiles cracking beneath his boots – then a sharp cry – a trick? – a crash, sliding. She looked back – he was sliding, going over the edge, the drop below him shear. He was grabbing at the tiles but could find no purchase, eyes so wide beneath his mask she saw the whites gleam. Then his feet were over, kicking in space, and he groaned, digging his elbows into the lead gutter at the very edge. He stopped, but with a creak the gutter started pulling away. She dropped the plate with a clatter and jumped, sliding down the roof after him, shaking the cloak clear as she did so. Just a few feet above him, but out of reach, a thin chimney pipe rose from the rooftop. She slid by it, and as she went, she whipped the cloak around, caught the other edge in her free hand.

'Darcy,' she cried, and kicked her legs towards him, her body stretched full.

She felt his fingers flailing at her boots, then one hand like iron wrapped around her ankle, followed by the other. She cried out as she took his full weight, fingers desperately tangling in the cloth of his cloak. With a strangled gasp, Darcy grabbed her trousers, fingers digging into the leather. She felt the seams give as he dragged himself upward, one hand then shooting up to grab her belt. She felt his bulk climbing up her, his face passing over her buttocks, lower back, then felt his hot breath on the back of her neck, sensed his clenched teeth. Then he had hold of the cloak himself, and rolled clear. On hands and knees they both climbed back to the flatter section and collapsed. Elizabeth sucked sweet night air back into her lungs, heard him blowing next to her. For a time there was no sound but their laboured panting.

'I suppose I owe you a debt of thanks,' he rasped.

'Do not mention it,' she replied, sitting up. Her joints all felt strained. She reached for the silver plate.

His hand came slamming down on top of it.

'Not that,' he said.

'It would have been mine if I had left you to fall.'

'That would not have been in your nature to do.' There was a pause, then: 'Perhaps I deliberately pretended to slip, just to thwart you?'

She laughed out loud at that, and the rich deep burble of his own laugh joined with hers. But then a picture came to her of Jane's pale, pained face, and she fell abruptly silent. She hugged her knees. Darcy also fell silent, seeming to feel the change in her mood.

'Take the damn thing,' he said, his hand sliding off.

She looked at him, but he rolled over and climbed to his feet, flinging his cloak back around his shoulders. She paused, then picked up the plate and picked her way back to the rear of the main house. She tossed the plate down onto the lawn, then sat and lowered herself into the corner, took hold of the drainpipe and slowly worked her way down.

No extra lights shone within. It appeared their chase had had no impact on the sleeping inhabitants of the house. She jogged around the corner, plate tucked under her arm. Once at the front, running down the grass alongside the drive, she turned and looked back. She could see his figure, silhouetted against the night sky, hands on hips, watching her, still as a statue.

She walked backwards along the drive, passed through the gateway, then held the plate above her head with both hands. When she was sure he was watching, she placed it upon the ground just outside the drive. The black figure bowed. She curtsied, then ran off into the dark.

Chapter 8

She would have slept in if she could, but Mr Collins' booming voice woke her and would not allow her to fall back asleep, despite Charlotte's quiet interventions. Thankfully, by the time she had dressed – her joints still felt sore and stretched this morning, and she was mottled in bruises – he had left the cottage.

Charlotte had errands of her own to run, and so Elizabeth was again left to her own devices. She decided a walk in the park would stretch out her tight muscles and give her the opportunity to think about the previous evening undisturbed. However, she had not gone far when she spied Colonel Fitzwilliam striding towards her.

'Miss Bennet,' he said, touching his hat. 'I am pleased to have found you. I was making a tour of the park and was then intending to head to the parsonage to see you. It is to say farewell, I am afraid. I will be leaving tomorrow.'

'You are being sent on another mission?'

He smiled. 'Of a sort. But not what you are thinking.'

'Does Mr Darcy accompany you?'

'He may. Or he may not. He arranges his business as it pleases him.'

'That doesn't surprise me. I do not know anybody who seems more to enjoy the power of doing what he likes than Mr Darcy.'

'He does like to have his own way very well,' replied Colonel Fitzwilliam. 'But don't we all?'

'Though we do not all have the power to act on it equally.'

They walked in companionable silence for a while.

'It is pleasing to walk in company,' said Colonel Fitzwilliam after a while. 'I tried to rouse Darcy to it this morning, but he threw a boot at me and told me to leave him to sleep. If I didn't know better, I would say he had been up half the night on a caper.'

Elizabeth said nothing, though she was sure Colonel Fitzwilliam was looking at her sideways.

'And is your mission tedious?' she asked. 'Are you permitted to speak of it?'

'Oh, it is far from tedious,' he replied. 'More of an honour, than anything. You see, I am joined with Darcy in the guardianship of Miss Darcy, his sister.'

'Are you indeed? And pray what sort of guardians do you make? Does your charge give you much trouble? Young ladies of her age are sometimes a little difficult to manage, and if she has the true Darcy spirit she may like to have her own way.'

As she spoke, she observed him looking at her intently.

'Why do you suppose she gives us any trouble?' he asked seriously, his keen eyes searching her face.

'Do not be alarmed, I have heard nothing but good things about her. She is a very great favourite with some ladies of my acquaintance, Mrs Hurst and Miss Bingley. I think you may know them?'

'I know them a little,' said Colonel Fitzwilliam, noticeably relaxing. 'Their brother, Bingley, is a pleasant fellow. He is a great friend of Darcy. There was some hope he may become a companion for the Dark Archer, but I am not sure if that is working out.'

'Oh yes,' said Elizabeth drily. 'Bingo Boy.'

'That's it,' said Colonel Fitzwilliam with a laugh. 'You know about that? That name was never going to catch on. Aunt Catherine loathed it.'

'I suppose she has the final say in such things?'

'Well, she is the founder and patron of the Best Men, so yes. With her connections and wealth, together we can accomplish much more than any of us could individually. And some of us are more serious about Vigilism, Miss Bennet. Men such as Darcy and myself. I don't believe Mr Bingley fits that category.'

'Though Mr Darcy has tried to involve him?'

'More like let Bingley have a run on a caper or two. But I suspect it is usually a case of the Dark Archer watching over Bingo Boy, both in a mask and without, too.'

'What do you mean?'

'Well, from something Darcy told me on our journey hither. I have reason to think Bingley very much indebted to him.'

'What for? Saving his life?'

'No, no. Nothing to do with Vigilism. It is a circumstance which Darcy would not wish to be generally known, because if it were to get round to the lady's family, it would be an unpleasant thing.'

'It involves a lady? You may depend upon my not mentioning it to anyone, I assure you.' It was as well they were walking, for that would explain the flush of pink in Elizabeth's cheeks at this news.

'I do trust you. Well, what he told me was merely this: that he congratulated himself on having lately saved Bingley from an imprudent marriage, without mentioning names or any particulars.'

A pulse was beating in her temple, a tiny drum of war. 'Did Mr Darcy give you his reasons for this interference?'

'I understand there were some very strong objections against the lady.'

'And what,' said Elizabeth, struggling to keep the heat out of her voice, 'gave Mr Darcy the right to so judge?'

'You think his interference was wrong? I am sorry, I do not have enough of the details to put your mind at ease on the matter. We must trust to Darcy's sense that he did what was right. Or at least, what he believed to be right for his friend.'

'Yes, but was it right for the lady in question? What of her?'

Colonel Fitzwilliam shrugged and the conversation shifted to lighter topics. Fortunately, they were close by the parsonage, so she did not have to keep up her side for long before they could go in and join Mr and Mrs Collins.

Later, when the visitor had left and she had retired to her room, she had time to think. She had always supposed Miss Bingley was the prime cause of her brother's removal from Netherfield, but now she saw it was Darcy who was the principal agent. His pride and caprice were the cause of all that Jane had suffered, and suffered still. He had ruined every hope of happiness for the most generous, affectionate heart in the world, and no one could say how lasting an evil he may have inflicted.

Very strong objections against the lady.

She should have let him fall.

They were due to take tea at Rosings, but by this time Elizabeth's agitation had brought on a headache. This, coupled with her unwillingness to endure Darcy's company, caused her to declare herself too ill to go. Charlotte did not press her, though Mr Collins could not conceal his apprehension of Lady Catherine's being displeased by her staying at home.

Elizabeth could not care in the slightest about Mr Collins' nerves, and it was only her care for Charlotte that stopped her answering him in a decidedly rude manner before they finally left. When she was finally alone Elizabeth pulled out all of Jane's letters that she had received since her sister had been gone. The more she looked at them, the more she sensed an unease, a cloudiness, within them. Mr Darcy's shameful boast about his actions gave her a keener sense of her sister's suffering.

The only comfort was that Darcy should be leaving soon, and so would she – her visit, and Jane's, were nearly at an end and they would soon be together again at Longbourn. Some of the tension appeared to be easing from her head – to be honest, the moment she decided to avoid going to Rosings that afternoon she had begun to feel better – when she was roused by the sound of the doorbell. For a moment she wondered if Colonel Fitzwilliam had come to speak to her one more time, but this idea was soon banished when, to her utter amazement, Mr Darcy walked into the room.

'Miss Bennet.' He slapped his gloves against his hand, then abruptly sat. 'How are you? Are you well? Is your current ill health due to the other evening?'

'It is not, sir,' she answered coldly.

'Good, good.' He nodded. 'I was worried that I may have inadvertently injured you.'

'No,' said Elizabeth precisely. 'You have not injured *me*.'

He did not seem to pick up on her meaning. Instead he lurched to his feet and began to pace the room. His agitation was quite infectious. Elizabeth had no idea what was going on, but had no wish to make things any easier for him, so held her tongue.

After a silence of several minutes, he came towards her, the sudden change in direction causing her to tense.

'In vain have I struggled. It will not do. My feelings will not be repressed. You must allow me to tell you how ardently I admire and love you.'

The air sucked out of her. He could not have done a better job if he had punched her in the stomach. She stared up at him, speechless, feeling the blood rush to her cheeks. Had she misheard? Was she dreaming?

'You are silent. You are surprised. As, I can tell you, am I. It isn't logical, yet here we are. I love you. I do not know precisely when it happened; it appears to be an incremental thing, like a slowly building fever. Certainly, I have always found you to be an attractive young woman. But there are many other equally attractive young women. There is something else about you which draws me to you. We have clashed, it is true, but I believe that has been due to differences in approach rather than any fundamental and irreconcilable differences in our nature. Your amateurism versus my professionalism, I mean.'

It hardly seemed possible – to be in this position again. Was she destined to forever be having to repel declarations of love she did not return?

'Still silent?' Darcy continued. 'You are thinking of the obvious problem. I am well aware, as I am sure are you, of the inferiority of your status. And as if that were not enough, there is the unbecoming behaviour of your closest relatives which sometimes crosses over into the scandalous. Connection with your family would thus be something of a degradation. This does provide some difficulty. Good judgement says stay clear but there is a spiritedness about you, which requires tempering, it is true, but which has infected me and urges me to cast reason and good sense aside.'

His words started to be drowned out by the roaring of blood in her ears.

'And I assure you, this is not just a reaction to your saving...to your efforts last evening. No, these are real feelings, the strength of which it is impossible to conquer, though I have tried, I assure you. Oh how I have tried! But they have defeated me, and so I hope to be rewarded by your acceptance of my hand.'

She forced herself to look at him, to meet his gaze. His eyes spoke of nothing but confidence. He had no doubt at all but that she should gratefully accept his offer. She felt as if she had to unstick her tongue from the roof of her mouth.

'In cases such as this,' she began slowly, 'I believe it is customary to express a sense of gratitude for the sentiments avowed, however unequally they may be returned.' A small scowl crossed his brow. 'But I cannot. I have never desired your good opinion, and you have certainly bestowed it most unwillingly, that much is clear. So, no, you will not be "rewarded with my hand". Especially when you have made it sound such a poor reward taken under such noble sufferance.'

She rose, and he stiffened, drawing himself up straighter as he stared at her with his dark eyes. He seemed more surprised than anything, then paled with anger as her words sank in. When he finally spoke, it was as if each word were bitten from ice.

'And this is the reply which I am to have the honour of expecting? I might, perhaps, wish to be informed why, with so little endeavour towards civility, I am thus rejected. But it is of small importance.'

'I might ask,' returned Elizabeth, 'why with so evident a design of offending and insulting me, you chose to tell me that you liked me against your will, against your reason, and even against your character? What other reaction could you possibly be expecting?'

'This is your issue? That in my honesty I have not asked you *nicely* enough? You, the woman who seeks to be a Vigile, requires *more gentle handling*?'

'I have other provocations! You know I have! Do you honestly think I'd accept the man who has been the means of ruining, perhaps forever, the happiness of my most beloved sister?'

This time he remained silent, and that silence condemned him. He may as well have been carved from marble for the want of movement in his face and the rigid stillness of his body. But his humanity was at least signalled by the changing colour of his countenance.

'I have every reason in the world to think ill of you. You provided some assistance rescuing the girls, true, but grudgingly. Then you dismissed the Wicked Man as a threat and I believed you because of your arrogant cocksureness! And no motive can excuse what you did to Jane. You dare not – you cannot – deny that you have been the principal there.'

She paused, but now he seemed to be hardly listening. He appeared to feel no remorse whatsoever, and even looked as if a slight smile was playing around the corners of his mouth.

'Can you deny what you have done?' she repeated.

With assumed tranquillity he replied, 'I have no wish to deny that I did everything in my power to separate my friend from your sister, or that I rejoice in my success. Towards him I have been kinder than towards myself.'

Insufferable. She stepped towards him before she knew she was moving, saw him instinctively drop back into a stance. There was a slight pause in which they both had to acknowledge how close they were to blows, and make a decision. With an effort, Elizabeth sought to relax her posture, and after a moment he did the same.

'But that is not all,' she continued. 'My dislike of you was already decided. Your character was revealed in the recital I received earlier from

Mr Wickham. What can you say about that? In what imaginary act of friendship can you here defend yourself? Do you dare rejoice in this as well?'

'You take an eager interest in that gentleman's concerns,' said Darcy, his voice harsh.

'Knowing what his misfortunes have been, one cannot help feeling an interest in him.'

'His misfortunes!' repeated Darcy. 'Yes, his misfortunes have been great indeed.'

'And of your infliction,' cried Elizabeth. 'You have reduced him to his present state of poverty. You have withheld the advantages left to him in your father's will. You have deprived the best years of his life of that independence which was his due. *You* have done all this! And yet you can treat the mention of his misfortunes with contempt and ridicule!'

'And this,' growled Darcy, 'is your opinion of me! This is the estimation in which you hold me! I thank you for explaining it so fully. My faults, according to your calculation, are heavy indeed.' He had commenced pacing as he said this, but then stopped, and turned back towards her. 'But perhaps these offences might have been overlooked had not your pride been hurt by my honesty as to the scruples that had long prevented my forming any serious design. These bitter accusations might have been suppressed had I concealed my struggles. But I am not ashamed of the feelings I have related. They are natural and just. What, could you expect me to rejoice in the inferiority of your connections? To congratulate myself on the hope of relations whose condition in life is so decidedly beneath my own?'

Enough.

She was before him, hands wrapping in his coat, one leg snaking around behind his, ready to take his balance, take his damned composure, and *throw him.*

But he braced, hands grabbing hers, his strong grip working to prise her fingers free. He widened his stance, and for a moment their foreheads tilted together and touched. Both snarled into each other's faces. She hooked at his leg, and he had to hop to stay upright. He pushed her, and she stumbled backwards, heels catching at the hem of her gown.

'If you were any kind of gentleman, you would wait here and let me put my armour on,' she hissed. 'I cannot fight you in this.'

'That sad, tattered thing? With the patches and the quilting half hanging out? That *costume?*'

Already, the aftereffects of the unexpected action were hitting her. Her limbs felt weak and quivery, and she suddenly felt so weary.

'Just leave,' she said, dropping into a chair. 'Just go.'

He hesitated. Seemed about to speak.

'Don't. You are the last man in the world who I could ever be prevailed upon to marry, Mr Darcy. And I don't even really have enough care to fight you, either.'

He exhaled. 'You have said quite enough, madam. I perfectly comprehend your feelings and have now only to be ashamed of what my own have been. Forgive me for taking up so much of your time.'

He strode from the room, and a moment later Elizabeth heard the front door slam shut.

She sat for a long while staring into the fireplace. She was not aware of any particular thoughts. She felt stunned. Raw. Some tumult was playing out behind her eyes. To her surprise she found she was crying, the teardrops pattering softly upon her breast.

In love with her?

Mr Darcy, in love with her?

Images sprang unbidden to her mind. His sneering contempt when he overlooked her at the first assembly. The press as he tested her balance at the later ball. The feel as he dragged her to him, his great cape sweeping about them in the blast from the shotgun. His arms about her as he sought to correct her aim with his bow. His weight as he dragged himself up along her on the roof...

The pressure of him on her legs...her buttocks...his breath on her neck...

If he had tackled her during the fight with her would-be kidnapper, if it had been him not Bingley, his hand reaching–

'I hate him!' She grabbed her temples in both hands and squeezed. 'Get out of my head!'

She cried. And later, when the sound of Lady Catherine's carriage alerted her to the return of the others, she fled to her room.

Chapter 9

When she woke the next morning, she was a little surprised: she had thought she would spend the entire night awake. She had feigned sleep when Charlotte's quiet knock at the door had come last night, but then lain with her eyes open to the dark. At some point, though, sleep had claimed her after all. But now the events of the previous evening crowded back into her mind. She found herself unable to think about anything else. She had already resolved not to speak with Charlotte of what had transpired, but found herself struggling to make conversation at breakfast. The repetition of Lady Catherine's main points from dinner the night before by Mr Collins did little to ease her agitation. At last she announced her intention to take a long walk.

Once she had closed the door to the parsonage behind her, tied her hat in place and begun to head briskly down the lane, she began to feel a little better. She caught herself about to enter the park, but not wishing the slightest risk of Darcy appearing, she continued down the lane instead.

She had gone maybe two miles, enjoying the morning sun, when a prickling feeling caused her to glance at the nearest stand of trees within the park. It felt like someone was watching her, but she could see no one there. Frowning, she turned to keep walking, and at that moment there came a humming in the air that caused her to drop to the ground in alarm. At the same time, there was a deep *thunk*, and a long black arrow stuck quivering in a tree ahead of her. She squirmed around to her front, one hand going to her waist to pull her dress up if she had to run. Where was the archer?

'Do me the honour,' called a voice from the distant copse, 'of reading that letter.'

Darcy!

She looked back at the arrow in the tree and saw that a piece of paper was tied about the shaft. She cautiously rose to her feet, brushing the worst of the dirt and leaves from her gown. The idiot, he could have just handed it to her. But she didn't want to read it.

She walked past it, making a point of ignoring it...then stopped. Cursing, she went back, worked the arrow free and pulled the letter from its binding. With no expectation of pleasure, but with the strongest curiosity, Elizabeth opened the letter. It was two pages long, closely written.

It said:

'Be not alarmed, Madam, on receiving this letter nor by the means of delivery: it does not contain a repetition of my offer which last night was so disgusting to you. I have no desire to pain you or humble myself by dwelling on a scene best forgotten. This was no easy letter to write, nor will it be easy, I imagine, for you to read it but nevertheless my character required it to be written and read. You must pardon my demand on your attention, including the aggressive method of delivery. I could not be sure you would allow me to approach close enough to deliver it otherwise. I have no doubt your feelings will mean you bestow your attention unwillingly, but I demand it of your sense of justice.

'Three offences of very different natures you last night laid to my charge. The first was that I did not care as greatly as you for the safety of the girls taken by the villain styling himself as the Wicked Man, nor advised you sufficiently as to the threat he represented. On this charge I must declare myself guilty. But it is inherent upon you to consider the broader context for my actions which, I point out, included following you to the canal and assisting in the disruption of the operation taking place there. You will have gathered from your time at Rosings that the work of the Best Men frequently involves action at a very high level. This is about more than the price of brandy, as you put it. It is about safeguarding the kingdom itself. Against this, the kidnapping of a few peasant girls cannot compare. True,

I believed that the disruption of the Wicked Man's operation would be enough to remove him from your neighbourhood, and here I appear to have been wrong. However, it has been my experience that these lower level villains are generally usually stopped in this manner. The fact that he remained, and sought to track you and I down, suggests a more personal motivation than I understood at the time. However, your subsequent dealing with him, which you state appears to have been lethal, removes our chance to understand him better.

'The second charge mentioned was that regardless of the sentiments of either, I had detached Mr Bingley from your sister. The accusation is somewhat true, but an explanation of my actions and motivations is necessary. This may be offensive to you, but further apology on my part would be absurd. I had not been long in Hertfordshire before I saw, as did you, that Bingley preferred your eldest sister to any other woman. I did not think much of it, for I had seen him in love before. But at the dance at Netherfield, where I had the honour of dancing with you, I saw that Bingley's attentions to your sister had given rise to a general expectation of their marriage. It appeared to be, in the eyes of such as Lord Lucas, a certain event. From that moment I observed my friend's behaviour more attentively, and saw that his partiality for Miss Bennet was beyond anything I had previously witnessed. Your sister I also watched. Her look and manners were engaging, but I remained convinced that while she received his attention with pleasure, there was no great depth of feeling on her part. Your passion last night suggests to me that I was wrong. Your superior knowledge of your sister must allow it to be so, in which case, in my error, I inflicted pain upon her, and your resentment is thus not unreasonable. However, surely you can admit that the coolness of your sister's countenance and air can make it appear her heart was not likely to be easily touched. Thus, I believed her indifferent.

'My objections to the marriage were not merely those. There are others, and these must be stated, though briefly. There is the situation of your family, but this, while objectionable, is nothing in comparison to the total lack of propriety so frequently demonstrated by your mother and by your three younger sisters, and occasionally even by your father. Pardon me for this, it pains me to offend you. Take some consolation from the fact that both you and your elder sister have conducted yourself in such a way as to avoid any share in this censure.

'That evening, before I left to follow you to the canal, my opinion of all parties was confirmed, and I determined to preserve my friend from what I esteemed to be a most unhappy connection – a wife who did not love him as much as he loved her, and a mother-in-law intent upon his money. The next day we left Netherfield for London, so that I could see my usual doctor for my back. Bingley, of course, wanted nothing but to accompany me.

'You may well realise that his sisters, too, were uneasy about the situation, and we shortly resolved on keeping him in London. Pointing out the familial problems had limited success – I believe he still had designs on returning to Hertfordshire. But assuring him of your sister's indifference was another matter. He had before believed that she returned his affection with sincere, if not equal, regard. But Bingley has a great natural modesty and a strong dependence on the judgement of trusted others such as myself. To convince him that he had deceived himself was no very difficult mission.

'On this subject I have nothing more to say, no other apology to offer. If I have wounded your sister's feelings, it was unknowingly done.

'Now we turn to the final charge: that I had, in defiance of various claims, in defiance of honour and humanity, ruined the prospects of Mr Wickham. I can only refute this charge by laying before you the whole of his connection to my family. Mr Wickham is the son of a respectable man who assisted in the management of the Pemberley estates, and whose good conduct in the discharge of his duty naturally inclined my father to wish to assist him. He therefore made Mr Wickham his godson and supported him at school and afterwards at Cambridge. More than that, my father was very fond of Wickham's society, describing him as a most engaging young man. He hoped the church could be Wickham's profession and intended to provide for him in it.

'As for myself, I was already forming a most different view. Being of the same age as him, I was able to observe him in unguarded moments, and noted certain vicious propensities he was able to hide from most people. There never arose a moment to talk to my father about my concerns before he died, about five years ago. In his will he desired that a valuable position be found as soon as one became vacant. There was also a legacy of a thousand pounds. Wickham's own father died not long after.

'Soon after, Wickham wrote to me to say that he did not wish to enter the priesthood after all. He wished for me to give him more money instead. He said he thought he might study law, and that a thousand pounds would not be enough. Since I firmly believed Mr Wickham had no place as a clergyman, I agreed and paid him three thousand pounds. All connection between us seemed dissolved. I thought too ill of him to try to maintain any contact. I believe he lived chiefly in Town, but his studying the law was a mere pretence, and being now free from all restraint, his life was full of idleness and dissipation. For about three years I heard little of him, but then the local priest died and Wickham applied to me for the position. He appeared to think I would just give it to him. When I demurred, he came to see me. He told me that his circumstances were very bad and that he was ready to enter the priesthood. And here a strange thing occurred. Before he came to see me, I had already resolved to refuse him. But as he stood talking to me, I began to feel myself yielding to his entreaties. It was only by the greatest force of will that I stuck to my original decision and sent him on his way emptyhanded. He was furious. I thought no more about the strange mood that had struck me at that time.

'I come now to a part of the story that I wish I could forget, and that I would not tell any human being but for the need to explain to you. Having said thus much, I feel no doubt of your secrecy. My sister, who is more than ten years my junior, was left in the guardianship of Colonel Fitzwilliam and myself. About a year ago, Wickham wormed his way into her life. He worked his charms upon her, and she was persuaded to believe herself in love and to consent to an elopement. She was fifteen.

'It was by pure chance that Fitzwilliam and I came to visit her a day or two before the plan was put into operation. I found her to be highly stressed, not herself at all. As the time came when she was supposed to leave and meet Wickham, she became feverish, almost delirious, and blurted out to me that she must go meet him. We confined her to her room, and she eventually acknowledged the whole to me. Here I made a great mistake and relaxed my guard, thinking that in her confession, Georgiana had woken from his spell. Alas, this was not the case and something terrible occurred. I do not wish to write more of this. Suffice to say I nearly lost all reason. Georgiana, at least, was finally safe.

'You may imagine what I felt and how I acted. I hunted Wickham at the set spot, but he must have had some warning of my coming and somehow eluded me. Regard for my sister's good name prevented any public exposure. And he has managed to avoid me these last twelve months until we both turned up by chance in Hertfordshire.

'Of course his chief object must have been my sister's fortune, which is thirty thousand pounds. But I cannot help supposing that the hope of revenging himself on me was a strong inducement. To take my beloved sister and make her his, to use her to satisfy his vicious appetites...his revenge would have been complete indeed.

'This, madam, is a faithful narrative of every event of concern. If you do not reject it as false, then you will, I hope, acquit me of any cruelty towards Mr Wickham. I know not in what manner, under what form of falsehood he has imposed himself on you, but his success is perhaps not to be wondered at. Given my own experience speaking to him, and his ability to sway Georgiana's good judgement, I believe it likely that he has been training in the art of mesmerism – no doubt when he should have been studying law.

'I should perhaps have told you this last night, but I was not then master of myself to know how best to explain it.

'I have taken enough of your time.

'Fitzwilliam Darcy.'

For a while, all she could do was stand, staring sightlessly, the pages scrunched in her hands, her mind a whirl of conflicting thoughts. Could it be true? Was this not some attempt to manipulate or suborn her? But would – could – he possibly use his sister like that, if it were just a tale? To place her reputation in Elizabeth's hands?

She smoothed the paper back out as best she could. He was not sorry. For the hurt he had done to Jane, he was not sorry. His writing was full of pride and insolence. For a moment, a bright spark of anger flared within her. But it could not be sustained. Her thoughts turned to her dear, sensitive sister, who, she must admit, tended towards a reserved manner. She had lost so much of her liveliness that dark night at the millhouse, become so much more guarded. She had not just stopped training with their father and Aunt Phillips – she had stopped being as open with the world. And that meant that, even when feeling a great depth of love, it was not to be too easily revealed upon the surface of her beautiful exterior.

Could Darcy, then, be speaking the truth? He did not suspect, did not know, that Jane really was very much in love. But would he have acted differently had he known? She read again his words concerning her family. Saw how dismissive he was, how arrogant. But this time, whereas the first reading had triggered hot anger, now, as she perused them a second time, she felt a deep sense of shame. The truthfulness of what he asserted could not be denied, however much one may wish. It was so. They were so.

As for the Wicked Man, now having a greater grasp on the culture of the Best Men, she could better understand his downplaying of the events at Hertfordshire. She still believed she was right – fiercely so – but she must accept that her view was in the minority. To her, the different care towards those of a different class or gender was obvious and wrong – but she could not claim to have always been so aware herself, so could she blame others whose position made it difficult for them to understand?

And finally there was Wickham. She felt as if two parts of her mind were grappling with each other for submission of the other. On the one hand there was that charming young man who had wooed her with his wit and manners. She had felt things for him that she had not felt for any other man before. She had delighted in his attention, sought him out. He had invaded her thoughts in ways that made her blush.

But, was he good? She tried to recollect some instance, something beyond mere charm. There was his acceptance of Aunt Phillips, which she had taken as a sign of great tolerance, but his inviting of himself to her place in the first instance made her uneasy. Was he doing so out of kindness or curiosity?

The visit…A sudden picture hit her – sitting and talking to him, Lydia coming over…'You want to go and play cards with Mr Collins,' he had said, *and she went*. Her stomach lurched. In the street…in the street he had said to her, improperly, 'Let us dance', and she *almost did*; her feet started moving before she was able to stop herself.

His eyes. His voice. The power of his charm, like a warm sun.

Mesmerising.

She felt like throwing up. She could see it. Could see the effect he could have, especially on a young girl, with plenty of time. What Darcy said about Georgiana had to be true. And if that was true, then the whole story had to be true, for whatever grounds could Wickham have to exact such a revenge?

She perfectly remembered everything that had passed in conversation between Wickham and herself that first evening. She was now struck by the impropriety of such communications to a stranger and wondered how it had escaped her before. She saw the indelicacy of putting himself forward as he had done and the inconsistency of his professions with his conduct. He had boasted of having no fear of seeing Mr Darcy, yet had avoided him in the street at Meryton and at the Netherfield ball.

An image came to her mind. Darcy, atop Rosings, his cloak billowing against the moon. If his actions had been as Wickham had described them, how could he maintain a friendship with a man so amiable as Mr Bingley or hold the respect of a man so honourable as Colonel Fitzwilliam?

She grew absolutely ashamed of herself. Of neither Darcy nor Wickham could she think without feeling that she had been blind, unjust. Prejudiced. And the thought that the cause of Jane's disappointment had in fact been the work of her family filled her with a sense of depression beyond anything she had known before.

She wandered along the lane for two hours, replaying the events of the previous months, trying to get her head around this sudden and painful change of perspective, when it occurred to her how long she had been gone and how fatigued she had become. She made her way back to the parsonage and entered as cheerfully as she could, repressing the thoughts that were loudly demanding her attention.

She was greeted with the news that the two gentlemen from Rosings had left but sent her their farewells.

Chapter 10

Mr Collins wasted no time in hastening to console Lady Catherine and her daughter on the loss of their guests. He returned beaming with satisfaction: her Ladyship felt herself so dull at the loss of her nephews that she demanded they dine with her to lift her spirits. To whatever extent they were able to, anyway.

Elizabeth could not see Lady Catherine now without considering that, had her answer to Mr Darcy been different, she could at this moment be presented as her future niece. She could not help but smile as she imagined the old lady's indignation.

When they were led through to the drawing room, Elizabeth's eyes went straight to the mantel – the silver plate was back in pride of position, seemingly unharmed. She should have scratched her initials on it somewhere.

'I believe nobody feels the loss of company so much as I do,' Lady Catherine told them. 'I am particularly attached to these young men, and know them to be so much attached to me! They were excessively sorry to go. Darcy's attachment to Rosings certainly increases.'

She looked towards her daughter, who was staring into space. Mr Collins rushed to echo her sentiments thoroughly.

So, thought Elizabeth, *he was that desperate not to see me again after delivering his letter...but who could blame him?*

'You are out of spirits, Miss Bennet,' declared Lady Catherine. 'No doubt you do not like the fact that you must soon return home. You must write to your mother to beg that you may stay a little longer. Mrs Collins will be very glad of your company, I am sure.'

Elizabeth felt Charlotte look at her. 'I am much obliged to your Ladyship for your kind invitation. But it is not in my power to accept it. I am afraid I must return home soon.'

'There can be no occasion for your going so soon,' said Lady Catherine. 'Mrs Bennet can certainly spare you another fortnight.'

'But my father cannot. I am sure he wishes me to hurry my return.'

'Oh, your father can spare you if your mother can. Daughters are never so much of a consequence to a father.'

'I can assure your Ladyship that we are of great consequence to my father. Indeed, my older sister and I trained to become companions to him.'

'Girls? As companions?' Lady Catherine snorted. 'Ridiculous. I understand that your father lacked a son to train to replace him, but the idea of using his daughters instead is preposterous. If he had been more sensible and aligned himself with me, I could have provided some support.'

'We did very well without any support,' returned Elizabeth. 'The Hound and Pack have kept the peace in Hertfordshire for many years.'

'I suppose there were indeed enough of you to form a pack. What was it again? Five daughters?'

'We were not all trained. My younger sisters do not...are not...And after Jane nearly...We...'

Lady Catherine let out a bark of laughter. 'You see? Girls have no stamina for the role. And your father revealed a weakness in reason by thinking they could. It is probably for the best that he is retired, even if it means your neighbourhood is unprotected.'

'My neighbourhood is still protected,' Elizabeth ground out between her teeth.

'Oh really? By whom?'

'By me.'

'I doubt that.'

'I saved four girls.'

'I heard nothing of this exploit.'

'You wouldn't have. They were ordinary girls.'

'Then *if* it happened, it is hardly significant. But I doubt it did. Miss Bennet, you are a fantasist.'

A heavy silence fell upon the room. Even Mr Collins seemed unwilling or unable to come up with a suitable compliment to shift the conversation.

'I killed a man.' Elizabeth threw the words into the room, her voice ragged. Charlotte inhaled like a hiss. 'Is that not significant enough?'

'Nonsense,' declared Lady Catherine. 'You did no such thing. This is not seemly. We will go through–'

'I wrenched his arm until it broke and threw him off a bridge!'

Miss de Bourgh clapped her hands to her ears, mouth open in horror. Elizabeth was aware of all of them staring at her. She was on her feet. There was a roaring in her head. Before she knew what was happening, she was heading for the door. Dimly aware of Charlotte calling after her, servants jumping aside as she strode to the main doors and threw them open. She grabbed at her skirts and ran down the stairs, onto the drive and away into the gathering night. The moon was rising, and that was as well, for as she ran, she threw her head back and screamed into the sky. The darkening sky that covered the earth like a giant black cloak.

She ignored Charlotte's gentle but insistent knocking for as long as she could. At first, when the house fell silent as everyone went to bed, and the first quiet tapping occurred, she could pretend to be asleep – though she was far from it. But then, when it became obvious that Charlotte wasn't going to give up, she threw back the covers and padded across in her bare feet to open the door.

Charlotte squeezed out a tight smile, then closed the door firmly behind her. Elizabeth drifted back to the bed and sat. Charlotte joined her.

'Are you hungry?'

Elizabeth shook her head. 'I'm sorry for the scene.'

'Yes. Well. Suffice to say, you are not in Lady Catherine's good books. Nor Mr Collins', either, I'm afraid.'

Elizabeth shot a sideways glance at her friend. 'And yours?'

Charlotte sighed. 'I am worried about you, that is all.'

'You do not need to worry on my account,' said Elizabeth automatically.

'Now Lizzy,' said Charlotte, a warm smile finally pulling at her mouth. 'We both know that isn't true. If you spent your days sewing and talking to officers that may be the case, but given your predilection for...alternative nocturnal activities...'

'Alternative nocturnal activities?' Elizabeth laughed lightly. Some of the tightness in her chest shifted.

'Well, I do not wish to get into an argument on what construes Vigilism, or even how the word is supposed to be pronounced. To be honest, I believe I have been cured of my interest in such matters.' She smoothed a strand of hair behind Elizabeth's ear. 'I wish I could say the same for you.'

'Charlotte...'

'I worry about the damage being done to you.'

'It is nothing. The tooth is the only lasting thing – everything else heals. It's just cuts and bruises.'

'I didn't mean on the outside. I meant the damage it is doing to you on the inside.'

Elizabeth stiffened. 'Perhaps that is just cuts and bruises, also.'

'And will heal in time?'

Elizabeth nodded.

'But you must give it time to heal, if that is the case. And that does not appear to be something you are very good at doing. Even here, on what was supposed to be a simple visit, you have brought that armour with you.'

'I...I feel naked without it.'

'And again, I am not just talking about that external leather.'

'You think me armoured on the inside as well?'

'So it seems.'

'If so, it is poor armour indeed. If you knew how things penetrated it... Can you blame me for trying to protect myself?'

'No. I just question whether you can allow yourself to open up when the time comes.'

'Dear Charlotte, I already told you, I–'

'I do not mean...I mean when you meet someone who may match you.'

'I see little chance of that happening any time soon.'

'Oh? What of that charming officer, Mr Wickham?'

'Hm. He is charming, true. But that may be the only positive quality he possesses.'

'Really? How did this change of mind come about?'

'I gained some more intelligence of him, which I am forced to believe to be true, against my own wishes.'

'Here? You learned about him here? How? Who from?'

'Mr Darcy.'

'Oh! I thought you hated Mr Darcy.'

'I do. I did...' She shifted uncomfortably. 'So, Mr Collins is very displeased at me?'

'Well. If you are very lucky, he may treat you to his most devastating disapproval. He may give you the silent treatment.'

Elizabeth stared at Charlotte's solemn face. 'Oh dear. How on earth am I to bear that?'

They both started giggling, and Charlotte pulled her into her embrace. And Elizabeth sighed.

The next morning at breakfast, it was as Charlotte foretold: Mr Collins maintained a stiff, aggrieved silence, only speaking to Elizabeth once, to enquire as to whether she approved of his plan to send to her father for the coach to collect her on the morrow. Elizabeth readily agreed. That subject concluded, Mr Collins fell silent again, decapitating his boiled egg in such a manner that suggested he wished it was some other in its place. Charlotte tried nobly to fill the space, speaking to both Elizabeth and Mr Collins in turn. Normally, Elizabeth may have enjoyed baiting the clergyman by talking greatly and laughing, but her heart was not in it. She was struck by such strong pangs of homesickness that she could barely eat.

And more than that – it was time to get to work.

Chapter 11

Her father's carriage was to meet her at an inn near the main road. As she approached in Mr Collins' trap, Elizabeth spotted Lydia and Kitty waving to her from an upstairs dining room. What on earth were they doing here? But then a third figure joined them, her hand raised in quiet greeting.

'Jane,' cried Elizabeth, and she jumped from the trap almost before it had stopped moving.

She raced into the inn and up the staircase to the dining room, and fell into her oldest sister's embrace. They squeezed each other tightly as Elizabeth fought to hold back tears.

'What about us?' cried Lydia.

'Yes,' said Kitty. 'We have come such an awful long way!'

Elizabeth reluctantly let go of Jane – she looked well – and gave each of her younger siblings a hug.

'Is this not nice?' asked Lydia. 'Is this not an agreeable surprise?'

'Very agreeable. But what are you all doing here?' she asked.

'We were bored,' answered Lydia. 'And Father suggested we might like to come meet you.'

'Mother didn't want us to come,' said Kitty.

Elizabeth looked at Jane.

'It was time for me to come home,' said Jane. 'And then Father sent a messenger informing me that you were to be meeting his carriage here, so the Gardeners kindly organised for me to meet you here too.'

'And now we mean to treat you,' said Lydia, gesturing to the table, which was set out with cold meats. 'Only, you must lend us the money, for we have spent ours at the shop out there. Look here, I bought this bonnet. I do not think it is very pretty, but I thought I might as well buy it as not.'

'Why ever would you buy a bonnet you did not think pretty?' asked Elizabeth.

'Because I can pull it to pieces when I get home and see if I can make anything prettier.'

'Besides,' added Kitty. 'It doesn't matter what we shall wear now. The regiment has left Meryton and gone to Brighton.'

'That's why we're so bored,' said Lydia with a sigh. 'No more officers.'

'That is probably just as well,' said Jane. 'Your conduct around them was most foolish and embarrassing.'

'Oh la, Jane. You are jealous because they gave us all the attention. Well, apart from Wickham, of course. He liked Lizzy best.'

'Did you see Mr Wickham?' said Elizabeth. 'Before they left?'

'No, we didn't get to see him. Oh, but Denny said he hurt himself. Fell off his horse.'

'Probably racing,' said Kitty, nodding.

Elizabeth felt an odd mixture of relief and regret. So there was to be no confrontation with him, no chance to allude to some of the things that Darcy had revealed and watch his response. Probably just as well. She was aware of how her heart still sped up a little at his name – better to sever that connection.

After they had eaten, and the elder girls paid (not best pleased to see how extravagant the younger girls had been in ordering), the carriage was ordered. With some difficulty, all four girls and their various chests and boxes, including Lydia and Kitty's unwelcome extra purchases, were at last all on board.

'How nicely we are crammed in,' cried Lydia. 'Let us talk and laugh all the way home!'

'I imagine that is fairly unavoidable anyway,' said Elizabeth.

'Don't be a stick-in-the-mud! Or I shall be forced to call you Mr Collins!'

'Pray do not! I have had more than my fill of that particular gentleman for a while.'

'Elizabeth,' said Jane, 'I am sure you do not mean that. I am sure he was a most amenable host.'

'If he were here, he could tell you all about that himself.'

'Lizzy!'

'If he were here,' cried Lydia, 'we should have even less room!' She jammed her knees far apart, causing Kitty to cry out in protest, and puffed out her cheeks. 'Listen to me, I'm Mr Collins! Blah blah blah!'

'Lydia,' cried Jane.

Lydia dissolved into gales of laughter until she started to hiccup, which only served to set off Kitty in turn.

'Oh, if Lady Catherine could see us all now,' said Elizabeth drily.

'Well, if she doesn't like laughter and fun she must be a terrible old bore!' Lydia turned to Jane. 'Tell us what happened to you, Jane. Nothing can have happened to Elizabeth, because she was just in the parsonage with Charlotte and Mr Collins. What about you? Have you seen many handsome men? Have you had any flirting? I was in great hopes you might come back engaged. You shall be an old maid soon! Fancy, almost three and twenty and not married! Lord, how ashamed I should be of not being married before I was three and twenty!'

Elizabeth sought Jane's hand and gave it a squeeze. She need not worry – Jane seemed to have the ability to absorb whatever unthinking and hurtful things her younger sisters said without rancour. For the rest of the trip, Elizabeth listened as little as she could. Lydia succeeded in her pledge of talking and laughing the whole way, assisted by Kitty. She was very glad when Longbourn came in view.

They were a noisy group at tea, for the Lucases came to join them. Maria seemed pleased to see Elizabeth again and insisted on sitting beside her. Lady Lucas wanted to know all about the welfare of Charlotte and that of her poultry – since Lady Catherine herself was showing such an interest. Mrs Bennet was doubly engaged, on the one hand collecting an account of the present fashions from Jane and on the other combatting Lady Lucas. Lydia was busy loudly enumerating the pleasures of the morning to all and sundry, with Mary her professed target.

'Oh, Mary!' said she. 'I wish you had gone with us, for we had such fun! As we went along, Kitty and me drew up all the blinds and pretended we were villains on the run! We collected pebbles and threw them at people as we drove by! I knocked a man's hat off!'

'You hit that boy in the eye, too,' said Kitty.

'Oh la, I am sure he is fine. Anyway, we behaved very handsomely and treated Jane and Lizzy to the nicest cold luncheon in the world, and if you had gone we would have treated you, too!'

'It is very easy to treat as many people as you like when you aren't paying,' said Elizabeth to Jane, who smiled and tapped her on the leg.

'And then when we came away, it was such fun! I never thought we would fit in the coach! And I pretended to be Mr Collins and even Lizzy laughed! And then we were merry all the way home! I was ready to die of laughter.'

Mary blinked gravely at Lydia, and said, 'Far be it from me to depreciate such pleasures. They would doubtless be congenial with the generality of female minds. But I confess they have no charms for me. I should infinitely prefer a book.'

Lydia stared at her for a moment, seemingly trying to comprehend what she had just heard, then turned to Kitty and Maria to talk about what they were to do now the regiment was gone.

Elizabeth was desperately impatient to get Jane alone and tell her all that had transpired at Rosings and the parsonage. But she was forced to sit through the rest of the evening before they could finally retire to their room undisturbed. As soon as the door was closed, she grabbed Jane's hand, pulled her down to sit beside her on her bed and told her of Darcy's proposal. Jane's mouth dropped open.

'He was so certain that I would accept him,' said Elizabeth, 'that I believe he fancied he had already heard the words come from my lips. When he understood I was refusing him, I doubt he could have appeared more stunned if I had kicked him in the side of the head.'

Jane winced, as she always tended to do when Elizabeth talked like that. 'It was wrong of him to be so sure of succeeding and to have allowed himself to appear so. But consider how much that must have increased his disappointment.'

'Indeed,' said Elizbeth drily. 'I am heartily sorry for him. But he has other feelings that will probably soon drive away his regard for me. You do not blame me for refusing him?'

'Blame you? Oh, no. You have always made your dislike of him very clear. I would not have you accept a proposal from a man you despise so, no matter how wealthy or connected he is.'

'I would never marry for money.'

'I know you wouldn't. Not for yourself. But I could easily see you agreeing to a match for the sake of the family, to safeguard the future of the younger girls.'

'After being trapped in a carriage with Lydia and Kitty for a whole morning, I believe I am quite ready to sell them to the highest bidder.'

As soon as the words left her mouth, she regretted them. An image of a murky barge sprang to mind, frightened white faces rising from the gloom. She made an effort to suppress it.

'I noticed,' said Jane, 'that you did not seem overly concerned by the departure of Mr Wickham?'

'Well,' said Elizabeth, and she proceeded to tell Jane what Darcy had revealed in his letter. The frown line in Jane's forehead grew deeper until Elizabeth felt obliged to reach forward and rub it with her fingertips. 'You know what Mother would say – one day it will stay that way.'

'I challenge anyone not to frown upon receipt of this news. Such wickedness! This certainly casts Mr Darcy in a more favourable light – his poor sister! And poor man, to have the guilt of failing in her protection! Still, I have trouble believing it of Mr Wickham. He seemed such a charming man. Such an openness and gentleness of manner. Could there be some error, some misunderstanding?'

'This will not do,' said Elizabeth. 'You will never be able to make both of them good. Take your choice, but you must be satisfied with only one. For my part, I am inclined to believe Mr Darcy. Something certainly went wrong in the upbringing of these two young men. One has got all the goodness, and the other all the appearance of it.'

'You must have felt terrible reading that letter, after the things you said to Mr Darcy about Mr Wickham.'

'I was very uncomfortable and unhappy, and with no Jane to comfort me and tell me I had not been quite as weak and vain and nonsensical as I knew I had! Oh, how I wanted you! And now I do not know what to do: what Mr Darcy thinks of me, I cannot imagine. I wish to expose Wickham's character before the world, but Mr Darcy has not given me leave to do so and is obviously trying to keep the matter quiet to protect his sister.'

'You must respect that.'

'Yes. Besides which, the general prejudice against Mr Darcy is so violent that it would be the death of half the good people in Meryton to attempt to place him in a positive light! And now, with Wickham gone, along with the regiment, well, I feel that someday hence it will all come out, and I must be content with that.'

'Perhaps he is sorry for what he has done and is now attempting to rehabilitate his character. We must not make him desperate.'

'Now, enough of Wickham, Darcy and I. What of you? How are you?'

Jane smiled at her, but Elizabeth could see the deep sadness behind it, and the knowledge of it tore at her heart.

'Do not worry yourself over me,' said Jane. 'I live.'

The next day Elizabeth was able to pay a visit to Aunt Phillips. After some tea, they retired to the training room.

'Some light sparring to start?'

Elizabeth nodded. They circled each other on light feet, sending out quick strikes and kicks.

'A little sloppy,' remarked Aunt Phillips, 'but not as bad as I expected, given the amount of time you have been away.'

'I was able to do a little training.'

'Oh? Partner work? Who with? Certainly not Mr Collins, I assume! Come, let us grapple. Take me down!'

Elizabeth lunged in, turning her back into her aunt, grabbed an arm and dropped forward. Her aunt rolled over the top of her shoulder and landed on her back. Elizabeth was on her straight away, lying across her and pinning her down, working to get hold of one of her arms.

'No, not Mr Collins,' she grunted. 'Mr Darcy, if you can believe it.'

Aunt Phillips tipped her off and sat up, astonished.

'Mr Darcy? You trained with Mr Darcy? How on earth could such a thing occur?'

'Well, I will tell you, but you must tell no one.'

'I cross my heart and hope to die if I should reveal anything about him! Now, tell!'

She hadn't told this part of the story to Jane, and so it felt good to speak of the rooftop chase.

'Mr Darcy, a Vigil? *He* is the Dark Archer you spoke of? I can scarcely credit it. Such a stern man. But then, we all have our secrets, do we not? Appearance does not always marry with reality. Shall we continue?'

Chapter 12

It was time to get started.

She could see now the benefit in teaming up with an investigator, who could do some of the initial legwork – especially if their character or occupation allowed them to travel about openly and ask questions. As it was, she needed to be circumspect. She could not use any of the family servants, for fear of discovery. But previous events had already introduced and placed in her debt a useful substitute.

Elizabeth loitered near the inn in Meryton, pretending to gaze into some shop windows, till she saw the innkeeper's daughter leave the establishment on some errand. Elizabeth strode swiftly after her, then passed her by and said out of the corner of her mouth, 'I need you to follow me, please.' She kept on, not stopping to look back, and turned a corner into a quiet lane. She was relieved to see the girl was just a moment behind her, a wary look on her face.

'There is nothing to fear,' said Elizabeth. 'You remember who I am? What I am?'

'Yes, miss,' said the girl.

'You remember what I did for you and the others that night?'

The girl coloured. She nodded.

'Good. There is something I need your help with. Don't look alarmed! I simply need some information.'

'What kind of information?'

'I want to know which men in the town mistreat their wives.'

'What do you mean, mistreat?'

'I want to know which ones hit them.'

'How am I supposed to know that?'

'Because I am sure there must be talk. Either amongst the men, while they are drinking, or amongst some of the ordinary women. I want to know which ones are cruel and violent.'

'Why?'

'So I can stop them.'

The girl looked at her. 'And how will you do that?'

'By reason, if I can.'

The girl snorted.

'By force, if I must.'

There was a pause as the girl studied her face.

'What's in it for me?'

'What do you mean? The knowledge that some of your sisters are sleeping more safely in their homes. Isn't that enough?'

'Should it be? What are they doing for me?'

Elizabeth blinked.

'I suppose I could pay you.'

The girl nodded. 'That's better.'

'Then you will help me? You will see what you can find out?'

'Yes, miss.'

'We will need to work out some kind of signal, to let me know when you have something to tell me.'

The girl stared into the distance for a moment, then glanced sideways at Elizabeth. 'Maybe I have something to tell you right now.'

Elizabeth looked at her, unable to read the girl's expression.

'Very well then.'

The bungalow sat on the far side of Meryton, down a winding lane. No light shone from within, though Elizabeth was sure the man was in there. Hopefully he had already retired for the evening – a man tangled amongst his bed clothes made an easy target. She shifted her weight from one foot to another, plucking at a thread in her armour. It was becoming increasingly worn. She would have to find a way to get a new set crafted soon.

But first there was the matter at hand. Another husband who wronged his wife and would now learn that there was a price to be paid. Let the word spread that the women and girls had a protector, and that the man who dared raise a hand against them would know fear and pain in return.

May as well go now.

She stepped from the shrub she had been concealed in and ran lightly across to the front door. Her lockpicks were in place beneath her jerkin, for the girl had said it was likely the door would be locked, but she tried the handle anyway – why waste precious time, in an exposed position, when it may be the door was open? – and was rewarded by a soft click as the bolt slid free.

She paused, feeling into the darkness within with her senses, then slipped inside, closing the door quietly behind her.

'And that's far enough,' said a voice that made her jump.

A match flared – a man sat at a table before her. He held the small flame to a candle, and the glow revealed the room. Just the two of them. The girl had said the woman would not be at home, and that there would be no others inside but him.

'William Bartle?' she growled. Weight spread evenly on the balls of her feet, baton smooth in her grip.

'The same.' He held up one hand in warning as she went to step forward, and she realised his other hand was out of sight beneath the table. She breathed out, thought of Darcy's words: *Some of them may have an interest in killing you.*

'Show me your hands,' she said in the most commanding tone she could muster.

'No.'

She hesitated. Rush him? Throw the club?

'Why don't you sit?' He kicked a chair out towards her.

'This isn't a social call.'

He let out a short bark of laughter. 'I know that. Come to deliver a beating, is that it?'

'Come to deliver a message. The form it takes is up to you.'

'Ah. And the message is?'

'Leave your wife alone.'

'Leave my wife alone. Now what could that mean?'

'You know what I mean. You beat her.'

'You're wrong.'

'I have information.'

'You have lies.'

'I trust my source.'

'What? Edith, from the inn? Ah, didn't think I'd know that, did you?'

Elizabeth paused. This wasn't going how she expected.

The man saw her hesitation and grinned. 'She isn't the most trustworthy of sources, young sir. Or the most discrete. Did she tell you we are related? No, I didn't think so. Tell me, what did she promise you, for you to come calling on me? A quick favour in the outbuildings?'

'Be quiet.' The baton came up, pointed at his face. She saw him tense, realised the risk she took if he was armed with a pistol, and fought to keep control. 'What do you mean, you are related?'

'She is my wife's cousin. She doesn't approve of me, to say the least. You see, she once tried getting a little too friendly, one Christmas gathering, and was more than a little miffed when I turned her down. I do have some honour, you see.'

'These could be lies.'

'Could be. But what are you going to do?'

'How did you know I was coming?'

'Like I said, she isn't discrete. She told Betsy, and Betsy told me. She loves me, you see.'

'Are you trying to tell me it is all lies then? If Betsy were here, and I asked her if you struck her, what would she say?'

He shrugged. 'Well, she is an honest lass, so she would tell you that yes, I sometimes knock her about a bit.'

So there it was. Cold resolve ran through her veins. If he did have a gun, he had one shot, and that from beneath the table, before she would be upon him.

'So that is it,' he said, voice empty. 'You think you know me.'

'I know enough.'

'You think yourself justified.'

'Justified enough.'

'You know nothing.' He suddenly pulled his hand from beneath the table and slammed it down upon the surface with a bang. She jumped, went to dive to the side, then saw his hand was empty. 'Too slow,' he said. 'In the old days, that would have got you killed, Vigil. Tell me, do you dream?'

'What do you mean?' she asked shakily.

'I do.' He was looking right through her. 'I sometimes dream of darkness, and screams, and fire. And when I do...when I do...' He looked at his hands, turning them over, frowning at them. 'She forgives me. She always says she forgives me. But I don't forgive myself. Why should I? So maybe I should just let you beat me. Another punishment. It's just that the thought of giving one of your kind the pleasure sticks in my craw.'

'I don't understand what you are saying.'

He looked up at her, eyes coming back into focus. 'It is quite simple. Once, long ago, I was a young man in London. Poor, with a young wife and a sickly child. I took whatever work I could. Whatever paid. That included some work for a gentleman that your kind would not approve of. A man you would see fit to judge, when to me he was a lifeline. And that night when it all came down...When you, in your masks, with your sense of bloody righteousness, when you burned it all down...And they...my dear and only...'

He pressed his hands down onto the table, breathing heavily.

Elizabeth's feet felt leaden.

'So, no. *No*! I will not subject myself to your judgement. I will not allow it. Beat me if you want, but I shall fight you with everything I have and will not stop until you or I are dead.'

'Then just stop hitting your wife,' said Elizabeth, then after a moment added: 'Please.'

'It isn't that simple. Tell me, do *you* fear falling asleep? Fear what will be waiting for you?'

She could feel she was grinding her teeth. Her grip was sweaty on the baton. The room suddenly felt small, stifling.

'You know, I feel sorry for you,' he said softly.

She jerked like he had shot her. 'Me?'

'You thought it was all so simple. But it isn't. Nothing ever is.'

He held her eye and slowly reached up, cupping one hand around the candle flame. He closed his fist, and the room was plunged into darkness. She spun, hand scrabbling at the door, heaved it open, and stumbled out into the night.

'Lizzy?' came the voice from Jane's bed. 'What is it?'

She was trying to be quiet, to hold everything in. But one of the buckles on her jerkin was coming loose, and so she had tried to slip the whole thing off without touching that one, but became stuck, and enraged, and a bitter surge of panic ran up her throat till she finally managed to drag it off and kicked it under her bed.

'It is fine,' she whispered hoarsely in response, and stood waiting. But already she could hear Jane's breathing deepening as she slipped back into sleep.

Sleep. That seemed far away at the moment.

She pulled on her nightgown, then a robe on top of that, and stole quietly out of the room. She was not sure where she was going, till she found herself outside her father's study. A faint light from within illuminated the edges of the door. She tapped lightly and turned the handle.

'Elizabeth,' said her father. He sat at his desk, also in his gown, a candle and book before him. 'You cannot sleep either?'

She shook her head. 'Am I disturbing you? I can go.'

'Sit down,' he said, closing the book. 'A little company in the middle of the night is as welcome as a candle. It lights us within. Depending on who the company is, of course.'

They smiled at each other.

'Old habits die hard, I am afraid,' he said. 'Too many nights spent patrolling. My body seeks the warm embrace of my bed, but I am afraid my mind is all too often out there.' He glanced at the darkened window. 'Have you been out?'

'I...I have. I know you do not wish it. I know you fear for my safety. But I cannot just...I am not like...'

Mr Bennet sighed, and nodded.

'Is all quiet?' His fingertips traced patterns in the wood of his desk. If you looked, you could still make out the hardened skin across his knuckles.

'It seems so.' She paused, unsure what she wanted to say. 'But everything seems so complicated now. Everything is changing. It isn't the same as when we...'

He looked up, his gaze piercing her from beneath his brow.

'It just seemed so much simpler then.'

'Tell me,' he said after a moment. 'Are there still ordinary people in the world? People who wish nothing more than to live their lives as peacefully as possible, to work their land, be with their families?'

'Yes, of course.'

'And are there also those who seek to make victims of them, to manipulate and cheat them?'

'Yes.'

'And if the ordinary cannot defend themselves from such villainy, are there still some who will do the extraordinary, who will stand for them, for what is right?'

The candle flared just then, a single spark shooting upward, like some tiny meteor.

'There are,' she said.

Mr Bennet nodded. 'Then the important things have not changed so much. Not beyond recognition. Not beyond us knowing what to do.'

He picked up his book then, calmly opening it to his page. She sat a while longer, then stood, came around the desk and kissed his head. Her hand was on the door knob when he spoke again.

'Lizzy. Just...be careful. That is all I ask.'

'Of course, Father.' She closed the door, not seeing the look of anguish that twisted his face as she left.

Chapter 13

'I am so bored!' Lydia announced at breakfast.

'As am I!' said Kitty.

'I am so bored I may die! Or kill someone!'

'Do not say that, Lydia,' said Elizabeth.

'But with the regiment gone away, what is to become of us?'

'I would recommend finding solace amongst books and–'

'Oh, do shut up Mary! Father, may we not go to Brighton?' asked Lydia.

'I'm not sure Brighton could cope,' said Elizabeth.

Lydia stuck her tongue out. Mr Bennet smiled, and Jane coughed into her hand.

'Girls, I know just how you feel,' said Mrs Bennet. 'I endured the same thing five and twenty years ago. I am sure I cried for two whole days when Colonel Miller's regiment went away. I thought I should have broke my heart.'

'Then you were very lucky Father came along to provide a cure,' said Elizabeth.

'Yes,' said Mrs Bennet, staring down the table at Mr Bennet. 'I suppose so.'

At that moment, one of the maids appeared by Elizabeth's shoulder and handed her a note. It was addressed to her, misspelled, in a hand she did not recognise. She excused herself from the table and went out into the garden to read it. She had assumed it would be from the innkeeper's daughter, but it was not so.

'Miss Elisabeth,' it read. 'I need you to meet me urgently at the Old Bridge this afternoon at 3. Come alone. I have news you must have.'

It was signed 'Meg' – the girl she'd rescued, who had delivered the Wicked Man's message to her house previously. What news could she have? The daytime meeting was difficult – she could hardly appear there in her outfit. And the girl had asked for *her*. Still, it would not hurt to be careful.

And so, when she set off that afternoon, while dressed in one of her gowns, she had her baton stashed down one sleeve and made sure she was wearing her sturdiest boots. She chose not to tell Jane or her father where she was going and made a point of avoiding the younger girls in case they decided to accompany her.

It seemed most likely to her that Meg had heard from Edith, the innkeeper's daughter, about her current plan and wanted to help. Maybe she would prove a more reliable source of information. The thought cheered her somewhat. Surely she ought not let one confusing setback deter her. As her father had said, there were still people in the world, especially women, who needed someone to stand up for them.

She kept her eyes open on the path to the bridge and stopped behind a tree once or twice to check if she was being followed. Once near the bridge itself, she moved more slowly and cautiously. She couldn't easily get into the same thicket she had observed the bridge from that fateful night, not in her dress, but she had deliberately chosen a dull colour so as not to stand out against the shadows. She was able to then pause and observe the bridge – there was a figure, a girl, sitting on the stone abutment in the middle of the span. She took a few more minutes to study the opposite bank and the girl – it did indeed look like Meg, and she appeared to be alone.

She stepped out onto the path, fingers of her right hand curling around the thong at the base of her baton, ready to whip it free. Meg was staring into the distance, her hands hidden beneath a shawl draped over her arms. As Elizabeth approached, she suddenly looked up, eyes big and black in her pale face.

'You came,' she said, voice shaking.

'Of course,' said Elizabeth, stepping forward. 'As you asked me to.'

'No,' cried the girl. 'Please don't come any closer!'

Elizabeth froze, a sudden stab of panic in her stomach, foot poised to step onto the bridge.

'What is it? What's the matter? Is it a trap? Meg, is this a trap?' She spun on the spot, eyes darting to all the possible hiding places for ambushers. No one, there was no one. She turned back to Meg. 'Is it the bridge? Is the bridge sabotaged?'

It looked solid as ever. She could see no sign of tampering. A bomb, perhaps? Was that possible?

'He has another message for you,' said Meg miserably.

'Who?' *But she knew, didn't she?*

'You should have killed him. I told you to kill him. Why didn't you?'

'I...I tried.'

'It wasn't enough.'

'I thought I had.'

'You only made it worse. You made him worse.' The girl shook her head, tears streaming down her face.

'Meg, what is going on? Where is he? When did you see him? Are you sure it was him?'

'He was waiting for me. I had to walk that way. I told you. I have to work. What else can I do? He was there. But this time, he wasn't alone.'

The cold knot in Elizabeth's stomach was sickening.

'Who was with him? What did he say?'

'He said that he knew now it was you. He worked it all out. He said that it took him longer to work out who your big friend was, and that they were very clever to go about disguised in plain sight, but now he knows, and now he is going to make you suffer.'

Her heartbeat was thudding in her ears.

'Wait, he knows it was *me*? He knows...my name?'

The girl curled over, sobbing. 'I didn't mean to tell him anything. I didn't want to come here. I don't want to do this.'

'Meg,' said Elizabeth slowly. 'Are you armed? Does he want you to kill me for him? In order to leave you alone?'

The girl shook her head. She looked upriver, took a deep shuddering breath, then looked deep into Elizabeth's eyes.

'Help me,' she said simply.

Elizabeth hesitated, then stepped slowly onto the bridge. Nothing happened. She stepped forward again.

'I want to,' she told Meg. 'I want to help you.'

'He just wants to give people what they want,' Meg said quickly, her eyes growing wide, the words tumbling out of her mouth as if learned by rote. 'He wants you to know that is all he does. But you made him suffer, and so now you will suffer. You will get the opposite. He will give you the opposite of what you want.'

Elizabeth hesitated, one hand reaching towards the girl. 'I don't understand. What do I want?' she whispered.

The girl looked at her sadly. 'You want to save people. So now you get the opposite.'

And the girl thrust her hands up into the air, the shawl falling free, and Elizabeth jumped back, not sure what was happening. The girl had something in her hands, then she saw that it was chains, a great ball of chain wrapped about her wrists. The girl thrust it up over her head, backwards, shoulders contorting – and the weight of it carried her over the abutment–

'NO!'

–down into the swift-running water. She vanished.

Elizabeth was at the edge, desperately looking, pulling at her dress, too hard to get it off, *no time*, clambered onto the abutment, jumped–

–hit the water hard, thrust herself under, hands sweeping through the cold – felt something, grabbed hold – her hair? Pulled, it came away, slimy – weed, only weed. Kicking with her heavy feet – her boots, her stupid boots – weight of her gown sucking at her. Eyes straining to stay open, the murk of the cold water pressing upon her. Lungs exploding, thrusting herself upward. Strength draining from her limbs, then her head breaking the surface, ragged great breath in. Turning, turning, turning. The water carrying her along. No sign. No sign. A life swallowed.

She struck out for shore, now fighting to save herself. The dress catching about her feet. Teeth set in a snarl as she fought the water's pull. The boots weighing her feet down, sinking, but then feeling her toes touch the bottom, and she could stand, and stagger up the bank, water pouring from her.

Too much. It was too much to take in. He was back, and he had killed the girl. How had he killed the girl? How had he convinced her to do that? It made no sense, it was as if she was – *mesmerised*.

She fell to her knees as if struck, and vomited. Could it be true? A whirl of images smashed into her mind.

That poor girl. The cruelty of it.

Darcy – *your big friend* – but he was safe, he was miles away. But how on earth had the Wicked Man worked that out?

She jerked upright.

Disguised in plain sight.

He didn't mean Darcy. He didn't know it was Darcy.

He thought...

She started to run.

Her boots were heavy. Her wet skirts stuck and tangled her legs. Her lungs were still burning from the river, and she coughed as she ran, a thin stream of water and mucous running from her nose. Then the cluster of buildings of Meryton were in sight. She started passing people, who stopped and stared. *Had to get there.*

'Lizzy!'

Jane – with Kitty and Lydia, standing and staring at her, open mouthed. She slewed, grabbed Jane by the wrist. Spun towards Lydia.

'You said he fell off his horse. Was injured. How?'

'Lizzy, what is–'

'*How* was he injured?'

'Who?'

'*Wickham!*'

'Oh, Denny said he broke his arm.'

His arm.

'Stay here. Jane, come; I need you!'

Dragging her away.

'But what is going on? Where are we going?'

'Aunt Phillips,' was all Elizabeth could gasp out.

She ran as fast as she could, but the words were there, beating their infernal rhythm in her head.

Run, run as fast as you can
But you can't get away from the Wicked Man.

Aunt Phillips carefully placed the tea tray on a small table and lowered herself into her favourite chair. It was overstuffed – *much like her*, she liked to joke with the girls. Her left knee was acting up again, feeling locked. A memory from a different life. She kneaded it for a few minutes before pouring a cup of tea. The cup was dwarfed by the hands that cradled it – a larger mug would be more practical, but the fragile beauty of the fine china appealed to her taste.

There was a creak from the door in the back room. Eyes narrowing, she placed the teacup carefully aside.

'Why don't you come in,' she said, 'rather than skulk about out there?'

'Delighted,' said a voice and a man stepped into the room. He was clad in grey. He wore a mask styled to resemble a human face. The mouth was pulled up in an obscene grin. One arm was held at an odd angle.

'Guests usually enter through the front door,' said Aunt Phillips, studying him. Her legs slowly drew under her, ready to launch her forward.

'Indeed,' said the man, voice muffled behind the mask. 'And so they have.'

She sensed movement behind her, and sprang to her feet, knee forgotten. Four more men were coming down the hall.

'What do you want?' asked Aunt Phillips.

She backed into the middle of the room – better to have space, put the chair between them.

The four men entered the room silently, fanning out into an arc, two very large, one mid size, one small but wiry.

'I beg your pardon,' said the masked man, and Aunt Phillips half turned, attempting to keep them all in view. 'I believe my face may be giving the wrong impression.'

He dragged at the mask and the smile melted into a scowl.

'I am very unhappy with you.'

'Who are you?' asked Aunt Phillips, though she had guessed. She was backing slowly. There was a short wooden staff hidden behind a bureau, if she could reach it.

'Of course, we must observe the niceties, mustn't we? Must stick to the façade? After all, you and I are all about the façade, aren't we? These are my Deadly Sins. I'm embarrassed to say that I do not yet have seven. They are a work in progress. It is hard to get good help when your previous gang has been attacked and roundly beaten. But these lovely men have had the foresight to believe in me and see the possibilities.'

'Get on with it,' growled a heavily muscled man sporting a thick moustache.

'That is Wrath, as you can see,' said the masked man. 'Terribly rude and impatient fellow. Do you want to know who the rest are?'

'Please,' said Aunt Phillips with a nod. Her back touched the bureau.

'The fat man is Gluttony, of course. That should be obvious.'

'That seems rather rude,' said Aunt Phillips, shifting sideways.

'I do not mind,' said Gluttony in an accented voice. Swiss or German. 'I do like to eat.'

'He was a chef, with some rather alarming habits that cost him his position. The well-dressed gentleman is Lust.'

'Enchanted,' grinned the man. He wore his hair long and oiled. His fingers were covered in gold rings. 'My, she is quite delicious, isn't she?'

'You know what it is?' grunted Wrath.

'I do not care in the slightest,' purred Lust. 'It's all one to me.'

'Jayzus, let's jest get on with it without all the talkin', can't we?' said the smaller man.

'And that brings us to Envy. He really can't help it. He's Irish, you see.'

'Feck you.'

'You see? They practically cast themselves. Now I just need the other three. Mind you, I'm not sure how much use Sloth will be in a criminal enterprise.'

'And you are?' She was beside the bureau now, hands behind her back, fingers feeling for the staff.

'How rude of me! Or is it, how rude of you? You do know me, after all. We have met on several occasions. On one, you nearly burned me alive, dispersed my henchmen and disrupted a lucrative deal I had going. On another, we had tea.'

Aunt Phillips nodded to herself. She cleared her throat. 'I'm sorry to say that you have missed my companion. He has gone to London. He will not be returning.'

The masked man shook his head slowly. 'Lies. I know your "companion". And it is not a "he" but a "she".'

'Oh my,' said Lust.

'You are mistaken,' whispered Aunt Phillips.

'No, I'm not. It took me some time to put the pieces together. But I had time, while they tried to put the pieces of my arm back together – not very well, as you will notice. I thought I was looking for a larger man and a youth. But then certain information came to light, from a most helpful poppet, and that led me to... Miss Eliza Bennet.'

'Touch her,' said Aunt Phillips, 'and I will kill you.'

Wrath guffawed.

'You have other things to worry about right now,' said the masked man. 'As do you...Mr Wickham.'

'Ah,' he hissed. 'Well done. Well done. I'd applaud your deduction, but this arm, you see-'

'You should leave while you can.'

'You are in no position to be making threats, you *freak*.'

'Ah,' said Aunt Phillips softly. 'And so you are revealed. You are no gentleman, sir.'

'Maybe not. But now we all see where we stand. Shall we see who amongst us will still be standing soon?'

'It would be my pleasure.' Aunt Phillips swept the staff from behind the bureau and ran at them.

At first, there was just a roaring blackness filling Elizabeth's head.

They ran up the path, through the opened door and into the chaos inside. That warm, welcoming space, invaded and defiled. Glassware smashed, cushions slashed, stuffing scattered like the feathers from a downed bird. Then the arcs of blood. Then their aunt.

Jane ran for the doctor while Elizabeth knelt and cradled the mighty head, her tears falling on the battered and bloodied features. She was aware of screams as Lydia and Kitty came in, then firm hands pulling her aside as the doctor knelt grimly, feeling for damage, listening to the faint gurgling breath.

Then, later still, her father – that the hardest of all. His face falling as sudden and shocking as a granite cliff giving way to a landslide. Sending such a sharp barb through Elizabeth's heart.

Under the doctor's direction, the wounds were bound, the broken bones set, some laudanum trickled into the swollen mouth. They gently lifted her, groaning, and set her in her bed. The doctor spoke to her father in sombre tones, and Mr Bennet nodded his head in weary understanding.

Elizabeth sat, staring at the mottled face, which twitched and frowned in unconscious sleep. Was she still under attack, in her dreaming state? She reached forward and took one of the bandaged hands, and Aunt Phillips' fingers curled around hers. That released the floodgates, and she sobbed and sobbed. It may have been that someone – Jane? – embraced her for a while, but there was nothing but this fragile contact with this beloved, damaged soul, and her anguish.

For was she not the cause?

The thought had to be clamped down, bitten down. It was unbearable. *The opposite of what you want.*

Then the roaring stopped, stilled. Quietened. She kissed Aunt Phillips' forehead, then went into the ruined drawing room. There were others there, whose conversations ceased as she walked in. At her feet lay a shattered staff. She picked up the pieces and put them aside. Then she began gathering the larger pieces of broken crockery, the flakes of delicate china with their fragments of floral designs. Jane knelt beside her, a brush in her hand, sweeping the debris away. Then there was Mary, quietly righting the pieces of furniture that were largely intact.

It was well into the evening by the time the house was in order. The doctor returned and administered more laudanum, a widow with some nursing experience with him, hired by Mr Bennet to sit through the night.

Elizabeth was silent on the walk home, though the younger girls talked, first in quiet tones, then gradually louder the further from the scene they travelled. Jane walked beside her, shooting her glances but respecting her desire to not speak.

At the house, she did not follow them inside. She headed for the old carriage house. She slipped inside, through to the back wall – then stopped. The sliding panel was locked in place by a new, heavy chain. She rattled it, but it was solid. There was no entry to the training room.

'Elizabeth.'

Her father, in the doorway.

'What is this?' she asked.

He stepped into the gloom, moving as if carrying a huge weight.

'An ending.'

'Why?'

'Do you really need to ask?' His voice was unsteady.

'But this is not the answer.'

'No more, Lizzy. No more masks, no more fighting. No more loss.' He rubbed his hands through his hair. 'I am so tired.'

'And I am not. This isn't over for me. After what he has done, he has to pay–'

'But where does it end? Do you not see how each violent act simply leads to another? And that meanwhile the butcher's bill grows ever higher? No. I may yet have lost my dearest friend. I will not risk my daughters. I will not allow them to risk themselves. It was a mistake to let you...After Jane, I should have burned all this to the ground. Stupid.'

'But you said – someone has to stand up. Do the extraordinary.'

'*I was wrong,*' he bellowed. 'This is no game. My God – it is all my fault.'

He slumped to the ground, and she sprang to him.

'No, no! It is my fault! Mine!'

'No,' he groaned, shaking his head. 'This is on me, Lizzy. This is my foolishness. What have I done to you?'

'To me?' She reared back. 'You haven't done anything to me.'

'Oh, but I have. Look at you. Look at what you have become.'

'What am I?' she asked softly, trembling.

'You are broken,' he whispered. 'You are in two halves, and I do not know how to put them back together again.'

He wept against her, and she stared into the darkness, into the place inside where the sea and the rock met with a seething, hissing, endless roar.

Chapter 14

Elizabeth was back by Aunt Phillips' bedside early the next morning. If anything, she looked worse, as the bruising came up in black and purple blotches. The widow reported that she had been restless but had not woken. It had seemed on occasion that she might speak, her swollen lips pulling back from her broken teeth.

'It may be that she was asking for her father, her da,' said the widow. 'People often call out to their parents when they are gravely hurt, no matter their age. Though usually it is their ma they call for.'

Elizabeth thanked her and took up position by the bed, taking up a damp cloth to gently soothe the troubled brow. It was hard to see Aunt Phillips like this. So strong. So full of knowledge and kindness. Such a fierce teacher.

'I hope you made them pay for this,' she whispered.

There had to be multiple attackers. The Wicked Man was a tricky fighter, but there was no way, she was sure, that he could overcome Aunt Phillips in a straight fight. That meant he had managed to recruit some new henchmen. She could ask around – surely someone saw a group of strangers slip into town.

She had to steel herself for the fact that Aunt Phillips may not recover.

Was she indeed calling out as she felt her life slipping away? Calling to her...da?

She frowned. That just didn't sound right. Aunt Phillips was not Irish, so it would be strange for her to adopt that diminutive. Unless...she was trying to say something else. *Da...*

Elizabeth sat forward, a slimy fear uncoiling in her belly.

Darcy?

The Wicked Man had come here, believing Aunt Phillips to be the other Vigil from the action at the canal. What if during the fight, or worse, at the end of it, while Aunt Phillips lay defeated and helpless, what if he had learned the truth?

What if he was now going after Darcy?

She had to warn him.

Darcy didn't know that Wickham and the Wicked Man were one and the same.

She must write at once – but where exactly was he likely to be? There was such an ache in her heart: the need to see him, tell him what had happened, was like a fist in her chest. It was like being whirled about by the dark river water, not knowing which way was up. It was Darcy that she needed now. He would know what to do.

When she returned home, it was to find that Fate had already provided a solution.

A letter had arrived from the Gardiners – of course! She had forgotten all about their plans to visit the Lakes. They were to call by in a day or two and still hoped she would join them on their tour. That meant travelling to the same vicinity as Pemberley. What better place to seek Darcy, or at least learn of where he may be, than his family home?

The forced inaction of the next couple of days was difficult, but she had to console herself with the thought that any letters she sent to London or elsewhere would take just as long or longer to reach him, and she would have no idea of when or even if he read them. The memory of their last meeting haunted her.

She felt guilty taking her leave of Aunt Phillips, who still lay unconscious. But there was nothing to do if she stayed but watch and fret. She felt the tug of action. The hound was sniffing the wind. Damned if she should sit and wait, like a sheepdog guarding the flock. She was the foxhound; she must hunt the prey.

When the Gardiners arrived, Mrs Gardiner took one look at Elizabeth and swiftly bustled her up to her room, citing the need to inspect her packing.

'My dear Lizzy,' she said when the door closed behind them, her eyes dark with concern. 'You look positively...well, I was going to say haunted.'

Tears pricked Elizabeth's eyes, and Mrs Gardiner took her into a warm, strong embrace.

'An accurate description of how I am feeling, dear aunt,' said Elizabeth. 'But I believe we are at a turning point now.'

'Well, I am pleased to hear that. Are you sure you still wish to come away with us?'

'Yes please, Aunt. I believe some time away is just what I need to clear my head.'

'Good. I agree. I...oh my dear, I do not wish to pry, but what on earth has happened to your tooth?'

Once on the road the next day, with all the farewells behind them, Elizabeth did indeed start to feel more herself. Aunt Phillips was showing some small signs of improvement, and Jane had promised to visit her daily and to watch over Mary and Kitty. Lydia had received an invitation from Colonel Forster's wife to visit and so was leaving shortly for Brighton. This had led to something of an argument with her father.

'Is this wise?' Elizabeth asked him.

Lydia was in raptures, flying about the house in restless ecstasy, laughing and talking with more violence than ever.

'She will be very safe with the colonel, you need have no fear.'

'But if you were aware,' replied Elizabeth, the words of Darcy's letter burned in her mind, 'of how her behaviour disadvantages the rest of us–'

'Disadvantage you!' said Mr Bennet. 'What, has she frightened away some of your lovers?'

That stung, too close to the mark. Sometimes, she disliked this part of his character. His teasing and mocking could go too far, come at the wrong moment. But she knew its source: his deep frustration. With his wife, his younger daughters. His age. A wilful second eldest daughter who seemed determined to sacrifice her happiness, even her life, in pursuit of wild ideals.

'I am speaking generally,' she said. 'She needs discipline. If she doesn't change soon it will be too late. She will forever be a flirt with an ignorant and empty mind and this...rage for admiration.'

For a moment she thought she had gone too far, spoken too reprovingly. Her father's face hardened, and he frowned. Her breath caught – it was the face she remembered, the face of the Hound.

'What would you have me do?' he asked harshly. 'Give her a mask? Is that the discipline you propose? No, Elizabeth.' He held up his arms. 'I can still feel her. Jane's weight in my arms, more dead than alive. I will not carry any of my other daughters. I will not steal another of my daughter's youth. Let her be a young girl for as long as she can.'

But then he seemed to deflate, and his hard chin sank into the cushion of his neck, the black light in his eyes faded. He sighed heavily.

'Do not make yourself uneasy, my love. Wherever you and Jane are known, you must be respected and valued. We shall not have peace at Longbourn unless Lydia goes to Brighton. Let her go then. Colonel Forster is a sensible man and will keep her out of any real mischief. At Brighton she will be of less importance – there will be plenty of other women better worth the officers' notice. Let us hope that her being there may teach her her own insignificance.'

Now, lulled by the clopping of the horses' hooves and the sway of the carriage, Elizabeth allowed herself to focus on what lay ahead. The Gardiners were ideal travel companions, content to sit in companionable silence, watching the countryside pass by.

The journey gave Elizabeth time to think. Two faces kept coming to her mind, and it was hard to reconcile them: Wickham's charming, easy smile, and the warped clay grin on the mask of the Wicked Man. Could they really be one and the same man? She wondered if he was also struggling to grasp that the Vigil who had thwarted his plan, broken his arm and nearly drowned him was also the young woman he had enjoyed flirting with. God, that he had sat drinking tea and talking so sweetly to Aunt Phillips, only to return – obviously with help – and beat her so viciously.

His desire for revenge on her – to go so far as to have Meg kill herself, just to punish Elizabeth – it revealed a propensity for cruelty deep within his character. Clearly, he was flawed. And dangerous. And she was sure it was worse because she was a woman. Wickham liked to be the centre of attention. The object of desire. The one in charge. He chafed at Darcy having power over him. And he believed fundamentally that he was above women. So to be brought down by one...It had triggered a murderous rage within him.

He was like a rabid dog. He had to be stopped.

She turned to the Gardiners.

'I believe we shall be passing very near Pemberley. Might we go and see it?'

'I would indeed very much like to see it again,' replied Mrs Gardiner. 'I know that Mr Darcy is not your favourite, but the house and grounds are truly exquisite.'

'Then we shall make enquiries with the head housekeeper for a tour,' said Mr Gardiner, knocking on the carriage roof. 'And if we do encounter Mr Darcy, I am sure you can ignore him.'

'Indeed,' said Elizabeth.

Chapter 15

Having spent the night at a comfortable inn, the morning saw them heading for Darcy's home. When they turned in at the keeper's lodge, Elizabeth was in a state of agitation. She needed to see Darcy to deliver her warning but keenly felt the awkwardness that must surely arise from seeing him face to face after their encounters at Rosings.

The park was very large, and once through the gate they drove for some time through a beautiful wood. The well-kept road gradually ascended in gentle sweeps until they came to a point where the trees thinned, and they crested the hill. The eye was instantly caught by Pemberley House itself, situated on the opposite side of a small valley. It was a large, handsome stone building backed by a ridge of wooded hills. Two wings stretched from the main house. The drive circled in front, containing a well-manicured patch of lawn. A natural stream ran along one side.

The beauty of the place relaxed her. An idle thought pictured what it could be like to live in such a place, but then she caught herself and shoved the thought aside – that wasn't something that was ever going to happen.

They descended the hill and drove around the circular drive to the main doors. They alighted, and the horses were led around the back by a solemn groundsman for watering while they climbed the stairs and were admitted to the hall. It was a grand space, with a split staircase before them rising to the upper floors.

The housekeeper met them and very civilly agreed to show them about. They followed her into the dining parlour, which was large and attractively furnished. Large windows looked out onto the grounds, allowing sunlight to spill into the room. They passed on, through a library lined with bookcases full of volumes. Each subsequent room was as lofty and handsome. Elizabeth saw with admiration that Darcy's taste was neither gaudy nor uselessly fine: it had less splendour but more real elegance than the furniture at Rosings.

'And of this place, I might have been mistress,' she mused, before mentally shaking herself again and reminding herself why she was here. This was a mission, not a sightseeing trip. She really needed to ask the housekeeper if he was present, but somehow her nerve failed her.

Luckily, at that moment, her uncle spoke up, asking if the master was at home.

'No,' said the housekeeper, 'but we expect him tomorrow.'

An absurd surge of relief ran through Elizabeth. She was off the hook today but could hope to return to speak to him tomorrow. Or possibly leave a note after all, despite her initial feelings that she should speak to him directly.

Her aunt wandered over to a series of portraits lining one wall.

'Which is your master?' she asked.

'This one. It was painted some eight years ago, but is still very like him.'

'It is a handsome face,' said Mrs Gardiner. 'Is it a good likeness, Lizzy?'

The housekeeper looked at her with greater respect. 'Does the young lady know Mr Darcy?'

Elizabeth coloured and said, 'A little.'

'And do you not think him a very handsome gentleman, ma'am?'

'Yes, very handsome.' She noticed a blank space beside it. 'Did there used to be another portrait here?'

The housekeeper's face darkened. 'Yes. Of the older Mr Darcy's protégé. I am afraid he turned out very wild, and the younger Mr Darcy directed the picture be removed. Would you like to see one of Miss Darcy? This one was done some time ago.' The housekeeper suddenly blinked rapidly – it appeared her eyes had filled with tears.

'Well,' said Mrs Gardner after a moment. 'It appears you think very highly of them both.'

'Yes, ma'am. I could not hope for better. Both are the sweetest tempered, most generous-hearted people in the world.'

Elizabeth stared at her – could this really be the same Darcy she spoke of?

After touring the upper floors, the housekeeper handed them over to the head groundsman, John, who met them at the hall door. The gardens were as exquisite as the house itself. They walked around the side of the house towards the stables, alongside a thick hedge, and came upon an open field with several archery butts set at one end.

'Your master likes to shoot?' asked Mr Gardiner.

'He is an uncommon fine archer,' said John.

'I rather used to enjoy archery myself when I was a lad.'

Mrs Gardiner patted her husband on the arm.

At that moment, Darcy walked around the corner.

Elizabeth could only stare, her face reddening. Darcy's eyes went first to the groundsman, and he lifted a hand in warm greeting. He then looked to her uncle and aunt, and a small polite smile crossed his face. Then his eyes scanned to her, and he stopped dead, the smile freezing then disappearing.

'Miss Bennet,' he said at last. 'The housekeeper informed me that we had visitors. But I had no idea that you were in the neighbourhood.'

'Mr Darcy, please allow me to present my uncle and aunt, Mr and Mrs Gardiner. I am touring with them in Derbyshire.'

Darcy bowed.

'I came on ahead a day early. A party follows behind, some of whom are known to you. And what of the house? Do you like it? And the grounds?'

'They are very beautiful,' said Elizabeth. He seemed to be only half listening.

'And your journey? Your family?'

'The journey was fine, and my family is well.'

'Good, good. Shall we all walk on? Allow me to escort you personally. Thank you, John.'

He drew the groundsman aside and the two spoke quietly for a minute, then clasped hands. Darcy clapped him on the shoulder as he walked off, touching his cap to Elizabeth and her aunt and uncle as he went.

'We do not wish to interrupt–'

'It would be my pleasure. There is a feature up ahead I believe you will enjoy.'

Mrs Gardiner looked questioningly at Elizabeth as they continued.

While Darcy proved an excellent guide, informative and interested, Elizabeth could not help but notice he seemed somewhat agitated beneath his cool exterior. Eventually, as they strolled alongside the stream, the Gardiners, arm in arm, pulled ahead, and she found herself alone alongside Darcy.

'I am sorry,' she said. 'I daresay I am the last person you wished to find wandering about your estate.'

He smiled a little. 'Hardly the last. I will admit to being somewhat surprised, however. I would have thought, given our last...meeting...that you would have done anything to avoid seeing me.'

'But I did want to see you. I need to warn you.'

'Oh?' His tone was casual, but she sensed a sharpening of interest beneath it.

'It is the Wicked Man. He isn't dead.'

'Ah. Well. You need not have bothered yourself, coming all this way, to warn me about a ha'penny villain like that. Indeed, he is barely worth the title.'

'It's Wickham.'

'Wait...What? What's Wickham?'

'The Wicked Man and Wickham. They are one and the same.'

He was silent. She shot a look at him. He was staring at the ground ahead, face white, brow furrowed. She could see his jaw working, like he was physically chewing over what she had said.

'How do you know this?' he ground out thickly.

'Because it all fits! And you do wrong to dismiss him so. He is evil and dangerous! He...'

Her words caught in her throat, and she stumbled, her vision suddenly blurry. She felt Darcy grip her arm, steady her. She sucked in a long slow breath, and told him of the girl on the bridge. The mesmerism. Aunt Phillips.

'Hellfire,' said Darcy after a minute. 'Damnation! I cannot...*Him?*' There was a long pause, then: 'I owe you a very great apology.'

'He has made an art of disguising himself. I did not see it myself. Not in time.'

'I should have killed him. I *would* have killed him, but, the situation is complicated. I am sorry that you have been drawn into it.'

'Well, in it we are. The question is, what do we do next?'

'Find him. And stop him.'

'How?'

'We will make use of the assets of the Best Men. Fear not, he will be located. Leave that to us. Meanwhile, we must look to your safety.'

Elizabeth shook her head. 'I do not think I personally am in danger. At least, not yet. He seems determined to teach me a lesson first, and believes you are in companionship with me.'

Darcy grunted. 'You need not worry about my safety. This estate is well protected. John and my other groundsmen are former soldiers. It is your own family's safety you should look to.'

She had no ready answer. She had come, when she could have sent a message instead. He was looking at her curiously, and she feared she was about to blush. What on earth was the matter with her?

They were forced to drop the conversation at that point, for the path had taken them around to the other side of the house to a beautiful large pond. The Gardiners were standing admiring it, and Elizabeth and Darcy joined them.

'Do you fish, sir?' asked Mr Gardiner.

'It was not made for that purpose,' replied Darcy. 'If you enjoy fishing, however, there is excellent sport in the stream.'

'Ah! I must say, I was admiring your archery ground, too.'

'Then you must come and shoot if you have time. Or fish. There is spare gear for both activities in one of the outbuildings. Go and have a look, if you wish.'

Mr Gardiner grinned at Mrs Gardiner. 'Do you mind, my dear?'

'Oh, come on then,' replied Mrs Gardiner, and they walked off.

'They are very nice,' observed Mr Darcy, then stopped, colouring slightly. Unspoken, the other words hung in the air: *unlike the rest of your family*. Elizabeth was searching for some way to say that she understood, that her family did indeed mortify her and fill her with embarrassment, but the pause was growing longer, more uncomfortable.

'There you are, brother!'

They both looked up at the sound of the high voice calling from the hedgerow. A girl was coming along the path, pushed in a wicker wheelchair by a servant. She appeared to be about 16. Darcy turned to Elizabeth with a sudden relieved smile.

'Miss Elizabeth, please allow me the honour of introducing you to one who has longed to meet you. May I present my sister, Miss Georgiana Darcy?'

Elizabeth smiled and stepped forward to take the girl's proffered hand. Georgiana looked up at her somewhat shyly as Darcy's words ran through her head: *she has longed to meet me?*

'I'm ready, brother,' said Georgiana.

'Of course,' said Darcy, then hesitated. 'Although we have guests.'

'Oh,' said Georgiana, her face falling. 'Yes, of course.'

'Please,' said Elizabeth quickly. 'Do not let me interrupt anything.'

Darcy looked at her gratefully. 'It is just that the doctors suggested it is the best thing for her. So if you do not mind?'

'Not at all. I do not wish to intrude. I will find my uncle and aunt and–'

'Oh please don't go just yet!' said Georgiana. 'Please stay. You can watch me fly!'

Elizabeth smiled at the girl, then looked away in some surprise as Darcy swiftly removed his jacket and pulled off his boots. Now clad only in his shirt and breeches, he removed the blanket that covered his sister's legs and scooped her from the chair.

'Ready?'

She nodded and hung onto his neck, and he waded into the pond. The girl shrieked as the water covered her. Darcy plunged on into the deeper water. He let go of her, swiftly catching her hands, and pulled her along behind him.

'Are you kicking?' he asked her. 'It does not feel as if you are kicking.'

'I am kicking,' she shouted, then looked up at Elizabeth gleefully. 'Do you see, Miss Eliza? I am flying!'

Elizabeth watched the older brother pull his broken sister through the water, struck dumb by the intimacy of the scene before her. The girl laughed, carefree, urging her brother to pull her faster, and he plunged about the pond, dragging her behind. Finally, Darcy led Georgiana to the shallows and bent to lift her again, her simple white shift clinging wetly to her. Darcy's own shirt was plastered to his body, and Elizabeth could see the definition of his musculature. He carried her dripping from the water – God, the strength and joy and light of the scene, such a counterpoint to that image that haunted her, that other man carrying a half-drowned girl down the drive – and set her gently back in her chair, before covering her with the blanket.

'Could Miss Elizabeth help me change?' asked Georgiana. 'If that is not too much of an imposition?'

Darcy looked at her.

'I can do that,' said Elizabeth. 'Please, allow me to help.'

'If you are sure.' He dismissed the maid. 'There is a change of clothing ready in that outbuilding.'

Darcy wheeled the girl to the doorway of the small building, and then Elizabeth manoeuvred her inside. The interior was neat and orderly, with towels and clean clothing arrayed on a bench. She helped pull the girl's sodden shift over her head, and something silver fell clattering from the chair. She bent to retrieve it and was surprised to find a small, thin dirk.

'Sorry,' said Georgiana. 'I should have tucked that away better.'

'Do you always carry a knife?'

'Yes. Fitzwilliam insists. He wishes me to be able to defend myself in case he is not around and...well...'

Elizabeth studied the earnest pretty face, reversed her grip and handed the weapon over.

'Do you know how to use it?'

'Somewhat. Fitz has shown me.'

She didn't ask the next question she really wanted to – *do you think you could*?

'Of course, I'm no Vigile, like you and Fitz,' said Georgiana shyly.

'What has he told you?' asked Elizabeth quickly.

'Oh. I am sorry. I probably shouldn't have let on that I know.'

'It is fine,' said Elizabeth, though inside she was reeling. That Darcy should discuss such an intimate thing about her. She realised Georgiana was watching her closely.

'What is it like? To be a female Vigile?'

Elizabeth paused. Her mind was crowded with images – the canal, the rooftop. The bridge.

'Oh, it is perhaps not as exciting as one might suppose.'

Georgiana nodded slowly.

'I expect you want to ask me,' said the girl. 'About my legs. Unless Fitz told you?'

'No, he did not tell me.' A strange pang here, that he had not trusted her in the same way he of course trusted his sister.

'It was the strangest thing.' The girl went still, her gaze sliding off into the distance. 'I was so sure I loved him; we were going to elope. But then Fitz and the colonel turned up. It seems like a dream, now.' She touched her cheek, then looked down at her thin legs.

Elizabeth squatted beside her. 'What happened, Georgiana?' she asked softly.

'I just...I just wanted to fly. I saw Fitz, and he was so angry. I could see how badly he wanted to hurt George. And this strange desire took hold of me. I remember walking to the window, and someone shouting at me, but I opened it – it was the second storey – and I...'

She wiped her eyes and smiled at Elizabeth, sniffing.

'Well, the doctors say if I keep exercising, I may be able to walk one day. I would dearly love to dance again. It is a hard thing, to be trapped in this chair all day.' Her small hands had formed into fists, and she lightly beat the arms of the wheelchair. 'I still wish to fly, you know. And I do, when I am in the water with Fitz.'

'I know,' said Elizabeth. 'I saw you. You fly very well.'

She took up a towel and gently rubbed the girl's hair. Georgiana reached up and squeezed her hand.

'He is so kind to me,' she murmured. 'He is the best of brothers. The best of men.'

'Here,' said Elizabeth, and she slipped a clean gown over the girl's head.

Chapter 16

Awaking at the inn the next morning, with the golden light pouring into her room, Elizabeth felt a sense of peace she had not experienced for some time. The knowledge of Wickham and all he had done was still there, but it seemed somehow a little more distant, less intrusive in her thoughts. When she joined her uncle and aunt at breakfast, she found she had a good appetite.

'Are you ready for the day, dear?' asked Mrs Gardiner. Elizabeth noted a knowing smile that passed between her uncle and aunt as she ate.

Darcy and Georgiana had insisted she return to join the party arriving that day for luncheon. And so leaving the Gardiners to tour by themselves, she found herself mid-morning being picked up by a carriage from Pemberley and escorted back to that house. She was led into a grand drawing room and within, she found Georgiana, who called out to her with delight, along with Darcy and several others. Bingley sprang to his feet when he saw her and bade her to come and sit beside him. Mrs Hurst and Miss Bingley were also in attendance, though their greetings were much cooler – thin smiles and bare curtsies. Darcy was seated between them – indeed, held hostage between them, such was their body language. It almost made her laugh aloud.

You cannot trap him.

In seeing Bingley, her thoughts flew to her sister – oh, how she wished to know if any of his own were directed in a like manner. All the anger she had felt towards him, at the ease with which he was dissuaded from Netherfield and Jane, evaporated in the face of his earnest delight in seeing her. It was a little awkward at first, which she first took to be a sign of guilty feelings, but as he spoke, at first barely looking her in the face for long, she realised it was something else. In a moment when the rest of the party were loudly discussing a mutual acquaintance, he leaned towards her and said:

'Miss Elizabeth, I wish to speak for a moment *in the open*. I wish to offer you my deepest apologies. Darcy has told me something of your... exploits. And that you, in turn, know that I am...that I am...' He glanced at the others, then whispered, 'Bingo Boy.'

'Yes,' said Elizabeth solemnly. 'I know.'

'Then, you may recall that I, when neither I nor Darcy knew it was you, that I grabbed...Well, I offer you my most sincere, deepest, humblest apologies.'

Elizabeth stared for a moment at his red face, then suddenly recalled what he must be referring to: Darcy, standing over them as Bingley pinned her to the ground. She blushed red herself, mumbled her acceptance of his apology, but neither could meet the other's eye for some moments.

'Are all your sisters at Longbourn?' he finally asked. There was not much in the question, but there was a look on his face that made her heart jump.

'Now, yes,' she replied. 'But did you know that Jane had been in London?'

'No! I would have called on her! She is...well, I do not need to tell you how beautiful she is.'

'She is that.' She hesitated. 'She is like a lake. No matter what you see on the surface, you do not know what depths lay beneath it.'

Bingley nodded thoughtfully. She glanced towards Mr Darcy and saw him looking back at her. At that moment Miss Bingley turned to speak to Darcy, and noticed with narrowed eyes the look being exchanged between them.

'Pray, Miss Eliza,' she called, causing the others to cease talking and look towards her, 'is not the regiment removed from Meryton? That must be a great loss to your sisters. No, wait, to yourself, too – were you not fond of one them as well? All the Bennets adore an officer in a red coat.'

She fought to control the surge of distress that rose within her at the ill-natured attack on her family. She could see Darcy stiffen and look towards Georgiana, who frowned in confusion. He rose to his feet.

'I believe we are being called through to dinner.'

The dozen or so guests readied themselves at the dining room doors, which were still closed. Elizabeth, a little ahead of Miss Bingley, heard her whisper to Darcy behind her: 'How very ill Eliza Bennet looks, Mr Darcy. I never in my life saw anyone so altered as she since we were trapped in that dreadful place. She is grown so brown and coarse! Louisa and I were agreeing that we barely recognised her.'

Elizabeth felt her jaw clench. She kept facing rigidly forward while straining to hear how Darcy replied but he remained silent. She wondered if she may feign falling sick, ask for a carriage and get out of this house and away from these creatures.

'I remember,' continued Miss Bingley, 'when we first saw her in Hertfordshire, how amazed we all were to find she was reputed a beauty! I could never see any beauty in her face, her eyes have a sharp, shrewish look, and her teeth – well! It is no small wonder you said that one evening at Netherfield, "She a beauty? I should as soon call her mother a wit." How we laughed.'

The air sucked out of her lungs. Then she heard Darcy clear his throat.

'Yes,' he said, 'but that was only when I first knew her, for it is many months since I have considered her as one of the handsomest women of my acquaintance.'

Then the doors of the dining room opened, and Darcy was brushing past her. She felt the heat of him as he passed, though they did not make eye contact. She stopped abruptly, dead in her tracks, half turned, braced, and Miss Bingley walked straight into her pointed elbow. The breath left her body in a loud surprised 'oof!'. Elizabeth cried out in feigned concern and grabbed her, apparently accidentally stepping right on her toes.

'How very clumsy of me,' said Elizabeth, fingers sinking into Caroline's soft arm. 'Forgive me. We must all *be careful how we go, mustn't we?*'

She looked into Caroline's eyes, let her mask slip, let the other woman *see her, really see her – all she had witnessed, all she had done.* Caroline Bingley went white as a sheet, stuttered out her forgiveness, found herself half-curtseying, then stumbled away down the table. She did not look in Elizabeth's direction once during the meal and barely touched her food.

Seated between Bingley and Georgiana, Elizabeth started to relax. The gentleman's good cheer and the quiet gratitude of the girl warmed her, and the rest of the afternoon passed by comfortably.

That evening, as she lay in her bed at the inn, her thoughts swirled around Darcy. Once, he had loved her. Wanted to marry her. And she, in her ignorance, had spat it back in his face. Yet instead of hating her for that, he had instead wanted nothing but to explain himself, get her to see past her prejudice. Instead of avoiding her, as he had every right to do, he had welcomed her. She rolled over, pulling the blanket beneath her chin. She had come, had seen him, had warned him, and now they were at... peace? Yes, that was where things stood, and she must be content with that.

In the morning, she found she had slept late and had been allowed to do so by her aunt and uncle, who left a note stating their desire to undertake a long walk before they continued their journey later that afternoon. When she went to take her breakfast, Elizabeth was pleased to see a letter waiting for her in Jane's handwriting. But her joy was quickly dashed as she read what the letter contained.

'Dear Lizzy,' wrote Jane, 'I hardly know what to write, but I have terrible news for you, and it cannot be delayed. Lydia is missing. She did not arrive in Brighton, and it now seems the whole thing was a fabrication. Colonel Forster and his wife were not expecting her. The letter had come from a different party, specifically to entice Lydia away from the protection of her family. Oh Lizzy, it is Wickham. He has proven himself as wicked as the character he adopts.

'Our poor mother is beside herself. She is very ill, and keeps her room. Our father bears it a little better, though I have never seen him so affected – not since the night of those events you know of. As far as they know, it is only that Lydia has run away with Wickham, which is bad enough. I have not dared reveal to them the extra intelligence of who he really is. I do not think they could survive the news...One of their own daughters in the clutches of such a villain. Bad enough that they think her run off with a cad.

'To Kitty it does not seem wholly unexpected, though she tries to dissemble, so there was secret contact between Wickham and Lydia before she left. She has been duped by him, obviously thinking he means to marry her. Perhaps he does, but a terrible part of me fears that this is not his intention. Oh Lizzy, how can a man be so evil as to target a young girl like this? I can scarcely believe that such blackness should reside inside him yet not show through his superficial charm. We are all fools. All fooled.

'All that is known is that they were seen on the London road. We learned this from Colonel Forster himself, who, upon learning of the deception, sought to trace them and ended up coming on to Longbourn. He says a number of his men have deserted, as well – I do not know if this is connected, but thought it best to tell you all that I know.

'I know that I should rise to this occasion, when the family needs me, but you have always been the stronger one, Lizzy. I beg you to return as soon as possible. Father is speaking of going to London to search for them. What he means to do, I know not, but his excessive distress will not allow him to pursue any measures in the best and safest way. We need you. Lydia, fool that she is, needs you. Come quickly.'

'Oh, where is my aunt, my uncle?' cried Elizabeth. Her stomach was knotted tight, acid rising in the back of her throat. She looked wildly about the room, ran to the window and looked desperately out left and right, but the figures of the Gardiners were nowhere in view.

It could scarcely be borne. She was so far away. She had let them down, left them defenceless. All because...because...Why was she here? *Stupid, stupid*! It could not be contained. She bent, and from her raw throat came a harsh roar of rage that shook her to her core.

The door burst open, and she spun towards it, eyes blurry with tears. *Darcy.*

'Good God, what is the matter?' he cried. He strode swiftly in, scanning the room. 'Is there someone here? Are you unwell?'

Elizabeth's knees buckled, but before she could fall, he was there, lifting her into a chair.

'Let me call a maid. Or get you some wine.'

'My uncle, my aunt...' she managed to gasp out.

'I will send for them.'

He was gone for a moment, then was back by her side. He noticed the paper crumpled in her hand.

'What is this?'

'Dreadful news from Longbourn.' She burst into tears and for a few minutes could not speak. Darcy could only wait in wretched suspense, observing her in silence.

'A letter from Jane,' she finally managed, 'with such dreadful news. My youngest sister is in the clutches of Wickham. Either eloped or kidnapped or some combination of the two. They are gone off together. You know him too well to doubt the rest. She has no money, no connections to tempt him to do the honest thing – she is lost forever. And it is all because of me.' Her voice began to rise in her anguish. 'It is my fault. I could have prevented this. I should have stayed home. Instead I...I thought only of myself. Oh, you are right, sir. I am no Vigil.'

Darcy made a chopping motion with his hand. 'No more of that. I am shocked. But is it certain? Absolutely certain?'

'Oh yes. They have been traced to London. But I do not know how we will find them.'

Darcy made no answer, but began pacing the room. Elizabeth hung her head. The shame of it, on so many levels. When it became public knowledge, the scandal would stain the family for decades. What did that mean for poor Jane? Everything was sinking. Must sink, under such proof of family weakness, such an assurance of the deepest disgrace.

And she...Her desire to come here, see Darcy. More weakness. And she could finally see, crystal clear, her selfish desire. She looked up at his brooding face and never had she felt so honestly that she could have loved him, as now, when all love must be in vain.

Here was an ending, as sure as the last page of the story having been turned and the volume tucked away on some untidy shelf.

As she watched, his face hardened, turned cold and fixed as stone. She felt her body turn to water, formless. A silly thing, to mourn the death of a hope so small she had scarcely acknowledged its existence to herself.

She covered her face with her handkerchief, craving some escape from this new existence. After a pause of several minutes, Darcy spoke.

'I am afraid there is nothing I can do now to relieve your distress. Your uncle and aunt cannot be far now, and so I shall take my leave.' She heard his quiet step move to the door then pause. 'I assure you that I will say nothing of this.'

And then he was gone.

His leaving was something of a relief, for now she could release the tears that welled behind her eyes. She cried for all of them: for Jane, whose fear to show the depth of her feeling had cost her a future with Bingley. For Lydia, whose shallowness made her such an easy target. For herself... How ridiculous she was, fancying herself some kind of hero when her hurt feelings had led her to suspect the innocent whilst allowing the actual villain to sway her with the compliment of his easy attention. Those same hurt feelings rebuffed Darcy, and then here she was, chasing after him just like Lydia and Kitty after any officer, when she should be home with her family, protecting them. She had proven her character to be as torn and battered as the armour she wore to hide her very weakness from herself.

She was wild to be at home. To hear, to see, to be upon the spot, to share with Jane in the cares that must now fall wholly upon her, in a family so deranged: a father absent, a mother incapable of sensible thought and action.

Then she heard hurried steps outside the door, and the Gardiners swept in, alarmed by the servant's somewhat garbled account of their niece having taken violently ill. Elizabeth quickly gave a truncated account of what had happened, punctuated by their cries of surprise and horror. Lydia had never particularly been a favourite, but they still saw the risk to her and the effect upon them all.

'Please,' said Elizabeth. 'I must go home at once.'

'Of course,' cried her uncle, and he strode from the room, calling loudly for the servants to make ready the carriage.

Within the hour, their luggage was packed and loaded, the account at the inn settled, and the three set off, grim faced, on the return journey to Longbourn.

Chapter 17

They travelled fast, stopping for one unrestful night at an inn and arriving by dinner time the next day. Elizabeth jumped from the carriage before it had come to a complete stop, at the same time as the front door opened and Jane flew down the steps. They embraced, both promptly bursting into tears.

'Is there news?' asked Elizabeth.

Jane shook her head, biting her lip.

'And how is our father? And Mother?'

'They shall both be the better for seeing you home safe. Oh Lizzy, I am so glad to see you!'

'It must have been very hard for you. I am so sorry I was not here. I should have been here.'

Jane gently cupped her face. 'I have no doubt you blame yourself, but you must not. None of us saw this coming. And I cannot imagine how terrible it must have been for you to receive such news in a letter, so far from home.'

'Dear Jane. You always think of others before yourself, don't you?' She suddenly thought of Bingley. 'I have so much to tell you, but first I must see Father.'

Leaving Jane with the Gardiners, she rushed into the house, which felt strangely quiet. At the closed door of her father's library she paused, listening, then knocked softly. When there was no reply, she knocked again a little harder and opened the door.

Her father was slouched in his chair, which he had turned to face the window. His head rested on one hand, an open volume held open forgetfully in the other, as he stared into space. Lizzy knelt at his side and kissed him, feeling the coarseness of his whiskers beneath her lips. He closed his eyes and for a moment pressed his head against hers. He coughed, then cleared his throat.

'He will want money, you can be sure of that. It will be a kind of ransom, for her good name.'

'Let us first find him,' said Elizabeth. 'And then we can see what must be done.'

'No.' Mr Bennet shook his head. 'There is no point in that. We must wait for him to make contact and tell us what he wants. We can only hope that it is an amount we can pay.'

'It is he who should pay, for what he has done.'

'None of that. I told you, we are done with that. Besides, it is a just punishment for my sins. I should have listened to you, shouldn't I, Lizzy? You tried to warn me. She is far sillier than I imagined. A silly daughter for a silly father.'

'You are not silly, sir.'

'Blind, then. I should have seen what this Wickham was. I used to pride myself on getting the measure of a man, but you seemed to like him.'

'He had me fooled, as well. If anyone was blind, it was I. I was in the better position to see his character but allowed my prejudice to colour my judgement.'

Mr Bennet stared at her, his eyes suddenly bright. 'I am so sorry, my dear, that you should be so much like me.'

The Gardiners determined to stay on at Longbourn to assist where they could. With Mr Bennet barely stirring from his study, Mr Gardiner took over the situation, declaring the young couple must surface soon for want of money. Meanwhile, Colonel Forster had sent parties to London and on the road north searching for news. The runaways were sure to be spotted.

Elizabeth was painfully aware that she knew more of the situation than the others apart from Jane. Like her, she could not decide if telling the truth about Wickham and his activities as the Wicked Man could do any good. Surely it would rather do nothing more than instil greater fear, since it made it even less likely that he intended to marry Lydia and salvage her name.

But she was sure that she would hear from him. For, was not making her suffer the very reason for the kidnapping? It seemed impossible to just sit still, to do nothing, but her reason told her that there was nothing to be gained by jumping on a horse and riding...where? To go and search London? No, hard as it was, there was nothing for it but to wait.

At least it gave her time to visit Aunt Phillips, who still lay unconscious, though sometimes she stirred and moaned. Her big, broad face was swollen and discoloured, but her breathing was easier and the doctor felt there was a good chance she would wake. Of course, what state her reason would be in was anyone's guess, as she had taken such heavy blows to the head. When Elizabeth touched her aunt's chin, she felt the rasp of whiskers and quickly called for a basin and razor. Aunt Phillips would be horrified to find herself in such a state.

The days passed in suffocating slowness, the air thick with foreboding. Longbourn was as quiet as a house in mourning.

Then one morning, a package arrived for her – a large, heavy cardboard box.

'Have you been ordering clothes without asking me if I wanted anything?' said Kitty with a pout.

Elizabeth excused herself and carried the parcel up to her room. Lifting aside the lid and folding back the paper within revealed a burnished gleam. Her fingers touched smooth stiffness, and she lifted out a leather jerkin. It was fashioned from deep-burgundy leather, almost black. Embossed upon the chest was a letter 'E'. There were laced leather leggings of the same colour and materiel, and a pair of light but sturdy boots. Parts of the armour were soft as butter, but key sections were stiffer, reinforced. Even the small steel eyelets for the laces were coloured the same dark red. She lifted it to sniff, then suddenly froze – who was it from? What if this was a trap, sent by Wickham? Perhaps the armour was sabotaged or poisoned.

But then she noticed a folded piece of paper tucked in the side of the box – she recognised the hand instantly.

'Although we must keep in mind that we cannot save everyone,' the note read, 'that should not dissuade us from trying. D.'

There was a postscript at the bottom: 'I hope the fit is correct. I largely had to guess.'

And below that, another: 'This, of course, is no costume. This is a uniform, as befits a true Vigile.'

She tucked the pieces back into the box, shoved it under her bed, then sat staring out the window. It was hard to grasp. She felt the need to rein in her mind, which was racing too far ahead, her heartrate beating an accompaniment. It seemed to signal such a reversal. She must be careful not to read too much into this. She had done nothing but misread him ever since she met him.

After dark, to the sound of Jane's fitful sleep, she slipped the box from beneath her bed and drew the contents out again. The trousers slid up her legs, the jacket cinched snugly about her torso. There was even a sheath for her baton on the left sleeve. She felt tight but not constrained: muscular, powerful. She thrust the window open, swung a leg out, marvelling at the smoothness of the leather. Down the trellis she went, her soft boots making not a sound. She dropped the last few feet and crouched, then stood, arms held out. The half moon shone, but the armour appeared black in the darkness. She ran lightly across the lawn, away from the house. The night belonged to her.

In a sheltered clearing, she ran through a range of movements – punches, kicks. Mimed throws. She dove at the ground, rolled, feeling the cushioning sewn within the armour take the brunt of the impact. She kicked and bucked and rolled, and the armour moved with her. So different to her stiff, battered old suit.

It was perfect. It was indeed no costume: it was a weapon.

Let Wickham come. Let them meet. It was not his place to give or withhold what she wanted.

She would take it.

Chapter 18

The family were sitting together in the dining room when their attention was caught by the sound of a carriage. It was too early in the morning for visitors, and Kitty, spying out the window, cried out that the chaise and four driving up the lawn was very expensive looking indeed and thus unlikely to belong to any of their neighbours.

'Could it be news about Lydia?' asked Jane.

Elizabeth squeezed her hand, her own heartrate suddenly rocketing.

'Someone's coming in,' cried Kitty, running to sit by Mrs Bennet's side.

Elizabeth heard the front door open and the swift steps of one of their servants, then the door was flung open and Lady Catherine swept into the room. She carried with her more than her usually ungracious air and made no other reply to Elizabeth's surprised salutation than a slight inclination of the head. She sat down without a word, making no request for introductions.

The Bennet family looked from Elizabeth to Lady Catherine and back again.

After sitting a moment longer, her Ladyship said stiffly to Elizabeth, 'That lady I suppose is your mother.'

'She is, madam.'

'And these, I suppose, are your sisters.'

'Yes, madam,' said Mrs Bennet, finding her voice. 'This is my eldest, Jane, and two of her younger sisters, Mary and Kitty. My other daughter is–'

'You have a very small park here,' said Lady Catherine.

'It is nothing in comparison with Rosings, my lady, I dare say, but I assure you, it is much larger than Sir William Lucas's.'

'This must be a most inconvenient sitting room for the evening. In summer the windows are full west.'

Mrs Bennet blinked, then assured her Ladyship that they never sat there after dinner.

'Lady Catherine,' said Elizabeth, 'do you perhaps have a letter for me from Charlotte?'

Delivery of a letter seemed the only probable motivation for a visit Lady Catherine obviously was not enjoying. But the lady frowned.

'I have not.'

'Oh,' said Elizabeth. 'Did she not know that you–'

'Miss Bennet, walk with me.' The old lady stood, looking about expectantly.

'Go, my dear,' cried Mrs Bennet. 'Show her Ladyship some of our different walks!'

Elizabeth obeyed, showing Lady Catherine outside. As they walked down the gravel path, there came the crunching of other footsteps behind them, and glancing back, Elizabeth was surprised to see Mrs Jenkinson following them at a discrete distance.

'Is Miss de Bourgh not with you?' Elizabeth asked, receiving nothing but a grunt in reply.

Lady Catherine walked swiftly on, and it seemed more that she was drawing Elizabeth away from the house than it was Elizabeth showing her the grounds. When they finally entered a clearing in the midst of a grove, Lady Catherine came to an abrupt stop and spun to face her.

'You can be at no loss, Miss Bennet, to understand the reason for my journey hither. Your own heart, you own conscience, must tell you why I come.'

Elizabeth could only frown in bewilderment.

'Indeed, you are mistaken, madam. I have no idea why you are visiting here.'

Her Ladyship's eyes narrowed, matching her pinched nostrils. 'Miss Bennet,' she hissed. 'You ought to know, I am not to be trifled with. There are many who made that mistake and paid the price. A report of a most alarming nature reached me two days ago. What do you have to say for yourself?'

'I would say I would need to know more about the nature of this report if I am to comment.'

'Really? Just so? You will still seek to obfuscate, still seek to hide how you have insinuated yourself into a world in which you do not belong? Even now?'

'Lady Catherine, I do not know what you are talking about.'

'I am talking about Darcy!'

Elizabeth's mind whirled.

'Do you deny it?' snarled Lady Catherine, her bony finger jabbing at Elizabeth's face. 'Do you?'

'Deny what? That I have seen him? That is no secret, we saw him at–'

'Do you deny you seek to marry him?'

The last had been delivered as a shout, and Lady Catherine fought to bring herself back under control. Mrs Jenkinson stood nearby, watching silently.

'I know it is a scandalous falsehood. I will not seek to injure my nephew by making inquiry of him, so I instead resolved to set off for this place, that I might interrogate you.'

'If you believed it impossible to be true, I wonder why you took the trouble of coming so far?'

'To insist upon having such a report universally contradicted!'

'Your coming to Longbourn,' said Elizabeth coolly, 'seems rather a confirmation of it. If, indeed, such a report exists.'

'*If!* You dare say *if* to *me*, with the intelligence-gathering resources I have at my disposal?'

'You mean Mr Collins?'

'I have more than just him! Now, you tell me – has not this report been industriously circulated by you?'

'It has not.'

'And can you likewise declare, with such easy certainty, that there is no foundation for it?'

'Lady Catherine, you may ask questions, but I shall not necessarily choose to answer.'

'This is not to be borne! Miss Bennet, I insist on being satisfied. Has he, my nephew, made you an offer of marriage?'

'Your Ladyship has declared it to be impossible.'

'It ought to be so. Yet for all his strengths, and his position in my organisation, he is still a man. And your arts and allurements may, in a moment of infatuation, have made him forget what he owes to himself and to his family. You may have drawn him in.'

'You make me sound like something of a villain.'

'In this, I believe you are. I do not like the way you have suddenly appeared. I do not like the influence you seem to possess. I do not like finding that some of my best agents have gone to London and appear to be doing your bidding. I am the nearest relation he has in the world. I should be the one who is closest to him. I am entitled to know all his dearest concerns.'

'But you are not entitled to know mine, nor will such behaviour as this ever encourage me to tell you.'

'Let me be rightly understood. This match, to which you have the presumption to aspire, can never take place. Never. Mr Darcy is to be engaged to my daughter. Now, what have you to say?'

'I do not understand. If, as you say, he is set to marry your daughter, why would you think he would make an offer to me?'

Lady Catherine hesitated a moment. 'There is no formal arrangement. The engagement between them is of a peculiar kind. They have been destined to be together since birth. Destined! It is something that he – that everyone – must just accept! For it to come undone now, because of a young nobody of inferior birth, of no importance in this world–'

'No importance?' asked Elizabeth quietly.

'None whatsoever!'

'It is true I have not attracted the attention of the rich and powerful. I have no royal plate. But in some smaller worlds, I have had, perhaps, some important part to play.'

'What are you talking about? What is this nonsense? You dare equate your sordid playacting with the work of the Best Men? Obstinate, headstrong girl! I am ashamed of you!'

'Lady Catherine,' said Elizabeth 'I believe we should be getting back. Your visit must surely be at an end.'

'No. I have not been used to submitting to any other person's whims. I have not been in the habit of brooking disappointment.'

'That will make your Ladyship's current situation more difficult, but it will have no effect on me.'

Lady Catherine's eyes narrowed. 'So be it. Then we must take some action that *shall* have an effect on you. Mrs Jenkinson!'

Elizabeth had practically forgotten the other woman was there, but now the serving woman strode purposely into the clearing, straight towards her. The way she walked, the set of her jaw, made it look like...

'You cannot be serious,' said Elizabeth – and then she had to spring back as the other woman made a lunge to grab her. 'Lady Catherine! Tell her to stop. I am not going to be forced to do your bidding, and I have no wish to hurt–'

But then the woman was grabbing at her again, and she was forced to wrench her arm clear and backpedal swiftly.

'Oh, there is no reason to worry about Mrs Jenkinson,' chortled Lady Catherine.

Elizabeth frowned. She did not like the sound of that. She adjusted her stance, hitching up her skirts, feeling faintly ridiculous. She looked to the older lady again.

'Lady Catherine, surely–'

Mrs Jenkinson hit her like a wall. They went down, the other woman landing heavily on her. She was fast – she had covered the distance between them incredibly quickly, and Elizabeth had the uneasy feeling that the other woman's first attacks had been deliberately slow to lull her into a false sense of security.

But now they were on the ground, in a tangle of arms and legs, and here, at least, Elizabeth was at home. She swiftly wrapped her legs around the serving woman's waist to hold her, and bent one of her arms backwards.

'Yield!' she hissed, putting pressure on the trapped arm.

But Mrs Jenkinson simply smiled, and butted with her forehead. Elizabeth twisted aside, feeling the blow glance off the side of her head – though it was still painful. She wrenched the arm further, but the woman's other hand was feeling for her ear, seeking to twist it. How was this possible? She should be begging for mercy by now.

'I found her in a travelling sideshow,' said Lady Catherine conversationally. 'Sticking pins in her arms and legs. She was born without the ability to feel pain. So all of your oriental trickery will not avail you, I am afraid.'

If she twisted further, she felt sure the joint would burst, and the thought sickened her. Instead, she thrust the other woman back, swiftly brought her feet in between them, and shoved her off. She scrambled to her feet, dropping into her fighting stance.

'I took her in. Gave her a purpose. Provided some training.'

Mrs Jenkinson came at her again. Elizabeth drew herself up tall, then abruptly dropped, punching hard for the solar plexus. Even someone impervious to pain needs to be able to breathe.

A clubbing forearm caught her in the side of the head, then another from the other side – she was moving too slow, this attack had caught her off guard. She needed to focus.

'She is quite strong, too,' continued Lady Catherine conversationally. 'As I am sure you are discovering.'

The woman came on, and Elizabeth punched her in the face. It didn't faze her in the least.

'All you have to do is swear to have nothing more to do with Darcy, and I will call her off.'

'Call her off? Is she nothing but a dog to you?'

Elizabeth was hoping to see some reaction in Mrs Jenkinson's eyes, but they remained as flat as ever.

'She is loyal. That is all that matters.'

'Good,' said Elizabeth. 'Then she won't want anything to happen to *you*.'

She sprang at Lady Catherine, who staggered backwards in alarm. She heard Mrs Jenkinson shout behind her, heard her thudding feet, turned, took told of the serving woman's reaching arms, fell backward, planted a foot in the other woman's stomach and propelled her up and over her head. *Tomoe nagi – circle throw*. Mrs Jenkinson landed heavily, groaning. Elizabeth somersaulted backwards and ended up on top of her. Mrs Jenkinson tried to roll onto all fours, and Elizabeth let her, then dropped back down, wrapping an arm around her neck, her legs around her waist. Somehow, the other woman still staggered to her feet, the weight of Elizabeth on her back not enough to hold her down. But Elizabeth's arm was buried beneath her chin, sealing off the blood flow on the sides of her neck. Mrs Jenkinson scrabbled to get her fingers around Elizabeth's arm, couldn't, then lurched backwards, crunching her into a tree. Elizabeth grit her teeth and squeezed. Mrs Jenkinson leaned forward, swayed, crumpled to her knees, then fell onto her side. Elizabeth rolled clear, gasping for breath herself.

'You've killed her,' said Lady Catherine, examining her serving woman.

'I have not,' said Elizabeth. 'She is merely unconscious.'

She pushed herself up onto her feet, brushing the worst of the dirt and bracken from her gown.

'Does her Ladyship wish to continue the argument herself?'

Lady Catherine narrowed her eyes and pursed her lips. If looks alone had the power to do harm...

'Then I will bid you goodbye. Go home, Lady Catherine, and bother me no more. When your woman wakes up, you can find your own way back to your carriage.' She started to limp off back to the house.

'I take no leave of you, Miss Bennet,' called Lady Catherine to her back. 'I send no compliments to your mother. You deserve no such attention. I am most seriously displeased.'

Elizabeth simply raised an arm in weary acknowledgement and kept walking.

When she was nearly back at the house, she saw the two women walking across the lawn towards the road. Lady Catherine was marching at a brisk pace while Mrs Jenkinson struggled on behind her, trying to keep up. Well, it did not appear she had suffered any lasting injury then.

Her mother met her impatiently at the door, looking past her.

'Where is Lady Catherine? Does she not wish to come in again and rest herself?'

'She did not choose it,' said her daughter. 'She would go.'

'She is a very fine-looking woman! And her calling here was prodigiously civil!'

'Prodigiously,' said Elizabeth, slipping by her mother into the house.

'I suppose she was just passing through? I suppose she had nothing else particular to say to you, Lizzy?'

'No,' said Elizabeth. 'Nothing in particular.'

Chapter 19

'News,' cried Mrs Bennet two days later, bursting into the drawing room and making Elizabeth jump.

'Lydia is found?' she asked as Jane clutched her hand.

'No, no,' said Mrs Bennet, frowning. 'It isn't that. You will never guess!' She paused expectantly, looking between them.

Elizabeth had been sitting with Jane, both pretending to sew. She had been deep in thought: if Lady Catherine had said that some of her best Vigils had gone to London, that must mean Darcy was hunting Wickham, which meant Lydia may soon be safe. That had led her back to the gift of the armour and Lady Catherine's visit itself. Her mind was a whirl, trying to make sense of it all.

'What is it, Mother?' asked Jane dutifully.

'Netherfield is being made ready!' said Mrs Bennet. 'Mr Bingley is coming back! Not that I care, though. He is nothing to us. But, however, he is very welcome to return to Netherfield if he likes. And who knows what may happen? But that is nothing to us. Such a spirited young man, one moment here, then gone, then back again.'

Elizabeth shot a glance at Jane, who had changed colour. Luckily, their mother only stayed a moment or two longer before bustling out to find

Kitty and Mary and repeat the news. No doubt she would then be off to the Lucases' for a third telling.

'I saw you look at me,' said Jane. 'I know I appeared distressed. It is only because I hope he brings word of Lydia. And because I knew you would look at me, and I didn't know how I should look.'

'Well,' said Elizabeth, 'let us hope it is indeed as you say, and he has some word.'

She was also wondering, but had not dared ask her mother – was Darcy with him?

At lunch, Mrs Bennet said to her husband 'As soon as ever Mr Bingley comes, my dear, you will wait on him of course.'

'No, no,' said Mr Bennet. 'You forced me into visiting him last year and promised if I sent to see him, he should marry one of my daughters. But it ended in nothing, and I will not be sent on a fool's errand again.'

'Mr Bennet! It is absolutely necessary that you should see him on his return. It is your neighbourly duty!'

'A duty I despise,' he replied. 'If he wants our society, he knows where we live. Now I shall take my post into my library, where I hope I may read it undisturbed.'

Seeing Jane's discomfort, Elizabeth drew her into the garden as soon as she was able.

'I'm starting to be sorry that he has come back,' said Jane. 'I can see him with indifference, I am sure, but I can hardly bear to hear it continually talked of. I know Mother means well, and it is a distraction for her from the worry she must feel about Lydia, but she does not know how much I suffer from what she says.'

It was on Elizabeth's lips to tell Jane that this was always the problem, that she kept her feelings too hidden away from others, but caught herself. No point in simply adding another blow upon the bruise.

At this point they were interrupted by one of the servants, who came running to tell them that their father wanted them both most urgently. They ran to the library and found their father, a stricken look upon his face, holding a letter. His fingers were shaking.

'I have news,' he said croakily, then coughed. 'It is not good. And I feel it best to inform you both. Lord knows, I have no desire to keep it to myself.'

'What is it, Father?' asked Jane.

'An express has come from my brother. I shall read it to you:

My dear brother,

At last I am able to send you some tidings of Lydia. Your old connections were helpful and on Saturday I was able to discover the couple's lodging house. I was at the point of going to speak to them, to ascertain whether a marriage had indeed yet taken place, when events took a very strange turn. I was prevented from entering the establishment by the arrival of a number of costumed men in masks, who bade me wait outside, as they had business within and did not wish me to come to any harm. I told them that I was there to see my niece, but they again told me quite firmly to wait, and entered the building themselves.

There was a great deal of shouting and mayhem. The various guests came running from the doorway, and I was fair swept away, trying to discern Lydia amongst them. At some point a fire started in the upstairs, and soon thick smoke was pouring from the windows. I fear I may even have heard a pistol shot.

Amid these scenes, the masked men withdrew, carrying one of their number who appeared injured. I tried to enquire whether they had seen a young girl and man, but they ignored me and went off.

I stayed while the fire was brought under control, and must admit to feeling a great deal of dread – but fear not, I am not writing you that sort of letter. No bodies were discovered in the lodging house, and I have it from one of the maids there that a girl matching Lydia's description was seen being led away by a man who must have been Wickham.

So, brother, be patient and optimistic. They are alive, and now must surely seek the comfort of family and friends. A pity that their very place of lodging should also have been the scene of such a fracas at that very time. A most strange and unfortunate coincidence.

Yours, &c

Edward Gardiner.

Jane's hand found its way into Elizabeth's and squeezed tight. Elizabeth felt a tremble within the grip.

Mr Bennet shook his head. 'This was no coincidence. Vigils arrive at that very moment to apprehend some villain? I cannot believe it to be pure chance. It had to have been Wickham they were seeking – but why?'

The girls were silent, but the question appeared rhetorical, and Mr Bennet continued.

'A terrible thought has struck me – that Wickham is the very same villain who had been seeking to establish himself here in Hertfordshire. And now he has my daughter. I thought he was just a young fool, but now I see I was blind, and there was more at play here. If I needed further proof that I am past any reason to see myself as the Hound, then this is it.'

'Oh, Father,' cried Jane, falling into a chair and reaching across the desk to take his hand.

'You are right,' said Elizabeth. 'He is the Wicked Man and is assuredly living up to the name he has chosen. But we are not alone, Father. We have friends. Powerful friends, who even now will be on his trail. Do not lose hope.'

'Elizabeth,' said her father solemnly, looking up at her. 'This is a kidnapping. Your sister has been kidnapped. We cannot take any chances with her safety. He must want money, and though it may ruin us, we will have no choice but to pay.'

'I thought the policy was not to negotiate with villains.'

Mr Bennet winced. 'In the past, I have said that, yes. And believed it. But not when it is one of my own daughters in peril. No, whoever these friends are, I do not want them involved. It is too risky. We must wait to hear his demands and hope he is sensible of my position and does not demand more than I can raise. And on no account must your mother be told the truth. Her nerves could not bear it. And we, I fear, could not bear *that*.'

To that the girls agreed. They kissed him on his bent head and left him in peace.

Some hours later a clattering of hooves on the drive alerted them to a visitor.

'Could it be another express?' wondered Jane. 'Perhaps–'

The door opened, and in walked Bingley.

He and Jane saw each other at the exact same moment, and both stopped dead in their tracks. Bingley recovered first and strode forward with a warm smile. He took Jane's hand in greeting, and Elizabeth saw her flush pink as she murmured a response.

Then Mrs Bennet swept in, with Kitty in tow, shepherding them all into the drawing room. Once seated, Bingley looked at the four ladies, frowning slightly and sitting forward on the edge of his seat.

'May we speak openly?' he asked hesitantly.

'Of course,' cried Mrs Bennet. 'I am sure there can be no topic of conversation that will not be agreeable to Jane – and the rest of us – should you wish to raise it.'

Elizabeth leaned back, caught his eye and shook her head sharply. He nodded imperceptibly and slowly settled back into his seat.

'Uh, I simply wished to say how pleasing it is to be back in Hertfordshire,' he said somewhat lamely.

'We hope to have good news soon, Mr Bingley,' said Mrs Bennet. 'One of my daughters may soon be married.'

'Oh?' Bingley's eyes shot to Jane, who looked down in confusion.

Mrs Bennet caught the direction of his look. 'Oh! You may not have heard the news.'

'Mother...' said Elizabeth.

'Oh hush, Lizzy. It will all end well, you will see.' Mrs Bennet turned back to Bingley. 'Lydia, my youngest, has eloped with an officer. Of course, we would have far preferred a more usual courtship. It has taken me some time to come to terms with it, but the ends justify the means, as they say.'

'Indeed, madam,' said Bingley.

Mrs Bennet smiled and looked from Bingley to Jane. 'It is a long time, Mr Bingley, since you went away.'

Bingley squirmed, and apologised for having been prevented from doing so by business.

'I had best go,' he finally declared, standing. 'I must...I am expecting... Perhaps Miss Bennet would be so kind as to walk me to my horse?'

'Of course!' said Mrs Bennet. 'Do not let us keep you. Jane, walk out with Mr Bingley.'

'And the other Miss Bennet too?' asked Bingley.

'Oh!' said Mrs Bennet. 'I am afraid I have need of Lizzy. Jane will suffice for company, I am sure.'

'Oh, she had better come,' said Jane.

'Why?' said Mrs Bennet with a frown.

'I'll bring your shawl,' said Elizabeth. 'It is likely chilly outside. Then I will come straight to you, Mother.'

Mrs Bennet pursed her lips, looking at them all, but assented to the plan. Once outside, Bingley spun to face the two girls.

'We found them!'

'Oh!' said Jane. 'How is Lydia? Is she unhurt?'

'And what of Darcy?' asked Elizabeth, feeling Jane shoot a look at her.

'Both are well, as far as I know.'

'What does that mean?' asked Elizabeth.

'Well, Darcy was fine when I left him yesterday.'

'So he was not injured?' The thought had been crawling around her mind like an insect since her uncle's letter. *Carrying one of their number…*

'And Lydia?' prompted Jane. 'Where is she? Does Darcy have her?'

'No,' said Bingley, frowning. 'They got away from us. But we saw her – briefly. She appeared unhurt.'

'Be quick,' said Jane. 'Mother will be demanding Lizzy goes back inside soon.'

'Well, our investigators tracked Lydia and Wickham to a lodging house. Darcy, the Blue Jack, some other chaps and I raided it. But Wickham is a wily one, he had taken precautions – he had someone on watch, and the floor was rigged with traps. He had allies, too: henchmen. Including some rather large and handy fellows. There was quite a brawl, and a fire broke out, and the Blue Jack was hurt – broken ribs, I'm afraid. It was too risky to chase them. But they were spotted fleeing London.'

'So Wickham still has Lydia,' Elizabeth said.

'Oh poor Lydia,' cried Jane. 'What suffering must she be enduring!'

'Do not worry,' said Bingley. 'Darcy is on his way here. We shall have her back to you soon.'

'Darcy is coming here?'

'Yes. We have reason to believe Wickham is headed back this way. A foolish, amateur move on his part, as he will face us where we have friends and he has none.' He went to put his hands on their shoulders, then thought better of it and awkwardly lowered them again. He grinned. 'The hunt is on! The noose tightens about his neck!'

Yes, thought Elizabeth to herself. *But cornered beasts are all the more dangerous.*

The front door opened, and Mary peered out.

'Ah! Sister Elizabeth. Mother wishes you to come in. Urgently.'

'Urgently?' asked Elizabeth, corner of her mouth twisting.

'I believe so,' said Mary solemnly. 'Those were her words. Would you like me to check?'

'No, I am coming.' She looked at Jane, who was looking into the distance. Bingley was looking at her intently. *Jane, say something.* 'Thank you, Mr Bingley. I look forward to seeing you again soon.'

She was barely back inside when her mother grabbed her arm in a pinching grip. 'Lizzy! Why were you out there so long, getting in the way?'

'I do not think I was much in the way of anything.'

'Oh, just leave them! Leave them!'

It was some quarter hour before the sounds of Bingley's horse could be heard, clattering down the drive, and Jane slipped back inside. She managed to bypass their mother and make her way back up to their room, where Elizabeth cornered her.

'So,' she said. 'Did Mr Bingley have anything else important to say after I left?'

'Important? No, not really.'

'You were certainly out there a longish time.'

Jane went faintly pink. 'He is a friendly man. And now that this first meeting is over, I feel perfectly easy. As you see, on both sides, we meet as common and indifferent acquaintances.'

'Oh I do see!' said Elizabeth. 'Very indifferent indeed!'

'You laugh at me, but you cannot think me so weak as to be in danger again.'

'I think you are in very great danger of making him as much in love with you as ever. If only you would–'

'If only I would what?'

Elizabeth sat by her sister and took her hand between both of hers. 'If only you would open yourself up to him, let him truly see you, then I believe he would love you even more than that. Almost as much as I do.'

Jane coloured again. It seemed she might draw her hand away, but then she softened. 'You are right, dear Lizzy,' she said, looking down. 'I do try. But sometimes...It is as if some part of me is frozen. Like there is a band of ice around my heart. It is as if the cold water of the mill pond crystallised something that ought not be, and ever since, I have this...'

Her voice choked and she fell silent.

'Oh Jane, Jane! How do I smash it? Or melt it? How do I help you?'

Jane met her eyes and smiled sadly. 'Thank you, dear sister, but I believe this is my fight. This is not one you can help with. But have faith in me. After all, I am – or was – one of the Pack.'

Elizabeth lifted her hand and kissed it. 'You are the best of the Pack.'

Why was it, she wondered, that humans must spend so much time at war with themselves, the contradictory pieces of self each fighting for control. She knew there was fire within Jane as well as ice – why must they be in opposition, why could they not reconcile? Perhaps this was the appeal for those who chose the path of villainy – to just surrender to their darker urges and live a simpler life. No debate, no divide.

What then of those who chose the mask of the Vigil? This was the opposite of that simpler existence, wasn't it? But did they all feel as she did, that the two halves of self were pushed further apart by the differing night and day aspects of their lives?

Did Darcy feel like this?

Somewhere, a wave was dashing itself to pieces on the rocks.

Chapter 20

The next day Kitty, again sitting looking out the window, rather bored without Lydia for company, and having been banned from walking into Meryton by herself, cried out:

'Mr Bingley is come again! And there is some other gentleman with him. Mr what's-his-name. That tall, proud man.'

'Good gracious!' said Mrs Bennet. 'Mr Darcy! Well, as a friend of Mr Bingley's, he is welcome, though I must say, I do hate the very sight of him. But I shall be civil to him, of course!'

The gentlemen entered and were soon seated in the drawing room. Elizabeth found herself quite nervous to see Darcy; she was both desperate to speak with him but also strangely reluctant. He was as serious as he had been the last time he had been in Hertfordshire. It was in fact hard to reconcile his stiffness with the loving brother she had seen splashing about the pond with his sister at Pemberley.

Mrs Bennet was all warmth towards Mr Bingley, which contrasted terribly with the cold and ceremonious politeness of her manner towards Darcy. Elizabeth recoiled inside at the lack of grace, thinking of the efforts Darcy had gone to in order to try to rescue Lydia and how his very presence here suggested his willingness to continue to do so.

Bingley and Jane, however, seemed oblivious, seated near each other and talking together with many shy smiles.

At some point, a suggestion was made to take a walk about the grounds – Mrs Bennet found a need to stay indoors, and urgently required the assistance of Mary and Kitty –, and the four naturally fell into two couples. Jane and Bingley walked on ahead, and Elizabeth was soon alone with Darcy, who paced silently alongside her.

'I owe you a great debt of thanks. We all do, though not all the family realise it,' she said, the words coming thickly from her throat.

'There is no debt,' he replied. 'I previously underestimated the risk Wickham posed and am merely seeking to right that mistake.'

Strangely, that answer stung. A dark part of her mind whispered '*nothing special, nothing special*'.

'I owe you further thanks,' she continued with some effort, 'for the gift of the armour.'

'Oh. That. You like it?'

'Yes. It is very well made.'

'Do you like the colour? I could have had it made in black, but thought, well...'

He fell silent.

'I am not sure what the "E" stands for?'

He grunted. 'Nor am I. You do not have a proper Vigile name.'

'I can hardly call myself "Elizabeth". It would be something of a giveaway.'

'No,' he said, 'and yet, it is very much who you are. I doubt the Vigile can be separated from the woman.'

They walked on for a few more steps. Her mind was spinning somewhat. She didn't know how to answer that, what he meant.

'I thought the "E" might stand for other things, too,' he continued. 'Things you value. Like "equality". That everyone matters.'

She smiled. 'That might be a lot to explain while I am in the midst of apprehending a villain.'

'Then let them wonder what it means. They will find out in the end.'

'The end. Are we drawing near to that now?'

'Yes. I believe so.'

'I...I can scarcely bear to think about Lydia.'

'Then do not, overly. You must discipline your mind. Compartmentalise it. Those things that rob you of strength must be locked up, put by. You must be able to focus on achieving victory in the mission.'

'I don't know if I can be like that. I believe the "E" also stands for "emotion".'

'He will seek to use that against you.'

'But, what if...' She swallowed. 'What if he kills her?'

'He will not. She is bait. He will use her to draw you out. He seeks to use your emotion to put you in a weakened position. You have defeated him twice now, and hurt him. That is more than enough to stir the fires of vengeance in a man such as him. Worse still, he now knows that you are a woman. That makes it all the more painful.'

'It is perverse that it should be so.'

'That is because you are not a man. You have no idea what it must feel like to be bested by a member of the weaker sex.'

An image flashed into her mind, of a moonlit night. A dark figure on a rooftop. A silver tray held high above her head.

Ah.

'And I don't think,' she said slowly, 'that men understand what it is like being in the position of a woman. To have less power, less control, less voice. It is the assumption of superiority that has helped feed Wickham's criminality. Probably that of many other villains, too. How often are women the main victims of their crimes? In the face of such hubris, someone must strike back.'

They were silent for a long moment. A burst of laughter came to them from Bingley and Jane, up ahead. The sound warmed Elizabeth's heart.

'Might I ask how you know that Wickham is returning to Hertfordshire?'

Darcy grunted. 'He told us, the idiot. As he was fleeing.'

'Why on earth would he do that?'

'It is the nature of those who are called to villainy. There is something missing in them, something that makes them crave recognition. They want to *matter*, but fear deep down that they do not. Part of that results in a desire for some kind of grand spectacle, even if it means their defeat. I believe Wickham knows he is at the end of his rope. His identity is out, there is nowhere left to run. Besides that, he feels he has unfinished business with you and wishes to humiliate you, as you humiliated him. So he will return and let you know, counting on your emotion to put you off balance.' Darcy smiled: a cruel, hard smile. 'But we will be here, too.'

Elizabeth nodded. 'And I am grateful for that, on behalf of all my family, whether they know they ought to be grateful or not.'

'It is nothing. I told you before, it is important that the Vigiles are always seen to win.'

'Do we...Are we not then much the same? Seeking to matter?'

'We are nothing like them. We are the opposite of them. Like opposite ends of a line. We do not act for our gain but for the good of the realm. For the good of the people, if you will.'

But still she wondered and felt troubled. Could not the opposite ends of a line bend towards each other, like a horseshoe, and so be closer than expected? She shook her head. She *was* off balance. She was teetering at the moment she needed to be most steady.

Later, when the gentlemen had taken their leave, Jane turned to Elizabeth with a smile.

'It has been a very agreeable day, given the circumstances. The party seemed well suited to each other indeed. Lizzy, do not smile so! You must not suspect me. I am simply learning to enjoy his conversation as an agreeable and sensible young man, without having a wish beyond it.'

'You are very cruel. You will not let me smile but are provoking me to it at every moment.'

'I...I do still worry for Lydia, of course. I do not wish it to seem I have forgotten her. But I wonder, is there any chance, do you think, that it is nothing more than an elopement and they may yet be married?'

Elizabeth's eyes widened. 'Married? To Wickham? To the Wicked Man?'

Jane twisted her hands together. 'But surely, there must be some chance of redemption. Must he necessarily be beyond saving?'

'Your desire to always find the good in people is certainly beyond help. But let us not quarrel about it. I don't wish to spoil this mood I find you in, as innocent as you would have me believe it to be.'

Elizabeth and Jane were not yet dressed when Mrs Bennet ran into their room the next morning, still in her dressing gown, her hair half finished.

'Jane! Jane! Make haste! He is come! Mr Bingley is come again! So early! Haste, haste, haste! Here, get your gown on!'

Jane turned to Lizzy, face full of anguish.

'Come down with me.'

'I'm not ready! Go down, you will be fine.'

'I will wait for you.'

'Jane,' cried Mrs Bennet.

'Go on,' said Elizabeth. 'I will be right behind you.'

When she did make her way downstairs some time later, she opened the door to the drawing room to find her sister and Bingley standing together by the hearth as if engaged in earnest conversation. As they heard her enter, they looked around almost guiltily and stepped apart. Elizabeth, feeling an odd tension in the air, was about to leave when Bingley leaned towards Jane and said, 'I will find your father at once!'

And with that he ran beaming from the room.

'What on earth?' Elizabeth asked. 'Is there news?'

'Oh Lizzy! I...I don't know what to say!'

'Wait,' said Elizabeth, mind reeling to catch up. 'Did he–'

'He did!' She grabbed her head. 'Oh, I am a terrible person! Lydia is still missing, yet I...I...'

'Please tell me you said "yes"!'

'Yes! But, I shouldn't have. Not right now. It isn't right, I don't deserve it–'

'Jane, stop it!' Elizabeth grabbed her sister's hands. 'Be happy! Let yourself feel it, let yourself be happy! You are allowed!'

Jane blinked, then promptly burst into tears, though she was smiling. 'Thank you. I must go to Mother! He is gone to Father already. Oh Lizzy, to have something to be happy about, when things have been so dark.'

She hastened away, and a few minutes later there came the sound of shrieking from Mrs Bennet's sitting room.

'I must go see Lady Lucas,' came Mrs Bennet's scream.

Elizabeth smiled, coughed out a laugh. She was so happy for Jane.

So happy for Jane...

So...

She was walking, walking. Striding across the field beside the house. Couldn't remember even leaving the room. She was laughing or she was crying. Dashed her arm across her face, came away wet with salt water. She was being lifted by an enormous swell. She was swept towards the rocks.

'Elizabeth!'

She turned, blinking her eyes clear. Darcy, striding across the grass towards her, face hard and stern.

'Where are you going?'

'I...' she said. 'I...'

'You should not go off by yourself. You–Whatever is the matter?'

She couldn't meet his eyes.

'I don't know. Nothing. Nothing is the matter.'

He stopped in front of her, close to her, and there was nowhere to look but at him.

'Yet you appear distressed. Have you not heard the news of your sister? Your older sister, I mean?'

'Yes! Yes. So, you know?'

'Yes. Bingley told me of his plan last evening and asked for my blessing. Which I gave.'

'That was good of you.'

Her eyes welled up again, and she looked away in embarrassment.

'Sometimes,' she heard her voice say softly, 'I do not know where I fit.'

She heard him exhale slowly. She cursed herself – why say such things to him? Why reveal her weakness? She looked at him, found him staring at her intently. Still as a statue.

'What are you thinking?' she asked shakily.

He shook his head. 'I wasn't thinking about anything. I was...looking at your eyes. I once described them as fine. But that...'

No, she said to herself. A man who has been once refused does not make a renewal. Does not subject himself to the indignity.

A drumming of hooves carried to them, and they both glanced towards the house.

'Were you expecting anyone else this morning?' asked Darcy.

'No. Do you think it could be an express?' Her throat constricted with sudden tension.

'It was ridden in fast. Perhaps we should–' He gestured towards the house, and they started walking, their pace brisk.

Her legs trembled with energy. 'This could be it?'

'This could be it.'

Their pace increased.

'I told you,' he said. 'He is weak and stupid.'

A question had been nagging at her. 'What exactly did he say to you? In London, as they fled? His exact words?'

Darcy thought for a moment. 'Something like 'see you back at the beginning'. Hence, Hertfordshire.'

Yes, where it all began. Where he appeared, all charm and grace on the outside, while inside he was rotten and depraved. Like an apple that appeared shiny and whole while a worm had been eating out the core. A worm that had been working away within him, filling him with anger and jealousy disguised as simply living as he pleased. Anger at the world, for the position he found himself in. Jealous of the things he could not have...

...growing up beside Darcy, living with Georgiana. A man he couldn't be. A girl he could not have...

'He isn't here,' she said breathlessly. 'This isn't where it began.'

'What?' said Darcy.

'It began in Pemberley!'

A scream split the air, coming from the house. They broke into a run. Darcy was fast, but Elizabeth, her skirts hitched, was his equal. Outside the front of the house, Jane was half collapsed in Bingley's arms. She saw them coming and thrust a piece of paper at Elizabeth with wild eyes. Elizabeth snatched it from her, held it with trembling hands, felt Darcy's breath hot on her neck as she read.

Dearest Heart-breaker and Hope-taker (Can you work out which is which?)

I would be delighted for you to join us at Pemberley, at your earliest convenience. Lydia, Georgiana and I (plus some friends) would love to show you what we have done to the place. And what more may yet be done. So do come.

And allow me to break your hearts and take your hope.

Wicked Man

'God,' roared Darcy. 'I will kill him! If he...I must—'

'What do we do?' asked Jane.

'I don't know. I don't know,' moaned Bingley. 'Darcy?'

Darcy grabbed his head, as if to keep it from splintering. 'I...I... Georgiana, God, what have I done? I left her there.'

'Darcy!' said Elizabeth. 'Stop! It is just as you said! He wants us off balance!'

Darcy sucked in a long, shuddering breath and drew himself up taller. 'He does not know what he has unleashed. The Dark Archer will finish him.'

'I'm with you,' said Bingley.

'And I,' said Jane.

Elizabeth looked at her sister and Bingley, their arms still wrapped about each other. 'You should both stay here. This may be a ploy. Twice before he has lured me away so that he could do evil – attacking Aunt Phillips, taking Lydia. This could be another trap.'

'Yes,' said Darcy. 'Stay here. It is Elizabeth that I need.' He turned to her. 'Get your armour. You will take Bingley's horse. Go!'

She ran into the house. Her mother stood at the foot of the stairs, sobbing.

'Oh, Elizabeth! What am I going to do? Mr Bennet is going to fight Wickham, and he will be killed, and what is to become of us all?' She grabbed onto Elizabeth as if she was drowning. 'Stop him, Elizabeth. He isn't young and strong anymore. Not like you.'

Elizabeth recoiled. 'Wait – *You knew?*'

'I just wanted you to be normal,' whispered her mother, 'but now, please...'

She collapsed back into helpless sobs. Elizabeth pulled her hands free and ran up the stairs. She burst into her room and pulled the chest from under her bed, fumbling at the lock before it sprang open. Within lay the gleaming red leather of her armour. And on the top, her mask. For a moment, the darkness of the eyeholes made it appear they were staring up at her. *Yes*, it seemed to say; *yes!*

Outside, her arms full, the baton swinging on its thong from one wrist, she heard a thud from her father's study and his voice, hoarse with emotion.

'Damn! Damnation!'

She pushed the door open. Her father was by his desk, a large open box upon it. His head was totally covered by a leather helmet, the visor fashioned like a dog's snout. He was struggling to cinch a leather bodkin about his midsection, fingers shaking as he tried to get the clasps to meet.

'Father.'

The snout swivelled towards her.

'Elizabeth,' he croaked. 'Come and help me. I cannot do up these damnable–*Gargh*!'

Placing her bundle on the desk, she went to him, placed a hand over his shaking fingers.

'Father. Stop.'

He froze, then slowly collapsed backwards into his chair, the wood squeaking beneath him. He slid his helmet up, revealing his red and sweating face.

'I must go,' he said. 'The Hound must protect the Pack.' He gulped. 'The father must protect his daughter. Surely.' The last word was whispered, almost a question.

'I will go. With Darcy.'

'Darcy?'

'Yes. He and I will bring her home. And...and make sure the Wicked Man can trouble us no more.'

'My responsibility–'

'Which you can pass to me.'

He took her hand, pressed it against his face, kissed it.

'I have been too absent. I should have been more...'

She shook her head. 'There is no time for that. Darcy and I must go. You must look after Mother and the girls.'

'Yes,' he said. 'Yes, I will do that.'

She bent and kissed his forehead, then scooped up her armour and strode from the room.

Outside, Darcy was already mounted, Bingley's horse ready beside him.

'Put that in the saddle bags.'

'Do you need your armour?'

He tapped his own saddlebags. 'It is here.'

'Of course,' she said, and mounted.

'I do not have my bow, but I do not want to waste time fetching it. If we ride hard, and cross-country, we can make it to Pemberley some time tonight. That may be earlier than he expects us and be to our advantage.'

'Let us make a start,' replied Elizabeth, 'but I will need to stop and change somewhere. I cannot ride the whole way side-saddle.'

'Oh. No, of course. But let us go now!'

Elizabeth looked to Jane, standing with Bingley on the steps, and gave her a tight smile. Jane lifted a hand, her other holding on to Bingley's.

They tapped their mounts and cantered away down the drive.

Chapter 21

For a while they were on the familiar roads of Hertfordshire, the lanes and ways that she would travel to gatherings, to teas, to balls. That other life. They rode side by side, the horses falling into a familiar rhythm, matching each other's stride.

Darcy rode without speaking. Whenever she glanced across at him, he was sitting rigidly upright in the saddle, face as fixed and grim as granite. The horses were fresh and spirited, and they made good time, eventually passing into parts she had less frequented. Eventually, more to break the silence than because of real need, she told him she wished to stop and change. He cast his eyes about, finally pointing to a small building in a pasture off to their left.

When they drew up to it, she saw that it was an old shepherd's hut – just four walls, a thatched roof and open doorway.

'You change first,' said Darcy. 'I will stand guard.'

She stepped into the small room, and Darcy immediately filled the doorway with his frame, staring out across the fields, his back to her.

'Have no fear,' he said. 'I shall not look.'

She shed her petticoats and drew on the leggings, lacing them tightly. Then she removed her gown. She stood for a moment, shivering slightly, skin prickled with goosebumps, her torso covered by only a thin chemise.

One of her arms came up automatically across her breasts, and she looked again at his back. A deeper shudder ran through her.

Did she wish he would turn around?

Cheeks burning, with fumbling fingers she roughly pulled the jerkin into position, noticing again its tight, smooth fit. She tied her hair back and slipped the mask into place. Like a visor, sealing her off. Armouring her.

'Ready,' she said.

Darcy slowly turned, eyes widening as he looked at her.

'The armour suits you very well.'

He stepped in, saddlebags in hand. The space felt very small with them both inside.

She took up his position in the doorway, looking out across the empty fields, the horses pulling strands of grass nearby. Her ears tingled with the sound of rustling cloth and the creak of leather. Surreptitiously, she allowed herself a quick glance over her shoulder. He was facing away from her, lacing his breeches. His back was bare. She watched the muscles bunch and move, saw the scattering of red spots from the birdshot, still healing. He turned and their eyes met. From behind her mask, it was easier to meet and hold his gaze. They stood like that for a second, maybe more, then he bent and picked up his jerkin, and she turned away.

She did not look again until she felt a light tap on her shoulder, and turned to see the cloaked, black-clad and masked figure that was so familiar to her.

They remounted, Elizabeth grateful to be able to ride properly in this guise. She wondered for a moment what Darcy would think of her as she swung a leg over the saddle, but did not dwell on it. Strange how something could be wrong in one context but normal in another.

They rode on, and despite the fact that they were slowly drawing closer to Pemberley and whatever awaited them there, the tension within Darcy seemed to have lessened. He rode more fluidly, his body moving with the motion of his horse. He was an excellent horseman.

'I am afraid,' said Darcy finally, 'that I have been a poor Vigil. I have underestimated Wickham several times now. It will not happen again. Are you smiling? What on earth are you smiling about?'

'I am sorry,' said Elizabeth. 'I do not mean to make it seem I am taking this lightly. It is just that you said *Vigil*, not Vigile.'

'I did not.'

'I'm afraid you did.'

Darcy grunted.

'But back to your point. I believe being underestimated is one of Wickham's best tricks.'

Darcy nodded. 'Yes. Perhaps a form of his mesmeric talents?'

'Yes.'

'Disappointing, though. I would prefer to think he did not have any power over...' He fell silent.

'You are thinking of your sister?'

He nodded, once, the line of his jaw setting.

They stopped briefly several times to eat, to rest the horses, and to stretch out their stiffening legs. But before too long the tug of action would urge them back into the saddle, the horses snorting in irritation. As the afternoon wore on and the light slowly began to fade, it was as well that they were able to travel on proper roads again and so continue on with greater speed.

And then, finally, with dusk turning the sky purple above them, they arrived at the walls of Pemberley.

Chapter 22

'It looks clear,' said Elizabeth.

They were squatting in the undergrowth across the road from the Pemberley gate, their horses tied further back around a bend. Lights burned warmly in the windows of the gatehouse, though it was not yet fully dark. Darcy shifted, peering across the road, and for a moment their knees pressed together.

A sudden panic hit her. 'What if this has had been another misdirection? What if Wickham isn't here at all, but was luring us away? Father...Jane...'

'No,' said Darcy. 'He is here.' He pointed. 'The shutters of the second window are fully open. John and I have a code for when I return – if all is well, he always half closes that shutter.'

'Then–'

'Something has happened to him,' said Darcy grimly. 'Come.'

He ran to the gates, with Elizabeth close behind. He paused to examine them briefly, glanced around, then pushed through and cautiously approached the gatehouse. He peered in a window, then recoiled, spinning away with a choking cry.

'What is it?'

'Don't look,' he croaked. 'Oh, John...' He straightened. 'We must hurry. He has shown himself willing to kill. I must get to Georgiana.'

'And I to Lydia.'

'Yes, of course. It is some distance to the house; we should get the horses. Wait here.'

His black form jogged back through the gate, leaving her alone. She turned slowly on the spot, ears pricked, right hand resting loosely on the handle of her sheathed baton. There was a creak from the house and she spun towards it. She moved towards the window and slowly leaned forward to peer inside...An ordinary room, lamp burning, but *feet dangling, a figure hanging from a beam*. She jerked back, bile burning the back of her throat.

The gate creaked – Darcy, pushing it further open and leading their horses through. She stepped quickly away from the window.

'John had weapons – a musket and a sword – which I doubt they would have left. But I gave him something else, which may still be inside. Wait a moment.' He gave her the reins and strode to the door. And there he paused, hand reaching for the doorknob. 'Come on, Darcy,' he muttered. 'Don't be a coward. He...'

Elizabeth put a hand on his shoulder. 'Let me. You were obviously very fond of him, and it is hard for you.'

'I cannot allow it.'

'Yes, you can. Vigils share what must be done. Now, what am I looking for?'

'Vigiles...Very well. It will appear like a thin six-foot staff.'

She pushed the door open and stepped inside. She kept her eyes averted, nostrils curling at the outhouse smell in the room. The lack of dignity of it all...She looked about, then moved into a small parlour and there found the long wooden staff Darcy wanted, propped behind the door, a cord wrapped about it. She left quickly, finding herself walking on tiptoe, as if fearing to wake something terrible that merely slept.

Outside, she sucked in a lungful of the clean night air.

'I am sorry,' said Darcy quietly. 'You must think me a poor specimen of a man indeed.'

'For caring? For being human?' She shook her head. 'I think you are the most complete man I know.'

She suddenly reddened, transferring her attention to the object in her hands.

'What is it? It is thin for a staff.'

'It is a thing of beauty,' said Darcy. 'An English longbow.' He took it from her. 'I gave it to him last Christmas. I was teaching him the art. A pity there would not be any arrows here, but there will be down at my range. We shall make our way there.'

They mounted and trotted down the white gravel path that threaded through the woods within the grounds. Their pace increased – Elizabeth could tell Darcy was barely holding himself back, that he wished nothing more than to whip his horse into a gallop and thunder down the road to Pemberley. She felt it, too. To be so near to Lydia and the chance to rescue her...But they had to be careful; Wickham was anticipating their reactions, trying to steer them – like leaving John hanging for Darcy to find.

'Stop,' she cried.

Darcy reined in his horse beside her. 'What? What is it?'

'I'm not sure.' She let her horse walk forward. There was nothing, nothing, but then – a line, strung across the road at head height. Almost invisible. If they had ridden into that at any speed, they would have been guillotined.

'Well spotted,' said Darcy. 'We cannot ride. The next is likely to be at knee height, to catch the horses. We will have to go on foot.'

'Should we go through the trees?'

'That will be very slow going. We will keep to the road, but keep our eyes open and be careful.'

They tied their mounts and moved off side by side down the road. They walked braced, their footfalls soft and quiet. The avenue was wide, the white gravel almost glowing as the rising moon's light fell softly upon it. A bird cried in the thick darkness of the tree line ahead of them–

'Down!' Darcy threw himself upon her.

Something thrummed above them – an arrow. Darcy rolled off her – he was heavy – and crawled into the undergrowth, behind a tree. Elizabeth squirmed on her belly after him. They spun about, came up on their knees behind a thick oak tree and peered cautiously around the trunk.

'Did you see where–'

An exuberant howling rose from the trees on the other side of the road, then subsided into wild high laughter.

'I'd say it came from there,' said Darcy drily.

'How many voices?' asked Elizabeth. 'Three? Four?'

'I think four. They are fools to give away their position. They must think they hit one of us.'

'And they may have, were it not for your quick action. I think you saved my life.'

'And you saved me from breaking my neck on that line. But I am not sure it is wise to keep score, lest one of us is sometime disappointed. I wonder...' Darcy stood and leaned out from behind the tree. There came that same flat thrum, and he jerked back as something *thocked* into the tree. He leaned around, grunted, then squatted back down. 'I didn't think these sort would normally go about armed with bows. They are using mine, from my range. Those are field arrows, not hunting arrows.'

'Is there much difference?'

'Field arrows are much easier to pull out of things.'

'Good to know, but an experience I would still prefer to avoid.'

'Yes. The good news is, I wanted some arrows, and they have just made that easier for me.'

'You are going to ask them to give you some?'

'More or less. Given the howls, I assume these are some of our friends from the canal. It is unlikely they are very skilled with bows, or disciplined. When presented with a seemingly easy target, they will all fire at once. I will be that target – when I say to go, I want you to rush them, from the side. They will panic and be unable to nock and shoot before we are on them.'

'You hope.'

'Indeed.'

Elizabeth drew her baton from its sheath on her forearm, wound the thong around her wrist. She touched Darcy's arm.

'Be careful.'

'Indeed,' he said again, then stood and took a pace forward into the empty roadway.

There was instantly a cry and howl from the trees further up the road, and dim shapes rose, loosed their arrows. Darcy, tall and black, swirled his cloak in a great spinning snap before him as he dropped to his knee.

'GO!'

Elizabeth broke from the trees, angling off to the right, running as fast as she could. She crossed the road in seconds, crashing into the thicket, a branch scratching at her cheek. She plunged into a narrow clear space. Men there, four of them. The closest turned, yelled, fumbling for an arrow, dropped it, bent to retrieve it. She launched forward, hoisting her knee, felt it slam into his face. He fell sideways, swearing. The next was aiming for her – faster than Darcy thought. She dropped to her knees – thanked the cushioning – the arrow flew by above her – threw herself forward, catching one of his ankles. He hissed, swatting at her with the bow. She spun about on the ground, wrapped her legs about his, twisted, brought him down, came up onto her feet.

Darcy crashed into the gap, barrelling straight into another henchman. The last threw himself on top of both of them, and they went down in a heap. Elizabeth, wanting more space, moved out of the trees, onto the road. Both of her opponents, one dripping blood down his chin, followed her. They wore wolf hides tied about their shoulders, the skin of the head forming a cap. The bleeding one licked his lips, tasted blood and threw his head back and howled. She kicked, caught him square in the chest; the cry ended in a strangled wheeze. A fist caught her in the side of the head. She blocked a second blow, struck back with her baton – he caught it on his forearm and yelped as the dense wood struck. He stepped back, cradling his arm, squinting at her.

There was a crashing, and three figures stumbled together onto the road. It looked for all the world like three drunken friends embracing after a long evening at the tavern. A steady stream of gasps and curses came from all three as two tried to hang on and one sought to break free to strike. She saw one actually trying to bite Darcy on the shoulder, thwarted by the thick cloak and the leather beneath. Darcy seized the opportunity to deliver a sharp butt with his head, and the henchman let go. Elizabeth grunted with approval. Aunt Phillips always said that there were no rules in fights.

Darcy delivered a series of hooking punches into the other attacker's side, and he, too relinquished his grip.

There was a strange pause as the four wolves shook off their injuries and circled about the two Vigils.

Darcy backed into Elizabeth, reaching behind to briefly squeeze her arm. She pressed into the comforting pressure of his back, and they stood, on guard, fists up.

'What are you waiting for, you curs?' snarled Darcy, and they rushed in.

No time for thought, for plans. Pure instinct and training kicking in. Arms up to protect the face, elbows in to guard the ribs. Looking for the gaps, punching and kicking into them. The satisfaction of solid connection. Elizabeth jabbed and punched with her left, chopped with the baton in her right, flicked out low kicks that made them swear and hesitate. Whenever she rocked back to avoid or soften a blow, she felt Darcy behind her, the swing of his arms, heard his deep measured breathing.

Things moved into focus again – one man was down before her, knocked out cold by a blow to his temple. She was aware of one of Darcy's crawling slowly away to her left, spitting blood. She was left facing the one with the bleeding nose, who was now also bleeding from a wound on this scalp. They made eye contact, and abruptly he took a step back and dropped his hands to his sides.

'Tommy!' he said.

'I ain't Tommy,' cried his mate. 'I'm a wolf!' And he howled.

'Tommy, it ain't worth it. Let's leg it. That freak ain't paying us enough for this.'

'Go if yer like, I ain't scared, I–'

There was a solid, meaty thwack behind Elizabeth, a groan, then the sound of someone crumpling into the dirt.

'Should keep your attention on your opponent, Tommy,' said Darcy.

The remaining henchman smiled briefly, his teeth stained with blood. He bowed to Elizabeth.

'He told us you was a woman. You sure don't fight like one.'

'I'm a new kind of woman,' said Elizabeth. 'And men like you had best beware.'

He pursed his lips, took two more steps backwards, then turned and ran down the road towards the distant gate. Elizabeth fought the urge to hurl her baton after him. Instead, she turned, flexing her sore fingers. A wild energy surged through her. She felt amazing. *This is what it is really like*, she thought. To stand together, to fight. This...'This is fun!'

Darcy smiled back at her with gleaming teeth. 'Yes.'

They stood looking at each other, then Elizabeth became embarrassed at the incredible intimacy of it and looked away.

'Any injuries?' asked Darcy.

She rolled her shoulders. 'I am sure I will be unbelievably sore tomorrow, but right now I hardly feel a thing.'

He nodded. 'The hunt.' He stepped closer to her. 'This is what no one else understands. The thrill of it. Testing yourself, and triumphing. It is better than dancing, better than racing, better than...better than anything.'

'Yes,' she said.

There was a moment. They stood close to each other, breathing hard. But then one of the men on the ground coughed, groaned and swore, and Darcy shook himself and turned away. He walked back to the side of the road and picked up the longbow and a handful of arrows.

'You retrieved some?'

'Yes,' He held out his cloak. 'The all fired at the same time, as I guessed, and the shafts became entangled in my cloak. The lacquer plates stopped most getting through.'

'Most?'

'Three. One did come through somewhat.' He put a finger through a hole in the black material.

'Did it hit you?'

'Yes. The armour stopped most of the penetration, but I have a small wound in my chest. Nothing to be concerned about. I don't believe it is bleeding much.'

'We must bind it.'

He shook his head. 'No, we must move on. There will be time for that later.'

They continued down the road, at first walking slowly, with great care, but after a time, tension built again and they could not help speeding up. What had been a fairly quick trip in a coach was a much longer proposition on foot, especially after a long day's riding and a fistfight.

Elizabeth felt her mood begin to slip. At first she was buoyed, striding along beside Darcy, feeling so *competent*. But as the journey went on, her mind started to drift, and as her energy levels fell in the wake of the combat, they seemed to drag down her mood with them. Yes, here she was walking beside Darcy, *with* Darcy, as Vigils, as equals, but what next? While she tried to stop herself thinking too far ahead – the greatest trial and danger still lay before them, after all – her mind could not be controlled. What lay beyond this night? At some point, her mask would come off, and it would be back to the world of assemblies and tea, of trying not to watch the days slip by and her age increase, every year subtly reducing her chance of a good match. And though she tried to always be herself, she could not shake the horrible feeling that when she took off this armour, she would be slipping on a different, less desirable mask.

This could not last.

'Where do I belong?' The words just slipped out, and she very nearly clapped her hands to her mouth in horror. She glanced sideways at Darcy's dim, dark shape, hoping that perhaps he hadn't heard. And for the space of a dozen steps or so, he said nothing. Then he stopped, causing her to do the same. He turned to face her. Behind his mask, his eyes were impossible to read.

'Strangely,' he said, 'there is some comfort in hearing you say that.'

'What comfort?' she asked miserably. Proof of his superiority, she supposed.

'It goes some way to describe how I sometimes feel myself.'

She shook her head. 'Please do not mock me, sir.'

'Mock you? Why on earth would I mock you? Do you not realise...' He faltered. 'Why do you find it so hard to believe that I should not, at times, feel out of place?'

'Because you always seem so sure of yourself.'

'I can say the same about you.'

'On the surface, maybe. But you do not know what is underneath.'

'Precisely.' He exhaled loudly. 'You do not know what it is like, to be constantly targeted by families seeking a match. Who see my wealth, my status, my form, but do not – *cannot* – see *me*. And yes, I know what you will say: I do not, perhaps, allow anyone to see. But how on earth do I explain...*this*? How do I find someone who can accept *this*?'

There was a moment of silence.

'I imagined I was the only one to feel that way.'

'Then it seems,' he said slowly, 'that which we thought separated us from all others, might actually have linked us to...another...if the circumstances had come to allow it.'

If the circumstances allowed it...

Then he snorted, which startled her. 'You are just like Fitzwilliam, you know. He is always inclined towards melancholia after action. Particularly if he has been drinking. You and he would make quite the pair after a fracas. Why, next time we should all...'

He abruptly fell silent, the sudden quiet like a frown.

'Our sisters,' said Elizabeth. *There could be no next time.*

'Yes,' said Darcy. 'Let us go on and do the things that must be done.'

They walked on, the road ascending. Then the trees thinned, and they crested the ridgeline. There before them lay Pemberley.

The house blazed with light. Lamps must have been lit in every room, and torches burned beside the entryway and in an arc around the drive. Against the deep darkness of the woods behind, it glowed golden. Elizabeth was surprised – she had expected it to be in darkness. Not that the light was welcoming – there was something about the wantonness of it, the excess, that rendered the house abnormal.

It also meant there was a band of light surrounding the entire front of the building.

'Should we work our way around the back?' asked Elizabeth. 'Find somewhere to sneak in?'

'Sneak in? This is my home. I am not sneaking in like some burglar. We shall enter via the front door, thank you very much.'

'You don't think–'

'No, I do not. We shall not show any fear of this villain and his henchmen. We shall not show any weakness.'

'A desire to gain whatever advantage we can is hardly a weakness, surely.'

'We do not need it. You have seen their calibre. I am the Dark Archer. I am their better.'

'I cannot help but think that pride such as that, while admirable in some situations, is possibly misplaced here.'

'Well. We shall see.'

And with that, Darcy strode down the slope, longbow in hand. There was nothing for it but to follow him.

There was not a soul to be seen as they walked up the drive. The torches crackled and flared. Elizabeth fought the urge to duck, though there was nowhere to hide. The sense that they were expected caused a shiver to run up her spine. If Darcy was at all perturbed by the situation, he gave no sign, so she copied him, forcing herself to walk upright.

The drive looped in a circle at the front of the house, and the crunching of their boots quietened as they started crossing the patch of lawn encircled by it. The quiet was abruptly broken by the sound of shattering glass – the windows in the room to the right of the doorway, three of them now gaping holes, musket barrels thrusting through.

'Down again,' cried Darcy, but Elizabeth was already diving to the ground.

The muskets boomed, and the balls hissed savagely over their heads.

'Must be some of the deserters,' said Darcy. 'They obviously took their firearms with them.'

'What now?' asked Elizabeth. 'Do we rush them too?'

'No,' said Darcy. 'Those muskets are designed for shooting en masse at a large target, like a battalion of soldiers. They are not very accurate at all at this range. But if we run at them, their chance of hitting us increases dramatically.'

The muskets fired again, and despite Darcy's words, Elizabeth could not help but try to thrust herself into the ground.

'You see?' said Darcy. 'They are shooting high.'

'But we're stuck,' said Elizabeth. She wriggled and looked back past their feet at the welcoming darkness further behind them. 'Do we retreat?'

Darcy looked across at her. 'I told you. I am going through the front door.'

'But how? Oh no.'

He was bundling the arrows he had collected from the Wolves into one hand, the longbow in the other.

'Do not do it. They will shoot you.'

'Not if I shoot them first.'

'But how fast can they fire?'

He considered. 'A good soldier can probably reload and fire every fifteen seconds. But these are hardly good soldiers.'

'But how fast can *you* shoot?'

His teeth showed like a snarl. 'Faster than them.'

'There are three of them.'

'And there is but one Dark Archer. Stay down.'

'Darcy–'

'Stay down!'

He slammed his hand down, thrusting the points of the field arrows into the ground, then rose, towering above her. He threw his cloak off his right shoulder, set the bow against his foot and bent it. She heard him grunt with the effort of stringing it, behind that excited yelling from the house, and then the muskets fired again in a stuttering line. She screwed her eyes tight against the noise and the acrid sting of the powder smoke that drifted in blue clouds across the lawn.

'*Now,*' said Darcy, and she had to look.

Silhouetted against the smoke and flame, she saw him pluck an arrow, nock it, and draw. She heard the creaking of the mighty bow. He paused for a moment, at full stretch, then loosed. She heard the tinkle of glass and a high, surprised cry. He selected another shaft, drew and aimed – two muskets fired this time. He loosed.

She felt something thwack into the turf close by, dirt showering her. She pressed her head into the ground, looking over at his feet. Another arrow was plucked from the ground. A second later came a terrible scream from the house. She gritted her teeth. Another gunshot, and Darcy grunted. She saw him rock back on his heels. She looked up to see him drawing the great bow again. The arrow streaked across the gap between them, disappearing through the hole in one of the windows. One musket fired, high, unsteady. Darcy had two arrows left – he fired one, reached for the final arrow, drew, paused...

Silence.

There came a faint tapping as the arrow shuddered where it lay resting on his left fist. The seconds passed, and she heard him hiss from the effort of holding at full draw. Then with a gasp he let go, and the final arrow splintered against the wall between the windows.

The bow dropped from his hand.

'Are you shot?' she asked.

'No,' he said.

'I thought–'

'I said no.'

'And...are they...'

'I believe I have hit them all. Even with field points, I do not think they will be troubling us further. Are you ready?'

She slowly levered herself up, brushing the dirt from her leather jerkin by reflex. She stared at Darcy intently, but he flicked his cape back off his shoulder and strode for the entrance. She jogged to catch up and fell into position alongside. She was relieved when he paused at the massive double doors and stood studying them – it would be awful to have come so far only to be felled by some trap at this point.

Abruptly Darcy reared back on one leg and let fly a massive kick, sending both doors crashing open. Cloak billowing, he strode into the entrance hall, the torches and lamps inside flaring in the rush of cold night air.

The grand staircase to the upper levels was in a T shape, with the first flight before them, then breaking off left and right to curl to the second storey. A mezzanine balcony above linked the two wings.

A number of figures stood spread upon this upper level, looking down upon them. Elizabeth's heart leapt as she made out Lydia amongst them.

'Well, well,' said the man standing in the middle, clad in grey, his face covered. 'Look who we have here.'

'Wickham,' said Darcy. His voice was cold and hard.

'The same.' Wickham bowed.

'Lizzy,' cried Lydia. She was standing at the top of the stairs on the left, her hands bound in chain before her. 'Is that you?'

'Yes, it is me.'

A very large muscular man with a frowning face stood behind her younger sister. She could see now that the chain ran from Lydia's hands and looped around the balustrade.

'Why ever are you dressed like that?' said Lydia. 'You look like a boy!'

'So, you are unhurt then?'

Elizabeth surveyed the rest of the balcony. Georgiana was there, too, on the right, not in her chair, but held upright in the bulky arms of the fattest man she had ever seen. She was staring down at Darcy, tears running down her cheeks. Wickham's clay mask was set in a wide smile. He was flanked by an elegantly dressed man with long black hair, and a smaller, sallow man with hard flinty eyes.

'See how pleased I am to see you? That you have made it this far?' Wickham pointed at his fake curved lips. 'But before you get any ideas, know this: at a word from me, my two large friends here twist your dear sisters' necks. You can't get up here fast enough to stop them.'

'Hurt Georgiana and I will kill you.'

'Stop growling and listen, Darcy. I have some things I wish to say before we get to the fun part. You've behaved perfectly so far, doing everything as I wished. Have the grace to go along with me a little longer. Lord knows I have had to spend more than my share of time listening to you.'

'My father gave you a good life and you have spat it back in his face.'

'No, your father gave me a life where I was constantly made to feel less than you. Do you know what happens, Darcy, when you are constantly reminded that you are not as good as everyone else? You stop caring about being good at all and start to crave the opposite. So here I am: *your creation*. Hello, Elizabeth. I like your new costume. Very fetching.' He turned to the long-haired man beside him. 'What do you think?'

'Delicious,' said the man.

Elizabeth shuddered. 'Let the girls go, Wickham.'

'I suppose you feel you have to say that, don't you, Lizzy? But we all know that isn't really what you want. You want to come and take them, with as much violence as possible.'

'Do not pretend to know me.'

'Oh, but I do. You may think your mask disguises you, but actually it reveals you – reveals what you want. Your desire to hurt people. Not very ladylike, I must say. And that is only one of your masks – take that one off, and there is another underneath. That fake one you wear about town. Good Miss Elizabeth Bennet. So witty. So gay. So false. At least I know when I am wearing mine–Wait a moment. Is that...Do you actually have an "E" on your bosom? Are you wearing monogrammed armour?' He cackled loudly. 'You really have no idea how this works, do you? *E* for *Elizabeth*, priceless.'

'E for the end,' she responded evenly. 'The end of what you have done. The end of you, if necessary.'

'No,' he said. 'This is just the beginning. I finally have my complete set, don't you see? My Seven Deadly Sins. That is Wrath, that is Gluttony. This is Lust and Envy. I wasn't sure how I was going to fill the last three, but then I realised they had chosen themselves. Little Lydia there is Greed – it was so easy to lure her away with the promise of some shiny baubles. My sweet Georgiana here is Sloth, because she does spend rather a lot of time sitting down, doesn't she? And you, dear Lizzy, you are Pride. You who come from a litter of bitches, with a hapless fool of a father who can't even provide you with a dowry. You who call a freak your aunt. Yet struts around as if she is so much better than everyone else.'

Darcy stirred angrily.

'And yes, that leaves you, *dear brother*. But there isn't any room for you, I have the set. Unless you would like to act as witness when I wed my three new members. Though of course, you realise, I am using "wed" in the more biblical sense.'

'I am going to kill you,' said Darcy.

'No, you are going to *try*. And you are going to fail. And when you fail, you will know that I have beaten you. I have bettered you. And you, dear Elizabeth, I have an additional score to settle with you.' He took hold of the wrist of his other arm, which had been hanging by his side, and waggled it. 'Do you see my doll arm? You are such a pretty dolly, I might give you an arm like this as well. Or maybe two. Probably a good idea, to keep you from trying to kill me all the time.'

Elizabeth drew her baton from its sheath.

'Enough talk,' said Darcy, and took a step towards the staircase.

'I've been working on Georgiana!' said Wickham quickly.

Darcy paused.

'Ever since I got here, I have been talking to her. Reacquainting her with her own deepest desires. Haven't I, my dear? And what is it you really want to do? Speak up in a big voice for your brother.'

'I...I want to fly,' said Georgiana.

'That's right. And fly you shall. We shall take you to the roof, and you shall have your heart's desire. And if you touch me, Darcy...If he touches me, my sweet, what will you want to do?'

Georgiana flushed pink.

'Say it.'

'I will want to do something to my face so it isn't pretty anymore.'

'You sick monster,' hissed Elizabeth. 'I wish I had killed you.'

'Yes. Well. You didn't. Though you gave it a merry try. Meanwhile, Lydia there isn't going anywhere. And I told Wrath, that if he impresses me by knocking out one of you, he can have her for himself. He seemed quite taken with the idea. Turns out one of the things that makes him really angry is pretty little poppets that he can never have.' He clicked his fingers, and Wrath took several steps down onto the left arm of the stairs, and the small man he'd called Envy did the same on the right. 'So. There you have it. This is the game for the evening. Pick a side and come on up. If you can.'

Darcy looked at Elizabeth. 'Take the right. I know you want to save your sister, but leave the big man to me.'

'I can take him,' snarled Elizabeth.

'I am sure you can. But leave him to me anyway.' He lowered his voice. 'I am going to need you against Wickham. I cannot touch him directly. I cannot risk Georgiana injuring herself again. His hold over her is... disturbing.'

Elizabeth nodded, the movement jerky with the flood of anxiety and energy coursing through her. Side by side, they mounted the steps of the first flight, their boots thudding in unison, then they turned back to back, facing their respective foes. Their fingers met briefly behind their backs, gripped, squeezed, released. The man called Envy grinned at Elizabeth and reached into his pocket. He slid a straight razor from within and flicked it open. Elizabeth tightened her grip on her baton and advanced up the stairs to meet him.

'Now this,' hooted Wickham, banging on the railing, 'is what I was waiting for. It's just like in the papers!'

Elizabeth surveyed the man on the step above her. Though small, he appeared to have a build that was all lean whipcord muscle. She guessed he was younger than his grizzled face suggested – aged by poverty. He stood balanced and ready, the razor held almost casually off to the side. He was obviously an experienced fighter.

'Well ain't you the pretty fine thing?' he asked in his lilting accent, the music of it at odds with his dead eyes.

Behind her, she heard a series of grunts and thuds, and a meaty slap. The Irishman's eyes flicked over to the other stairs, and at that moment she struck, lunging to smash her baton down onto the toe of one of his boots. But the club jarred away, numbing her hand – steel caps! – and he laughed at her. She lunged with her left hand, trying to catch his other foot, to trip him, but fast as a snake the razor slashed at her, and she pulled back – her sleeve now bearing a deep cut, the leather parted almost right through. She could not let him catch her like that twice in the same spot or he would be cutting into her flesh.

A man bellowed behind her – she couldn't tell who – and then came the sound of two heavy bodies tumbling down onto the landing. She didn't turn, but was momentarily distracted, and Envy took a step down and sliced at her face, so fast. She jerked back, stumbled, barely kept her balance. It was close – the blade must have missed by the barest of margins. She shivered, mind picturing the skin of her face opening, the burn of the cut. An image sprang forth: the assembly room, everyone dancing, and her sitting unchosen on the side, amongst the old ladies, her face latticed with scars...It must have shown in her eyes, for he laughed, a throaty rough chuckle.

He was fast and reacting to everything she did. She had to change things.

'It makes sense that you are in here, not outside with the Wolves,' she said quietly. His eyes narrowed. 'For this is just the place for an Irish dog – at the feet of his English master, ready to lick his boots. Or whatever else he desires.'

The colour drained from his face, and he came at her, furious. The silver blade flashed, but she stepped back, parrying with her baton. On the third time she had his rhythm and caught him across the hand, felt the impact, heard him gasp. The razor clattered from his nerveless fingers. But he came on, swinging his fists, and now he was inside her reach, aiming vicious punches into her ribs. The leather and padding beneath cushioned the blows somewhat, but she felt the strength of him. She dropped the baton, letting it hang on its thong, took hold of him and turned side on, thrusting her hip into him. Being on the step below him, it was a simple matter to pull him over her back and keep turning, throwing him down the stairs. He yelled as he fell, the staircase pitch causing him to fall all the further. He tried to catch himself but had no skill in tumbling, landed partially on his head, and slid down onto the landing like a rag doll.

Elizabeth spun – Darcy and Wrath were back halfway up the other staircase. Both had blood dripping from their faces. As she watched, Darcy landed a solid jab into the other man's chin, but the height difference robbed it of some power. Wrath shook his head, then lunged, taking hold of Darcy – he obviously had realised that the Vigil was the better boxer. He butted with his head, and Darcy cried out – he appeared stunned. Wrath laughed, and reared back to butt again, but as he came in, Darcy suddenly dropped his head forward and thrust – he had been faking! – and caught the bigger man's face on his forehead as he smashed it down. Wrath roared wetly, thrusting Darcy away, his nose gushing blood. Darcy swung hard at his stomach, doubling him over, then launched upward with a vicious uppercut to the chin, and Wrath went down like a felled tree.

'Disappointing,' said Wickham above them. 'Oh well, I suppose you had better claim your prize – if you can free her. I'm afraid I have misplaced the key. No matter, she is a bit annoying. But if you want Georgiana, you will have to follow us to the roof.'

He gestured to the man he called Gluttony, who easily lifted Georgiana in his thick arms. She whimpered as she hung in his grasp. They headed to the right, down the hallway. The long-haired man trailed after them, smiling over his shoulder at Elizabeth as he sauntered off.

'Lizzy,' screamed Lydia. 'Please! Get me out of here!'

Elizabeth started forward, but Darcy, bent over and breathing hard, held up his hand.

'I will get her,' he said hoarsely. 'Follow them.'

He wearily mounted the stairs on the left, and Elizabeth, after one last glance at Envy – he appeared to be out cold – carefully started ascending the right. Lydia held out her bound wrists to Darcy, who inspected them briefly, then flicked his cloak aside and slowly bent to peer at where the chain ran through the railings – then, with an awful cry, he took one staggering step and fell to his hands and knees.

'What is it?' cried Elizabeth, then stared in horror.

Lydia stood over Darcy, a thin stiletto held in her two bound hands.

'I did it,' she shrieked. 'I did it, Wicky! It was easy, just like you said! Right in the side!'

'Lydia, no!"

Wickham came striding back down the hallway, almost dancing with delight.

'Good girl! I knew he wouldn't be paying attention! Too busy being the big hero!'

'Darcy,' cried Elizabeth, frozen on the staircase.

'God damn it!' spat Darcy. 'God damn it, stabbed in the back by a stupid...' He moaned in pain, clapping a hand low onto his back. Elizabeth guessed that his jerkin had ridden up as he bent over, making a gap between it and his leather trousers.

'I'm not stupid!' said Lydia crossly. 'What shall I do now, Wicky?'

'Stab him again, dear!'

'Where?'

'Lydia, no! Stop! You don't know what you are doing!'

Lydia paused, looking at her. 'Yes, I do.'

'You are mesmerised! Fight it!'

Wickham laughed. 'Oh, Lizzy! What makes you think she didn't want to do that? I told you: I give people what they want. And Lydia wants excitement. Now go on, poppet, stab him again. Anywhere you like.'

Lydia looked down, knife in hand – Darcy spun, flinging out an arm. The stiletto went spinning out of her grasp.

'Ow! You hurt me,' cried Lydia.

'Lydia,' said Elizabeth shakily. 'I don't understand–'

'What's to understand? Being good is just so...boring.'

'Speaking of boring,' said Wickham. 'Let's heat things up.'

He snatched up a lamp from a side table.

'Wicky! Wait! You said...You said–'

'I said a lot of things, you clot. I am a little sorry, but you have to finish serving your purpose – to break your sister's heart.'

He flung the lamp across the landing. It smashed into the wall behind Darcy and Lydia. The lamp oil sprayed flaming across wall hangings, chairs and side tables. Yellow flames ran swiftly up the walls, and black smoke billowed. The ignition was so fast, the area must have been soaked already in some accelerant.

Then a flame licked up Lydia's gown, igniting it in a sudden burst of orange, and she screamed.

'Lydia,' cried Elizabeth.

A dark shape rose, towering behind Lydia. *Darcy*. His cloak opened like a pair of mighty black wings and furled around her, enveloping her and bearing her to the ground, extinguishing the flames.

Wickham cursed and spun on his heel, disappearing down the hall.

Elizabeth ran partway up the stairs, which were alight in several places as burning lengths of wall-hanging dropped upon them.

'Darcy,' she called. 'Darcy!'

Through the smoke she saw him roll over, heard him groan.

'How badly are you hurt? Is Lydia – God damn her – is she all right?'

'She is fine,' he rasped. 'I have rendered her unconscious, for all our sakes. Where is Wickham? Where is Georgiana?'

'They have gone down the hallway. What's down there?'

'Stairs to the third floor. And from the third, a servant's way to the roof. Go after him,' hissed Darcy through gritted teeth. 'I will save Lydia then follow. Go!'

'Let me help–'

'Lizzy, please. I will see your sister safe. I give you my word. Now please, go and save mine.'

She nodded tightly and stepped back. Flames were spreading down the hallway. Darcy took hold of the chains in his hands, sat facing the balustrade, and kicked at it with both legs. He gasped in pain, but the wood shook. He looked at her, eyes fierce. She turned before he could say anything else and ran to the hallway. A haze of smoke had already filled the air, the acrid haze making her cough.

The hall turned to the left, and she found a narrower staircase to the next level a short way along. She paused, but could hear nothing above, and so took the stairs two at a time. At the top, the long-haired man waited. He had removed his frock coat and shirt and stood bare chested, clad only in a pair of leather trousers somewhat like her own. He held a flask in one hand.

'Ah,' he said upon seeing her. 'My turn.' He lifted the flask and oil poured from it across his body. Here, as throughout the rest of the house, lamps burned brightly, and she stepped back in alarm. He laughed. 'Do not be alarmed. It is olive oil.' He dropped the flask and rubbed his hands across his torso, which glinted in the light. 'Are you familiar with the *Yagli Gures*? No? Well, you are not the only one with some training from the East. Yagli Gures is the noble art of Turkish oil wrestling. I am pleased to give you an education in it. Perhaps,' he purred, 'after I have defeated you, I can give you another kind of education. The Wicked Man needn't know. It can be our little secret.'

'I am so tired,' Elizabeth said, 'of listening to men like you.'

She threw her baton, and it struck him squarely in the forehead.

He cried out, falling to his knees and clutching his head. Blood from his split scalp ran between his fingers, spattering onto the carpet.

'My face,' he screamed. 'What have you done to my face?'

She heard yelling up ahead.

'Move!' came Wickham's voice.

'I am trying!' said the surprisingly high and accented voice of the fat man. 'It is very narrow.'

The servant's way up to the roof...She stepped forward and bent to retrieve her baton.

Lust's bloodied hand seized her by the wrist. He yanked her towards him, eyes wide and crazed in his mask of red.

'I will kill you!'

She twisted her hand, and it slid free of his slippery grip, but he was already on his feet, arms outstretched, barring her way. He came at her, fingers clawing for purchase in her armour. She swatted them away, tried to get a kick into his stomach, but he turned and her boot slid past him. She tried to grab him for a throw, but his oiled skin slipped in her grasp. His hand found a grip in her hair. He twisted it viciously, cocking her head to the side. She reached back, trying to grab his oily fingers – he spun, used his momentum to ram her face first into the wall, his whole weight pressed up against her from behind.

'Do you like this? I do,' he hissed in her ear, the stink of his breath filling her nostrils. He ground into her from behind.

She grabbed onto his arm, lifted her legs off the ground, got her knees up against the wall and shoved backwards. They staggered away from the wall, and she spun in his grip, launched a knee into his groin. He made a strangled sound in the back of his throat and bent over, releasing her.

'Do *you* like this?' she said, and, stepping back, swung her boot in a sweeping kick that caught him flush on the temple. He hit the floor hard and lay unmoving.

There was a crash below and behind her – the smoke was rising thick and black from the lower floor. She felt a stab of uncertainty – should she go back, make sure Darcy and Lydia were not in trouble, make sure she herself was not trapped by the fire? But Georgiana was still somewhere up ahead, still in the grasp of Wickham.

She took up her baton and ran down the hall to where the door to the servant's way hung ajar. It was a narrow, steep staircase – cool night air was rushing down from an open doorway at the top. She pressed herself against the wall and took the stairs as quietly as she could, though it seemed that her heart was beating loudly as a drum. But then she heard Wickham's angry voice coming from out on the rooftop.

'Why aren't they all lit? Whose job was this?'

'I don't know,' replied the thick voice of the one called Gluttony – it sounded like he was panting. 'I think the people with the masks came too early.'

'They have to be able to see, otherwise there is no point!'

'I think they can see good enough.'

Elizabeth peered onto the roof. The central section, over the entrance hall, was flat with a low parapet running around the edge. About a dozen lamps were lit and stationed across the expanse, while a cluster of unlit ones sat near the hatch where she was. Worryingly, she could see sparks shooting up into the night sky from somewhere below.

Gluttony stood halfway to the edge, his arms still wrapped around Georgiana, who hung helplessly in his grip.

Elizabeth stepped out onto the roof.

'Why, Miss Eliza Bennet! Shall we dance?'

Wickham paced forward into the circle of light from the lamps. He held a sabre in his good hand.

'George,' said Elizabeth. 'Let the girl go.'

'George? *George*? How overly familiar of you, *Lizzy*. But there is no "George" here. You have forced another name on me. You have forced the smile from my face and left me frowning.'

'No. Everything that has happened has occurred because of your choices. Your weakness.'

'Weakness! No, no. Freeing oneself to live according to what one truly desires takes strength in this age. In this time when misguided savages such as yourself and that cretin Darcy try to hold us all back, to constrain us.'

'Giving in to base impulses can hardly be considered progress. It is the opposite. It is allowing the worst of ourselves to hold sway.'

'Ah, Lizzy. How I miss our little chats. Such a pity you have chosen the wrong side. We could have...but no, you had to choose *him*. Now, where is Darcy? Is he coming? Doesn't he want to watch his dear sister take wing? You still want that, don't you, dear Georgiana?' He called across to the girl. 'You would still like to fly?'

'Yes,' she replied meekly.

'Go put her on the edge.'

'No! Stop!' Elizabeth stepped forward as Gluttony turned towards the building edge. Wickham rushed at her, sword raised. She gave ground before him, conscious of the extra reach the sabre afforded him.

'You would love to save her, be the hero, wouldn't you?' snarled Wickham, slowing to a halt between her and Gluttony. 'Well, guess what?

You are going to fail! Unless, of course, you allow yourself to be the savage you wish to be, deep down, unleash all that violence that is simmering there beneath the surface, *and tear me apart*.'

'Why?' she groaned. 'Why must you do this?'

'To free you. Or to punish you. It is hard to say which. You made me think you were something different, something special. But you're not, are you? Even dressed like that, you're still just another boring, conventional, parochial girl, desperate to avoid becoming an old maid. You are just so *ordinary*. Strip away your masks, one by one, and there is just *nothing there*.'

'Hey,' called Gluttony. 'Do you want me to drop her over?' He was standing close by the edge now.

'No, set her down. I want her to step off herself.'

'She cannot walk, Wickham!'

'Then she can crawl over.'

Elizabeth went to run by him – he was expecting it, and sidestepped into her path, raised the point of the sword towards her. She swatted at it with her baton, but he twirled it around her attack and stabbed. The point bit into her bicep, penetrating the leather sleeve. She gasped, fell back. She flexed her fingers – they still worked, but the wound burned with a deep, numbing pain.

By the drop, Gluttony was trying to set Georgiana on her feet. She was staring down at the ground, three stories below.

'So high,' she said, her voice trembling.

'Georgiana,' Elizabeth screamed. 'Georgiana, fight it!'

The girl looked around at her. Elizabeth tried to hold her with her eyes. Wickham moved, but she felt if she broke the eye contact, she would lose the girl.

'Georgiana,' she said again, conscious of the black shadow of Wickham coming at her, sword glowing in the lamplight. '*Do not let this man tell you what to do*.'

And then instinct told her to fall back, and her baton came up, just catching the sabre as it descended. The blade bit into the wood, the impact wrenching her wrist sideways. She fell backwards, took her weight on her left hand flung out behind her, and kicked with her right foot, feeling it sink into Wickham's midsection, and he staggered back with a loud grunt.

She looked desperately across at Georgiana – the girl, hanging limply in Gluttony's grip as he tried to swing her feet over the parapet, was fumbling at her skirt. Then her hand emerged, something slender and silver glinting in the light. The stiletto! With a cry, she jabbed it into the side of Gluttony's neck. He squealed, snapped upright, clapped a hand to his neck and dropped Georgiana in a heap at his feet.

'She stabbed me! She stabbed me,' the fat man shrieked. He took his hand away for a moment – the hilt of the thin knife jutted from his neck. 'Ah! It is still there! It is stuck in me!'

Wickham was bent over, breathing hard. 'Well, don't pull it out, you fool, or you'll bleed out like a stuck pig!'

'I will kill her!'

Elizabeth looked desperately about – and caught up one of the unlit lamps. She hurled it at Wickham, and in a reflex move he slashed at it with his sabre. Glass shattered and lamp oil splashed across his mask. Already she was launching a second, and he smashed that one too, reacting to the movement, and more glass and oil rained upon him. He cried out and clapped his sword hand to one eye. She threw a third, and this time he covered his face with his arms, and it broke upon his head.

Georgiana screamed, punching at the huge doughy hands of Gluttony as he reached for her. Elizabeth ran at him – his hands were on the girl's neck, her face. She threw the baton – it sailed straight and true, and cracked into the hilt of the stiletto, jerking it sideways. He made a sound deep in his chest, half cry, half hiccup. He staggered sideways, and a jet of blood arced from the wound, spattering upon the rooftop. He stared about with crazed eyes, breath coming in wet blubbers. His gaze fell on Elizabeth, and he screamed with rage.

'Georgiana,' called Wickham, still rubbing at the eye holes in his mask. 'Georgiana, you want to go over the edge. Do it now.'

'I don't want to,' Georgiana said, crying, but dragged herself towards the drop.

'No,' cried Elizabeth.

Gluttony came at her, flailing wildly with fists as big as hams. She ducked beneath them, punched for his diaphragm, hand rebounding off his girth. Georgiana now had her head over the low parapet. She was sobbing.

'I want to, but I don't want to.'

Elizabeth spun, landing a round kick to Gluttony's knee, and he staggered. He went to put a hand out to catch himself, and she kicked that away, making him fall onto his face. He was weakening, a pool of blood spreading beneath him – she doubted he would have the strength to push himself back up onto his feet.

She heard a deep crash, and a large shower of sparks shot into the night sky. A patch of roof had caved in.

She ran to Georgiana, pulled her away from the drop.

'Georgiana, stop this. Stop it! You won't fly, you will fall. If you want to fly, you must come down with me, down to the pond.'

'The pond?' said the girl, frowning.

'Yes, you remember. Darcy helps you fly there.'

'Fitz...'

'That's right.'

Georgiana stared at her, then suddenly slumped back, eyes rolling back in her head.

'So. Just you and me at the end, Lizzy. How poetic.'

She whirled around. Wickham faced her across the roof. One of his eyes was swollen shut within his mask. He looked terrible – half the putty was smeared from the mask base, making him appear like some grotesque gargoyle come to life.

'All Vigils need their nemesis, don't they?' He held his sword again. 'No little stick. No room to run. Fire below you, nothing but air behind.'

'You should flee,' she said, more calmly than she felt. 'The roof is caving in. Pemberley is lost. Let me take Georgiana down, and you can just go.'

'No, I don't think so.'

'I warn you.'

'You warn me?' He laughed, high and wild.

'I told you,' she said. 'I am the end.'

He shook his head. 'This is just the beginning.' And he came at them, raising the cruel steel.

There was a lamp at her feet. She kicked it straight at him.

It was alight.

He slashed it with his sword. It shattered.

And he was engulfed in flame.

He cried out, first in rage, as he realised what had happened, then in mad pain, and he came at her, flaming, arms outstretched, seeking to catch her in his crazed grasp and send them both hurtling like a comet through the night sky.

There was nowhere to dodge. Nowhere to fall back.

So, as he came at her, she stepped forward to meet him, took his flaming hands in hers, and fell backwards, one of her feet coming up into his stomach, thrusting, lifting him up.

She kicked.

Tomoe nagi. Circle throw.

Wickham flew up and over her. Over the edge of the roof.

Aunt Phillips was a good teacher. She drilled you and drilled you until the move became instinctive. So just as she had practised, Elizabeth held on, to ride Wickham's momentum and end up on top of him–

–so she, too, went over the edge.

A sickening feeling, of space yawning open below her. In that fleeting moment, she gazed down in horror, watched the twisted face falling between her legs, his one arm twisting violently to grab her but slipping from the leather of her trousers.

Looking up then, desperately flailing, she caught at the edge – hard, jarring impact, shoulders wrenched. Heard Wickham's angry scream, cut short as he landed heavily many feet below. Her finger tips. She was hanging onto the wall by her fingertips. She was going to fall.

'Georgiana,' she gasped, but there was no reply from the girl. An angry sob escaped her.

It was over. She was going to fall, and Georgiana was going to die in the flames, and Darcy and Lydia must already be dead. It was fact. It was written. So why did she still hold on? Better to just accept...Just let go, just let go...

A black shape loomed above her, and a hand gripped her tightly by the wrist.

'Darcy.'

'Elizabeth,' he groaned. 'Give me your other hand.'

'You're too badly hurt. Save yourself. Save Georgiana.'

'Just give me your hand.'

'No!'

He sighed deeply, looked her in the eye. 'Miss Elizabeth Bennet, won't you do me the honour of taking my hand?'

She took it. She took it and cried for him as he hauled her up, and she heard the sounds he made as he took her weight and dragged her up and over the parapet. He fell backwards, panting.

'Lydia is safe,' he gasped. 'Now take Georgiana and go.'

'No, I can help you. And her.'

He shook his head, coughing, and reached for the collar of his cloak. 'I need you to take my sister. I will follow behind.'

He rolled onto his side with a groan, pulling at the cloak beneath him. Elizabeth helped him tug it free.

'Wrap this about her. It will shield her from the flames.'

He closed his eyes. Elizabeth leaned over him, cradling his head with its sweat-matted hair, tears pattering down upon his black mask.

'You must allow me,' she said. 'You must allow me to tell you how ardently I admire and love you.'

He chuckled, and lifted his hand, gently touching a finger to her lips.

'I believe that is my line.'

She kissed his forehead, then stood. She staggered. Her eyes appeared to be deceiving her, for it seemed that rivers of sparks were flowing across the dark grounds towards the house. Or else they were stars, falling, and she was upside down. But then she heard distant shouts and knew them for torches and lanterns – the villagers, Darcy's tenants, drawn to the flames of Pemberley.

She had to get Georgiana out.

She knelt, spread the cloak and rolled the younger girl onto it. Georgiana whimpered as she wrapped it about her.

'I don't want to go. I don't want to go.'

Elizabeth shook her.

'Georgiana! Wake up! I need you to help me. Put your arms around my neck. Can you do that?'

The girl nodded, though her eyes remained tightly closed. She lifted her arms, and Elizabeth took them and wrapped them around her neck.

'Tight!' she grunted, pressing the girl's arms against her. She felt the grip tighten a little.

She wrapped her arms around Georgiana's slim waist, squatted, and brought to mind her exercises in the training room at Longbourn – all those hours spent lifting bags of grain. She straightened, bringing the girl up with her, stood swaying. She felt quite lightheaded. Her arm throbbed, and she remembered the wound there. She manoeuvred Georgiana to her side and took a couple of steps, the girl's toes dragging on the roof.

'Darcy! Darcy, get up, we have to go.'

She heard him grunt, and at first that seemed all he was going to do, then slowly he turned over and pushed himself up onto his hands and knees.

'Go on,' he rasped. 'I'm coming.'

Somewhere, there was a loud crack and a roar. She had to go.

She tottered towards the hatch to the servant's way, feeling Georgiana slowly slipping through her grasp. The girl at least kept her fingers locked, but now her grip was pulling on Elizabeth's neck, unbalancing her. Finally she had to let her down and instead grab her under the armpits and drag her to the staircase.

Darcy crawled slowly behind them.

The narrow staircase was a nightmare. It was a wonder that Gluttony had managed to get the girl up it. She had to feel blindly with one foot for each step, blocking Georgiana from just sliding down head first. The closer she got to the bottom, the thicker the smoke became. Sharp tendrils made her breath catch and choke. Her eyes watered and stung.

In the hallway, the thick carpeting made it too slow to drag the girl. At least Georgiana seemed to be coming to. Elizabeth sat her against the wall and looked into her eyes.

'Can we try pig-a-back?'

Georgiana nodded, biting her lip. Her face was white with fear. Elizabeth dragged her up the wall, holding her in place, then turned around. Georgiana wrapped her arms around her, and she leaned forward, taking the weight. She fumbled to catch hold of the girl's legs as they dangled behind her but couldn't reach them, and felt a quivering in her own limbs as the last of her strength started to go. She gripped the thin arms instead and staggered onward, bent over.

'Darcy,' she called behind her. 'Come on!'

She thought she heard him answer, but couldn't be sure. She wanted to look behind her, but going back, even a few steps, seemed impossible. She staggered down the hall to the staircase to the second floor. Somewhere, somehow, she half turned and finally caught hold of one of Georgiana's legs and got her up across her shoulders, as she farmers did with heavy loads. And somehow, like that, legs screaming, she descended the stairs.

Don't fall, don't fall.

The second floor was in flames. She rounded the dogleg in the corridor and saw the central hall before her, engulfed. There would be other ways down, towards the rear of the house, but she didn't know them, feared getting lost. Besides, she did not have the energy for that. The stairs were right there, just ahead, and she could hear voices calling. Or at least imagined she could.

'Hold your breath!'

She went forward, as close to a run as she could. Her leather would protect her to an extent, and Darcy's cloak would help shield the girl's skin from the scorching heat.

She must not fall. Must not fall.

She leaned into the wall as she hit the stairs, using it to help hold her upright, keeping as far from the flames as she could. Knees jarred as she came unexpectedly to the landing, almost buckled, screamed as she thrust herself upright again. The last flight down, just there, the darkness of the main door beyond, smoke pouring through it.

She charged for it, down the last steps, across the hall, and burst out into a sea of worried faces. Would have fallen but kind, rough hands caught her, lifted Georgiana from her back. She gasped as someone poured a bucket of water over her. Steam rose from her armour. The earth tilted beneath her feet.

People ran about, there was shouting. A line of men passing buckets of water. Someone with a hose and pump. She scanned the ground amongst the chaos – she couldn't see Wickham's body.

'Miss? Miss?' An older woman, familiar – the housekeeper. 'Where is the master?'

Darcy.

She spun, rocking on her heels. And plunged towards the orange-glowing doorway.

'Miss, no! *Come back*!'

Back inside the flaming hell that was the main hall.

'Darcy,' she screamed into the roar of the fire. '*Darcy*!'

And then he was there, swaying at the top of the stairs, his armour smoking. He stared down at her, and his face twisted in rage.

'Elizabeth,' he bellowed. '*Get out*!'

Something cracked above her. There was a rushing roar. A terrible impact.

Blackness.

Chapter 23

The river took her.

It kept her down deep for a long time, before she woke enough to be aware of it.

Its waters were black, and icy, and she shivered uncontrollably in its uncaring, encompassing embrace.

She was afraid. For she wasn't alone down here, she was sure. Meg was here somewhere, wrapped in chains, her terrible remains dragging along the riverbed, and she did not want to see her, did not want to feel her skeletal grasp, nor see the reproach in her empty eye sockets.

And Wickham would be down here too, burned, ruined arm languid as water weed, clutching at her. Just as the weeds were even now wrapped about her legs, defying her feeble kicks. His twisted mask would leer at her, and she would clutch at it, only to find it was not a mask at all, but his own deformed face, ugly as his soul.

No, he wasn't here...He fell from the roof...

No, you threw him off the roof.

No, he wasn't there, wasn't lying on the drive where he should have been.

He could be anywhere.

She whimpered.

A cool hand touched her face, and she pressed up against it.

Then she was not in the water, but walking up the darkened slope at Pemberley. This time *he* was beside her. Strong and stern as a standing stone. Ahead, the ridge line glowed orange with the mocking lights of the great house on the other side, but when she finally crested it, it was different. The house was dark and cold. She did not wish to approach it, but suddenly she was there before the gaping empty doorway, the shattered windows. Like standing before a great leering skull. She was alone. He was no longer beside her, and she knew it was because he was in there. It was his tomb.

Someone wiped her face with a cloth.

It seemed to her that a great crowd had gathered, watching her. Jane and Bingley. Charlotte and Mr Collins. Others. She reached up – where was her mask? She was exposed.

Then it seemed Aunt Phillips was sitting wrapped in a shawl by her bedside. But that wasn't right, it was supposed to be the other way round. Everything was upside down.

Then, finally, the light caught her, and slowly lifted her up.

Elizabeth opened her eyes. The ceiling above her was white with daylight. She swallowed, aware that her mouth was dry and her tongue thick and swollen.

'Water,' she croaked, and she heard a chair creak, and a cup was held to her lips. She swallowed gratefully, then sank back, slowly letting her eyes grow accustomed to the light.

'Father,' she said at last.

'I am here,' said Mr Bennet.

There was pain. Her head throbbed, as did her arm. But worse was the sharp knife that speared her heart as memory and realisation settled across her like mourning lace.

'He is dead,' she said.

There, the awful words were spoken aloud.

'Yes,' said her father heavily.

Her eyes screwed tight, hot with tears.

'You did well,' continued Mr Bennet. 'Very well indeed. I am so proud of you.' His voice caught in his throat.

She shook her head. 'Wasn't enough.'

'You saved your sister. And saved Georgiana Darcy. I think that is enough for one day, don't you?'

She lay silently for some moments.

'Where is Jane?'

'She is at Netherfield. A situation we shall have to get used to into the future. She has been by your side day and night, exhausting herself. But I sent her away. You are out of danger, and it is only right that she spends some time with her betrothed.'

'That's right,' said Elizabeth. 'She is to be married...I forgot...Dear Jane. Wait – you said "day and night". How long have I been unconscious?'

'Three full days, not counting the slow trip back from Pemberley. You took quite a blow to your head and had also lost a great deal of blood. Not to mention sundry other pieces of wear and tear. But you are a strong girl. I have always known that about you.'

'I do not feel strong. I feel broken into a thousand pieces. Did...I dreamt I saw Aunt Phillips. Can it be so?'

'Yes, she has been here. She woke from her state two days ago. Demanded to come and see you. As you know, there is no arguing with her when she has made up her mind.'

'I am glad. I wish to see her with all my heart. And where are Lydia and Georgiana?'

'Miss Darcy is also at Netherfield. She will be very glad to see you. Lydia – well, she has been somewhat subdued since her return. If I had known that kidnapping might have had that effect on her, I might have arranged it much earlier.'

Elizabeth shot him a dark look.

'I do not see any humour. She...she...I am not sure. I think she knew more than we thought. Was more willing to join W–To join that man than we thought. We must watch her.'

'I can assure you, I doubt I will ever give her permission to leave the house again. Even if she just wishes to visit Meryton. She is a foolish girl, but perhaps she has learned her lesson.'

'You don't understand. It is worse than that. I fear there is a proclivity within her. You must watch her, teach her.'

He bowed his head. 'I will endeavour to encourage more restraint within her. And in Kitty and Mary too.' Mr Bennet hesitated. 'I also hope you will think seriously about your own future in all this. With Vigilism, I mean.'

Elizabeth stared up at the ceiling. 'I do not know what to think. There are so many who need help. But I am so tired. I don't know if I...'

She had to be careful. There was a deep whirlpool of black grief at her centre. She could feel herself skirting its edges. It would be all too easy to go plunging downwards, and she did not know how she would ever be able to rise again.

And there was something else, too – a terrible fear. A weary sense that this was not over. Meg had said Wickham came back worse, that time after the bridge. What would he be like now? Burned and broken, he must surely have lost whatever human feeling yet remained. He would be a monster – one that she had helped create. Her nemesis…It was different to how the newspapers and pamphlets framed it. There was nothing exciting or heroic about it.

But then, as she contemplated the days ahead, their emptiness, their purposelessness, she saw that she needed something if she was to survive. This hunt would have to suffice, then, though it was as sustaining as a mouthful of ashes. What had she labelled vengeance, once before? Before she knew better? It was when she was talking to…

No. Hold it down.

'Is Pemberley lost?' she asked.

'The central hall sustained great damage, but the efforts of the villagers succeeded in saving most of both wings. It can be rebuilt in time.'

No, her mind cried, *let it remain his tomb.*

'That is good. Georgiana shall have somewhere to call home.' She could feel her eyes burning. 'Though I fear she will never feel truly safe till I have found him.'

Mr Bennet frowned. 'Found who?'

'Wickham.' The name was bitter as poison on her tongue.

'But he is dead.'

'What?' Her mind swam. 'No, he isn't.'

'Elizabeth, I can assure you, he is.'

'But he was gone…I remember. I looked, but he was gone.'

'They had moved his body. My child, he is dead. He will trouble neither you nor Miss Darcy nor anyone else ever again. I thought you knew that – you said "he is dead".'

She could barely utter the words. 'I meant Darcy.'

Mr Bennet's face softened, tears glinting in his eyes. 'Oh dear child. Forgive me. I did not know what you meant.'

'It doesn't matter.'

'Elizabeth, Elizabeth! *He* is alive!'

A terrible rush of hope. She fought to hold it back. She could not survive this.

'No, he isn't. He died in Pemberley.'

'He did not. He survived. Who do you think carried you from the house?'

She stared at him. She could not speak, could not think. She searched her mind for some scrap of memory. Was there something? Some sense within the blazing flames, of a dark presence taking her, lifting her. He had been so badly injured – how could he have?

'I understand that some of the men were about to follow you in when part of the ceiling fell. They were rallying themselves to go in after you when Darcy came staggering out with you in his arms.'

'Where is he?' she asked shakily.

'At Netherfield, with his sister and Mr Bingley. And Jane, of course.'

Elizabeth threw back the covers and stood, head swimming. She reached for a gown.

'Elizabeth, wait. He was very badly injured. Really, it is a miracle that he survived. Though of course he was always a stubborn man; I think he just refused to die.'

She pulled on her boots. She glanced at her mirror – she was a tousled mess, face pale and bruised. She headed for the door.

'Elizabeth!'

Her father's tone brought her to a stop, her hand upon the knob.

'You need to know...The fire...He was badly burned. His face...He isn't the same.'

She looked at him.

'Do you,' she said, 'honestly think I give one damn about that?'

And then she was running down the stairs, calling for her horse.

There were voices behind her, calling her name, begging her to wait, offering her the carriage, but she could not stop.

Once mounted, she urged the horse down the drive, down the lane. As she turned into the park, she nearly fell, reeling drunkenly in the saddle, but she pulled herself upright, hung on. She could hang on. She tapped the horse, and it leapt forward, ears twitching, catching the urgency of her mood.

They cantered across the grass, her hair flowing in the wind. Her blood screamed within her – no, rather, it was singing. A primal note of longing. Siren's song on the shore. Rising within her. Carrying her forward.

Across the fields, towards the house.

Clattering up the drive, to the entryway.

Sliding from the saddle, pounding up the steps.

Throwing open the door, into the hall.

Across to the stairs.

Up, up. Jane at the top, pointing down the hallway.

Down the corridor, to his room. Bingley there, throwing the door open wide.

Through the door...

Where he lay, swathed in bandages. Waiting.

He looked up; he looked up and he *saw her.*

A pause of a moment, an intake of breath, a heartbeat, dust motes swirling in the sunlit air between them in celebration.

Then she ran to him, and she flowed into his outstretched arms

Like water.

Like the sea, the rising tide, swirling about the rocks of the shore.

Filling all the gaps.

       All the spaces.

        Natural.

         Seamless.

Complete.

Epilogue

The girl sat at her bureau, examining her own beautiful reflection in the mirror. It was late, and the house was still and quiet. Her family was asleep, but slumber evaded the girl. She had been thinking.

Now she sat, her face heavily powdered and seeming to glow white in the candlelight. She liked the effect. She dipped her fingertips in a pot of lip rouge and held them up before her. Red as blood. With a sharp motion, she drew her fingers down across her lips at an angle, leaving a jagged red smear. She turned her head back and forth to admire the effect. Like a cut across her face.

Next she swirled the fingers of her other hand in some dark eyeliner. Black as the night. Black as hearts. She closed her eyes and drew her fingertips across her lids. Blinking, she smiled at how the dark smear set off her eyes. So pretty. Like a mask.

She hardly recognised herself.

'It is a truth universally known,' said her reflection, 'that a Vigil, especially a smug, self-important bossy one who always thinks she is right, must be in want of a villain to oppose her. Otherwise, whatever is the point?'

She paused. Her eyes glinted in the candlelight.

Like diamonds.

Like ice.

'Well,' said the girl, smile like a snarl. 'Wait until she gets a look at me.'

Afterword

On the martial arts described in the book:

There really was a man named Barton-Wright who travelled to Japan as an engineer and studied jui jitsu while working there for several years. On his return to London, he opened his own martial arts school for gentlemen. He added techniques from boxing, French savate and stick fighting to form his own style, which he modestly christened 'bartitsu'.

It was this fighting system that Sir Arthur Conan Doyle gave to his most famous character, Sherlock Holmes. It was also the style utilised by the suffragette bodyguards of Emmeline Pankhurst, including Edith Garrud.

The only problem? This all happened a good 80 to 90 years after the time that Jane Austen was writing *Pride & Prejudice*. But this chance for the Vigils to have a realistic source of martial arts training was one I could not ignore, so I took the liberty of moving the date of his journey (and his birth, therefore) to this earlier time.

Acknowledgements

The first person I wish to thank is a man whose name I can't actually remember. He was an author being interviewed in a newspaper about how to get published. In the article he said it came down to three things: talent (you have to have some, obviously), luck (you need to get your manuscript in front of the right person at the right time) and persistence (you can't give up) – and of those three, the most important is the last, because it is the one most in your control. That resonated with me, as at that point I was starting to receive the first of a flurry of rejections, shaking my faith. I clung to his words of wisdom and persisted.

Which brings me to the second person I need to thank: Lindy Cameron at Clan Destine Press. Definitely a case of the right person at the right time. I am grateful that Lindy saw something in this story and my writing, and was willing to provide it with a home. My thanks extends to the rest of the gang at Clan Destine as well.

I also want to express my gratitude to my editor Jason Nahrung, who has helped hone the manuscript into something sharper and brighter. When the suggested changes just seem so right, you know you are working with someone who really gets your work. I do find him very biased against the humble ellipsis, but we shall let that pass...

I enjoy writing fight scenes. If they sounded at all good, then that is due in part to a number of people who have shaped my knowledge over the years as either instructors or training partners, and so I think they have earned a mention. First thanks goes to Liz Mahler (she said on the hardest day 'accept that you belong here', which was something I needed to hear). Second goes to Joshua Marks (a joyful warrior who helped me lose most of my fear of sparring). Third goes to Rod Mattocks (who patted my head and kept me going when I just wanted to weep and give up). Later came Kyle Martinez (who created just the space I needed to continue to train but also terrified me with the circle throw), and Zac Greenfield (whose calm, relentless energy made him an absolute pleasure to roll with).

If any of the action sequences aren't so good, then that is down to me not them.

Josh Cotter can also get a mention for his continued interest in the process. Thanking him here might mean he has to read actually read the book, too.

And finally, I would like to thank my wife Sandra, for her ongoing support and belief.

It's all for her, really.

About the Author

Timothy Bowden was a high school English and History teacher for 14 years before becoming interested in psychology and retraining as a school counsellor. He has worked in that field ever since and, along with his wife Sandra, created two graphic novels for young readers introducing the concepts of Acceptance and Commitment Therapy. Together they have also presented at conferences on that topic nationally and internationally.

He always enjoyed writing stories. Once in Year 6 at primary school, he wrote a 12 page murder mystery – his teacher's only comment was "You are restricted to two pages from now on". Luckily that didn't dissuade him.

Timothy lives on the Central Coast of NSW with his wife, two demanding cats and a cheeky house rabbit. Apart from writing, he enjoys reading, nerdy boardgames and has a totally amateur interest in martial arts.

Pride & Justice combines his interests in literature, human psychology and martial action into one classic reimagined story.